W9-ASW-894
TREASURES OF THE HEART
CONNIE MASON
LEISURE BOOKS
NEW YORK CITY

A LEISURE BOOK®

Published by
Dorchester Publishing Co., Inc.
276 Fifth Avenue
New York, NY 10001

Printed in the United States of America.

TREASURES
OF THE HEART

Prologue

St. Louis, April 1868

The house was dark but for a thread of light escaping from beneath the study door. The children crept up the stairs, their soft tread inaudible on the wooden steps. Voices, raised in anger, drew them toward the closed door, until the frightening words spoken by their step-uncle could be clearly heard. It was obvious the man thought them asleep in their beds and felt in no danger of being overheard.

"I'll accept no excuses, Conrad, do you understand? If you bungle it this time you'll get nothing more from me."

"What's he mean?" Seven-year-old Brady's

hoarse whisper was directed at his ten-year-old sister.

"Hush and listen," Amy hissed into her small brother's ear.

"It wasn't my fault those blasted brats were pulled to safety at the last minute," Conrad complained. "They would have been dashed beneath the wheels of that runaway carriage if some damn good Samaritan hadn't interfered. I swear they lead a charmed life."

"Charmed life or not, see to it that no one interferes again," Julian Masters grumbled.

"Does he mean us?" Brady's voice was shaky as he recalled their near tragic accident the day before. Though still young, the lad was old enough to understand the imminent danger to their lives.

"Of course he means us," a much more astute Amy said with a hint of exasperation. "Uncle Julian wants us dead."

The breath escaped from Brady's lips in a slow hiss and his eyes grew luminous as a shiver crept down his spine. "I thought he liked us. What are we going to do?"

"Leave it to me, Mr. Masters, I'll not fail—"

"Shhh, do you hear something?" Julian halted Conrad's speech with a chopping motion of his hand.

Both men stood motionless, waiting for the sound to repeat itself. When nothing further was heard, Conrad continued. "I'll take care of it, don't you worry."

"See that you do, I've paid you handsomely enough. Now get out of here before the brats take it into their heads to wander the halls at this late hour."

The children looked at one another in panic when they heard footsteps approach the door. Amy reacted instinctively as she grasped Brady's hand and pulled him down the darkened stairway. They barely had time to slip beneath a table against a wall in the foyer before the door to Julian's study opened, spilling light down the entire length of the staircase and into the foyer.

Shaking in fear, the children hovered beneath the table, unable to see anything but Conrad's legs as he descended the stairs and quietly let himself out the door. Their step-uncle remained at the top of the stairs for several minutes, his face pensive as he peered down into the foyer. He sensed another presence, yet saw nothing. His dark, penetrating gaze searched the foyer, finally settling on the only piece of furniture in the entranceway. A slight movement in the shadows beneath the table caught his attention, and he knew immediately that the children had been sneaking about and had overheard him and Conrad plotting their deaths. It wasn't the first time he had caught them roaming the halls at night.

"You can't hide from me," he rasped in a threatening voice. "What are you brats doing out of bed? Were you eavesdropping? How much did you hear?"

Realizing their hiding place had been discovered, Amy poked her head from beneath the table and said, "We—we were hungry and came downstairs for something to eat. We didn't hear a word you and Mr. Conrad said."

Julian tensed, realizing immediately that Amy wouldn't have known Conrad's name if she hadn't heard everything. "So, you did hear. Too bad, now I'll have to take matters into my own hands. Only this time there will be no mistakes, or anyone coming to your rescue. Why should you two brats have all the money when I need it more than you do?"

Though only ten years old, Amy knew that their dead parents, Joseph and Dora Trenton, had left them wealthy, and that their step-uncle had been granted guardianship. But what she wasn't aware of was that Julian Masters, as the only surviving relative, would inherit their money should they not live to collect it when they reached their majority. If they hadn't awakened hungry and crept downstairs to pilfer a snack from the kitchen, they would never have heard Julian and Conrad plotting their death.

"What's he going to do to us?" Brady whispered to Amy. He had never been so frightened.

"I don't know."

"Does he want to hurt us?"

"I won't let him. I'll think of something." Wise beyond her years, Amy had been her little brother's protector since their parents' tragic accident over two years ago and she knew he depended on her to see them safely through this danger. "Give me your hand, and we'll make a run for it through the front door."

It was useless to call for help, for none of the servants spent the night in the house; her uncle was too cheap to pay for live-in help, even if it was the children's money footing the bills.

"Come out of there," Julian cajoled as he started down the stairs. "I was only teasing, I'm not going to harm you."

His menacing expression told them otherwise and Amy decided they shouldn't wait to find out if he meant what he had said. "Now!" she hissed, grasping Brady's hand and pulling him from beneath the table. When they lunged toward the front door, Julian's rage exploded.

"You sniveling little brats! Ungrateful wretches! When I get my hands on you you'll be sorry you didn't listen to me."

He leaped down the stairs after them. A big man whose bulk made him clumsy, Julian lost his balance on the very first step and tumbled head over heels down the long staircase. The children watched in dismay as he bumped and bounced his way to the foot of the stairs and rolled nearly to the door, stopping inches from where they stood. He lay still as death, blood seeping from his nose and ears.

"Is—is he dead?" Brady asked in a tremulous whisper.

"I think so," Amy replied, as shaken as her brother.

"What do we do now?"

Amy's small face grew somber, burdened far beyond her years. Would the man named Conrad come looking for them when he learned their uncle was dead? Would the police hold them responsible for Uncle Julian's death and put them in jail? She thought they would. Her youth and the shock of hearing their uncle plot their death, followed in short order by his own death, robbed her of logic. She feared they would either be arrested or sent to an orphanage. Neither choice was palatable. When she finally made a decision, her child's mind believed it the right one.

"We have to leave." Staunch conviction lent her the courage to make the choice.

"Leave? Where will we go?" Brady's dismay was obvious. This was the only home he had ever known.

"I don't know, but anyplace is better than jail. Would you prefer an orphanage?"

Brady shook his head in vigorous denial.

"C'mon, then, before the servants arrive and discover us. You know they wouldn't protect us. Uncle Julian hired all new servants when he came here to live with us and none of them like us very much."

His warm brown eyes glowing with absolute trust, Brady placed his small hand in Amy's and followed her out the door.

Chapter One

St. Louis, April 1868

Cody Carter was rather fond of St. Louis. It was a thriving, bustling city on this fine April day in 1868. Some called it the gateway to the West, and the sprawling metropolis had certainly been the jumping-off place for many an expedition to western destinations. Today it was large enough to offer sophisticated diversions, and urbane enough to pay little heed to his obvious Indian origins.

Dressed in buckskins and fringed jacket, his hat pulled low over his eyes—holdovers from his Army days—Cody paused a moment before Sal's House Of Pleasure before pushing open the gate and trudging up the walk to the front door. It was just seven o'clock in the evening but already sounds of revelry were wafting through the open windows.

After spending the war years as a scout with the Army in the West, Cody had drifted on to greener pastures once peace was declared. Two years ago he had arrived in St. Louis and promptly accepted a position riding shotgun for the Butterfield Stagecoach Lines. It was as good a job as any for a man like him. And the pay was good.

A loner, Cody Carter had one too many strikes against him for a more stable job. Not only was he a half-breed—his mother was full-blooded Cheyenne—he was the bastard son of a prosperous Kansas rancher. He could outshoot and outswear any man crazy enough to tangle with him. To his credit, Cody had never been in trouble with the law. He had been scrupulously careful to remain within the law in all his dealings, aware of how justice worked in regards to half-breeds.

Tall, broad-shouldered, and deep-chested, Cody filled out his buckskins in ways that constantly caught the interested eyes of the fairer sex. His bold, handsome features were enhanced by shoulder-length black hair clubbed at the back with a rawhide strip and startling blue eyes totally unexpected in one so swarthy.

The door to Sal's establishment was opened immediately and Cody stepped inside, his cool gaze sweeping the room's scantily clad occupants with casual interest. Cody had learned the hard way that "decent women" had no use for half-breeds. When he first arrived in St. Louis he had been smitten with a sultry, dark-eyed beauty named Lisa Paxton. So smitten in fact that he felt an unaccustomed yearning for respectability and the kind of stability normal people enjoyed. He had stupidly believed that Lisa was different from the type of women who scorned his kind.

He had courted lovely Lisa, foolishly assuming she returned his affection, until the day he proposed. Laying bare his heart to her, he had confided that he was a half-breed and a bastard. Cody could still feel the sickening humiliation of her laughter. And hear the words that had hardened his heart against all "decent women."

"Paxtons don't marry bastards," she had said. "Why didn't you tell me sooner? I wouldn't marry you if you were the last man on earth. I'd be the laughingstock of the entire town."

The experience had taught him a valuable lesson. From then on he had restricted his socializing to whores. Who needed a wife and children anyway? Children. Ugh, the very word brought back memories of his own childhood and how his half-brother Wayne had made his existence a living hell.

"If you're looking for female companionship, cowboy, you've come to the right place. Come in and make yourself at home." Sal Sparks looked Cody up and down, liking what she saw. "Haven't I seen you in here a time or two?"

"Yeah, a time or two," Cody allowed, flashing the coquettish woman a devastating smile. He didn't smile often, but when he did it lit up the room.

Dazzled by the tall, dark stranger's virility, the woman closed the door behind her and asked, "What's your pleasure, cowboy? You got anyone special in mind?"

"Yeah, a woman."

The woman grinned saucily. "Will I do? The name's Sal."

Cody's glittering gaze traveled over Sal with slow relish. He had seen her before but had never met her personally or bedded her. She was slightly older than he would have liked, but he couldn't fault her where looks were concerned. Small and daintily made, she was nonetheless full-breasted. Her curly hair was colored a rich auburn and her features were still smooth and flawless. He placed her age at around thirty.

"You'll do just fine, Sal."

"What's your name, cowboy?"

"My friends call me Cody." He almost laughed aloud at that remark; there were few men he'd call friend.

"Well, Cody," Sal said, savoring the taste of his name on her tongue, "would you like a drink first or—"

"If it's all right with you, Sal, I'd just as soon go upstairs first and drink later." He gave her another grin, and suddenly Sal couldn't wait to get upstairs with this handsome cowboy. Though his proud, bold features and swarthy complexion gave subtle hint of his Indian blood, Sal couldn't have cared less. He was still the most attractive, virile man she'd seen in a damn long time, and that was saying a lot for a woman in her business.

"A man after my own heart," Sal tossed back as she grasped his hand and led him up the stairs.

Cassie Fenmore hurried through the upstairs hallway, anxious to leave Sal's before the nightly crowd of men descended upon the popular house of pleasure. She had remained later than usual this night because Sal had asked her to mend a hem for her before leaving. Normally Cassie's hours were from six in the morning until six in the evening, ending before the clients converged for their night's pleasures. It wasn't easy being a maid in a whorehouse, but Sal had been the only person willing to pay Cassie the kind of money needed to buy Nana's medicine when her beloved grandmother had taken ill. And after her grandmother died, Cassie had remained with Sal, she supposed out of loyalty.

Not that Cassie wasn't beautiful enough to be mistaken for one of Sal's girls. She was young and stunning, with wheat-colored tresses and vivid green eyes. At twenty, her lush figure was the envy of many of Sal's girls, and most of them were thankful Cassie had no inclination to give them competition. She was happy—as happy as a young woman could be without kith or kin—to remain a servant in Sal's House Of Pleasure. There was only one person whom she could call kin, and he hadn't shown the least interest in her in years. She had been just a small child when he sent her away to live with her grandmother after her mother had died. He hadn't wanted to be bothered with raising a young girl.

Cassie rapped lightly on Sal's door. When she received no answer, she entered the room and walked briskly to the wardrobe. The dress she had hemmed for Sal was draped over her arm and she quickly hung it in place. Then she turned and hurried out the door. These garishly decorated rooms always made her nervous, Sal's more than the others. Just imagining what went on in this room made her shudder with dread. Since working at Sal's she had observed enough of men and their depravities to know that she'd never allow a man to touch her in that way. She'd die an old maid before succumbing to a man's lust.

Once in the hallway she headed directly for the servants' stairs, since the front stairs were reserved for guests and the women of their choice. On more than one occasion when she had failed to leave the house at her usual time, she had been mistaken for one of Sal's girls. Those had been embarrassing encounters and she preferred to avoid such situations.

Cody grinned all the way up the stairs, anticipating a most enjoyable evening in Sal's bed. He reckoned she'd be an accomplished lover and looked forward with relish to a few hours of sexual relaxation. It had been a long time since he'd had a woman. His job kept him on the road and afforded him little opportunity to visit Sal's or any other bawdy house.

At the top of the stairs he paused for a brief moment, totally enthralled by a lovely creature who had just exited a room farther down the hall. He was sorry, then, that he had accepted Sal's offer before looking over the rest of the girls available for the night. The blond beauty was the loveliest woman he had seen in a long time. The brief glimpse he'd had of her face had been unforgettable. It was too late now, but he fully intended to ask for her the next time he visited Sal's. Intrigued, he watched as she started down a flight of stairs at the opposite end of the hallway, obviously unaware of his presence and the fact that she was being stared at. Cody was certain he'd never forget the sway of those slim hips or the flash of shapely ankles as she swung out of sight.

"Are you coming, Cody?" Sal had suddenly noticed that Cody was no longer behind her and she turned to see what had detained him.

"Who is that woman?"

Sal looked in the direction of Cody's gaze and caught a glimpse of Cassie hurrying down the stairs. "That's just Cassie. She's not for the likes of you." Though Sal didn't elaborate, she assumed that Cody recognized Cassie's drab uniform and understood that she was merely a servant and not one of the whores.

Since Cody had paid little attention to Cassie's mode of dress, he put an entirely different meaning to Sal's words. He assumed that the young beauty was reserved for special customers, those with enough money to afford someone as fresh and tempting as Cassie. Before following Sal into her room, Cody made a mental note to bring enough money with him the next time to buy Cassie's favors for the night, no matter how dear her price.

The following morning when Cody returned to his boardinghouse he found a telegram waiting for him. It had been sent from Dodge City by a lawyer named Cornelius Willoughby. Willoughby had hired a Pinkerton man to track him down.

Later that same day a similar telegram was delivered to Cassie Fenmore at her place of work.

Cody's first reaction was to ignore the telegram, but after much deliberation and soul-searching he went to the railway station and bought a ticket for Dodge City on a train leaving the following day. Then he went to the Butterfield Stagecoach Lines and asked for a leave of absence in order to attend to family business.

Cassie's initial inclination was to forget that she had ever received a telegram. But curiosity got the best of her and she bought a train ticket to Dodge City on her way home from work. Her next stop was the mercantile, where she purchased special clothing for her trip the next day.

Cody leaned against a shady corner of the depot, smoking a long, thin cigar and watching the people who had gathered at the station to await the arrival of the train. He pulled his watch out of his pocket, checking the time. He frowned in annoyance. The train was late. So what else was new? His gaze wandered aimlessly over the crowd, then across the street where the delicious smell of freshly baked sweet rolls wafted from the door of a bakery. The scent made his mouth water and he debated whether or not he should walk across the street and buy one of the sticky buns the baker had just placed in the display window.

From the corner of his eye he saw two grubby, ragged children appear out of nowhere and sidle into the doorway of the bakery. They loitered there until the baker's back was turned; then the smaller of the two darted inside, snatched two sticky buns from the window, and ran like hell. The older child was close behind. Cody found himself cheering for the two ragged waifs as they darted across the street toward the depot. But unfortunately for the children, the baker had seen them from the corner of his eye and had taken off after them. Cody thought the boy probably would have escaped if the baker hadn't nabbed the girl. But when the lad saw that his companion had been apprehended, he skidded to an abrupt halt.

"Don't stop! Run, Brady, run!"

The boy paused, looking confused and frightened. Then he turned and ran.

Cody had stepped out from the wall to get a better view of the action, and was nearly knocked from his feet by the small bundle of energy who smacked into him, clutching the sticky buns in his filthy little hands as if they were gold. The baker caught up with him a moment later, dragging the small girl by the collar.

"Damn thieves," the baker muttered, grabbing Brady and giving him a violent shake. "You both deserve a good beating and I've a mind to give it to you. But why should I dirty my hands? Stealing is a crime, let the police take care of it."

"No! Not the police! Please don't call the police!" Amy begged.

Cody had never seen anyone more terror-stricken in his entire life than those two children, and something inside him snapped.

"Can't you just call their parents?" he suggested when the baker would have dragged them away.

"We're orphans," Brady offered timidly. Amy groaned in dismay. It was the worst possible thing he could have said.

"Then you belong in an orphanage," the baker replied.

"No! I won't go!" Drawing back her foot, Amy released it with telling force against the baker's shin.

"Damn you!" In retaliation the baker let Brady loose and clouted Amy aside the head, stunning her. Brady reacted by biting the baker's hand.

When the baker raised his fist to strike Brady, Cody intervened. He hadn't meant to get involved, but he couldn't tolerate the baker's abuse of defenseless children.

"Just a damn minute," Cody said, grasping the man's wrist in his powerful fist. "There's no need for violence. They're only kids, for God's sake."

"Thieves today, murderers tomorrow," the baker muttered, glaring at Cody.

Being called a murderer hit too close to home for Brady. "We're not murderers! We didn't kill anyone!"

"Of course we're not murderers," Amy concurred, attempting to protect her brother by shoving him behind her.

"Nevertheless, I'm taking them to the police. If these brats don't belong in jail then they certainly belong in an orphanage."

"I'll pay for the damn buns," Cody said, pulling some coins from his pocket and shoving them at the baker. Then he looked the man straight in the eye, conveying a silent message that caused beads of sweat to pop out on the baker's brow. "If I were you, I'd forget this ever happened."

The baker found himself staring into a pair of the coldest blue eyes he had ever seen. He wasn't stupid. He recognized a threat when he heard one. And he had suddenly realized that he was talking to a half-breed, one of those savage men who would just as soon slit your throat as look at you.

"If—if you say so, mister," the baker stammered, backing away. "But you'd best convince those kids to keep away from my shop. The next time you might not be around to protect them." Coward that he was, he made certain he was a respectable distance away from Cody before he threw out those last words.

Cody watched him reenter his store, then turned to glare down at the children. They were wolfing down the sticky buns as if they hadn't eaten in days.

"When was the last time you kids ate?"

Amy swallowed a mouthful of bun, looked at him with soulful brown eyes, and said, "Two days ago. We raided the garbage can behind the saloon."

Cody groaned. "She-it!" Brady looked at him with round eyes. Cody coughed and amended, "I mean, shucks. Where's your family?"

"Don't have one," Brady said, chewing thoughtfully. "You're not going to send us to an orphanage, are you?"

"That's where you belong." Suddenly Cody took a hard look at the children, wondering where he had seen them before. They looked familiar but he hadn't been able to place them, until now. "Say, aren't you the two kids I pulled from beneath the wheels of that runaway wagon a couple of weeks ago?"

Amy had recognized Cody immediately, but thought it best not to mention the "accident" unless he mentioned it first. She nodded, admitting they were the same two children.

"You sure do seem to attract trouble. Haven't you anyplace to go?"

"No," Brady piped up. "No place."

"What are your names?"

"I'm Brady and she's Amy. We're brother and sister."

"I thought so." Both had the same dark curly hair and warm brown eyes. "I'm sorry, kids, there's nothing more I can do for you. I'm leaving town on the next train." He pulled several wadded-up bills from his jacket pocket and handed them to Amy. "Here, buy some food. And try to stay out of trouble. I wouldn't be surprised if the police are looking for you."

Brady paled. "You mean they know?"

"Know what?" Cody couldn't figure out what in the hell these two kids were talking about, or why they were so terrified of the police.

"Pay no attention to Brady, mister," Amy said, sending Brady a silent warning.

"The name is Cody, Cody Carter." Now why had he told them that? It wasn't as if he'd ever see them again.

"Thank you for the money, Mr. Carter," Amy said politely. "C'mon, Brady, it's time we left."

Brady stared at Cody with such a wistful expression, the hard-boiled half-breed found himself assailed by feelings totally foreign to his experience. Why should he feel this overwhelming surge of compassion for them? It just didn't make sense. He'd had enough problems in his own childhood; he didn't need to take on these two waifs. His half-brother, Wayne, had hated him with such consuming passion that his youth had been a nightmare. Things might have been easier if his mother hadn't died in a tragic accident when he was about the same age as Amy. But he couldn't change things, and looking back brought only bitterness.

"Good-bye, kids," Cody said, giving a jaunty wave. "Take care of yourselves." Cody turned back toward the depot just as the train whistle sounded in the distance.

"He seems like a nice man," Brady said as he stared at Cody's departing back. "Why is he so dark?"

"Uncle Julian seemed like a nice man when he first came to live with us," Amy replied in a wise voice. "Mr. Carter looks like one of those Indians in our picture book. Do you suppose he *is* an Indian?"

"I don't care if he is," Brady defended staunchly. "I still like him."

Cody waited until the locomotive let off a blast of hot steam before retrieving his bag from the depot and joining the other passengers boarding the train. He was wishing he could have done something more for the kids when he noticed a woman walking briskly toward the train. Her trim form was swathed in black mourning, and Cody's eyes followed the intriguing sway of her skirt. She seemed in a hurry, and he stepped aside to let her pass.

Her unrelieved black dress enveloped her slim figure from head to toe, but not even a gunnysack could disguise the womanly curves beneath. A wisp of blond hair straggled from the black hat sitting atop her head, its dense veil stopping just short of a pair of lush red lips. Intrigued, Cody fixed his gaze on those shapely lips as she passed within inches of him. Never had he seen anyone who fascinated him so thoroughly or exuded such an air of mystery. The swish of her skirt in passing captured his attention, and he stared in open admiration of the subtle swivel of her hips. When she entered the train he quickly followed, choosing a seat directly opposite her.

The mysterious lady in black turned her head once to stare at Cody, but since the upper part of her face was veiled, he could not read her expression. Then she quickly turned away. Cody settled back in his seat, pulled his hat down over his eyes, and let his imagination run wild. It pleased him to try to picture what the woman behind the veil looked like. She appeared to be young and shapely, and the mystery of her face fascinated him.

The engineer gave two long blasts of the whistle, warning lingerers on the platform to board the train. Then the conductor pulled up the steps and followed the last of the passengers inside.

Two children stood in the shadows of the depot, their expressions pensive as the train wheels began churning, slowly pulling the locomotive forward.

"I wish we could have gone with Mr. Carter," Brady said wistfully.

"You don't even know where he is going," Amy replied.

"It doesn't matter. Not when we've no place else to go. Besides, he was a nice man. I wonder if he's married. Maybe he has kids our age."

Amy looked skeptical. "I doubt it. Mr. Carter didn't look like the kind of man who'd be married and have kids. Forget him, Brady. I'll take care of you. C'mon, let's get out of here. We've got some money now. We can buy a decent meal."

Brady had just turned to follow his sister when he caught a stealthy movement in a corner of the depot. A man was advancing toward them, waving his arms in the air in a menacing manner.

"Hey, you there, wait up!"

Brady tugged on Amy's dress. "Amy, look! That looks like Mr. Conrad. He's coming to kill us!"

Amy swiveled her head and saw a man running toward them waving his arms. Without pausing to think, she grasped Brady's wrist, jerking him forward.

"Where are we going?"

"Don't talk, just run," Amy gasped as she took off at a run.

But their frantic flight had been anticipated. To their dismay, another man was rushing to intercept them from the opposite end of the depot. With the train in front of them, the depot at their back, and men coming at them from both right and left, the children were trapped. But their pursuers hadn't counted on Amy's ingenuity.

"The train!" Amy cried, recognizing the only way out of their dilemma.

By now the train had picked up speed and all the cars had passed but for the baggage cars. Pulling Brady toward the moving train,

Amy urged, "Climb up, Brady!" Brady obeyed instantly, grabbing on to the car and scrambling nimbly inside.

"Hurry, Amy," Brady cried as the train gained momentum. He held out his hand and Amy reached out. Their fingers touched, parted, touched again, and then Brady was hanging on to her for dear life as she pulled herself into the baggage car. Their faces were white and strained as they glanced out the door and saw that the two men who had been chasing them were standing on the platform, cursing and shaking their fists. The children grinned at each other in perfect understanding, then sat back to rest and catch their breath.

"Where do you suppose we're going?" Brady asked as they left the station behind.

Amy remained thoughtful for a long time. "I don't know. I suppose anyplace is better than St. Louis. Do you think Uncle Julian is really dead?"

"He looked dead."

They both chewed on that for a while.

"What if they find us here? How will we pay for our tickets? I'll bet that nice Mr. Carter will help us if we ask him." This from Brady, who tended to be more optimistic than his practical older sister.

"Perhaps." As young as she was, Amy had no illusions about Cody Carter. "Don't worry, I'll think of something. Don't I always?" Abruptly she turned her head. It wouldn't do for her little brother to see her trembling chin. She had to be brave, for Brady's sake.

Chapter Two

Cody felt the train jerk, heard the chugging of the engine, and let his mind drift back to Dodge City and his unhappy childhood. Fifteen years melted away as if they were just yesterday.

He was fifteen. His beautiful Indian mother had been dead five years and his father, Buck, had returned from a trip to St. Louis with a new bride and her five-year-old daughter. The past year had been rather peaceful at the ranch, with his half brother, Wayne, still away at college and Buck involved with the sprawling cattle ranch just outside Dodge City. Without Wayne around to taunt him with his bastardy and Indian blood, Cody had been almost content.

Of course he would have been happier if Buck had married his mother before her untimely death. But Bright Star had been given to Buck in exchange for cattle by a Cheyenne chief whose starving tribe had wandered onto Buck's property. Since Buck's wife, Wayne's mother, had died in childbirth a few months earlier, Buck eagerly welcomed Bright Star into his home and bed. That Buck had never seen fit to marry his mother was something Cody would never forgive him for.

Cody's childhood hadn't been an easy one, given Wayne's penchant for cruelty and his hatred for his half-breed half brother. Nearly ten years older than Cody, Wayne persisted in his violence toward his younger brother until Cody gained height and weight that far surpassed the smaller and weaker Wayne. When Cody turned fifteen he put an end to the abuse. Since Cody wasn't a tattler, he had never run to Buck with his troubles, choosing to handle them himself. Not that Buck would have interfered. It was obvious to Cody that Buck preferred his legitimate son to his half-breed bastard.

Shortly after Wayne had been sent off to school in Denver, Buck made a trip to St. Louis and returned with a stunning blond wife. Linda brought a five-year-old daughter with her from a previous marriage. Funny, but Cody couldn't even recall the child's name. What he did remember was that she was blond and chubby with the face of a cherub. Less than half Buck's age, Linda settled her roving eye disconcertingly on fifteen-year-old Cody, who was swiftly maturing into a ruggedly handsome man. Then Linda climbed into Cody's bed one night and proceeded to initiate the untried youth in the ritual of love, shattering Cody's world.

The next morning, shock and embarrassment at what had happened nearly destroyed Cody. Unable to face his father with his guilt, he had packed his bag and crept away in shame, vowing never to return to the Rocking C Ranch as long as Linda remained. Since Buck had Wayne and a new wife, Cody reckoned his father would not miss him. It wasn't as if he was going to inherit the ranch or any part of Buck's fortune, Cody told himself. That was reserved for Buck's legitimate son and any children he might have with Linda.

In fifteen years Cody had never looked back. He had drifted west, all the way to California, making a living cowpunching, joining trail drives and performing general ranch work. He had grown and matured the hard way, defending himself against men who thought half-breeds were fair game. He had made a name of sorts for himself by becoming a crack shot. He had done it out of self-defense, realizing he needed to be proficient with a gun if he wanted to discourage those who thought half-breeds were savages who didn't deserve to walk the face of the earth.

Finally Cody joined the Army as a scout, spending most of his days helping to quell uprisings by renegade Indians in Arizona and New Mexico. When hostilities between the states broke out, Cody thought it a senseless war and remained with the western branch of the Army. In all that time he had never contacted Buck, not once. Nor had he returned to the ranch. He still couldn't face Buck after betraying him with Linda, even though he had been a mere lad at the time and vulnerable to Linda's wiles.

Though Cody had plenty of women in those intervening years, his experience made him distrustful of women in general and wives in particular. He had been neglected by his father after his mother's death and had seen how Linda's little daughter had been shunted aside by her self-serving mother. Those experiences had made him decide never to marry or father children. At thirty, he was still footloose and fancy-free. And since he had no idea whether or not Linda was still with Buck, he had never returned to the Rocking C. After resigning from the Army, he had drifted to St. Louis and found a new job, where he had finally been located by Buck's lawyers.

Now Buck was dead and Cody had been summoned for the reading of the will.

Chapter Three

Cassie glanced surreptitiously at the buckskin-clad man in the seat across from her. He seemed to be sleeping, so she tilted her head back and gazed openly at him. She had seen him watching her, his startling blue eyes roving speculatively over her mourning clothes and veil. From the corner of her eye she had seen him step back and allow her to board the train ahead of him; she had felt the heat and intensity of his gaze as he tried to look beyond the veil to her face. When he had chosen a seat directly opposite her and his riveting eyes settled disconcertingly on her lips, she had deliberately lowered her head. His eyes were too intense, too mesmerizing.

Cassie didn't need to be told that the man was

a half-breed. His features were bold and compelling, his complexion a golden bronze. The dark slash of inky brows rose above brilliant blue eyes, contrasting vividly with his shiny ebony hair and swarthy skin. Her eyes lingered on his callused brown hands where they rested on muscular thighs that strained the confines of his buckskin trousers. He was broad of shoulder, thick of chest, narrow-waisted and slim-hipped. Somewhere in the deep recesses of Cassie's brain a dim memory fought to emerge, but she was unable to bring it forth. If the man looked familiar, she reasoned, it was because she probably had seen someone who resembled him at Sal's.

Since they wouldn't reach Dodge for nearly two days, Cassie resigned herself to looking at and being observed by the man whose commanding presence caused an unfamiliar sensation in the pit of her stomach and brought a flush to her cheeks. Thank God he couldn't see past her veil. Could he be a gunslinger, she wondered, or a down-and-out cowboy? Did his mixed blood make him an outcast to white and Indian society alike?

Realizing she was all too interested in the mysterious half-breed, Cassie directed her gaze out the window, watching the scenery slip by without really seeing it. When weariness and boredom grew unbearable, her eyes closed, her head dropped back, and she drifted off to sleep.

Cody hadn't been sleeping as Cassie had thought. Beneath slitted lids he had seen her looking at him, watched her speculate on his origins and occupation, and grew warm beneath her searching gaze. Did she know what she was doing to him? he wondered, moving his hands to cover that part of him stirred by her bold perusal. Even though he couldn't see her face, what he did see was damn enticing. He almost smiled when she tore her gaze from him to stare out the window. Then her head tilted to the side and he knew she had fallen asleep.

Once Cassie was asleep, Cody felt free to study her more thoroughly. His hot blue gaze slid with slow relish over her breasts where they strained her bodice, then slid lower to her tiny waist, admiring the way her hips flared out in perfect symmetry. He wished he could see her legs but they were folded primly beneath the long black skirt of her dress. He'd be willing to bet they'd be long and shapely.

While he studied the lush line of Cassie's lips, her head, relaxed in sleep, started to slide horizontally against the backrest. She would have fallen sideways if Cody hadn't moved beside her so that her head dropped against his shoulder and her body wedged comfortably against his. Feeling her weight resting against him was so damn stimulating it was all he could do to keep his hands off her. What in the hell was wrong with him? Cody wondered sourly. It wasn't like him to get excited over a woman he'd never seen before, especially one swathed from head to toe in widow's weeds. She might be ugly as sin beneath her veil, for God's sake!

Cassie squirmed into a more comfortable position, unaware of the agony she was inflicting on her seat mate, or that she even had a seat mate. It was dusk when she awakened, and the train was just pulling into a small town where passengers could buy food and refresh themselves. The first thing Cassie noticed was the softness beneath her cheek. Then her vision cleared and she saw that she was resting most comfortably against a buckskin-clad shoulder, her slight weight supported by a body much larger than hers.

Bolting upright, Cassie gasped, embarrassed that she had allowed herself to fall asleep and be taken advantage of. "How dare you, sir!"

Her voice was low, with a husky quality that sent shivers of awareness through Cody. She stiffened her spine, set her hat straight on her head with an angry motion, and glared at him through the black veil.

"I meant no harm, ma'am," Cody drawled. The corners of his lips slipped upward into an unaccustomed smile. Cassie wasn't prepared for its devastating effect. "You fell asleep and would have fallen if I hadn't moved so you could rest against me."

"Nevertheless," she said crisply, "it isn't decent. I don't even know you."

"I can remedy that."

"No, thank you."

He was on the verge of telling her his name whether she wanted to know it or not when the conductor came down the aisle, advising the passengers that they had thirty minutes at the depot before departure. Sending Cody a baleful glare, Cassie stood, shaking out her skirts. When the other passengers started leaving the car, she followed. When everyone had departed, Cody unfolded his long frame from the seat and made his way out the door.

"Why are we stopping?" Brady asked when the train chugged to a halt at a sleepy little station in the middle of nowhere.

"Probably so the passengers can buy food," Amy replied.

"I'm hungry."

"So am I but we can't get off now. It's too close to St. Louis. Maybe at the next stop."

Disappointed, Brady settled back against some large sacks piled in the back of the baggage car and conjured up all his favorite foods.

"There goes Mr. Carter," Amy said excitedly when she saw Cody exit the train. Brady was beside her instantly.

"Do you think he'll get back on the train?"

"Probably. He isn't carrying his bag."

They watched through the partially opened door of the baggage car until the train whistle blew and the passengers began reboarding the train. When they saw that Cody was among the returning passengers, they smiled at one another and settled back. For some obscure reason, Cody had become very important to them.

* * *

Cassie boarded the train in a state of agitation. It seemed as if the handsome half-breed was stalking her. Though he knew better than to accost her in public, he seemed to be constantly at her elbow. Couldn't he see she didn't want to be bothered? She had seen too many men like him. He was bold, brash, too damn sure of himself. Even dressed in deep mourning, with her face concealed, she could sense his interest and was annoyed by it. She had deliberately waited until the last minute to board the train so she could take a seat as far away from the half-breed as possible. Only it hadn't worked out the way she had planned.

More passengers had boarded at the small town and only one seat remained unoccupied—the one directly opposite the half-breed. It seemed that she wasn't the only one who wanted to steer clear of the dangerous-looking breed. Heaving an exasperated sigh, Cassie yanked her skirts aside and slipped into the empty seat across from Cody. Then she forced herself to stay awake the entire night so as not to invite a repetition of his inexcusable behavior earlier.

Cody awoke the next morning just as the sun was peeping from behind a bank of fluffy gray clouds. His lips curved into a cynical smile when he saw that the lady-in-black—that was how he had come to think of her—was still sitting ramrod straight, just as she had been last night before he had fallen asleep. Her prudish behavior amused him. Did she think he'd attack her right here on the train? Didn't she know she was making an otherwise boring trip most enjoyable?

The train made another scheduled stop early that morning at Kansas City. After a hearty breakfast, Cody returned to his seat. The passengers had been advised to purchase food for lunch because another stop wasn't scheduled until dark, and he had followed that advice. He set the neatly wrapped bundle of food beside him on the seat and leaned back to continue his surreptitious perusal of the mysterious lady-in-black.

Clickity clack, clickity clack. The wheels had an almost mesmerizing effect as Cassie fought to keep her eyes open. Thank goodness she'd be in Dodge tomorrow and rid of the offensive half-breed for good.

The hot afternoon sun and choking prairie dust made the journey almost unbearable as the train left Missouri and crossed the Kansas border. Cassie wrinkled her nose at the fine sprinkling of dust coating her black dress, and she imagined she could almost smell the acrid odor of her own perspiration. How wonderful it would be to soak in a warm bath and get out of the mourning clothes she had chosen to wear for the trip to Dodge. Although Buck's death had entitled her to wear them, they were hot and stifling.

Cassie steered her thoughts in various directions, carefully keeping them from dwelling on the half-breed sitting across from her. By keeping her mind averted from his magnetic presence, she hoped to avoid further conversation with him. Even eye contact, despite the barrier of her veil, gave her a tingling feeling, and she had no idea why.

Most of the passengers were napping in the late afternoon heat after their sack lunch, and Cassie finally succumbed to drowsiness. Before sleep overtook her, she noticed that the half-breed was also napping and felt much better about surrendering to weariness.

The commotion at the back of the car was loud enough to awaken Cody—and nearly every other passenger. Cody swiveled his head in the direction of the ruckus, and what he saw caused his mouth to drop open in shock. The conductor was advancing down the aisle, dragging two children by the scruffs of their necks. Screeching at the top of their lungs, the children dug in their heels, resisting wildly. Seeing those two homeless waifs on the train was the last thing Cody had expected. He was in for an even greater shock.

To Cody's dismay, the conductor stopped directly before him, thrust the children forward, and asked, "These your kids, mister? I found them hiding in the baggage car. They said they belonged to you."

"What!"

Amy, having already told the lie, carried it even further. Thrusting her thin little arms toward Cody, she cried, "Papa, why did you leave us behind?" Her voice was pathetically provoking.

"What!" Cody repeated, thoroughly confused.

A loud murmur traveled through the car as the passengers voiced disapproval of what they thought was a heartless father who had abandoned his children.

Brady added his pitiful voice to his sister's. "Papa, we didn't want to go to the orphanage. Why did you leave without us? I'm hungry and thirsty."

Cassie couldn't believe her ears. What kind of monster would abandon his own children? She couldn't imagine the dangerous-looking half-breed fathering these adorable children, or any children at all, but stranger things had happened. "Heartless beast," she hissed. "How could you abandon your own children?"

Tired of the game, Cody said, "Don't look at me, lady. These kids aren't mine."

"Are you saying that these kids don't belong to you, mister?" the conductor asked. He sent Cody a skeptical glare. "Are you sure? Or are you trying to get out of paying for their fare?"

"I repeat," Cody said, his lips compressed so tightly they were white, "I don't have any kids."

Amy began sobbing, her big brown saucer eyes brimming with tears. "We love you, Papa, even if you don't want us." By now Amy's tears were very real. She was only ten years old and there was only so much she could bear. Since she and her brother had caused her uncle's death, they had lived precariously, struggling to keep from starving to death or being apprehended. Being discovered in the baggage car by the conductor had burst the dam of her emotions.

Cody was speechless. What had he done to deserve this? Why had these two homeless waifs chosen him to latch on to? Him, of all people, a hard-boiled drifter who hadn't even spoken to a child in his entire adult life until the other day.

"Is that your last word, mister?" the conductor asked, unconvinced that Cody was telling the truth. The kids certainly seemed sincere enough. "If it is, the kids will be put off at the next station."

Brady began to cry in earnest, wishing desperately that he and Amy could remain with Cody Carter. "Please, Papa, don't let the conductor put us off the train. What will we do? Where will we go?" His sad little face, dirty and smudged with tears, touched the heart of every passenger.

Suddenly Cody found himself on the receiving end of abusive language and pointed insults, and he didn't like it. Nor did he like the way the lady-in-black was glaring at him. He could feel the potent heat of her disapproval boring into him through the protection of her black veil.

"Dammit to hell, I'll pay for their damn tickets but I won't be responsible for them. Just what I need," he grumbled sourly as he counted out the money, "two brats hanging on to my coattails."

"You should have thought about that before you had them," Cassie charged hotly. "Only a black-hearted devil would abandon his own children. And watch your language around the children." She turned to Amy, who was drying her tears on her ragged sleeve. "Where is your mother, honey?"

"D—dead," Amy gulped, immediately intrigued by the kind, husky-voiced lady.

Cassie shot Cody a venom-filled glare, then asked Amy, "Are you hungry?"

"We're both hungry," Brady piped up. "We've had nothing to eat for two days. Not since—Papa left us."

Cody's black brows came together in a fierce scowl. "Here," he said, shoving the remnants of his lunch at the kids.

Contrary to what the lady-in-black thought, he wasn't a heartless bastard. Scooting over, he made room for the children beside him on the seat. Cassie added her leftovers to the hoard of food and soon the two waifs were happily engaged in demolishing every morsel.

Cassie studied the children while they ate, trying to discover something of their half-breed father in them. Though their hair was the same dark ebony, their eyes were a warm brown, not the brilliant blue of their father's. She thought their noses were the same, and that the boy's mouth was shaped exactly like his sire's. She wondered what their mother had looked like and what had provoked her to marry a half-breed who would callously abandon his own children.

Cody knew the lady-in-black thought him a hard-hearted bastard, and it rankled. He didn't deserve her poor opinion. There were many things he did deserve, but not this. As soon as he got to Dodge he'd park the kids in an orphanage and forget them. It couldn't be too soon to suit him. They were lying little thieves who were trying to con him into offering something he wasn't prepared to give. He had challenged men for lesser offenses.

"They're sleeping."

Startled anew by the silken huskiness of the woman's voice, Cody glanced down at the children. Huddled together in a heap against him, they had indeed fallen asleep, looking like two grubby angels. It suddenly occurred to him that they must have been terrified alone in the baggage car all night.

"What are their names?"

"Amy and Brady," Cody said without thinking. Cassie glared at him, and Cody realized too late how incriminating his words must sound. How could he know their names if they weren't his children? Damn! What could he say after that?

"They're beautiful. Their mother must have been lovely."

Cody's eyes lingered on Cassie's lips, wishing he could see the rest of her face. "I have no idea what their mother looked like."

"You don't have to lie to me. Any fool can see they love you."

"Look, lady, I don't know much about kids, but I do know these two aren't mine."

"I'd be proud to claim children like yours."

"You want them, they're yours."

Cassie gasped in dismay.

Disgruntled, Cody turned away to stare out the window. Soon they would stop at another of those endless little towns, and he supposed he'd be obliged to buy supper for the kids.

Brady jerked awake just as the train let off a long blast of steam. He looked around him, disoriented by his surroundings, until his eyes lit on Cody. Then he smiled with such sweetness, Cody's breath caught in his throat despite his agitation. "Where are we, Papa?"

"At some godforsaken town in eastern Kansas," Cody growled crossly. "And don't call me Papa."

"What should I call you?"

"Nothing, kid, don't call me anything. We're not going to be together that long."

By now Amy had awakened, her grimy little face screwed up into a frown. "Are you going to leave us again, Papa?"

"No!" This from Cassie, who couldn't help but overhear the conversation. "Your father isn't going to leave you, children. You're going wherever he's going."

"Where are you going, Papa?" Amy asked curiously.

"Dodge City," Cody replied, wondering why in the hell he felt it necessary to divulge that piece of information.

Somewhat startled to learn that the half-breed was getting off at the same town she was, Cassie said, "I'm going to Dodge City, too, and I'll make certain your papa doesn't try to abandon you again."

Amy gave Cassie a brilliant smile, but the child wasn't deluded. She knew that somewhere along the line Cody Carter would rid himself of the unwanted encumbrance of two orphaned children. But until he did, she and Brady would make the most of it, enjoying the nice lady and their adopted "Papa" until they parted company. Who knew what the future held?

Chapter Four

Cassie just barely remembered her mother. She was eight years old when Linda died giving birth. The child, a boy, had died along with his mother. All Cassie could remember of Linda was that she had long blond hair and was beautiful. She had tried to forget those days when Linda had no time to devote to her small daughter and had shunted her aside or plain ignored her.

Cassie vaguely recalled Buck Carter, her stepfather. When she had first come to the Rocking C with Linda, Buck appeared quite taken with the little blond cherub. But after a few months the novelty of having a stepdaughter wore off, then disappeared altogether.

If memory served, there was a son named Wayne, much older than she, who was away at school when she and Linda had arrived at the ranch. She thought there was another son who had left soon after her arrival; she couldn't recall his name or what he looked like except that he was as different from Wayne as night from day.

Life was rather pleasant for Cassie at the Rocking C, until something happened between Linda and Buck, something so terrible that things were never the same again. Not even Linda's pregnancy seemed to appease Buck—it had made things worse, in fact. The atmosphere was so tense that Buck's anger even extended to Wayne. Cassie had no idea why bad feelings existed between father and son, but because Buck needed Wayne's help running the ranch, and Wayne was his heir, they made the best of it. Even a young child like Cassie could sense the tension and animosity between Buck, Wayne, and Linda.

The worst moment in Cassie's young life had been when Buck stood beside Linda's grave and spoke with such hostility that eight-year-old Cassie had been shocked and frightened by his strange anger.

"Serves the bitch right," he had muttered before turning and walking away.

Not long afterward Cassie was shipped off to St. Louis to live with her grandmother. She was nearly grown before she learned that Buck had never sent a penny to that dear woman to help support his stepdaughter. She and Nana had existed the best they could on what her grandmother earned from sewing for the rich. Until this day Cassie had never forgiven Buck for his blatant neglect. She had even written and asked for help when Nana had taken ill, but Buck had ignored her letter. In order to afford the medicine necessary to keep Nana alive, Cassie had taken a job at Sal's. But age had taken its toll and Nana had died anyway.

When the telegram had arrived, Cassie felt little remorse over Buck's death. How could she?

"Dodge City next stop!"

The conductor's words brought Cassie abruptly from her reverie and she prepared to debark. She wondered what life had in store for her at the Rocking C, and why she had been summoned for the reading of Buck's will. After years of neglect, had Buck made some kind of provision for her?

She seriously doubted it, and wasn't certain she would accept it if he had.

Chapter Five

"Is this Dodge City, Papa?" Brady asked excitedly.

"For God's sake, kid, I'm not your father," Cody said, gnashing his teeth in frustration. "Once I find a place to dump you, we're quits with one another, got it?"

"The nice lady said you're going to take us with you," Amy said, aiming a soulful look at Cody.

"The *nice* lady can go straight to—"

"Sir!" Cassie heard the remark and rounded on Cody. "Please watch your language in front of the children."

"Take us with you, Papa." Brady's voice held a tremulous note that went straight to Cody's heart. Was he going soft in the head? He sure as hell didn't need the aggravation of two grubby waifs.

"For God's sa—" The word disintegrated when he recalled Cassie's rebuke. His language sounded fine to him. "Aw, what the heck. C'mon, kids, let's get off this damn—er—blasted train." Grinning from ear to ear, Amy and Brady scrambled to obey.

In the commotion of arrival, Cody lost sight of the lady-in-black, and cursed beneath his breath. He had spent two miserable days wondering what she looked like beneath her black shroud and had every intention of looking her up after his business was settled at the ranch. But all he caught a glimpse of now was the enticing line of her shapely back as she hurried away. He didn't even know her name, or who she was mourning.

"Where is the nice lady going, Papa?" Amy asked, sorry to part company with Cassie.

"Not too far away, I hope," Cody muttered with a hint of vexation. He didn't mention it to the kids, but when the business at the ranch was taken care of and he was rid of these two pests, he fully intended to find the mysterious lady-in-black.

"What are we going to do now?" asked Brady. He wasn't impressed with the raw cow town known as Dodge City. Compared to St. Louis it was small, dirty, and overrun with dangerous-looking men who frightened him. And Brady was correct in his fears. Dodge City was a gathering place for every gunslinger in the territory, where the law had little impact and murder was a nightly occurrence.

"First I'm going to find an orphanage where I can leave you two. Then I'm going to the Rocking C—alone."

"What's a Rocking C?" Amy asked curiously.

"It's a ranch, and a damn prosperous one."

"The nice lady said you weren't to curse in front of your children."

Cody leveled a quelling glance at Brady. "Look, kid, you can stop pretending now. I'm not your papa. I don't have any children."

Amy's face lit up. "Would you like some?"

"No more than I'd like a wife," Cody grumbled with growing impatience. "Do you kids always ask so many questions?"

"Only when someone answers them," Brady said, grinning impishly.

"Look, kids, I'm going into the sheriff's office over yonder. Wait outside while I talk with him. Do you think you can do that?"

"Will you promise to come back?" Amy suspected that being abandoned in this rough town would be much worse than being on their own in St. Louis.

"Yeah, I'll come back," Cody growled in a voice meant to convey his impatience. But somehow it didn't come out like that. Hidden someplace in that gruff voice was a compassion he had no idea he possessed.

"Then we'll wait," Amy replied.

Setting his bag down on the wooden boardwalk outside the door, Cody walked into the sheriff's office. The sheriff, a large man whose muscles were already going to fat at age forty, looked up from the wanted posters he was perusing. He frowned, recognizing Cody's mixed blood immediately. The town already had enough trouble without a mean-looking half-breed mixing things up.

"I'm Sheriff Hermann. What can I do for you, mister?"

"I need some information, Sheriff. Can you direct me to the local orphanage?"

Hermann sent Cody a hard look, realized he was serious, and burst out laughing. "Are you joshing? There's no such thing in Dodge. Maybe Wichita, or Kansas City, but not here, not in this town."

"Sonuvabitch!" What was he going to do now? He couldn't just drop the kids off in a hellhole like Dodge to fend for themselves. "Do you know of a family that would like a couple of kids?"

The sheriff gave Cody a narrow-eyed look. "Are they yours?"

"No, they're just a couple of orphans who latched on to me in St. Louis. Can't seem to shake them."

Just then the door opened and Brady peeked inside. "What's keeping you so long, Papa?"

Cody groaned.

The sheriff made a disgusted sound deep in his throat. "What's your name, stranger, and why are you trying to get rid of your kids?"

Cody dragged in a ragged sigh. Would this nightmare never end? "The name's Carter. Cody

Carter. And I told you before, these aren't my kids."

"They seem to think so. Carter, you say? Well I'll be damned. Aren't you old man Carter's bastard by an Indian squaw? Heard tell they're waiting out at the ranch for you to arrive so they can read the will. Sorry about your pa. Doc says it was his heart, been bad for years."

"Watch your language in front of the kids," Cody growled. Suddenly he blanched, realizing what he had said. Not only were the kids growing on him, but the prissy lady-in-black had gotten to him as well.

"Sorry," Hermann mumbled. "But you are old Buck's son, aren't you?"

"Yeah. I'm on my way out to the ranch now, just as soon as I find a place to park the kids."

Amy joined Brady in the doorway, looking solemn and forlorn. Sheriff Hermann searched their grimy faces. "What did you do, Carter, roll them in dirt?"

"It's a long story," Cody said tightly. It was a wonder he had held on to his temper this long.

"Seems to me the best place for a pair of kids like these two is out at the ranch. Plenty of room for them to roam. Irene will welcome them with open arms."

"Who is Irene?"

"Irene Thompson, old Buck's lame housekeeper. Been with him nearly ten years. Damn shame about her leg. Kept her from finding a husband. Where've you been? Obviously you haven't been home to see Buck in a long while."

Not wanting to delve too deeply into his past, Cody said, "I've been busy."

"Are we going to the ranch, Papa?" Brady asked, excited at the prospect of remaining with Cody.

"We're going to the ranch," Cody replied in a tone that gave vent to his vast annoyance. "But don't get your hopes up. You're not going to stay." He turned to the sheriff. "Is there a livery in town where I can rent a wagon?" His original intention had been to rent a horse, but with two kids in tow that would hardly do now.

"End of the street, you can't miss it," Hermann directed.

Cody nodded and left the office, the children hard on his heels.

"What kind of ranch is it, Papa?" Brady asked, barely able to contain his excitement as he skipped beside Cody. "Are there horses? I've never ridden a horse. What other animals are there at the ranch? Can I—"

"For God's sa—For Pete's sake," he amended, "be quiet. Your tongue wags faster than wash hanging out on a line on a windy day."

Brady's dirty little face fell as he recalled the many times his Uncle Julian had told him to keep quiet and stop asking so many questions. When Cody saw how his rebuke had subdued the little fellow, he was instantly contrite.

"There's the livery," he said, hoping to lift Brady's spirits. The little fellow perked right up as he ran to the nearest stall to inspect one of the horses. Amy joined him, more cautious of the animal than her daring brother.

Cody found the stableman shoveling hay in one of the stalls. He remembered the man from his youth. Franz Vogelman had been old before Cody had left the ranch and he appeared ancient now.

"I'd like to rent a wagon, Mr. Vogelman."

Franz Vogelman straightened from his task, rubbed his back, and peered up at Cody through myopic eyes. "Got one out back. How long will you be needin' it?"

"I'll send it back tomorrow. I'm just going out to the Carter place."

"Say, I remember you. You're old Buck's bast—er—son. Sorry about your pa. You gonna stay a spell?"

"I don't think so," Cody replied, recalling how nosy the old man could be. "About the wagon . . ."

"Sure thing. Say, you got a couple of nice-lookin' younguns there. Where's their mother?"

"There is no mother and these aren't my—oh, hell, what's the use?"

Avoiding the old man's questions, Cody quickly hitched a horse to the wagon out back, threw his bag in, lifted Amy and Brady to the seat, and leaped up beside them. After paying Vogelman, he guided the horse down Dodge City's main street. At the edge of town, almost opposite the Longbranch Saloon, something occurred that added to Cody's already considerable woes. A small, dirty white mongrel darted out into the street directly into their path.

"Watch out for the dog!" Amy cried as the mongrel, who was being chased by the butcher waving a wicked-looking cleaver, ducked beneath the wheels of the wagon.

Brady screamed.

Amy clapped her hands over her eyes.

"Aw, she-it!" This from Cody, who sawed on the reins so hard the horse reared in protest. But it was too late. A long, loud howl told them that the dog had been hit. The butcher didn't wait around to learn the dog's fate. He merely nodded as if to say, "That's that," and turned back to his shop.

The moment the horse was under control, Brady scrambled down from the wagon and ran after the dog, who had limped into an alley, whining pitifully.

"Wait," Cody cried as Brady disappeared into the alley. "Don't touch him, he might bite!" But it was too late, Brady was already hard on the mongrel's heels.

"Blast and da—darn!" Feeling much put upon, Cody set the brake and leaped from the wagon. He started forward and suddenly remembered Amy, who was sitting white-faced on the seat. "Don't move!" he warned. "Stay where you are until I come back."

"But Brady—"

"I'll take care of Brady."

Sprinting into the alley, Cody hoped Brady hadn't attempted to touch the injured animal. Lord only knew what the pain-maddened dog would do to the kid when cornered. His heart flew into his mouth when he spied Brady at the end of the long alley, standing as still as a statue, holding the injured dog in his arms. He was staring down at the ground, apparently terror-stricken by what he saw.

"Brady, what is it?" Cody asked anxiously when he reached the boy. "Did that da—blasted dog bite you?"

Regarding Cody with stricken eyes, Brady shook his head from side to side.

"What is it?"

No answer was necessary when Cody glanced down and saw a man lying atop trash and empty bottles littering the ground. He was unconscious, bleeding from a head wound, and his right leg was twisted beneath him at an odd angle. His right hand was curled around an empty whiskey bottle, cradled against his chest.

There was no left hand. Or forearm. His left arm was missing below the elbow.

Cody knelt beside the man, ascertained that he was still alive, and decided that his leg was broken. The odor of alcohol was strong on the man, and Cody surmised that he had gotten staggering drunk, fallen down, injured his head, and broken his leg. He looked up at Brady, still clasping the injured dog in his little arms. His face was ashen.

"Is he dead?"

"No, but he needs a doctor. Do you remember where the sheriff's office is, Brady?" Brady nodded. "Run there as fast as you can and bring the sheriff back with you. And put that damn dog down. He's probably diseased."

Brady's eyes grew round. "The nice lady said you shouldn't curse."

Cody gnashed his teeth in frustration. "Just do as I say, Brady. Do it now!"

Turning on his heel, Brady ran as if the devil himself was after him. But he refused to put the dog down; he cradled him protectively in his thin little arms, his short legs churning furiously.

Ten minutes later Brady returned with Sheriff Hermann, minus the dog, which he had placed in Amy's tender care before summoning the sheriff.

"What do we have here, Carter?" Hermann asked. "Couldn't make heads or tails out of your kid."

Cody moved away from the unconscious man, allowing the sheriff to take his place.

"Aw, hell, is this what you called me out of my office for? It's just Reb Lawrence on one of his regular binges. He'll sleep it off and be ready to start another one tomorrow."

"The man's injured, Sheriff," Cody said, pointing out Reb's head wound and oddly bent leg. "How did he lose his arm?"

"War injury," Hermann grunted. "Fought on the losing side."

"Does he have a family?"

"Naw. Had one, though. When he returned from war with one arm his wife up and left him. He's got no relatives far as I know. Old Reb don't bother nobody. Works some when he's sober. Lost his small farm a while back when he couldn't pay the taxes. Wasn't much, but it earned him a living before the war."

"The man is injured. Help me carry him to the doctor's office where he can be treated."

"Doc Striegle is out of town. Won't be back till next week. Went to see his married daughter and new grandchild in Denver."

"Who else in town can treat him?"

Hermann scratched his balding head. "No one that I know of. The good folks of Dodge don't cotton to Rebs. There was a lot of hard feelings when Lawrence joined the Confederate Army back in '62. His folks were from around Atlanta and owned one of those fancy plantations. Everything's gone now, for all the good it did him."

When Hermann turned away to return to his office, Cody grabbed him by the arm and spun him around. "You going to leave him here to die?"

Hermann gave Cody a searching look. "You got any other ideas? You could take him out to the ranch." At Cody's horrified expression, Hermann said, "Heard tell Irene is pretty good at doctoring. Takes care of all the ranch hands."

"She-it! I'm already saddled with two orphans who stick to me like glue and a lame mutt I'll probably never get rid of. I sure as hell don't need a drunken, one-armed Reb with a broken leg added to my list of responsibilities."

For a moment Hermann looked confused. Then he shrugged and said, "Suit yourself. I'm too busy upholding the law to worry about it. But if it makes you happy, I'll ask around and see if anyone wants to take care of him." He turned to leave.

"Wait! Help me carry him to the wagon."

Cody couldn't believe he had said that. His life was slowly going from bad to worse. A week ago he had been happy with his carefree existence, lonely though it might be. And he was content with his reputation as a tough, hard-boiled half-breed who handled a gun better than most. No one messed with Cody Carter, not if they wanted to live, or so he led them to believe.

"Are we taking the poor man home, Papa?" Brady asked.

For a moment Cody had forgotten that Brady was standing on the sidelines, listening with rapt attention to the conversation.

"The ranch isn't my home, hasn't been for a long time. But if Sheriff Hermann says Irene can help him, then I guess that's where we'll take him. After that I wash my hands of him."

Still unconscious, Reb Lawrence screamed once when Cody straightened out his leg, then fell silent. His face was white as paste, his breathing shallow. He still clutched the half-empty bottle of booze against his chest. With a snort of disgust, Cody took the bottle from his hand and dashed it to the ground. Then he and Hermann carried

Reb back to the wagon where Amy still waited, clutching the small mutt Brady had thrust into her arms.

Once Reb was settled into the back of the wagon, Cody placed Brady on the seat beside Amy, jumped up, and slapped the reins against the horse's rump.

"I can't persuade you to leave that mangy mutt behind, can I?" Cody asked hopefully.

"She's got a hurt leg," Amy said, as if it explained everything. "Our wagon is the one that ran over her." She turned to Brady. "What shall we name her?"

Cody gave a snort of disgust. "The damn mutt's a male, not a female."

Brady ignored him. "Let's call him Blackie."

"Blackie!" Laughter exploded from Cody's chest. It was so unexpected it startled the children. "The mutt's pure white. Or would be if he was clean."

"So what?" Brady said with childish logic. "I always wanted a dog, and I always wanted to name it Blackie."

"I think it's a perfect name," Amy announced, petting the dog's matted coat as if it were the purest silk. If her brother wanted a dog named Blackie then he would have a dog named Blackie. "We can keep him, can't we, Papa?"

"Don't call me—aw, she-it, keep the damn mutt if you want. I won't be around long enough to worry about it. I'm leaving soon as the will's read. I've got a damn good job waiting for me in St.

Louis and I doubt Wayne will want me around."

"The nice lady said—"

"I don't give a damn—darn what the prissy—er—nice lady said."

The ranch lay ten miles west of Dodge. It was a large spread, boasting several hundred head of cattle and countless acres of knee-high grass, which was cut several times a year and used for fodder. Except for the sound of Reb's moans coming from the back of the wagon, the trip progressed quietly. Cody's last outburst had plunged the children into silence. They were both aware of how much they depended on his goodwill. He had already done more for them than any person since their parents' deaths.

When they came in sight of the ranch house, painful memories assailed Cody. He recalled his mother's love for him, and the gentle woman's devotion to a man who had refused to marry her. He remembered Wayne's cruelty and Buck's indifference toward his half-breed son. And he recalled how much he had loved the ranch and missed it despite his abrupt leaving all those years ago. And he remembered Linda and his initiation to sex.

He wondered if Linda was still alive.

"It's a big house, Papa," Brady said, suitably impressed.

"Does all this land belong to you?" Amy asked.

"None of it belongs to me," Cody said resentfully. "It belongs to my brother Wayne. Maybe he'll take you in after I leave." A moment later he realized how stupid his words were. Only a miracle could change Wayne from the disagreeable person he had been, and Cody didn't believe in miracles.

"I won't stay here without you," Brady said. His stubborn little chin jutted out at a defiant angle, challenging Cody to contradict him.

"Neither will I," Amy declared, in complete agreement with her brother.

"Lord deliver me from such a fate," Cody muttered, raising his eyes heavenward.

Cody guided the wagon close to the house, hopped from the driver's seat, and tossed the reins around the porch rail. Despite the fact that the sprawling two-story house needed a fresh coat of paint, it was still impressive with its floor-to-ceiling windows and wraparound porch. He was staring at the imposing structure, thinking that Buck had made a great success of ranching during his life, when the door was flung open and a slim, handsome man stepped out onto the porch.

"Well, the prodigal has returned. Welcome home, *brother.*" The way he said brother made it sound like an insult.

"Hello, Wayne," Cody said evenly. "I wouldn't be home now if I hadn't been summoned by Father's lawyer. Where's Linda?"

"Linda? Haven't you heard? Linda died three years after you left. We would have told you had we known where to contact you."

Cody looked startled. "Dead?" Had he known that Linda was dead, he might have—no, he told himself, he wouldn't have returned. Buck didn't really care about him, and Wayne sure as hell didn't want him around. "I'm sorry."

"Can we get down, Papa?"

Wayne's eyes bulged grotesquely when he saw the children sitting in the wagon. "Don't tell me you're married! Those kids don't look like breeds. You sure as hell didn't marry a squaw. What decent white woman would marry a half-breed?"

"These aren't my kids," Cody said tightly.

"No? What are they doing with you if they aren't your kids?"

"They're a couple of—aw, hell, it doesn't matter. Their names are Amy and Brady." He swung the kids from the unsprung seat and set them on the ground. Amy still clutched the injured mutt in her arms. "This is my brother Wayne, kids."

"Half-brother," Wayne corrected nastily. "Haven't you ever heard of soap and water, Cody? The kids are filthy. Where's their mother?"

"Their mother is dead." Cody swiveled his head toward the sound of a voice so familiar he felt his gut contract. "Hello, children."

"The nice lady!" Brady squealed, delighted by the unexpected appearance of the nice lady.

"You and Cassie know one another?" Wayne asked suspiciously.

Astounded, Cody could do little more than stare. Standing in the doorway, swathed in unrelieved black, but minus the concealing hat and veil, stood the lady-in-black from the train. "Cassie?" Where had he heard that name before?

Cassie was stunned. Seeing the handsome half-breed and his two children at the Rocking C was a complete shock. Why hadn't she guessed that he was Buck Carter's son? Vaguely she recalled the brooding, dark-skinned lad she had known so briefly. She'd had no idea he'd grow into such a ruggedly handsome man. Just looking at him sent her senses reeling, even if he was an exasperating devil. Any man who'd abandon his own children had to be a devil. In a moment of insight, she decided to keep that piece of information from Wayne, at least until she learned why Cody Carter had denied his own children.

"Don't you remember?" Wayne explained. "Cassie is Linda's daughter."

The picture that came to mind was of a chubby blond cherub. Then the scenario changed abruptly and he was inside Sal's House Of Pleasure, ogling a stunning blond with the face of an angel and a body to match. Her name was Cassie, he had been told by Sal, and she wasn't for the likes of him. Now here he was, looking upon that very same Cassie, appearing as prim and virtuous as an untried virgin.

Cassie, Linda's daughter.

Cassie, his stepsister.

Cassie, the high-priced whore.

Cassie.

She-it, he wanted to puke.

Suddenly he became aware of Amy pulling on his coattail. "Papa, Mr. Reb is awake."

"And what about Blackie?" Brady asked petulantly. "He's hurting. And we're all hungry."

"She-it!"

Chapter Six

Cassie stared at Cody, her eyes clinging to his with a tenacity that produced an almost painful tension. The air between them crackled with emotions neither of them understood. She grew breathless just looking into his dark, intense face with those startling blue eyes. Something in his expression gave her the distinct feeling that he didn't approve of her. What had she done? Was it because she'd had the nerve to rebuke him for abandoning his children? He certainly deserved her rebuke. What decent woman wouldn't disapprove of what he had attempted to do to two innocent children?

Against her will, her eyes lingered on the wide slope of his shoulders, rippling with thick muscles; on his broad chest, narrow waist, and slim hips; on the bold thrust of his groin, where her eyes paused almost brazenly. Suddenly realizing the dangerous direction of her gaze, she pulled her eyes back to his face. She saw little resemblance to his half-brother. She recognized Cody's strength and determination in the unyielding set of his square jaw; in the stubborn lift of his firm, full lips; in the searing heat of his blue eyes as he watched her slow perusal of him.

It took every ounce of Cody's willpower to keep his body from reacting to Cassie's bold scrutiny. When her eyes lingered with slow deliberation on his loins, he clenched his fists and vowed to get even with her for treating him like a stud bull on display. Once a whore, always a whore, he thought disgustedly. Was she so eager for a man after the long train trip?

It was the first time Cody had seen the unveiled splendor of Cassie's eyes, and their unusual color startled him—intrigued him—drew him so deeply into their torrid depths that it took gigantic effort to withdraw. Did she know what she was doing to him? Of course she did, he assured himself. And she was damn good at it. She was an accomplished seductress who used her body to make a living. The woman was a real beauty; long-limbed, slim, yet exquisitely endowed. Her exotic eyes sloped upward at the corners, so innocent yet filled with the age-old knowledge of Eve. The bones of her face were delicate, with high cheekbones and chiseled nose, framed by a wealth of waist-length golden curls. She was a compelling combination of haughty reserve and sultry temptation—part lady, part tart, and all woman.

Why the widow's weeds? Cody wondered. Surely she wasn't wearing mourning for Buck, was she? Why had she been living in St. Louis instead of at the ranch? All kinds of questions flitted through his brain as his body reacted violently to Cassie's thorough inspection. Questions that demanded answers. And he *would* have answers, he told himself as he deliberately broke eye contact.

While Cody and Cassie were engaged in their rapt study of one another, Wayne, alerted by the children's words, walked over to peer inside the wagon. "What in the hell is Reb Lawrence doing in the wagon? Why have you brought the town drunk to the Rocking C?"

Dragging his thoughts and eyes away from the enticing blond, Cody said, "He's injured and the doc is out of town."

"What are you, some kind of do-gooder? You haven't gone and found religion, have you? Lord, that would be something. A half-breed zealot."

"Not hardly. Sheriff Hermann suggested I bring him here so Irene could treat him. His leg is broken. If it isn't set immediately, he'll never walk again."

"No big loss," Wayne said nastily. "Of what good to society is a one-armed drunk?"

"Wayne!" Cassie gasped, shocked by Wayne's callous words. "I just met Irene but she seems like a kindly woman who wouldn't mind helping an injured man. Why don't we ask her?"

"Ask me what?"

Irene, a petite, raven-haired woman in her mid-thirties, had come out onto the porch from the house in time to hear Cassie's words. She saw Cody and Wayne standing beside the wagon and limped down the steps to join them. Cody felt a jolt of compassion when he noticed that the woman was crippled. Upon closer inspection he noted that her right foot was twisted.

"Reb Lawrence," Irene said quietly as she looked into the wagon bed. "What's wrong with him besides being drunk?"

"Broken leg and head wound," Cody said tersely. "Can you help him?"

Irene stared hard at Cody. "You must be Mr. Buck's other son. He talked of you often." Cody doubted that. "I'll do what I can for the poor man. I know what it's like to be crippled. Carry him into the house."

"The bunkhouse," Wayne countered harshly. "I won't have him in the house. You have Cassie to thank for this, Cody. If not for her tender heart I'd order the man driven back to town and dumped in the gutter where you found him." He turned abruptly and stomped into the house.

"I appreciate the warm welcome," Cody muttered beneath his breath as he stared at Wayne's departing back. Then shoving Wayne from his mind, he lifted Reb from the wagon bed and carried him to the bunkhouse.

Irene turned to follow, but halted abruptly

when she noticed Amy and Brady hovering in the shadow of the wagon. Her expression softened. Never had she seen such forlorn-looking children. "Whose children are these?" she asked, her brown eyes filled with pity.

"They belong to Cody," Cassie explained. "Their names are Amy and Brady."

"Mr. Cody's children? Mr. Buck would have liked that," Irene said wistfully. "Why are they so dirty?"

Cassie flushed, unwilling to divulge all she knew about Cody and his children. "It's a long story."

"They look hungry," Irene noted.

"We are hungry," Amy admitted, finally finding her tongue. "But my brother would like you to look at his dog first."

Both Irene and Cassie stared at the incredibly dirty mutt Brady was holding in his arms.

"What's wrong with him?" Irene asked.

"Blackie ran beneath the wheels of the wagon and Papa ran over him," Brady said tearfully. "Papa said we could bring him to the ranch. Will you help him? He's hurt his leg."

"After I take care of Reb," Irene promised. "While you're waiting, maybe Cassie can take you into the kitchen and fix something to hold you over till supper." Then she turned and followed Cody to the bunkhouse.

"I like her," Amy said as Irene walked away.

"So do I," Cassie concurred.

"Why does she limp?" Brady asked guilelessly.

"She's crippled," Cassie explained with exaggerated patience, "but it isn't polite to talk about another person's afflictions. Didn't your father teach you that?" Brady merely stared at Cassie. "Come along, children, into the house." She gave the dog a dubious glance. "You'll have to leave your dog behind."

Brady's arms tightened around the mangy mongrel. "No, Blackie goes where I go."

"Blackie?" The name was so utterly inappropriate for the filthy white dog that Cassie laughed aloud. "How about if we leave Blackie on the back porch and feed him something while you're eating? Then we'll see that you all have baths, and maybe find you some clean clothes."

Brady nodded in reluctant agreement.

Cassie saw little of Cody the rest of that day, which was fine with her. Looking at the handsome half-breed gave her unfamiliar twinges in the pit of her stomach. His blue eyes were relentless, hiding secrets that confused and frightened her. Secrets that had nothing to do with their chance meeting on the train. It was almost as if he was warning her to watch her step, that he was watching her.

Irene returned to the house several hours later, exhausted from setting Reb's leg and binding his head wound. Cassie offered to help her prepare the evening meal. She had already bathed the children and washed their hair, and when she had asked Wayne about clothing for them, he grudgingly told her to take whatever she needed from the attic. In an old trunk she had found cast-off clothing that had once belonged to Wayne, Cody, and herself. The clothes were wrinkled and musty, but a far sight better than those they had been wearing.

It was amazing what soap and water could do, Cassie thought as she watched the children pick at their food, too tired to do justice to the meal. Once the dirt and snarls had been washed from their hair, their curly locks were as sleek and dark as their father's. They really were beautiful children, she reflected, recalling their handsome father. She wondered if their mother had been a beautiful woman, then chided herself for thinking otherwise. Cody would never marry an ugly woman. Thinking about Cody making love to another woman and producing adorable children like these two made her uncomfortable.

Cody failed to show up at the evening meal. He had decided to remain with Reb in the bunkhouse that night in case he was needed. But Wayne was seated at the table, as nasty as ever. Cassie wondered what in the world made the man so disagreeable about everything.

"Put those brats to bed, they're falling asleep over their soup," Wayne complained. "I still find it astounding that a white woman would marry a damn half-breed. Ah, well, I don't imagine he'll be around long after the will is read. I've sent word to Lawyer Willoughby and he's coming tomorrow to read the will. I can't imagine why you and Cody were summoned for the reading. The old man must have left you each a small token."

Sending Wayne a withering glance, Cassie retorted, "I want nothing from Buck Carter. He gave me nothing in life. Why should I expect anything from his death?"

"Why, indeed," Wayne agreed complacently.

Having had just about all she could take of Wayne, Cassie rose abruptly. "Come along, children, I'll put you to bed since your father doesn't seem concerned about your welfare."

Cody dozed in the chair beside Reb's bunk. Irene had brought out a delicious supper for him and he had savored every morsel. She had also included a rich broth for Reb, but he hadn't been conscious long enough to eat it. It was the head wound that kept him unconscious, Irene had told Cody after she had treated Reb's injuries to the best of her ability. Cody came fully awake when Reb began thrashing around in the bunk. Leaning over the gaunt, one-armed man, Cody held him down to keep him from doing himself serious harm.

Cody was surprised when Reb opened his eyes and looked directly at him. "Who are you?" His strained whisper gave hint of the pain he must have been suffering.

"Cody Carter."

"Where am I?"

"At the Rocking C."

"Old Buck's place?"

"Yeah."

"Why?"

"Damned if I know. I guess I've got a soft spot in my heart for drunks and orphans." Self-derision made his voice rough. "Rest now. You don't know how lucky you were when my kid found you in that alley." *My kid?* Where in the hell did that come from?

"I could use a drink." Reb's voice was shaky and softly pleading.

Cody's expression hardened. "That's the last damn thing you need. Go to sleep!" Disgusted by the man's insatiable need for alcohol, Cody rose abruptly and left the bunkhouse. He met Irene on his way to the house.

"Is he awake?" she asked.

"Awake and asking for a drink."

"Go see your children, they've been asking for you. I'll try to get Reb to take some nourishment. Mr. Wayne told me which room was yours as a child and it's still empty if you'd like to use it."

"Much obliged, Irene."

Cody trudged into the house, weary to the bone. So much had happened during the last several days that his head was spinning. He had encountered a beautiful, desirable whore who turned out to be his stepsister, been adopted by two orphans on the run, and gained dubious custody of a dirty white mongrel with the unlikely name of Blackie and a drunken one-armed Reb with a broken leg.

Cody quietly let himself inside the house. A light was burning in the parlor and he looked in, surprised to see Cassie curled up in a chair reading a book.

"I'm surprised you can read." Startled, Cassie looked up as Cody sauntered into the room with a rolling gait that made her aware of the lithe sleekness of his body. She looked askance at him when he closed the door behind him.

"Why should that surprise you? My grandmother was a learned woman; she taught me to read and write and even sent me to school."

"Your grandmother?"

"Mother died when I was eight. Buck sent me away almost immediately. Nana raised me."

So that explained how she had ended up in St. Louis. "Did your grandmother know you are . . ."

"What am I?"

"Don't spar with me, Miss Innocent," Cody said harshly. "I saw you at Sal's. When I inquired about your availability I was told I couldn't afford you, that you were only available to high-class clients."

Cassie gasped in dismay. "Sal told you that? I don't believe you."

"So, it *is* true," Cody said, mistaking her dismay for guilt. "What in the hell ever possessed you to become a whore? If you needed help, why didn't you ask Buck?"

"Buck!" Cassie spat derisively. "Your father found it convenient to ignore me. I did write him, after Nana fell ill and was unable to ply her needle to support us."

"There were other options. Decent jobs, for

instance. I'm not condoning Buck, but you should have tried harder. You're just like your mother." His voice was ripe with disgust. "Linda needed more than one man to keep her satisfied. I should know, I was only fifteen when she seduced me."

All color drained from Cassie's face as she leaped from the chair. Her hand lashed out at his face before he could stop her. "Liar! My mother wasn't like that! She wasn't."

"I hate to be the one to disillusion you."

"Arrogant bastard! What does a half-breed know about the kind of problems I faced? Who are you to judge me?"

Cody's face stung from her blow as he fought to control his temper. "You're right, Cassie, I am a bastard. Buck's bastard. And a half-breed. I've never tried to deny it."

Cassie was instantly contrite. "I—I didn't mean it that way."

"Which way did you mean it? Are you saying I'm not a bastard? Or a half-breed? We both know that's a lie."

"I didn't mean to suggest that your blood was tainted. It isn't your fault that Buck didn't marry your mother. What I meant is that you have no right to suggest things about me that aren't true. Abandoning your children is worse than anything I have ever done."

"Those aren't my kids. Why won't anyone believe me?"

"You can't deny them, Cody. They love you so. They're waiting for you to tuck them in bed."

Cody couldn't seem to take his eyes off Cassie. The lamplight shining on her blond hair turned it to pure gold. She looked like an angel—he knew she wasn't—and his hands itched to drag the length of her body against his, to feel her breasts pressed against his chest, her legs molded to his, their loins meshed. He wanted to see her naked, without the black shroud concealing her lovely body.

He wanted her spread beneath him, open, inviting, displayed wantonly for his pleasure alone.

He wanted to be inside her.

His face grew warm; he could feel his groin swelling as his body responded to the mere thought of all those arousing things he wanted to do to her.

He loved her lips. He wanted to kiss her. He strained toward her.

Suddenly feeling threatened by the dark half-breed, Cassie retreated, until the edge of the chair bumped against the back of her knees. "Cody, did you hear what I said? The children are waiting for you."

"Let them wait. I suddenly find myself wondering what your lips taste like. I spent hours on that damn train staring at them. And wondering about the color of your eyes. Your voice intrigued me. Did you know that? You've got the sexiest voice I've ever heard."

Cassie's eyes grew round, mesmerized by his words and lazy drawl, fearing what he would do and yet wanting him to do it. "Don't touch me."

"Touch you? Oh, baby, I want to do a damn sight more than touch you. Come here." Reaching out, he dragged her against him. Their lips were a breath apart.

Cassie stiffened. "Cody, please, why are you doing this?"

"You may not realize it, but I've wanted you from the first moment I laid eyes on you at Sal's and was told you weren't for the likes of someone like me. If you're afraid I can't afford you, don't worry, I've got plenty of money to pay for your services, no matter how expensive you are."

"Dammit, Cody Carter, this has gone far enough. I'm not a whore! I was working as a maid for Sal."

Cody laughed harshly. "Sure, baby, and I'm lily white. You don't expect me to believe that, do you? A girl as stunning as you working as a maid? Ha! Tell me another story."

For the second time that night she raised her hand as if to strike Cody, but this time he was prepared. Catching her wrist in his fist, he imprisoned it behind her back, using it as leverage to press her more closely against him. From breast to thigh they were pasted together so tightly Cassie could feel the rampant thud of his heartbeat, the throbbing pressure of his sex. Or was it her own heartbeat she heard? Her own sex vibrating against his? The way he was staring at her lips made them tingle and burn, and she knew instinctively he was going to kiss her. Her mouth opened in silent protest.

Cody smiled to himself when he saw Cassie's mouth open in anticipation of his kiss. Hot little baggage, he gloated in mute satisfaction. She could deny it all she wanted but he knew exactly what she liked—what she needed. The little tart wasn't so different from her mother. If she was, he wouldn't have found her working in a whorehouse. Then all thought ceased as his mouth covered hers and he became lost in the sweet, taunting essence of her.

Trapped in the vise of his arms, Cassie was experiencing the first kiss of her life. Though twenty years old, she had never even had a beau. Fiercely protected by her grandmother while she was growing up, she'd had no opportunity to meet boys. And when she'd started working at Sal's she'd seen too much of men to ever want to be used by one. She doubted if the man existed who could interest her enough to make her want to surrender her heart or offer her body. But her response to Cody's kiss was something she hadn't expected.

She couldn't breathe, couldn't think, could barely support herself on her two legs. Did she even have legs? Cody's mouth was soft, coaxing, hot, demanding, encouraging . . . Taking her open mouth as invitation, his tongue slipped inside, searching, seeking, hot . . . *She* was hot.

Cody was shaken by the kiss. If he didn't know better he would swear there was smoke coming out of his ears. Had his body turned to ashes yet? Hot damn, Sal was right. This little number would be wasted on ordinary cowboys; the madam had been right to reserve her for "special" customers. And during his short stay at the ranch, he was claiming her as his own.

Suddenly he wanted more of Cassie, *had* to have more of her. His big, callused hands slid around her tiny waist, then slowly upward to her breasts. He groaned, feeling the soft mounds swell beneath his palms, their nipples hard little nubs that pushed pertly against his fingertips.

"Oh, God, baby, we're wasting time here. Let's go to bed where I can take your clothes off and make love to you slow and easy. You like it that way, don't you?"

Panting raggedly, she struggled out of his arms and pushed him away, catching him unaware. "How dare you! I'm not what you think. Don't ever touch me again."

"So, you're pretending to be Miss Prissy again," Cody said as he fought to bring his rampaging lust under control. Cassie seemed to bring out the worst in him. He rarely lost control where women were concerned. "You might fool Wayne but you can't fool me. Don't forget, I *saw* you at Sal's. But I can understand your desire to pretend you're respectable while at the ranch. Very well, Cassie, I'll go along with your pretense . . . for now. But if you suddenly find yourself with an itch and nobody to scratch it, you know where to find me. I've been told I'm damn good at making a certain kind of itch go away."

"Conceited jackass!" Cassie hissed, working her way around him so she could escape from the room. "I feel sorry for your children, Cody Carter. They love you so, yet it's obvious you care nothing for them."

"Now wait a damn minute, Cassie, I've done some despicable things in my life but I'd never abandon my own flesh and blood. Those two kids aren't mine."

She placed her hands on her hips, glaring at him. "Whose are they?"

"They're—"

"Yes?"

"She-it! What does it matter? You won't believe me anyway."

She flashed him a smug smile. "Good night, Cody. Don't forget to look in on the children. They're in the room next to yours." Abruptly she turned and fled out the door.

"She-it!" Cody repeated. Just when things were getting interesting, Cassie had to go all innocent on him. He still ached with urgent need, his loins were still full and heavy, and his body felt as if it had been slammed into a brick wall. If it was just any woman he wanted, he'd go into Dodge and find someone, but to his regret, no other woman but Cassie would do.

Cody paused before the door to the children's room, wondering why he bothered. Catering to the kids wasn't in his best interest or theirs. It would be to their advantage to forget him instead of depending on him. He wasn't going to be around forever. By making himself available to them he was placing himself in an awkward position. He wasn't their father, nor was he likely to become their father. He had his own life to live.

But despite that reasoning, Cody couldn't stop his hands from opening the door, or his steps from carrying him into the room where the children slept. Amy heard him and raised herself up on her elbows.

"Is that you, Papa?"

"It's Cody," Cody hissed through the darkness. "You know damn well I'm not your papa. Why aren't you asleep like your brother?"

"I was waiting for you. I—I wanted to thank you for bringing us to the ranch. Not for myself," she was quick to add, "but for Brady. He's still little, and living in the streets worried and confused him." Her selfless words, so brave, so utterly heart-wrenching, brought a lump to Cody's throat. "I know we can't stay, but until we have to leave, it would make Brady happy if he could call you Papa."

Silence. Cody couldn't have spoken had he tried.

"Did you hear?"

Gruffly. "Yeah."

"Brady was so young when Mama and Papa died. It makes him feel good to call you Papa. You aren't mad, are you? I know you weren't expecting us to show up on the train and tell everyone you were our papa, but—but—they were after us."

Cody's attention sharpened. "Who was after you?"

"I can't tell you."

"Look, kid, maybe I can help you."

"Nobody can help us. Please, Papa—Cody, please don't be mad at us."

Cody cleared his throat, surprised to find himself strangely choked. "I'm not mad. But you know I'm not the kind to hang around long in one place. One day I'll leave and you'll be on your own."

Suddenly Amy brightened. "Do you think Cassie would want us? I know she likes us. Maybe she could be our temporary mama."

Cody laughed harshly. What would a whore do with two kids? He didn't want to give Amy hope where none existed. "I doubt it. Look, Amy, let's just take it a day at a time. You can stay at the ranch until I leave. Then I'll try to find a family willing to take you in."

Even in the darkened room Cody could see the happy smile on Amy's solemn little face. "Then it's all right if we call you Papa? For Brady's sake," she added in a small, pleading voice.

Cody sighed in weary surrender. He was too tired to argue. "I reckon, if it will keep you from bothering me."

Then Amy did something that utterly flustered Cody. Reaching out her thin little arms, she found his neck and drew his head down to hers. Then she planted a wet kiss on his cheek.

Inhaling sharply, Cody bolted upright, backing out of the room as if he had just been bitten. He was shaking from head to toe when he finally reached the hall. He leaned against the closed door for support, his face white, his heart pumping furiously.

He'd rather face a room full of wildcats than go through that again. If some of his rough friends could see him now, he'd be the laughingstock of the entire country. Cody Carter, Army scout, sharpshooter, drifter, loner, half-breed—bastard. Lord, what had he ever done to earn the title of foster father, protector of drunks and mongrels and—soiled doves?

Chapter Seven

Lawyer Willoughby arrived at the ranch the next afternoon. Irene accompanied the children to the bunkhouse to see Reb while Cody, Cassie, and Wayne met with the lawyer in the small office Buck had always used to conduct business in. Ever since Buck's failing health had forced him to give up control of the ranch, the room had become exclusively Wayne's domain.

Willoughby seated himself at the desk, flanked by the three heirs, opened a leather portfolio, and withdrew a thick sheaf of papers. He peered owlishly over the rim of his thick glasses, cleared his throat, and began shuffling the documents in a rather distracted manner.

"For God's sake, Willoughby, will you get on with it?" Wayne snapped impatiently. "I've waited too damn long for this reading for it to be delayed another moment. Father died over a month ago; you should have had everything in order."

Willoughby sent him a withering look. "In good time, Wayne, in good time." A personal friend of the family for many years, Willoughby knew good and well what was going to take place once Buck's last wishes were made known, and he didn't look forward to the ruckus it would cause.

When everything was assembled to his satisfaction, Willoughby picked up a sheet of paper and began reading. The opening paragraphs followed the usual course of a will, with Buck declaring himself of sound mind and stating that the will was unbreakable and irrevocable.

Cody fidgeted in his seat, wondering what in the hell he was doing here when he didn't need the pittance he expected Buck to leave him. He was young and healthy and had earned his own living since the age of fifteen. He wished he had remained in St. Louis, returned to Sal's, and purchased Cassie's favors. By now he would have had his fill of her and not be driven by raging lust every time he looked at her.

Still wearing the black garb of mourning, Cassie sat with her hands folded neatly in her lap and her eyes downcast. She didn't want the small bequest Buck had probably left her. She had received nothing from him when she needed it and she could damn well do without it now. Coming here had been a mistake, she realized with a jolt of insight. If she had remained in St. Louis she'd never have met her arrogant, exasperating, bullheaded stepbrother. Or experienced the devastating allure of those compelling blue eyes.

Wayne waited nervously for Willoughby to begin enumerating Buck's bequests. There had been bad blood between him and his father for many years, since the day Buck had returned early from a trail drive and found him cavorting in bed with Linda. It had happened after Wayne returned home from college and learned his half-breed brother, Cody, had left home suddenly. The moment Wayne met Linda he suspected that Cody had left so abruptly and without explanation because he had been too immature to deal with their beautiful young stepmother.

Restless, insatiable Linda. Wayne grew hot just thinking about her. She had a whore's appetite and body, often leaving Buck's bed when he was asleep to be with Wayne. When Buck had discovered them, he became so angry he had suffered his first heart attack. After that, Buck had never enjoyed the robust health of his early years.

Several months later when Linda died in childbirth, neither Wayne nor Buck had been sure who had fathered her dead child. But since Cody had never bothered to return to the ranch or apprise Buck of his whereabouts, Buck, because of his failing health, had reluctantly allowed Wayne to take on more and more responsibility for the ranch. But Buck had never forgotten—or forgiven Wayne.

"Ahem," Willoughby said loudly in an effort to recapture the straying attention of the heirs. "Buck left specific instructions as to the distribution of his earthly goods. 'To my illegitimate son, Cody, who, had he seen fit to return home, would have been welcomed with open arms. I never meant to neglect you, son. I loved your mother dearly and regret not marrying her.' "

Cody made a sound of disgust deep in his throat.

Willoughby continued, " 'To Cody, I leave three-quarters interest in the Rocking C Ranch.' "

"Three-quarters! Father had to be out of his mind to leave his bastard three-quarters of my ranch!" This from Wayne, who leaped from his chair in violent protest.

"Sit down, Wayne," Willoughby admonished in his sternest voice. "I repeat, 'To Cody, I leave three-quarters interest in the Rocking C Ranch and three-quarters of all monies and profits thereof.' " Cody was in a state of shock. All he could do was stare at Willoughby as if the man had lost his mind.

" 'To my stepdaughter, Cassie, I ask forgiveness. I was still too angry with her mother to offer help when she asked. I hope to make up for it now. To Cassie, I leave the remaining one-quarter interest in the Rocking C and one-quarter of all monies and profit thereof. Should either Cody or Cassie die, their heirs will inherit their share. If there are no children on either side, the surviving heir will inherit the other's interest. And if they both should suffer an untimely death and leave no surviving children on either side, then with great reluctance on my part, my son Wayne will then inherit the whole.'"

His face white with shock, Wayne was reduced to silence.

"'To my son Wayne,'" Willoughby quoted before Wayne could find his voice, "'I leave a modest house in Dodge City and a yearly stipend of one thousand dollars. He alone knows why he has been disinherited. May the knowledge haunt him the rest of his days."

The silence was stunning as Willoughby enumerated generous bequests to Irene, who received ownership of the cottage she lived in, and several other loyal employees. When he finished, he set the will aside, removed his glasses, and waited for the storm to break.

It came within seconds. "I'll have the will broken!" Wayne shouted, shaking his fist at Willoughby.

"The will is unbreakable," came the lawyer's calm reply.

"Father was mad."

"Your father was as sane as you or I. It was his heart that failed, not his mind."

"I've worked and slaved for the ranch for as long as I can remember, while Cody left to live the wild life. I sacrificed my youth, thinking I'd inherit everything, just as it should be. Father never loved Cody. I am the legitimate son. As for Cassie," he sneered derisively, "he knew she'd probably turn out like her whoring mother; that's why he sent her away in the first place. It isn't fair!"

Cassie froze. Why would Wayne call her mother a whore?

"It might not be fair, Wayne, but these are your father's last wishes," Willoughby said, "and they will be carried out to the letter. Now, Cody, Cassie, there are some papers that need signing to make everything legal and binding." Willoughby had already dismissed Wayne from his mind, which made Wayne even angrier.

Cody was slow to respond, still too stunned by his sudden change of fortune to react. He was still digesting Buck's statement suggesting that it was Wayne's own fault he had been disinherited. Without being told, Cody knew that Buck's anger with his son involved Linda, and he was assailed by guilt. He had been seduced by Linda too, only he had been a callow youth of fifteen, too young to resist, but smart enough to know he couldn't remain on the ranch as long as Linda lived there. Ten years older than Cody, Wayne should have known better and kept his distance from the seductress. Now his half-brother was paying the price of his betrayal of their father.

Cassie's mind was running in the same direction as Cody's. This whole thing was so preposterous she felt as if she were an actor in a play. It was inconceivable that Buck would have remembered her after all these years, and even more astounding that he regretted his stinginess and neglect. Not that Buck was her real father—that man had died before she had been born—but for a short time Buck was the only father she had known. She had even grown to love the man, until he had cast her aside. One-quarter of the Rocking C. Co-owner with Cody Carter and his children. The thought was mind-boggling.

"If you two will sign these papers, I can be on my way," Willoughby repeated when neither Cody or Cassie seemed inclined to move.

"Sorry," Cody muttered, moving with alacrity. Willoughby pushed the papers under his nose and handed him the pen.

"This document is the deed, which is made out in both your name and Miss Fenmore's, making you co-owners of the Rocking C." Cody signed with a flourish. "And this document gives the bank authority to change the names on the bank accounts. Tomorrow you and Miss Fenmore will have full access to all the ranch's bank accounts as well as Buck's personal account." Cody signed quickly.

The papers were passed to Cassie, along with the pen. She was still in a daze as she signed them where Willoughby indicated.

"Is that all?" Cody asked.

"For now. Come to the office at your leisure and we'll go over the recent business transactions you should know about." He turned to Wayne, who stood nearby glowering at Cody and Cassie. "This one is for you to sign, Wayne. It's the deed to the house in Dodge. It's unoccupied at the present time and can be moved into immediately."

Wayne signed the paper in a huff and literally threw it back at Willoughby. "You haven't heard the last from me, Willoughby. Neither has Cody." Turning abruptly, he stormed from the room.

"He'll cool down," Willoughby predicted, gathering up his papers. "Things haven't been right between him and Buck for a long time. He should have expected this."

"I don't think Wayne will cool down any time soon," Cody drawled in an amused voice. Suddenly he found all this quite hilarious. Wayne had made life miserable for Cody when he was a child, and it tickled him to think that Wayne was being paid back in full. By his own father, no less. Never in his wildest dreams did Cody ever imagine he would own the Rocking C. Three-quarters of it, anyway. Hell, he didn't even want it!

He wasn't the kind to be tied down to one place, or shoulder responsibilities of such an enormous nature. Cody knew that the running of the ranch would fall entirely to him since Cassie couldn't be expected to know anything about a cattle empire. She-it! Two orphans, a mongrel, a one-armed drunk, a tart, and now a ranch. What next? He glanced at Cassie, wondering how she was taking this sudden change of fortune. From whore to ranch owner, quite a step upward.

Cassie felt the heavy weight of Cody's blue gaze on her and squared her shoulders. Having to deal with the arrogant half-breed on a day-to-day basis was something she didn't look forward to, although being near his children did please her. She had grown quite fond of the endearing little creatures and was pleased with the prospect of seeing more of them in the future. But Cody was another kettle of fish entirely.

Though inexperienced, she knew enough about men from viewing them firsthand at Sal's to know that Cody wanted her sexually. He'd made no bones about demonstrating how far his lust had driven him last night in the parlor. Living in the same house with Cody was like living with a time bomb. You never knew when it would explode, and the waiting was excruciatingly painful. Although she had to confess it wasn't pain she'd felt when Cody kissed her. It was far worse than pain. It was agony. The kind that came with the knowledge that kissing Cody had been the most devastating experience of her life. Surrendering to him would be a worse kind of torment, because she knew he would only be using her to sate his healthy male appetite.

"Well, I'll see you two in my office in a few days," Willoughby was saying as he let himself out of the study. "Contact me sooner if you have any questions, and I'm sure there will be questions. Give yourself a day or two to get over the shock." He closed the door behind him.

"Well, I'll be damned," Cody said, dropping into the nearest chair. "Whatever I expected, it wasn't this."

Cassie nodded mute agreement.

Cody gave her a searching look. "Do you need to wire Sal and tell her you won't be back? Look, if you'd miss the life and your—men friends too much, I'd be willing to buy you out."

His words brought Cassie abruptly out of her state of shock. "Buy me out? Never!" She shook her head dismissively. "There's no one I care about in St. Louis. I only remained with Sal because I felt a certain obligation. She gave me a decent-paying job when I needed it most. No one else could offer me half as much as she paid."

"I'll bet," Cody said snidely. "Look, Cassie, I'm going to be brutally honest with you. If you're going to remain at the Rocking C, I'll expect you to behave. Even if you're tempted to resume your—er—profession, don't expect to do it in Dodge. Lord knows I'm no saint, but there are some things I won't tolerate."

A mottled red crept up Cassie's neck. "You're right, Cody, you're definitely no saint, I can attest to that. Besides, you're too dense to see the truth if it was staring you in the face. But as long as you're laying down rules, I'll make a few of my own."

Cody smiled, thoroughly unsettling Cassie. Would she ever be prepared for the devastating effect his smile had on her? "Go ahead." His amused drawl told her he had no intention of following her rules.

"I expect you to treat your children as if you really cared for them." Cody gave her a startled look. "And you're to keep your hands off me. I won't be threatened by you."

"Threatened? You mean like this?" Before she knew what he intended, Cody uncoiled his long length from the chair and pulled her hard against him. Tilting her head with a forefinger under her chin, he took aim toward her lips. Ever so slowly, tauntingly, his mouth moved closer, hovering over hers until her lips tingled and she felt the warm brush of his breath mingle with hers. She heard a rumble deep in his chest and knew he was laughing.

Then his lips were searing hers. Burning. Hard. His tongue demanding entrance and getting it. He found her tongue and sucked it into his mouth, savoring her essence as his hands roamed freely over her back and trim buttocks. When he finally released her lips, he was still smiling. Cassie was furious.

"That's exactly what I mean, Cody Carter, and you know it!" Her shaking voice made it sound weak and ineffectual.

"Sure, baby, if that's what you want. Only don't let me catch you making eyes at any of the hands. I told you before, if you get an itch you can't scratch, I'll gladly oblige." Giving her a jaunty salute, he left the room.

"Conceited jackass!" Cassie called after him.

The children were romping in the yard later that day when Wayne came bursting out of the house, bulging saddlebags slung over his shoulder and a carpetbag in one hand. They watched curiously as Wayne disappeared into the stable. He came out a few minutes later, whipping his mount into a hard gallop and riding hell for leather away from the house and toward the children. Apparently Wayne's anger had blinded him, for he didn't see Amy and Brady playing near the stable, directly in his path. He was nearly upon them before he noticed them, and by then both children were so frightened by the huge animal bearing down on them that they froze in their tracks.

Cursing viciously, Wayne sawed on the reins, causing the poor animal to rear and paw the air just inches away from the terrified children. "Misbegotten brats!" he shrieked, shaking his fists at them. "If not for your father I'd still be in control here. The world would be a better place if none of you existed." Gaining control of his mount, he thundered away, leaving a badly frightened Amy and Brady staring after him in mute astonishment.

Cody had just walked out the back door when he saw Wayne's horse bearing down on the children as if the devil were after him. Cody's heart flew into his mouth when it looked as if his vindictive half-brother would trample the children beneath his horse's hooves. Cody's long legs seemed inadequate as he sprinted toward the stable. Just when he realized he was going to be too late to save the kids, Wayne reined in his horse, causing the animal to rear, missing the kids by scant inches. By the time

Cody reached them, Wayne had already galloped away.

"Are you kids all right?" Cody couldn't remember when he had been so frightened for another human being.

The pupils of Amy's limpid brown eyes were dilated, her face white as a sheet. When she saw Cody she acted instinctively. Flying to him for protection, she hugged him around the waist so tightly he could scarcely breathe. Nearly as frightened as his sister, Brady grasped one of Cody's legs and hung on for dear life. Embarrassed, Cody looked around to see if anyone was looking. He could well imagine how silly he looked with two children hanging on to him as if their lives depended on him. For lack of anything better to do, he reached down and clumsily patted their heads.

Watching from the kitchen window, Cassie witnessed the whole thing. She had been terrified for the children and angry at Wayne for frightening two helpless kids unable to defend themselves. She wanted to go out and comfort them but saw that Cody had taken them in hand. She was amazed by his tenderness and compassion and realized she was seeing a side of Cody she never knew existed.

She saw that his act to appear tough and uncaring was just a sham, that he was really a tender-hearted father who truly cared for his children, although she still couldn't come to grips with the fact that he had tried to abandon them in

St. Louis. Perhaps she wasn't aware of all the facts, she tried to tell herself. Either that or unusual circumstances existed that she wasn't aware of.

The children were still shaking when Cody dropped to his knees beside them. He wanted to make certain the horse's sharp hooves hadn't hurt them. He asked again, "Are you kids okay?"

Amy nodded, finally losing some of her glassy-eyed fright. "Why did he do that, Papa?" she asked shakily. "Where is he going?"

"Wayne is a thoughtless man who cares for no one but himself," Cody replied tightly. His words startled him, for he could be describing himself. "You needn't worry about him again. He's leaving the ranch."

"For good?" Brady asked, pleased with the prospect. He hadn't seen much of Wayne, but what he had seen he didn't like.

"For good. There's something else you kids should know. I won't be leaving the ranch anytime soon. Due to circumstances I hadn't expected, the Rocking C belongs to me. Well, mostly to me anyway. Cassie owns a small part of it. It's not exactly what I want, but then again, it's a damn sight better than what I expected."

Amy grew thoughtful. "Does that mean we don't have to leave?"

Cody's fingers tunneled through his crisp black hair in an exasperated motion. He stared hard at the children, confused by his lack of direction where they were concerned. What he should do was find them a good home with a couple who could be a real mother and father to them. What did he know about kids? Since he never intended to have kids of his own, his possessive feelings in regards to these two particular waifs threw him into a state of panic.

"I'll make a deal with you. You tell me what or who you're hiding from and I'll think about letting you stay until I can find someone willing to take you in."

Amy and Brady exchanged furtive glances. "We—can't," Amy whispered. Her child's mind worked furiously. How could she admit to Cody that she and Brady had killed their uncle? They depended on Cody's goodwill, and that might end if he found out the police were after them. They wanted Cody to like them enough to keep them around, not feel obligated to turn them over to the authorities.

Cody snorted in disgust. "Can't or won't?"

"Both," Brady piped up. "Can we stay anyway? We won't be any bother, will we, Amy?" Amy shook her head. "We like you, don't you like us?"

Cody groaned in dismay. "Listen, kids, I'm a helluva father figure. You need someone to look up to, someone who can lead you in the right direction in life. It's not that I don't like you, it's just that you won't get the proper upbringing at the Rocking C."

Amy brightened visibly when a thought suddenly struck her. "You said Cassie owns a part of the ranch. Is she going to stay, too?"

"I reckon," Cody mumbled. "Until she gets hankering for Sal's place and itching for all the men—er—excitement she left behind."

"Who's Sal?" This from Brady.

"Aw, she-it, forget it, kid. Let's just say that Cassie isn't any more a proper mother than I am a proper father."

"We think so," Amy contradicted. Her faith in him was unshakable. It frightened Cody.

"Aw, she-it."

"Papa," Amy said, pursing her lips primly, "you know you aren't supposed to use that kind of language in front of children." Her imitation of Cassie was astonishing.

Thoroughly shaken, and more than a little annoyed, Cody merely stared at her. She stared calmly back at him. Then he threw up his arms in mock surrender and said, "Aw, she—uh, darn, what's the use."

An experienced ranch hand, Cody took over the reins of the ranch without a hitch. In the days that followed he made friends with the hands, met with the ramrod, inquired about all phases of the ranch operation, and pored over the account books. On those nights he burned the midnight oil in the study, examining the ranch records, he discovered a trend that had occurred with frightening regularity during the past ten or twelve years. Whenever cattle were sold and a large sum of money deposited in the ranch bank account, some of that amount had been siphoned off with no record showing where it had gone or what it had been used for. According to Cody's calculations, the ranch should be making considerably greater profit than the books showed. Actually, it was barely holding its own for all its look of prosperity.

Cody began to suspect that Wayne was the culprit, since he was the only one besides Buck who had access to the books. And as Buck's health failed, keeping the accounts had fallen exclusively to Wayne. Why Wayne had stolen from his own father was a mystery, until Cody examined the issue more closely.

Evidently Buck and Wayne had had a falling out, and despite Wayne's expectations to inherit the Rocking C, a small doubt had nagged at him. Obviously Wayne was protecting his future and covering all angles in the unlikely event that Buck changed his will at the last minute, which he had indeed done. Though the ranch was in fair shape financially, the books showed that it would be a whole lot healthier if Wayne hadn't been feathering his own nest. The missing money accounted for more than Wayne would have earned as his share of the profits throughout the years.

Cody couldn't fault Wayne's thinking. If Buck decided to disinherit him, Wayne's future was secure, and if Buck had named Wayne sole heir, his future was still secure. Either way he won. Though Cody and Cassie had inherited the ranch, they were still big losers, for the amount of money Wayne had siphoned into his own pocket over the years was considerable.

Since Cody could prove nothing, and Wayne could claim that he had earned the money, he avoided mentioning it to either Cassie or Lawyer Willoughby. Taking over the helm of the Rocking C was enough to keep him busy for the time being without delving too deeply into past transactions. The time would come, however, he promised himself, when he'd bring Wayne to account for the thousands of dollars he had taken from the profits.

Reb Lawrence improved to the point where he could hobble from bed and sit outside. The doctor had returned to Dodge and the sheriff had sent him out to the Rocking C to look at Reb's leg. He found that the break was a simple fracture, and since Irene had done everything right, he informed them that Reb would heal without any lasting effects.

Reb wasn't a docile patient. His craving for alcohol had turned him surly and uncooperative. Irene was just about the only person who could talk to him with any success. And the children. He seemed to calm right down when Amy and Brady, accompanied by Blackie, came to visit.

One day Reb crawled from his bunk after the hands had left the bunkhouse for work and raided their lockers, searching for alcohol. When they returned he was roaring drunk. The men were livid. When Cody was told about Reb's fall from grace, he decided the time had come to talk to the man. Until now he had been too busy to concern himself with Reb, relying on Irene to keep him informed of his progress.

Cody found Reb seated on his bunk, his splinted leg poked out in front of him. His face was pasty, his eyes bloodshot, and he looked like the very dickens. Though he was not an old man, alcohol and hard living had aged him. "It's time you and me had a little talk, Reb," Cody said, pulling up a chair.

"I'm in no condition to talk," Reb grumbled sourly. "Why in the hell didn't you let me die in that alley? I ain't good for nothing or no one."

Cody regarded him sternly. "It's never too late to make something of yourself. Liquor isn't going to solve anything. You're not too old to change."

Reb gave a sarcastic hoot. "Take a good look at me. I'm forty years old and have only one arm. Even my own wife couldn't stand the sight of me."

"She wasn't the right woman for you or she wouldn't have left," Cody contended. "It could have been worse. You could have been killed."

"Would of been better," Reb muttered. He eyed Cody narrowly. "Who are you anyway? You look like some damn Indian."

That stung. Maybe Wayne had been right. Maybe he *was* turning into some kind of do-gooder. Still, he couldn't help but feel that there were some redeeming qualities in Reb. He just hadn't found them yet.

"I'm Cody Carter, Buck's son. I'm the new owner of the Rocking C."

"You? What about Wayne? Thought he was Buck's only son."

"Now you know differently. What do you intend to do once you're on your feet again?"

Reb shrugged. "Same as always, I reckon. What's it to you?"

"You owe me and Irene for looking after you. I figure that once you're on your feet three months' work ought to about cover your room and board and medical expenses."

Stunned, Reb gaped at Cody in disbelief. "Three months! What in the hell are you talking about? Who'd want a one-armed man working on a ranch? Do I need to remind you that I'm a cripple?" He held up his stump, waving it in Cody's face.

Cody neither flinched nor seemed impressed by the fact. "There's lots of things you could do. You still have one good arm, don't you? And two legs, once you're healed. You're not getting off that easy, Reb Lawrence. I'll expect a day's work out of you, just like I do from any other hand I hire on." He rose abruptly, ending the interview.

"You'll probably enjoy seeing me make a fool of myself, won't you? I'll bet you're one of those damn bluebellies, just like everyone else hereabouts."

"I was an Army scout in the West," Cody admitted, "but I took no sides in the war. I don't care what you were, Reb. What I do care about is being repaid for all the trouble I've encountered on your account. When you're able to work, I'll see that there's plenty for you to do around here."

Cody strode from the bunkhouse, hoping he had given Reb a good deal to think about during the remainder of his recuperation period. He certainly had enough to keep his mind occupied. But that was the way he wanted it. He needed to be too damn exhausted at night to think about that enticing little baggage who shared his house, trying to pretend she was a prim and proper lady when they both knew exactly what she was. If he wasn't tired enough to fall asleep immediately each night, he knew he'd find his way to Cassie's bed and make love to her until he'd had his fill of her.

Cody had no idea that the object of his thoughts had entered the bunkhouse while he spoke with Reb, having come to check on Reb's progress. Cassie had arrived to find Cody and Reb deep in conversation and would have left if she hadn't heard Cody's last sentences and been shocked by them. She was angry. Damn angry. She hurried to catch up with him.

Placing a hand on his arm, she swung him around to face her. "How dare you treat that poor man as if he was dirt! How can you expect him to work when he has only one arm? Just when I was beginning to think you had some redeeming qualities, you go and do something despicable. I'll never understand you, Cody Carter!"

Chapter Eight

Cody's black brows slashed upward as he stared at Cassie. "What in the hell are you blathering about, woman?"

Tossing her mane of golden hair in a show of angry defiance, Cassie fixed Cody with the turbulent fire of her green gaze. "I heard what you told Reb. Where is your compassion? Have you no heart? The man is a cripple, for heaven's sake."

"He's an emotional cripple," Cody said dismissively. "By suggesting that he work for his keep I was merely trying to instill self-respect in the man. If someone doesn't take him in hand, he'll just drink himself to death when he leaves here. Would you rather see him lying drunk in an alley or doing an honest day's work?"

"That sounds all well and good, Cody, but what

is he capable of? He doesn't have two good legs to stand on and is missing one arm."

Exasperated, Cody said, "You'd be surprised what a man with only one arm can do. And he'll soon have two good legs. What he needs is the opportunity to discover his own worth. Otherwise he'll just lapse into his old ways. Look, Cassie, I don't really like the man, but I can't let him return to his old ways after I picked him up out of the gutter and took him in."

"You don't like him because he's a Reb, is that it?" Cassie accused hotly.

"Dammit, Cassie, why can't you trust me to do what's best for the man?"

"I can't trust you to do what's best for anyone, not even your own children."

Keeping a firm grip on his temper, Cody asked, "What's that supposed to mean?"

"Can't you see that Amy and Brady need new clothes? And shoes? I've been dressing them in things I found in the attic, but they're sadly inadequate."

"How in the hell am I supposed to know what kids need? Take them to town and buy whatever they need. Charge it to me. And while you're at it, buy yourself something decent to wear. Sal must not have paid her girls very well. So far you've worn clothing fit for the rag bag. Thank God, you finally discarded those widow's weeds. They didn't suit you at all."

Cassie flushed, stung by his insulting words. Most of the clothes she owned were drab, shapeless, and old, purchased with the knowledge that they served the purpose for which they were intended. While working for Sal she didn't want to appear in clothing that drew attention to herself or placed her in competition with the girls. Whenever she purchased anything new, which was infrequently, she stuck to grays and tans a size or two larger than necessary and sporting high necklines and long sleeves. Since she never went out anywhere, she owned nothing fancy. It rankled to have Cody remark on her choice of plain, unflattering clothing.

"What I wear is my business." In an effort to conceal her hurt, she lifted her chin an inch or two in the air.

"Charge your clothes to me; I can afford it. Take the wagon. One of the hands will hitch it up for you if you don't know how."

"Take the wagon?" Cassie squeaked. "I—I . . ."

Hands on hips, Cody shook his head in obvious disgust. "What's wrong now?"

"I—I've never driven a wagon. Or ridden a horse."

"She—"

"Papa, look what Blackie can do."

Brady appeared at Cody's elbow, grinning from ear to ear. He held a stick in his hand and when he threw it, Blackie, still limping from his accident, bounded after it. Obviously the mutt was well on the way to recovery.

"Isn't he smart, Papa?" Amy asked, coming up to join them.

"Yeah, smart," Cody agreed with a hint of sarcasm. He'd never admit it, but the damn mutt was beginning to look almost normal now that he had a little meat on his bones and his coat was growing sleek from constant brushing. "Are you kids up to a ride to Dodge to buy some new clothes?"

Amy's eyes lit with pleasure. Like most girls her age, she relished the thought of shopping, especially for pretty clothing. "Are you going to take us?"

Cody sent Cassie a baleful glance. "I reckon, since Cassie has never learned to drive a wagon. I need to visit the bank and see Willoughby anyway, so I might as well do it while I'm waiting for you and Cassie to finish your shopping."

By now Brady was jumping up and down in excitement. "When, Papa? Can we take Blackie with us?"

"That damn mongrel stays home," Cody grumbled. "Be ready in an hour."

The children were in such high spirits during the ride to town that even Cody was infected by their exuberance. He couldn't help but laugh at their antics and childish bickering as they argued over who could teach Blackie the most tricks. To his dismay, Cody found himself smiling more than he had in years, and he even enjoyed answering the children's nonstop questions. If not for Cassie's stimulating presence beside him, he would have found the ride to Dodge rather pleasant. But Cassie disturbed him in ways that left him questioning his own sanity.

The heady scent of her warm flesh stirred his manhood. Just the sound of her throaty voice sent ripples of awareness racing through his body. If he didn't have a woman soon he feared he'd be unable to keep his hands off Cassie. His problem was that he didn't want anyone but Cassie Fenmore, his own stepsister, for God's sake. He cast a surreptitious glance at Cassie, sitting so prim and proper next to him in a dull gray dress two sizes too big for her. Even dressed in rags she was one desirable woman. A silent groan lodged in his throat. Maybe there'd be enough time for him to visit one of the whores at the Longbranch while Cassie and the kids were shopping.

Cassie's instincts were intact. She could feel Cody's sidelong glances when he thought no one was looking, and her body reacted instinctively to his provocative looks. Warm. She was so warm she began fanning herself with her hand. What was he thinking? she wondered distractedly. Did his thoughts match hers? Lord, he was attractive. Lowering her eyes to where their legs were nearly touching on the seat, she was aware of his vibrant animal appeal, the rippling muscles of his thighs that jumped reflexively beneath her gaze—and his arousal.

Good Lord! She had done nothing to arouse him and was stunned to think that simply sitting beside him could cause that kind of reaction. Dragging her eyes away from the awesome sight, she scolded herself mentally and concentrated on the road ahead. Unfortunately for her peace of mind, her body hummed with the naughty thought of how that hard masculine part of him would feel inside the soft feminine part of her.

Cody parked the wagon, left Cassie and the kids at the dry goods store, and went directly to the bank. His business took only a short time. Then he visited Willoughby's office where they spent considerable time discussing the ranch's stability and why profits weren't as great as they should be. Willoughby promised to investigate the possibility that the ranch had been drained of profit by someone. Though neither man mentioned his name, both knew that Wayne was the only person who could be responsible for such a loss. They both knew it would be difficult to prove.

"I want to know for my own peace of mind," Cody told Willoughby. "I don't know what, if anything, can be done, but I feel that Wayne has made damn certain he's financially secure despite being disinherited by Father."

"Buck suspected Wayne was siphoning off profits, but his poor health prevented him from doing anything about it. He lived for the day you returned home, Cody, and when he realized he was close to death, he changed his will in your favor. It was his way of making up for past mistakes."

"I—never knew," Cody said. His voice was laced with guilt. "I should have kept in touch. But it's too late now for recriminations. The best I can do is run the ranch as Father would have wanted."

Shortly afterward they parted company and Cody headed over to the Longbranch. He bellied up to the long polished bar, ordered a whiskey, and sized up the women with a jaundiced eye. A couple of whores were young and attractive, but their eyes were older than sin. Most had seen more wear than a hallway carpet. One of the younger ones noted his interest and sauntered over to join him, her short skirts swishing jauntily about her dimpled knees.

"Would you like some company, mister? My name is Holly and I'm mighty thirsty." Cody motioned for the bartender to pour Holly a drink. She took a generous gulp and asked, "I haven't seen you around. Are you new in town?"

Cody's eyes dropped to Holly's breasts, nearly bursting from the top of her scanty bodice. At least she doesn't wear clothes two sizes too big for her, he thought sourly. "You could say that. I own the Rocking C. Name's Cody Carter."

Holly's eyes grew round. "You're Wayne's half-brother! He told me all about you. Was your mother really an Indian?"

"Full-blooded Cheyenne," Cody said with grim amusement. "How well do you know Wayne?"

Holly hesitated a moment too long.

"So, my esteemed half-brother isn't above using whores. Well, Holly, no matter what Wayne told you, I'm the legal owner of the Rocking C. Me and Miss Fenmore."

"Wayne said you were a bastard." Her frank words startled him.

"In more ways than one." He was growing extremely agitated. "What else did Wayne say?"

Cody's fierce look frightened Holly and she retreated a step. Though he was more handsome than any man she had ever seen, she sensed a dark side to Cody, and a quiet, brooding danger. She backed off immediately. "He didn't say much else," she purred in an effort to placate him. "You need a woman, Cody? I'll bet you're good in bed."

"Would you compare me with my brother? No thanks, honey, no woman is worth it." He gulped down his whiskey and walked away, his muscles beneath his tight buckskins rippling powerfully, his rolling gait reminiscent of a magnificent cat, lithe, sleek, completely sensual.

Keen disappointment brought a sigh to Holly's painted lips.

Cassie bought several outfits for the children from the ready-to-wear section, and material to make several more, especially for Amy. For Brady she purchased Levi's, knickers, and a variety of shirts. She also bought heavy jackets for cool weather and an outfit each for special occasions. Brady balked when Cassie picked out a tie, but despite his protests it was added to the growing pile of clothing. Amy received a pair of soft slippers and a pair of ankle-high boots. Brady was particularly happy with a pair of cowboy boots almost like Cody's.

For herself, Cassie was less extravagant. But since she had been taught to sew by her seamstress grandmother, the problem was solved when she bought a wide variety of material, thread, needles, and trim. In a moment of madness she bought two of the popular split skirts in soft suede and denim, and several blouses. She couldn't resist new underwear to go with her new clothes. Before she left, she bought a soft linen shirt for Cody in the same blue as his compelling eyes. She intended to embroider his initials on it before presenting it to him.

They had just left the store, their arms loaded down with packages, when they came face-to-face with Wayne.

"Well," Wayne said nastily, "if it isn't my beautiful stepsister and Cody's two little brats. What brings you to Dodge?"

"We bought new clothes," Brady said, proudly displaying the packages he carried.

"Spending the ranch's money, I see. What happened to your mother? Did she become disenchanted when she realized she had married a half-breed?"

"Leave the children alone, Wayne," Cassie warned as she stood protectively before them. "They love Cody and don't understand vicious people like you."

"I'm sure they've heard it all before," Wayne said, giving a careless shrug. "I don't know where they were living before coming to Dodge, but most communities have little love for Indians and half-breeds. Have you named yourself their protector, Cassie?"

"If need be."

He sidled closer. "Team up with me and together we'll find a way to seize the Rocking C for ourselves. We'd make a good team, Cassie." The gleam in his pale blue eyes sent a shiver of apprehension down Cassie's spine. She knew that look. He wanted her, not in a brotherly way but sexually. He grasped her arm and tugged. "Ditch the brats and come with me. We'd be good together. I don't think you're as innocent as you pretend."

Angry, Cassie attempted to pull from his grasp. "Let me go!"

"Damn Cody to hell, has he gotten to you already? If Father hadn't sent you away, I'd have trained you to please me. In no time at all you'd be as good as your mother. And believe me, *sister* dear, Linda was the best."

"I suspected Father's reason for disinheriting you and now I know for certain. Take your hands off Cassie, Wayne."

Wayne hadn't seen Cody come up behind him. He swiveled around, saw the look on Cody's face, and knew a moment of raw fear. His hands dropped helplessly to his sides. "You even sneak up on people like an Injun," he said in a show of mock bravado.

"If you want to pick on someone, pick on me,"

Cody advised harshly, "not defenseless women and children."

Coward that he was, Wayne had no desire to initiate a fight he knew he couldn't win. He knew damn well he wasn't in Cody's league. If he did anything it would have to be done by stealth, or better yet, he'd hire someone to do his dirty work. "You'd like to goad me into fighting, wouldn't you, Cody? You know I can't compete with your superior strength. But I'm too smart to fall for your tricks."

Cody's hands clenched at his sides as he struggled to keep from pounding Wayne with his fists. If Wayne wasn't so puny he wouldn't think twice about flaying him to within an inch of his life. "Get the hell out of here, Wayne, before I lose my temper and forget we're brothers."

"Half-brothers," Wayne reminded him as he backed away. "I don't know how the old man could have slept with a squaw." Before he turned and fled he gave Cassie a searching look. "Think about what I said, Cassie."

"Are you and the kids okay?" Cody asked. Wayne was already halfway down the street.

Cassie nodded. "He didn't hurt us." Her face had a pinched look. "Cody, that wasn't the first time Wayne hinted that my mother was—was—not very nice. You said the same thing yourself. Is it true? I was so young when she died, I never really knew her."

Cody's reply was to grasp her by the arm and lead her toward the wagon. "We'll talk about it later." He had no idea why the knowledge that her mother was a whore should bother Cassie. Hadn't she chosen the same profession?

"What's a half-breed, Papa?" Until now the children had been too frightened by what was taking place between Wayne and Cody to speak.

Cody stopped dead in his tracks. "A half-breed is someone who is half Indian." Cody decided that being honest with the children was the best policy since both Amy and Brady were intelligent enough to figure it out for themselves once they put their minds to it. He resumed walking toward the wagon.

"If you and Wayne had the same father, then your mother must have been an Indian."

Cody smiled, realizing that Amy was quick to grasp the truth. "Does that bother you?"

Cassie couldn't believe what she was hearing. "Cody, you mean your own children aren't aware that you're—that you are . . ."

"A half-breed?" A cynical smile curved his lips.

"Do you care that Papa is a half-breed, Cassie?" Brady asked with the naïveté of a seven-year-old.

Cassie really was flustered now.

"Well, Cassie? You heard Brady. What are your feelings about that?"

"Why—why, it doesn't make any difference to me," Cassie stuttered. "I don't think any less of you children or your father because you have Indian blood."

Amy, aware that they shared no blood with Cody, flew into a fit of giggles, joined by Brady, who immediately grasped the reason for her laughter. Luckily, they reached the wagon before Cassie could ask why they were laughing, and the kids clambered inside, bringing the conversation to an end.

"What is this?" Brady asked, holding up an object that Cody had placed in the wagon bed.

"It's a crutch. I borrowed it from Dr. Striegle. He said Reb could probably bear some weight on his leg now without too much discomfort. He promised to visit the ranch tomorrow and remove the bulky splint and replace it with a smaller one."

Cassie sent Cody a searching look. Did that mean Cody would expect Reb to pull his weight around the ranch now that the poor one-armed man was mobile? As if reading her mind, Cody said, "He can begin earning his keep by teaching you how to drive a wagon and ride a horse. And it wouldn't hurt for you to learn to shoot. Since he was in the Army, I assume he knows how to do those things."

Cody was driving the wagon out of town when a woman, standing on the balcony above the Longbranch, began waving and calling out his name. All four occupants of the wagon glanced upward. A groan slipped past Cody's lips when he saw the scantily clad Holly leaning over the railing, trying to catch his attention. She had succeeded admirably, for not only had he seen her but so had everyone else, including the children, who were gazing up at Holly with open-mouthed interest. Cassie groaned in dismay and slanted him a disgruntled look that spoke volumes. Slapping the reins against the horse's rump, Cody left Dodge behind in a flurry of dust.

After the children had donned their new clothes the next day, Cassie insisted on trimming their hair. Amy's long curly locks were constantly becoming snarled, and Brady was beginning to look more like a girl than a boy. Meanwhile, Cody had entered the house to tell Cassie that Reb had reluctantly agreed to begin teaching her the skills she would need to ride and shoot. He found her in the kitchen, snipping away at Brady's tousled curls. A carpet of shiny black hair lay at her feet. Amy, having already been shorn, watched the proceedings with utter boredom.

"Hold still, Brady," Cassie admonished, "you're almost finished. I can't believe Cody would let your hair get so shaggy. Did your papa take no interest in your appearance?"

"Their mother probably took care of all that."

Cassie started. "I swear, Cody, you do have a way of sneaking up on people."

"Are you finished, Cassie?" asked Brady, who saw Cody's appearance as a means of escape. Sitting still for more than five minutes at a time was asking too much of the active lad.

"All done, Brady. You and Amy can go out and play until lunchtime." They didn't need a second invitation. Joining hands, they ran out the back door where Blackie sat waiting for them in forlorn abandonment.

Cody's eyes followed them out the door. "They really did need new clothes, didn't they? I think they've grown two inches in the past few weeks."

"They've filled out, too," Cassie observed. "When I first saw them they looked as if they weren't eating regularly. I don't know what your circumstances were, but judging from the appearance of the children, they couldn't have been very good."

Cody frowned. If they were truly his kids, he wouldn't have neglected them as Cassie was suggesting. For the moment he let her remark pass. "I've just spoken with Reb. He's agreed to start your riding lessons tomorrow. Meet him at the corral at ten tomorrow morning."

"Did you give him the crutch? How does it work?"

"Well enough, but Reb's not too happy about earning his keep. He wants to go back to town."

"You're not going to let him, are you?"

"I can't force him to stay if he has his mind set on leaving. I think Irene has more influence over the man than any of us. Have you noticed how often she finds an excuse to visit him in the bunkhouse?"

"You don't think . . ."

Cody shrugged. Abruptly he changed the subject, stunning Cassie with his directness. "I like your new outfit." She wore a split skirt in soft buttery suede and a white linen blouse, open at the neck to expose the vulnerable softness of her throat and the upper curves of her breasts. "You have a beautiful body, baby." His voice was low and provocative.

"Is that what you told that whore at the Longbranch? Did you find time to scratch her itch?"

Cody laughed. "Jealous?"

"Hardly."

"I offered to scratch your itch, baby. Whenever you've got the hankering. It's been a long time for you, Cassie. I can tell because you ignite into flame whenever I touch you. Or are you always that hot for a man? Tell me the truth, baby, are you hankering yet?"

"What's Cassie hankering for, Papa?"

Cassie looked horrified. "Oh, you, you . . ." Mortified that the children had picked that moment to return to the kitchen, Cassie whirled and fled, her cheeks burning with shame. What if it had been Irene who walked in on their sexually charged conversation instead of the children? She was going to have to be more careful in the future, but it wasn't going to be easy. Cody unleashed something in her she didn't even recognize. She went up in smoke whenever he looked at her, and he hadn't been wrong when he accused her of bursting into flame when he touched her. Was she like her mother in that respect?

That was something else that needed explaining. Both Cody and Wayne had intimated that her mother was a whore. And she had never forgotten Buck's mystifying statement that day long ago when he had stood over her mother's grave.

Meanwhile, back in the kitchen, Brady repeated his innocent question. "What's Cassie hankering for?"

Throwing caution to the wind, Cody said, "Me, I hope." Then, realizing what he had just said, he abruptly changed the subject. "How do you kids like your new clothes?"

"Aren't they beautiful?" Amy cooed, whirling before Cody to show off her new checkered pinafore.

"What about you, Brady? Are you satisfied with your new clothes?"

"Aw, she-it!"

"Brady!" Amy gasped, horrified. "You know what Cassie said about using bad language."

"Papa says it."

A stunned look flitted over Cody's face. "Aw, she—horsefeathers, Brady, you know better than to repeat what I say. Is something wrong with your new clothes?"

"Cassie bought me a tie. She said I have to wear it to church. I don't wanna wear no damn tie."

Cody groaned.

Amy gave an exaggerated shrug and looked at Cody as if to say, "You handle it, I give up."

"You'll wear a damn tie if Cassie says you will!" Cody thundered. "And if you use that kind of language again I'll tan your damn hide."

"You did it again, Papa," Amy scolded.

"Did what?"

"How do you expect Brady to stop cursing if you don't?"

"Aw, she—horsefeathers, I wasn't cursing. Not that I'm aware of, anyway." Suddenly his patience fled. Being a man with responsibilities was new to him and he wasn't sure he liked it. "Besides, I'm not your father so stop trying to reform me. First Cassie and now you. There's only so much a man can take."

Amy's pointed little chin quivered and her doelike brown eyes grew luminous with unshed tears. Of course she knew Cody wasn't her father, but she was only thinking of her little brother. Adopting Cody had given Brady a sense of security he hadn't had since their parents had died. At first, calling Cody "Papa" was something they'd done out of necessity and desperation. Later, it just seemed right to keep up the pretense. But now, after Cody's outburst, Amy knew she and Brady had driven him too far, taken too much for granted.

"I'm sorry, Pa—Cody, I didn't mean to make you angry." Tears began sliding down the velvet smoothness of her cheeks. "You can cuss all you want." Her sentence ended in a sob. Then she turned and fled.

Brady didn't follow immediately. He stood his ground, glaring at Cody with such a ferocious look on his face that Cody was shaken to the roots of his hair. "We know you're not really our papa, but Amy isn't strong like I am. You shouldn't have scolded her like you did." Then he whirled on his heel and followed his sister out the door.

Thunderstruck, Cody stared after the children in confusion. What had he done to deserve this?

"She—" He almost bit his tongue off to keep from completing the word.

"Horsefeathers!"

Chapter Nine

Cassie's riding lessons began immediately. Hobbling on his crutch, the stub of his left arm waving in the air, Reb was a demanding instructor. Cassie was surprised that the town drunk showed such remarkable aptitude for horses, until she learned that he had been in the cavalry during the recent war. Within days she was riding around the yard on a rather placid mare named Lady. Sitting on a nearby rail, Amy and Brady usually could be seen lending their encouragement as Cassie rode by. Soon she was proficient enough to ride to the nearest pasture and back without supervision.

Cody was satisfied with Cassie's progress. He had watched her a time or two, but the sight of her enticing little bottom bouncing against the saddle soon sent him fleeing in another direction. She sorely tried his sanity. After that, he had made certain he was occupied elsewhere whenever Cassie had a riding lesson.

Learning to drive a wagon followed the riding lessons. By now Reb had discarded the crutch and was walking gingerly on a leg blessedly free of restraint. On the doctor's last visit he had removed the splint and proclaimed Reb's leg healed. When Cassie had her first shooting lesson, the children weren't allowed to accompany her to the shooting range hastily set up for Cassie's use in one of the pastures.

It was about that time that a succession of strange accidents occurred. First, a gate to one of the holding pens had been left open and nearly a hundred head of cattle, due to be transferred to a feeding lot, escaped. It took three days to round them up and herd them back into their enclosure. Then an unexplained fire broke out in the barn, but fortunately it had been discovered before it did much damage. Another near disaster brought Cody to the reluctant conclusion that all these "accidents" weren't acts of God or nature. This time the accident involved the children.

They were playing in the barn when a bale of hay fell from the loft, missing them by scant inches. If not for Blackie, who barked and nipped at their heels, which made them turn and give chase to their pet, they would have been struck down. Cody had been thoroughly shaken when he learned of the "accident."

Since Cody had lost his temper with the children, they had deliberately been avoiding their adopted father. They lived in fear of the day Cody would send them away. But seeing how close the kids had come to death had affected Cody in ways he never thought possible. After their brush with death they became uncharacteristically subdued, and Cassie insisted that Cody console them.

"They need sympathy, love, and reassurance," Cassie told Cody after the kids had gone to bed one evening a few nights after the incident. They were sitting in the parlor on one of those rare evenings when Cody didn't go out to the bunkhouse or retire immediately after supper, as was his usual habit.

"What am I supposed to say?"

Exasperated. "You're their father, how should I know? Haven't you noticed their strange behavior lately? I don't think I've ever seen them so quiet. Have you scolded them recently? They act as if they're walking on eggs when they're around you."

Cody recalled exactly what had led to their subdued manner. He just didn't want to admit to himself that their coldness and fear bothered him. "They should have picked a father better suited to raising kids," he grumbled sourly.

Confounded by his words, Cassie looked at him blankly. "What a dumb thing to say. Children don't pick their fathers."

"These kids did."

Cassie frowned, unable to make heads or tails out of that remark. "Why don't you go talk to them?"

"I'd rather talk to you."

"What is there for us to discuss? Within five minutes we'd be at each other's throat."

She felt the heat of his compelling blue eyes bore into her and grew flustered. Would it always be thus with her?

Cody sent her a sizzling glance. "If you'd rather not talk, there are far more pleasant things we can do."

Fearing where this might lead, Cassie rose abruptly. "Cody . . ."

The intensity of Cody's gaze sent the blood pulsing through her veins. "Don't go."

The breath slammed from her chest and her legs gave way beneath her. She promptly sat down beside him, suddenly unable to move one leg before the other. He was staring at her lips now, memorizing their shape, their lush fullness, the way they trembled beneath his penetrating gaze.

"I want to kiss you, Cassie. I'm *going* to kiss you, and no amount of pleading is going to stop me."

Cassie swallowed hard. She was dismayed to realize it was exactly what she wanted too. Unable to speak, she lifted her face in blatant invitation as the pink tip of her tongue flicked out to moisten her suddenly dry lips. It would be dishonest of her to deny how much she wanted to experience the bold brand of his kiss again.

Cody groaned, his body reacting violently to her unexpected willingness. And the sight of her provocative little tongue nearly sent him over the edge. He fought for control, realizing how close he was to tossing her on her back, flipping her skirt up, and thrusting into the silken crevice of her receptive body. By welcoming his kiss, Cody hoped she was inviting more, much more. A thrill of anticipation shot through him. He nearly went up in smoke when it occurred to him that Cassie's startling compliance was tantamount to admitting that she wanted him.

"Oh, baby," Cody muttered on a sigh as he reached for her. His hands were hot, hard, as he pulled her against him. Starved, he crushed her lips with his, groaning from the pleasure of so simple an act. It wasn't a tender kiss, but a bold taking as his tongue forced her lips open. The moment their tongues met, a raspy sigh escaped his throat. His lips softened and the kiss deepened. Cassie's hands discovered the long hair at his nape and her fingers tunneled through the dark silken mass as she returned the kiss with a passion surprising in one so innocent.

His hands released her waist and found her breasts, molding them, pressing them upward to meet the hot demand of his mouth as he broke off the kiss and lowered his head to them. She felt the warm moistness of his mouth as he licked her nipples through the material of her blouse. A moment later his fingers slid beneath her skirt and up the silken inside of her thigh, searing her flesh. When he reached that moist throbbing place between her legs, encountered her drawers, and attempted to slip his fingers beneath the offending garment, a frustrated moan slid past his lips.

"Too damn many clothes," he muttered as he began to frantically work the small buttons on her blouse through the smaller buttonholes.

His words brought a sense of reality to Cassie's befuddled mind. "Cody, wait, we can't do this!" She tried to stop his hands, but Cody was too aroused now to be put off.

"You said you wanted this."

"N—no, I said you could kiss me."

Cody grinned wickedly. "I am kissing you. I aim to kiss you all over. But it's difficult to do through all these damn clothes."

"Cody, I admit there is something between us. I feel it every time you look at me, but that doesn't mean I—"

"It's called lust, baby. Think of me as just another man coming to see you at Sal's. Hell, I'll even pay you if it will make you feel better. I think of you day and night; you're never out of my mind. I picture you spread beneath me, all naked and rosy, and me thrusting into you."

"Cody, stop!" She clapped her hands over her ears, his erotic words sending her into a slow burn.

"Not now, baby." Gripping the edges of her blouse, he ripped it apart, sending the remaining buttons flying in all directions. Then he released the ribbon on her chemise and shoved it aside, baring her breasts to his appreciative gaze.

"What if Irene comes in?"

"Irene is with Reb. Besides, she has her own little cottage and is unlikely to return to the house tonight." He shoved her skirt up to her hips.

"The children might wander downstairs," Cassie gasped, nearly senseless with a strange, titillating yearning. It didn't really surprise her to learn that she wanted Cody nearly as desperately as he wanted her. What did shock her was her willingness to become his victim. She had seen firsthand how men used women and how little most of the girls at Sal's thought of the act they performed for money, and had vowed never to be used in such a manner. Now here she was, as hot for Cody as he was for her.

Cody seemed oblivious to her words. "You're not going to put me off again, baby. This time we're going to do it and do it right."

"No! I won't let you use me that way." She struggled to escape from his determined embrace.

"We'll be using each other. It won't be as if this is your first time."

"But it is!" Cassie cried.

Cody grinned. "Sure it is. Mine too."

"Cody Carter, I could shoot you!"

"If you do you'd own the ranch free and clear." Before she had time to consider his words, his lips came down hard on hers, scattering her thoughts. Without breaking off the kiss, he lurched to his feet, pulling her up with him. Gripping her rounded bottom in his callused palms, he pressed her against the throbbing hardness of his loins. "Oh, Cassie, can't you feel how desperately I want you? Don't deny me now."

Deny you? Cassie reflected irrationally. *To deny you would be denying myself.* She struggled desperately to retain her sanity. Someone had to. "Let me go, Cody!"

At that moment Cody couldn't recall ever seeing anyone as magnificent as Cassie, her green eyes snapping angrily and her pale breasts heaving in delicious invitation. He didn't care how many men she'd had before him. He had wanted her the first time he set eyes on her at Sal's and he still wanted her. "Not on your life, baby."

Betrayed by her own surging passion, Cassie made one last effort to escape Cody as she spun out of his embrace. Her unexpected rebellion caused him to lose his balance and fall to the floor. Cassie squawked in surprise as he dragged her with him, cushioning her with his big body. Lying atop him, their bodies pressed together, Cassie felt her resistance slip away as her own need suddenly matched Cody's. Grasping the back of her head, he brought her lips to his, coaxing them open with his tongue so he could taste her sweetness. With his other hand he stroked her breasts, her hips, pressing his loins against hers in desperate need. Excited beyond endurance, he lifted her skirt, shoved her drawers aside, and touched her, finding her wet and slick.

"Cody, my God!"

"You're wet and hot for me, baby. Do you want me?"

"No!" Her mind denied that which her body demanded.

One thick finger slipped inside her hot pulsing moistness. He waited for her face to reflect her pleasure before repeating his question. He didn't have long to wait. "Do you want me, Cassie?"

"Damn you, Cody!"

"If you still want to shoot me you can do it afterward." His words were light and teasing but his intense blue eyes were like twin flames, scorching her everywhere they touched.

He knew the exact moment Cassie's desire matched his, and his loins surged powerfully against her.

As she realized that Cody was not a man to be denied, and that she no longer wanted to deny what they both wanted, the tension left Cassie's body and she relaxed in mute surrender. This moment had been building between her and Cody since that fateful day they had encountered one another on the train. He'd find out soon enough that she wasn't a whore, and if his conscience smote him afterward, it served him right. Not that she expected Cody to suddenly realize he needed a wife and mother for his children. Where did that thought come from? she wondered, startled that she should consider Cody and marriage in the same breath. The thought of marriage to the handsome half-breed was intimidating.

Actually, it would serve the bounder right, she thought resentfully, since he seemed so unwilling to accept the responsibility of a wife and children. Lord, what was she thinking of? She wouldn't marry Cody if he was the last man on earth.

When Cody released the heavy fullness of his manhood from the confinement of his trousers, Cassie's good sense returned. "Not here, Cody, upstairs." He might not care about his children walking in on them, but she did.

With little effort on his part, Cody swept Cassie off the floor and into his arms, bounding out of the room and up the stairs, taking them two at a time. He carried her directly to his room, booted the door shut behind him, and let her slide down the long length of his body until her feet touched the floor. She gasped in breathless wonder at the burning sensation created by the simple rubbing together of their bodies. Every inch of her skin was so sensitive that his mere touch set her afire. Then, with more gentleness than he'd heretofore shown, Cody began to strip her. Slowly, each sensual movement carefully orchestrated to thrill and titillate, each caress sending her deeper and deeper into a state of suspended bliss.

Her blouse fell to the floor, followed by her skirt. Her chemise went next, then her bloomers, stockings, and shoes. When she stood naked before him, his avid blue eyes raked the length of her body and back with slow relish. "I knew you'd be beautiful but had no idea just how ravishing you were beneath those shapeless clothes you wore."

Nearly undone by his words, Cassie took a step toward him. "No, don't move, not yet. I want to look my fill."

The hot melting fire of his penetrating gaze aroused Cassie in ways she never thought possible. Her skin burned with the fires of hell, her churning innards turned to quivering jelly. She felt an intense tingling sensation in that soft place where Cody's eyes had settled. As if aware of her yearning, he reached out and palmed entirely that aching place covered by golden fleece. He heaved a sigh so immense that Cassie felt the reverberations where his hand rested against her womanhood.

Caught in the throes of tormented agony, Cody fought to control his desire. He knew it had been a long time since he'd had a woman but he'd gone longer periods in the past without going to pieces the first time he touched soft woman's flesh. Spacing his breathing in a deliberate effort to still his racing heart, Cody lowered his head, pulled Cassie hard against him, and drew a swollen nipple into his mouth. The tugging of his mouth at her breast triggered rhythmic shudders within her. Small mewing sounds erupted from deep in her throat as she grasped his head and drew it closer against her. When he raked his teeth lightly against the tender nub, Cassie jerked violently, threw her head back, and cried out.

"You like that, baby?"

"Yes . . ."

He still clasped her between the legs, and she could feel herself throbbing heavily against his hand. She was utterly enthralled by what was happening to her body. She hadn't expected such overwhelming pleasure. Why had no one told her?

When he slid one finger inside her, her body trembled as if from ague. "You're hot as a firecracker," he whispered hoarsely. With determined purpose, he bore her backward toward the bed. Then he eased her onto the soft surface and followed her down. He rested his full length atop her for a moment before she felt his weight leave her. She cried out in protest.

Cody grinned, realizing she was as far gone as he was. No wonder she was highly prized by Sal, he reflected. Not only was her tempting body fashioned for love, but she enjoyed her work with an eagerness that must have pleased her customers. Her reason for holding him off so long puzzled him, for obviously she needed it as badly as he did.

"I won't leave you, baby," he rasped as he began tearing off his clothes. Before he rejoined her, he turned up the lamp. He wasn't going to lose a moment of this due to darkness.

Turning from the lamp, he faced Cassie, pausing just long enough to give her a look at his fully aroused manhood. Her eyes flew open, her chin dropped down to her chest, and a terrible fear seized her. He was too *big!* He'd kill her. His manhood, thick and stiff, rose at full mast to his belly button. With great effort she dragged her eyes upward, away from the awesome sight of magnificent masculinity, so potent it robbed her of her breath.

Too late she discovered that sliding her eyes over other parts of his nude body didn't help return her sanity as she had hoped. His shoulders were massive, his chest corded with muscles. His hips were narrow, his waist lean, and his legs long and shapely in a purely masculine way. Everything about him stirred her, from the bronze perfection of his skin to the stark artistry of his proud face with its high cheekbones, flaring nostrils, and full lips.

Cody stood proud and tall before Cassie, aroused by the blatant way in which she was looking at him. "If you keep looking at me like that I'm going to explode." His voice was a low, sexy growl.

Cassie blinked and looked away.

"How do I compare with the others?" he couldn't help but ask.

Her gaze returned to his face. "Others?"

"C'mon, baby, you know what I mean. The men at Sal's."

"There were no others."

"Have it your way. It really doesn't matter. I can't recall when I've ever wanted a woman as badly as I want you."

He knelt on the bed, bending down to kiss her. His lips were soft and oh so teasing. "I've waited a long time for this." He slid more fully atop her, bringing their bodies into stunning contact as he nudged her legs apart and settled between them.

When he slid the tip of his manhood an inch or two inside her, Cassie stiffened and cried, "Wait!"

"Wait? Are you crazy? Don't tell me you're not ready. You were already wet for me before we hit the bed." He slid inside her a little deeper.

Cassie gasped. "You're too big!"

Cody paused, a look of intense pleasure softening his features. "That's quite a compliment coming from you."

"I mean it, Cody, you'll hurt me." She was growing desperate now, realizing that he could cause her intense pain if he didn't believe she was a virgin.

"I've never hurt a woman yet."

"Have you ever had a virgin?"

"Virgins don't interest me. They're not my style." He shoved himself in farther, surprised at the muscle control she employed as he felt the walls of her femininity grasp and squeeze him. "Oh, baby, you *are* good." She was giving him more pleasure than any woman in his recent memory.

When Cassie opened her mouth in silent protest, Cody seized the moment and covered it with his own. As he thrust his tongue into her mouth, he flexed his hips and sheathed himself fully. Cassie stiffened, her scream of agony lost in the dark cavern of his mouth. He grew still, rearing up and looking at her in disbelief. He knew there was no way she could be pretending that portrayal of utter shock and pain.

Finding her mouth free, Cassie gasped. "Stop, please."

A pained expression flitted over Cody's dark face. "I can't. It's too late, the damage is already done. The hurt will go away very soon, I promise." His voice held a note of tenderness Cassie hadn't expected.

When his hips moved again, he deliberately kept his strokes slow and even and careful, in complete opposition to the wildness raging within him that made him want to thrust hard and deep until blissful completion burst upon him.

Cassie gritted her teeth, waiting for the terrible pain to end, and to her utter surprise it did. The dull ache inside her faded into a small glow, which ignited into the torrid heat of renewed arousal with Cody's expert stroking. She had thought the pleasure of foreplay had ended with Cody's powerful shattering of her maidenhead, but once the initial pain had subsided the pleasure returned. With a vengeance.

Small, inarticulate sounds gurgled in Cassie's throat as Cody thrust into her again and again, his sweat-slicked body vibrating from the terrible strain of containing his stampeding passion. It was the first time in his memory that he had wanted so desperately to please a woman. He always tried to give pleasure, but Cassie was different. Not only was she his first virgin, but he wanted to make her first time memorable. And he didn't want her to hate him for refusing to believe she was an innocent.

Intense delight shivered through Cassie. With a will of their own her hands traveled the length of Cody's back to his hips, to his buttocks, gripping the taut, heaving mounds in her two hands, bringing him more deeply inside her.

The heat.

The hunger.

The unexpected pleasure.

The heat. It continued to rise feverishly within her.

He plunged deeper, stronger. She could hear the harsh rasp of his breath in her ear, feel the slippery sweat of his body anointing her. From somewhere deep within came the urge to reach for something . . . something just beyond her grasp . . . something that would change her life forever. She was close . . . so close.

"Cody!"

"You're almost there, baby."

Splendor. It burst upon her in shimmering waves of blissful contentment as tiny contractions began deep in her loins where their bodies were joined and spread outward with every driving thrust of Cody's surging body.

Beautiful, she thought dazedly as she gazed up at his stark face hovering inches above her. The moment of her climax had been like nothing she had ever experienced before, but the look on Cody's face was even more thrilling. His expression was fierce, magnificent in masculine fulfillment as release thundered through him. Beautiful . . .

He fell against her, his elbows braced on either side to spare her his weight. His chest heaved as he sought desperately to catch his breath. She felt him flex within her, listened to his heartbeat thudding against her breast, and knew a moment of supreme satisfaction. She had given him as much pleasure as he had given her.

He arose slowly, his eyes hooded, his movements jerky. He sat beside her on the bed, staring at her in silence. His face wore a stunned look.

"She-it! Why didn't you tell me? If I had known you were a virgin I wouldn't have been so rough."

"I did tell you," she replied earnestly. "You didn't believe me."

"How in the hell was I supposed to believe you after I saw you at Sal's? Sal herself told me you weren't for the likes of me. I thought she meant you were reserved for 'special' customers, that a half-breed wasn't good enough for you."

"What Sal should have said was that I wasn't for the likes of anyone," Cassie said on a ragged sigh. "I was a maid, nothing more, nothing less. And paid well for doing my job. Sal knew I wasn't interested in any other kind of work and protected me. That's what she should have said."

"But she didn't." He gave her a long inscrutable look. "I'm not going to apologize. I don't know when I've ever enjoyed making love to a woman more. If I didn't feel the proof of your virginity myself I would have sworn you were experienced. You're so responsive. I've never had a virgin before," he admitted in a hushed voice.

"Are they so different?" Cassie asked curiously.

"You're different. I can't attest to anyone else." He slid down beside her, pulling her roughly into his arms. "Do you still want to shoot me?"

"More than ever," Cassie said testily. "Do you realize you've just spoiled me for marriage? It was the only thing of value I had."

"You've got one-quarter interest in the Rocking C."

"Yes, I do have that. Too bad Buck didn't see fit to leave it *all* to me."

He merely grinned, his eyes settling disconcertingly on her breasts. She sensed his renewed interest, saw the potent proof of his passion stir between his thighs, and her pulse quickened. He looked so irresistibly handsome, so hungry, so dangerous, that she deliberately tried to provoke his anger as a means of diffusing his growing lust. She'd probably never recover from another round of his lovemaking.

"Would I really own the entire ranch if you weren't around to collect your share?" Her honeyed voice literally dripped with venom, startling Cody.

He stared at her narrowly, wondering what she was hinting at. "Do you hate me so much? It's true I probably wouldn't have made love to you if I had realized you were innocent, but that's no guarantee. You said before there was something between us that wouldn't go away. Knowing you were a virgin would have merely postponed the inevitable. The plain truth is that I wanted you, Cassie. I still want you. That damn ache inside me won't go away." He reached for her.

Cassie shrugged from his grasp. "What about tomorrow?"

"I'll want you tomorrow too." Exactly what in the hell did she want him to say? "And the next day and the next after that."

"What about your children?"

"They're not—What about them?"

"They're not stupid. They'll know what's going on between us. Maybe I should leave. If I remove myself, perhaps the temptation will disappear."

"Like hell it will!" The thought frightened him. Where would she go? What would she do? "You're not going away, Cassie. Holler at me, curse me, shoot me if it will make you feel better, but you're not leaving." He recalled how he had offered to pay for her services and winced inwardly. He hadn't meant to hurt her. Suddenly a thought occurred to him, and he smiled slyly. "What if you're carrying my child? It could happen, you know."

Cassie paled. "It won't happen!"

"What if it does?"

"I'll cross that path when I come to it."

"Of course you will." He reached for her again, this time making sure she was in no position to resist as he trapped her arms between their bodies.

"What are you doing?"

"I'm going to make love to you again, baby. As long as you're mad at me you might as well be good and mad. I wouldn't want you to shoot me for no reason."

"If I shoot you, Cody Carter, I'll have a damn good reason. Tonight I broke a promise I made to myself. I vowed I'd never let a man use me like the men who used Sal's girls."

"Promises are made to be broken," Cody whispered against her lips. "But as long as we're discussing promises, I'll make you one. I promise to bring you pleasure every time we make love."

"If I decide to remain here I promise this won't happen again," Cassie returned tartly. Lies, all lies. "If I wanted to be a whore I would have stayed on at Sal's and joined her stable of girls."

Afterward, Cody had no idea what perverse demons prompted his next words. They appeared from nowhere, without thought or consideration.

"You could marry me. For the children's sake," he added thoughtlessly. "And in case tonight should bear fruit neither of us is expecting."

Cassie's stunned expression turned into uncontrollable rage.

"When I get married it will be for love!"

Chapter Ten

Cody reared up from bed as if it were on fire. Wouldn't you know it, he thought derisively, the two women he'd asked to marry him treated him as if he were a social outcast who had just made an improper proposal. He'd never forget the humiliation Lisa had handed him. Of course, he told himself, he'd rather have Cassie as a bedmate with no strings attached, but he was considering the possibility that she could become pregnant. He knew what it felt like to be called a bastard all his life.

"Why in the hell are you so upset?" he roared. "You act as if I just insulted you. Forget I ever asked you, it won't happen again."

Cassie hadn't realized her thoughtless outburst would make Cody so angry, but she couldn't help it. She knew Cody didn't love her, he just enjoyed making love to her. Good Lord, she had enjoyed it as much as he, but that didn't mean they loved one another. She wasn't even certain that Cody loved his own children. And if he didn't love them, he couldn't have loved their mother either. Yet to his credit, there were times when she actually believed him a good father, wonderful even, and the kids obviously adored him. But marriage to the handsome half-breed? It just wasn't possible.

"We don't love each other, Cody."

"What's love got to do with anything? I don't believe in it."

"Love has everything in the world to do with marriage," Cassie said, exasperated. "Why did you marry your children's mother?"

"I've never been married," Cody muttered, leaving his implication dangling in the air.

Cassie was thunderstruck. "Then your children are—"

"Dammit, Cassie, don't put words in my mouth. I don't want to talk about the kids' mother, I want to talk about us."

"Another time, Cody, I'm tired." She sighed wearily, reached for her discarded clothing, and put on her chemise and bloomers.

"Aw, she—horsefeathers," he amended, hoping his tepid oath would please her. Reaching for his pants, he pulled them on, then sat on the side of the bed. "Is that your last word?" he asked, giving her a lazy smile. "I bet I can make you change your mind." He touched her cheek, then deliberately lowered his hand to caress her breast.

The moment his fingers stroked her breast, a clap of thunder rattled the windows and brilliant lightning charged the air with electricity. At first Cassie assumed that Cody's touch had set off fireworks in her body but she soon realized that they were in the midst of a brief but violent spring storm. As thunder rolled overhead and jagged bursts of lightning turned the room to daylight, Cassie fought the sensations Cody's touch had roused in her. Cody felt the strength of her response and sent her a roguish grin. He slid down on the bed beside her, fully intending to initiate another satisfying round of lovemaking.

"I still want you, baby, even when you say things that get my dander up." He lowered his head, his lips moving over hers with such heated passion that Cassie wasn't certain whether the next clap of thunder was the result of the erratic beating of her heart or nature's violence.

The door to Cody's room flew open with a resounding bang. "Papa, Papa! We're scared." Amy and Brady bounded into the room, Amy landing on Cody's chest while Brady's lunge placed him solidly between Cody and Cassie.

"What in the hell is going on?" Cody gasped as the breath exploded from his chest. He wouldn't have guessed that Amy was so heavy.

"The storm," Amy cried, burying her head against Cody's shoulder. "I'm frightened of storms."

"I told her she was being a fraidy cat," Brady said, feeling much braver now with his body cradled in the warm gap between Cody and Cassie.

Cody plucked Amy off his chest and placed her beside her brother. He glanced at Cassie, noted her embarrassed blush, and gave a helpless shrug. It wasn't his fault the kids had burst into his bedroom and found them in bed together. He should have locked the door, but at the time he hadn't thought it necessary. It was Amy who broached the question of what circumstance had placed Amy in Cody's bed.

"Were you afraid of the storm, too, Cassie? Is that why you're in Papa's bed?"

Cody choked back a laugh while Cassie searched futilely for an answer, her face growing redder by the minute.

Amy didn't seem to notice Cassie's confusion as she remarked innocently, "Isn't this fun? All of us in the same bed. Does this make Cassie our mama?"

Cody made a strangled sound deep in his throat. To Cassie it sounded suspiciously like laughter. She sighed heavily. "I hope you don't think that I—that I sleep here all the time," she managed to say.

Brady looked at her with complete understanding. "Just when it storms? Does sleeping with Papa make you feel better too?"

Cody could hold back no longer. He howled in laughter. "You're damn right sleeping with me makes Cassie feel better."

"Cody!" Cassie hid her flaming face beneath the sheet.

More laughter. "Sleeping with Cassie sure as hell makes me feel better."

"Cody!"

His face was almost composed when he said, "Excuse the damn and hell. I'm trying hard to clean up my language, but it's not easy to lose old habits."

"That's not what I mean and you know it," Cassie seethed angrily.

"Don't be mad at Papa," Amy pleaded. Suddenly she remembered that Cody didn't like being called Papa and turned to see if Cody was angry at them. It was difficult to tell in the darkened room. She turned to whisper in his ear, "You're not still angry at us, are you? Calling you Papa seems so—so natural."

"It's all right," Cody said gruffly. "Call me whatever you want."

"Did you hear that, Brady?" But Brady had already fallen asleep, his head resting comfortably on Cassie's shoulder. "Oh, well, I'll tell him tomorrow."

"Tell him what?" Cassie asked sleepily.

Amy smiled mysteriously. "It's a secret." A few minutes later she was blissfully asleep, her dark head resting against Cody's broad chest.

"Cody, are you awake?" Cassie's whisper reached him over the rumble of thunder.

"No. Go to sleep."

"Tomorrow you've got to explain to the children about this."

"What should I tell them? That you and I were indulging our passion just moments before they burst into the room?"

"Must you be so vulgar? You deserve to be shot."

"Go to sleep, Cassie. You can shoot me tomorrow if you still want to."

Cassie glanced briefly at Cody and the children the following morning when she crawled out of bed, then quickly looked away. Somehow during the night Brady had climbed over his sister and found a comfortable resting place on Cody's chest. The intimacy of the scene brought a lump to her throat. She might hate Cody for seducing her but she couldn't deny the loving bond that existed between him and his children. What made the situation so distressing was the fact that she was beginning to feel that same kind of closeness with the children.

Washing and dressing quickly, Cassie went downstairs to help Irene with breakfast. She found the kind-hearted woman in a somber mood. "Is something wrong, Irene?"

Irene shook her head.

"You can tell me. Sometimes it helps to talk about it. Does it concern Reb?"

"Am I so transparent?"

"Well, you do seem quite fond of him. Or am I mistaken?"

"No, you're not mistaken, Cassie. I saw something in Reb that no one else saw. I've never felt this way before. I never allowed myself to hope

I'd feel this way about a man."

"Why? You're an attractive woman."

"I'm a cripple," Irene said succinctly.

"Oh, Irene, that won't matter to the right man."

Irene blushed, abruptly changing the subject. "I'm worried about Reb."

"Why? What happened?"

"Nothing yet, but it might if Reb goes to town Saturday night like he intends. I'm afraid Reb won't be able to resist the lure of liquor. Cody has done so much for Reb, I hate to see his life destroyed by a cheap bottle of booze."

"Saturday is three days away," Cassie said consolingly. "Maybe he'll change his mind by then."

"I hope so, Cassie. Reb is a good man. So much has happened to him that he couldn't cope; that's why he turned to drink."

"It doesn't matter to you that he has only one arm?" Cassie knew it wasn't a fair question but she asked it anyway.

"No, I don't care about that," Irene replied. "I have only one good leg."

"Have you told Reb how you feel about him?"

Aghast, Irene said, "Oh, no, I'd never do that."

"Perhaps you should," Cassie suggested.

The conversation ended when Cody walked into the kitchen, looking sleepy-eyed and quite pleased with himself. He sent Cassie a slow, sizzling look that flustered her so badly she fled from the kitchen, her skirts flying. If Irene wondered what had caused the furious blush that crept up Cassie's cheeks she kept her thoughts to herself.

After breakfast Cassie consented to another lesson in handling a gun, and she and Reb headed out toward the north pasture where the shooting range had been set up for her use. The children, advised to remain near the house until Cassie had become proficient with the weapon, romped in the yard with Blackie while Irene baked cookies for their midmorning snack. Cody had taken off immediately after breakfast, voicing his intention to inspect fences.

Cassie practiced for two solid hours. When Reb's leg started paining him, she suggested he return to the bunkhouse without her. She was still so upset with Cody that shooting at bottles seemed a good way to work off her anger. Reluctantly Reb agreed. Cassie was doing so well he felt she no longer needed supervision.

Cody was in the north pasture when he heard the shooting. Startled at first, he started to ride hell for leather toward the sound when he recalled Reb telling him earlier that he intended to take Cassie to the shooting range for another lesson. He saw her a short distance away, taking aim at a row of bottles lined up atop a bale of hay. He watched her squeeze off a few rounds, then slowed his mount to a sedate walk, focusing his attention on the fence he had been inspecting. When he noticed a section that looked as if it had been deliberately snipped with wire cutters, he dismounted to inspect it more closely.

Cody was so angered over the malicious destruction to the fence that he paid the shot little heed. Just as he bent to have a closer look, a bullet whizzed over his head, missing him by scant inches. It had come so close he felt the heat of its passing as it parted the air above his head. Instinctively he dove to the ground.

Turning his head slowly, he saw Cassie pointing the rifle in his direction. He opened his mouth and spit out a string of vile oaths. Never in his wildest dreams did he imagine Cassie would actually try to shoot him. She had threatened it often enough last night, but he had laughed it off, assuming she had meant it teasingly. He should have known she was serious.

"Damn you, Cassie," he shouted, still hugging the ground. "What do you expect to gain by killing me?"

Feeling quite smug about her prowess with a rifle, Cassie paused a moment to take aim on the last bottle. She was so intent upon her target that she hadn't noticed Cody down by the fence. She was about to squeeze off a shot when she heard a rifle report that had nothing to do with her own weapon. In a purely reflexive movement, she swung the rifle toward the sound just as Cody dropped to the ground.

Her face wore a stunned expression as she slowly lowered the gun. What was Cody doing on the ground? she wondered. Then she heard his words and gaped at him in disbelief.

When Cody saw Cassie lower the weapon, he rose shakily to his feet, his hand testing the top of his head where the bullet had parted his hair. His strides were jerky and uneven, his face a mask of rage as he advanced toward her. He didn't want to believe she had intended to kill him, yet if he hadn't bent over at that precise moment he would be dead meat.

Cassie stood frozen to the spot, devastated by what Cody had accused her of. Kill him? What kind of woman did he think she was? Having Cody dead would serve no purpose. Did he think she'd kill his children too? Didn't he realize that killing him made no sense whatever?

Obviously not, for when he reached her he was absolutely livid. He pulled the rifle from her hand, flung it to the ground, and proceeded to shake her until her teeth rattled and her hair flew from its neat bun at the back of her neck.

"If you try anything like that again, I promise you won't like the consequences!" His teeth were bared in a feral snarl. Cassie had never seen him in such a rage, and she could well imagine his enemies fleeing for their lives before his ferocious temper. At the moment he looked like a savage on thc warpath.

"C-C-Cody, s-s-stop," she stuttered, helpless against the powerful hands that squeezed her shoulders in their hurtful grasp. "Y-y-you're h-h-hurting me."

The shaking stopped but his hands remained clamped on her upper arms. "Why did you do it? Was it because of last night? You were as eager to make love as I was."

"What are you accusing me of? I didn't fire the gun at you."

"The hell you say! If you didn't fire the gun, who did? The prairie is so flat you can see for miles in every direction."

"What about the cornfield?" she pointed out. "It's dense enough to conceal a dozen men. And the trees over there by the creek. I have no reason for wanting you dead."

"Sole ownership of the ranch is as good a reason as any," Cody hinted darkly. "You stand to gain a helluva lot by killing me."

"Have you forgotten the children? According to Buck's will they would inherit your share."

"Yeah, if I had kids," Cody intoned dryly. "I'll give you the benefit of the doubt this time, Cassie, but you can bet your boots I'll be watching you closely from now on."

Releasing her, he turned abruptly, his angry strides carrying him back to where his horse was tethered. Cassie was so mad, she was tempted to shoot him in earnest. "Damn contrary man," she muttered to herself as she watched him stomp away. She was still muttering a short time later when she reached the house.

"Have you seen the children, Cassie?" Irene met Cassie at the back door, her face anxious. "They haven't returned for lunch and the little scamps rarely miss a meal."

Cassie smiled despite herself. It wasn't the children's fault they had an overbearing jackass for a father. "I'll go look for them," she offered. "They're probably in the bunkhouse with Reb, or in the barn playing with Blackie."

She walked into the yard just as Cody came riding up. He reined his horse in, dismounted, and watched her narrowly as she strode toward the bunkhouse. "Reb isn't there. I just saw him going into the barn. Did you want him for anything in particular?"

"I don't want him at all," Cassie sniffed haughtily. "I'm looking for the children. Irene said she hasn't seen them all morning and it's lunchtime."

Looking concerned, Cody tied up his horse. "I'll help you look." He matched his steps to hers as she turned in the direction of the barn.

"It sure is hot today." Brady wiped the perspiration from his brow with a sweaty forearm as he squinted up at the shimmering sun. With both Cody and Cassie gone about their own business that morning the children were bored.

"We could go down to the creek and soak our feet," Brady suggested hopefully. "That might cool us off some. I'll bet Blackie would like to go, too."

Amy gave Brady's idea careful consideration. "We've never been down to the creek alone before."

"Papa won't care."

"We should ask him."

"He'd probably rather not be bothered. He's not too happy with us anyway."

"I suppose you're right."

"Then we can go?"

"I guess so. There's probably only a couple of inches of water in the creek, so I can't see why we shouldn't."

Amy was wrong. The spring had been an unusually wet one and over two feet of water was rushing down the creek toward the river some distance away. After a month or so of normal summer drought the creek would once again be a placid stream a few inches deep, but not now.

"Wow! Look at that!" Brady gushed as he stood on the bank staring into the churning water. "It wasn't like this the last time we were here."

"Remember the storm last night? The stream must be swollen from all the rain we had."

"Can we go in? It looks so cool."

Amy had serious reservations. "I don't know, Brady. It might be way over our heads."

"We could just wade in a little ways." He scrambled down the bank and removed his shoes and stockings. Before Amy could stop him he stood in the shallows with water lapping at his ankles. "C'mon in, it feels good."

Seeing that Brady had come to no harm, Amy kicked off her own shoes and stockings and tested the water. She wiggled her toes, smiled blissfully, and waded in. Blackie joined them, romping between them and the bank, barking playfully. Soon they were splashing one another with childish exuberance, all their troubles forgotten in the pleasure of the moment.

* * *

"Looks like them brats saved us the trouble of findin' 'em, Conrad."

Two men lurked in the tall cottonwood trees lining the bank of the creek, spying on the children with avid interest.

"We've been waiting to catch those two brats alone for a long time, Dooley," Conrad confided eagerly. "Mr. Masters is probably fit to be tied waiting for word that they have met with an unfortunate 'accident.' He would have come himself, but his broken leg wasn't healing properly. The doc said he had some kind of infection in his blood."

"You know, killin' kids don't seem right," Dooley complained.

"I'd kill my own mother for the kind of money Masters is paying us. You knew what had to be done when you hired on for this job. C'mon, Dooley, standing here jawing isn't going to get the job done."

"Reckon you're right."

Stealthily they crept from the concealment of the trees. Since they were behind the frolicking children, their presence went undetected until they were nearly upon the unsuspecting brother and sister.

Brady saw them first and tugged frantically on Amy's sleeve. "Amy, look!" He gestured toward Conrad and Dooley. "I don't think those men belong to the Rocking C. They do look kind of familiar, though."

Amy whirled, her brow furrowed as she watched the men approach. Suddenly she gasped and reached for Brady's hand. "Run, Brady! Those are the two men who tried to catch us at the depot in St. Louis. And one of them is Mr. Conrad!"

Hampered by the pull of the current, they made scant progress. Within minutes the two men had them caught fast. Amy screeched at the top of her lungs, "Let us go! You'd better not hurt us or our papa will kill you."

"You ain't got no papa," Dooley laughed, giving Amy a vicious shake. "You got an uncle though, and he ain't too happy with you right now."

"Uncle Julian is alive?" Brady squeaked.

"No thanks to you two," Conrad said. "That fall down the stairs damn near killed him. He still ain't a well man, but he aims to live high off the hog with money from your estate once he's recovered."

After hearing Conrad's words, Amy thought it a good time to scream again. She did, louder than before, until Conrad clapped a dirty hand over her mouth.

"How we gonna do it, Conrad?" Dooley asked.

Glancing down at the churning water, Conrad grinned evilly. "Drown 'em. That way it will look like an accident and no one will come looking for us."

Dooley nodded, then plunged Brady head first into the swollen stream. Conrad did the same with Amy. But they hadn't counted on Blackie. The faithful white mongrel tore into Conrad with a vengeance, causing him to lose his grip on Amy. She popped to the surface, coughing and sputtering. With a vicious snarl, Blackie turned his attention to Dooley, who was having difficulty protecting himself against the dog while holding Brady beneath the water. In self-defense he released Brady. Amy was beside her brother instantly, pulling his head above the water and trying to drag him to the bank. Both children knew it was only a matter of time before the men would subdue the brave little mongrel and come after them again.

"That sounded like a scream." Cody and Cassie had searched the yard, barn, and stable without finding a trace of the kids. They were already on their way to search down by the creek when they heard Amy scream. When the cry ended abruptly, only to be replaced by Blackie's furious barking, they exchanged worried glances, came to the same frightening conclusion, and broke into a run.

They burst from the line of cottonwood trees in time to see two men lunge for the children, who were in the stream scrambling desperately to reach the bank. Blackie lay stunned, half in, half out of the water. Cody's blood froze as he sought a way to divert the men from the children so that he could fire off a shot without endangering the kids. He let out a shrill war cry that would have done his Cheyenne relatives proud.

"What the hell!" Dooley gasped, certain they

were being attacked by savages. When he saw Cody's dark features and heard his bloodcurdling cry, he knew damn well a savage was after him. "I'm gettin' outta here! We'll get the brats another time."

Turning on his heel, he sprinted from the water and ran downstream to where the horses were tethered. Conrad was close behind him. Cody gave chase, firing off two shots in quick succession before the men were lost amid the cottonwood trees. Moments later he saw them burst from the trees and gallop off across the prairie. Since he was without a mount, he watched helplessly as they made good their escape. It rankled that he hadn't gotten a good look at them. Had Wayne hired them? he wondered, putting nothing past his half-brother. He knew that Wayne would do anything to get his hands on the Rocking C. He let out a few good curses, then turned back to where Cassie was bending over the children.

"Are they okay?" he asked, squatting down beside them.

Both children looked like drowned rats. Though tears were streaming down Amy's cheeks, she appeared unhurt. But Cody's heart contracted with fear when he looked at Brady. The lad's face was white, his breathing almost nonexistent. Cody wasn't sure how long Brady had been underwater, but he knew that if something wasn't done immediately the boy might cease breathing. Flipping him over on his stomach, Cody began gently applying pressure to his back. He grunted in satisfaction when water gushed from the boy's mouth.

"Breathe, dammit, breathe!" The terrible urgency in Cody's voice sent arrows of fear through Cassie's heart. Who would want to harm two innocent children?

Silent tears coursed down Amy's cheeks as she watched Cody labor over her little brother. Brady was all she had left in the world. Her voice quavered when she asked, "Is he going to be all right?"

"Don't worry, darling," Cassie soothed, hugging the small frightened girl to her breast. "Your father won't let him die." She wasn't certain that Cody could work such a miracle, but he was a strong-willed man who would do everything in his power to save the boy.

All attention focused on Brady as he gasped, choked, and began coughing. Cody sat back on his heels, a glimmer of a smile on his lips when Brady began breathing on his own. Then he flipped Brady on his back, slipped an arm beneath his neck, and lifted his head. "Are you all right, son?"

Brady slowly opened his eyes and squinted up at Cody. For a moment the sun shining through the trees blinded him. He blinked, then blinked again. Then his lips widened in a slow smile as a trembling sigh shuddered through him. "For a minute you looked just like my father."

"He's delirious," Cassie said, her own fear for Brady finally abating. "You *are* his father."

"Only if he wants to be," Amy added, her voice barely audible.

Confused, Cassie wanted to ask Amy what she meant, but the child seemed so distraught she didn't want to add to her distress. Instead, she looked at Cody, searching for the key to the puzzle. What she saw stunned her. His expression was a mixture of vulnerability, confusion—and longing? His eyes met hers, and he flushed when he realized that Cassie had been privy to his innermost feelings. No one had ever gotten that close to him before.

Suddenly the spell was broken by Amy's hysterical cry. "Papa! Blackie's not moving!"

Chapter Eleven

Exhausted from their harrowing experience, the children were brought back to the house, fed lunch, and tucked into bed for a nap. Normally they didn't nap, but Cody insisted upon it today. To the children's delight, Blackie had merely been stunned and revived a short time later, as playful as ever. In honor of his survival, the mongrel was thoroughly dried and allowed to lie at the foot of Brady's bed during their nap. Despite their protests that napping was for babies, they dropped off to sleep almost immediately.

When Cody left their room, his face wore a grim expression. The children were in no condition yet to be questioned about their would-be assailants, but he had his own theory. Knowing Wayne's vindictive nature, Cody was convinced that his half-brother was behind the attack. Once the children were disposed of, Cody suspected that Wayne would turn his attention to him and Cassie. Human lives meant nothing to Wayne if they got in the way of what he wanted. Convinced there was only one way to stop Wayne, Cody stopped off at his own room before returning downstairs.

Cassie thought it best not to interfere while Cody tucked the children in bed so she paced the length of the parlor, intending to get some answers from the taciturn man before he left the house. She heard his footsteps on the staircase and rushed to meet him as he reached the bottom landing. She gasped in dismay when she saw him buckling his gunbelt around his narrow hips. The cold, hard glint in his blue eyes was frightening, causing Cassie to take an involuntary step backward. This determined, flint-eyed man was one she had not seen before.

"Where are you going?" Her gaze shifted upward from his gunbelt to search his face.

"I have business in Dodge."

"You'll never find those men, Cody. There were two of them. Do you want to get yourself killed?"

"I reckon that wouldn't make you too unhappy," he said succinctly. "It would spare you the bother of having to do it yourself. If I don't return, the ranch is yours to do with as you please. My only request is that you place the children with a good family."

"Damn you, Cody! I've never run across a man

as bullheaded as you. You're barking up the wrong tree. I never tried to kill you."

"Save it for the judge," Cody said harshly.

"Let the sheriff handle the attack on the children."

Cody laughed harshly. "You don't know much about frontier justice, do you? I'm perfectly capable of doing what needs to be done."

His gaze lingered a moment on her face, thinking he'd never seen her more beautiful, with her green eyes snapping and her breasts heaving with the force of her anger. She sounded so damn convincing he almost believed that she hadn't shot at and nearly killed him. But his own eyes had seen her standing there pointing a gun at him. He turned abruptly and strode toward the door.

"Go ahead," Cassie sputtered, "see if I care. Don't worry about the children, I'll take good care of them. And the ranch, too. I don't need you."

Cody stopped in midstride, spun on his heel, and walked back to where Cassie stood, looking angry enough to spit nails. "You're just full of surprises, aren't you, baby? Take last night, for instance. You might not have been the whore I thought you were, but you sure acted like one in bed. You were panting for me, and so hot that just touching you set you aflame. Don't try to tell me you wouldn't miss me if something happened to me in Dodge, 'cause I wouldn't believe you."

Cassie's face turned fiery red. "I can see I was wrong to express concern for you. You're certainly no gentleman. Get yourself killed for all I care.

I was just thinking about the children, anyway."

His lids narrowed, his hot blue gaze sweeping the length of her with an indolent sensuality that brought a strange tingling to her blood. Damn him! she fumed in silent rage. Why should he affect her that way? Just thinking about Cody touching her as he had last night made her body burn with internal fires. The expression on her face must have revealed her thoughts, for Cody's lips spread in a lopsided grin.

"Are you sure your concern is for the children?" he drawled lazily. "I suspect you were thinking about last night. Deny it all you want, baby, but you enjoyed making love with me. I sure as hell enjoyed making love with you. Once you get over your crazy desire to kill me you might discover you want to do it again."

"Conceited jackass!" Cassie hissed, stunned by his vulgar language and sexual innuendoes. "It's a shame whoever shot at you missed."

"I'll bet you're real sorry."

With a swiftness that startled her, Cody's arms snaked out, grasped Cassie behind the neck, and dragged her up against him. Before she could protest, his mouth seized hers in a bruising, crushing kiss. She whimpered softly as the hard spike of his tongue pushed past her teeth to explore the delicate lining of her mouth. When his hands slid down her back to her buttocks, pulling her hard against his straining erection, the blood pounded in her ears. Struggling desperately to dispel the memory of his hard, throbbing length filling her, bringing her to panting ecstasy, she doubled her fists and pounded his chest. He gave her a provocative, knowing smile and set her away from him.

"That's what you'd miss if you had succeeded in killing me."

Against her will her gaze traveled down to the thick bulge straining his trousers. Did just one kiss do that to him? Not only was he bullheaded and conceited, she thought sourly, but he had the sexual appetite of an animal. She was living proof of that. He had seduced her with incredible ease last night. Worse yet, she had enjoyed it. When she offered no reply to Cody's infuriating remark, he sent her a leering smile, then abruptly turned and strode from the room. She stood rooted to the spot until she heard the front door slam behind him.

"Damn half-breed," she muttered thickly. At the moment it was the most disparaging remark she could think of. It stung to know he was aware of how profoundly he affected her, how his touch made her tingle and burn. He was so cocksure of himself that she felt the inexplicable urge to rush after him and bash some sense into him.

Cody's face was grim when he mounted and rode away from the ranch. What existed between him and Cassie defied his knowledge of relationships. The little witch might want to kill him but she couldn't deny the almost magical attraction that pulled them together.

By the time Cody reached Dodge, his thoughts

were channeled to more serious matters. In his mind there was only one man who could be responsible for the attack on the children. To his knowledge, only Wayne would profit from their deaths. It would be interesting to learn how Wayne intended to do away with him and Cassie.

Wayne wasn't home when Cody arrived at the door of his modest house on the outskirts of Dodge. But Cody wasn't discouraged, despite the fact that Wayne might have left town after the abortive attempt on the children's lives. He vowed to hunt the man down no matter where he tried to hide. Following a hunch, Cody headed over to the Longbranch. If Wayne wasn't home, he'd bet his boots that Holly knew where his half-brother could be found. His dark face sported a grim smile when he entered the dim interior of the Longbranch and spied Wayne sitting at a corner table, talking earnestly with two rough-looking men. Were they the same men who had attacked the children? Cody wondered, annoyed that he hadn't gotten a good look at the assailants.

Cody approached the table with the smooth gait of a panther—poised, watchful, determined. His passage was so silent he stood beside the table before his half-brother or his companions knew he was there. Wayne started violently when he glanced up and saw Cody glaring down at him, his face dark with menace, his blue eyes as cold as ice. Wayne knew a moment of raw fear. Never had Cody looked more like a savage.

Wayne swallowed past the lump of panic rising in his throat and said, "Hello, Cody, what brings you to Dodge?"

"You know damn well what brings me to Dodge." Cody nodded toward Wayne's companions. "Get rid of your friends. What I have to say is better said in private."

The two men seated at the table with Wayne didn't wait to be told to leave. The dangerous glint in Cody's eyes gave them all the incentive they needed as they quickly vacated their chairs. Without a second glance at the fleeing pair, Cody kicked one of the empty chairs into place and sat down facing Wayne. With deliberate slowness he placed both his hands on the table, palms down.

Finding his lips suddenly dry, Wayne rubbed moisture in them with the tip of his tongue. He was staring at Cody's hands as if they were poisonous snakes. Wayne couldn't take his eyes from them. He swallowed convulsively, found his voice, and asked, "What's on your mind, Cody?"

"You know damn well what's on my mind. If your hirelings try to harm the kids again, you'll not get a second warning. I'll come gunning for you."

"Are you loco? What in the hell are you jawing about?" Wayne looked so utterly shocked that Cody might have believed him if he didn't know his brother so well.

"You know damn well what I'm talking about. Two of your thugs tried to kill the kids this morning. Probably the same two who just ran out of here."

"You're hallucinating, Cody. If someone tried to kill your brats, it wasn't me."

"Forgive me if I don't believe you. You've got too much to gain by their deaths. But what I'm going to tell you will change your mind about wanting them dead."

Beads of perspiration gathered on Wayne's brow as he watched Cody's hands coil into fists. He'd be foolish to admit that he was indeed planning the children's demise, but as yet the plan hadn't been worked out to his satisfaction. It would be interesting to know who besides himself wanted them dead. He also wondered why Cody had failed to mention being shot at that morning.

"You're still talking in riddles, Cody."

"Then listen carefully, *brother,* I'm only going to repeat this once. Since those kids aren't mine, it will gain you nothing to kill them. I've never been married, and to my knowledge none of the whores who have serviced me have ever given birth to a child of mine. Amy and Brady are a couple of orphans whose lives I saved in St. Louis. They took it into their heads to adopt me and followed me aboard the train. I didn't have the heart to have them put off so I paid their fares. When we reached Dodge there seemed to be no place to leave them, so I brought them out to the ranch."

"They call you Papa," Wayne observed, only half convinced.

"That's their idea, not mine. If you don't believe me, check my Army records. I served as Army scout in Arizona and New Mexico from '62 through '66. You'll find no record of a wife or children."

"If that don't beat all," Wayne guffawed, finding humor in the situation. Having two less to kill made things a lot easier for him. "I'll be damned, you *are* some kind of do-gooder. When did you go and get religion?"

Before Cody could form an answer, Holly appeared at his elbow, bending low to give him the full benefit of her lush breasts.

"Howdy, Cody, can I get you a drink?"

Cody barely spared Holly a glance. "Get lost, Holly. My business is with Wayne."

Holly's painted lips came together in a lush pout. "Is that any way to treat a friend? I thought you might have come to Dodge to see me."

"I repeat," Cody said tightly, "my business is with Wayne."

Realizing it wasn't going to be easy to get rid of Holly, Cody reached into his pocket, found a gold ten-dollar piece, and tucked it into the cleavage between her breasts. He was immediately sorry he'd been so generous when Holly squealed in delight and planted a wet kiss on his mouth.

"Go away, Holly, we'll talk later."

"Maybe more than talk," Holly hinted as she flounced off with a naughty swish of her skirts that exposed a good deal of white thigh.

Cody turned back to Wayne, Holly already forgotten. "If I see you or your men sneaking around the ranch I won't be responsible for the consequences. Keep away from Cassie and the kids, Wayne."

Wayne smiled nastily. "I wondered when you were going to mention our tempting little stepsister. Is she good, Cody? Are you enjoying screwing her? I wouldn't mind trying her out myself. If she's anything like Linda she'd be a hot little piece."

Seething in uncontrollable rage, Cody surged to his feet, reached across the table, and grasped Wayne by the collar. Cody's chair crashed to the floor as he dragged Wayne across the scarred surface of the table, bringing them nose to nose. "Keep your dirty thoughts to yourself. If you so much as look crosswise at Cassie, I'll tear you limb from limb. She's too good for the likes of you."

Throwing caution to the wind, Wayne laughed derisively. "Too good for me! Ha! I did some inquiring, sent a few telegrams, and learned just exactly how our esteemed stepsister earned her living in St. Louis. She worked in a whorehouse, for God's sake! She's probably bedded half the men in St. Louis. That's the kind of woman who inherited a share of the Rocking C."

A slow smile spread over Cody's dark features. "You're a fool, Wayne. Cassie is no whore. She was working as a maid at Sal's place." He released Wayne so abruptly he fell with a thud onto the tabletop. Wayne saved himself from further embarrassment by catching the side of the table before falling to the floor. By the time he gained his feet, Cody was striding out the door.

"You all right, honey?" Holly asked, sauntering over to Wayne. "What happened to your brother? He sure is a gorgeous specimen. I'll bet he's great in bed, too." Her eyes fixed greedily on the taut mounds of Cody's buttocks.

As he tried to pull himself together, Wayne's frustration grew in leaps and bounds. Unfortunately for Holly, she found herself the recipient of Wayne's rage. Drawing back his arm, he slapped her full across the face. Grasping the table for support, she licked the blood from her lips and asked shakily, "What in the hell was that for?"

"Damn whore," Wayne muttered, feeling better already. It felt good to vent his frustration on someone too weak to offer more than token resistance. "I don't want to hear how good Cody is in bed."

"What's the matter with you?" Holly whined, rubbing her cheek. "You're not jealous of the other men who buy my time. Hell, that's how I make my living. You never complained before."

"Cody is different," Wayne snarled. "He's a dirty half-breed. Don't ever let me catch you going upstairs with him."

"You are jealous!" Holly smiled coyly, sidling close to Wayne. "Hell, honey, you know I prefer you to anybody. I even let you do it for free."

"Oh, yeah?" His eyes fixed on Holly's breasts.

"Get your tail upstairs and show me how much you prefer me." He turned her roughly and shoved her toward the stairs. Holly obeyed with unaccustomed meekness. She'd bedded Wayne often enough in the past to know he had a mean streak and she didn't relish being made his whipping boy. Wayne followed her upstairs, his eyes overbright with lust and barely suppressed rage.

Lying naked beneath Wayne, her thighs spread wide as he unleashed his anger on her body, Holly smiled up at him and pretended it was Cody thrusting into her with unbridled lust. Instead of pale eyes narrowed in frustrated fury, she imagined Cody's compelling blue eyes encouraging her to previously unknown heights.

Grunting and gasping above Holly's nude body, Wayne imagined it was Cassie's pale body splayed beneath him. Maybe that was the secret of getting back at Cody, he thought darkly. Cody seemed so taken with Cassie that he'd be devastated if she had an unfortunate accident. Or if she suddenly preferred Wayne to Cody. It was something to think about. Then all thought ceased as climax shuddered through him.

As soon as he returned to the ranch, Cody set up night patrols around the perimeter of the house and set about repairing the fences that had been deliberately cut. It might not have been necessary to organize night patrols, but he'd never forgive himself if anything happened to the children due to his own negligence.

Then he set out to question the children about the men who had attacked them. The children had gone into the barn to feed Lady an apple. Cody saw them and followed. He rested a few moments against a bale of hay as he watched the children feed Lady and eavesdropped on their conversation. They hadn't seen him in the deep shadows, and he decided not to make his presence known just yet.

"I wish I could ride Lady, Amy, don't you?" Brady said.

Amy had to think about that. Horses still frightened her. "Lady seems gentle enough, but I'm still not sure I'd like to ride her."

"Sissy."

"Am not."

"Are, too."

Tiring of the game, Amy grew serious. "Brady, I think we should leave here."

"Leave the ranch?" Brady's face wore a stunned look. "I don't want to leave. I like it here. Did Papa say we had to leave?"

"Cody really isn't our papa, Brady, no matter how badly we might want it to be so. It wouldn't be right to get him into trouble with Uncle Julian. He knows where we are now, and those men will come back to kill us. I couldn't stand for Cody or Cassie to get hurt because of us."

"Cody wouldn't let anyone hurt us," Brady said with staunch conviction. "Maybe we ought to tell him about Uncle Julian now that we know the law isn't after us. Maybe he can help us."

"No one can help us," Amy said.

Her small, forlorn voice was filled with such overwhelming sadness that Cody's heart went out to the child. He'd always suspected the children hadn't told him everything but he'd resisted the urge to question them. He wasn't certain whether it was because he was afraid he wouldn't like what he heard or because he didn't want to become too involved in their lives. It was too late now to analyze his feelings, for he suddenly found himself smack dab in the middle of a mystery. If it wasn't Wayne who had made the attempt on the kids' lives, who was it?

Deciding it was time to make his presence known, Cody said, "Try me, you might be surprised what I can do. It's about time you kids confided in someone. It might as well be me."

"Papa, where did you come from?" Brady asked.

Cody stepped from the shadows into full view. "I thought it was time we had a talk. I want to know the truth, kids. Don't try to talk your way out of it this time, it won't work. Come over here and sit down. We won't be bothered for a while."

Reluctantly the children trudged over to where Cody stood. He lifted them atop a bale of hay and leaned against it, relaxed yet attentive. "Okay, start with St. Louis and that accident with the carriage. Or was it an accident?"

"Mr. Conrad arranged it," Brady blurted out, glad to get it out in the open. He wanted no secrets from Cody.

"Who in the hell is Conrad?"

"He's the man who tried to drown us in the creek," Amy explained. "He and the man with him were the ones who chased us at the depot in St. Louis. Don't you see, we couldn't let them catch us. Uncle Julian wanted to kill us."

"Whoa, start from the beginning," Cody said, thoroughly confused. "I thought you were orphans."

"We are," Brady contended. "Our mama and papa were killed a long time ago in a riverboat accident. It blew up. We were with them, but someone pulled us from the water."

"Uncle Julian is our guardian," Amy said, taking up the story where her brother left off. "But he's a bad man. He wants the money Mama and Papa left us. We heard Uncle Julian talking to Mr. Conrad one night when he thought we were sleeping. He paid Mr. Conrad to kill us so he could take all our money."

Cody found all this difficult to believe. He'd heard that kids were fanciful creatures who often made up stories and wondered if that could be the case with Amy and Brady. "Why didn't you go to the law?"

"'Cause we thought we killed Uncle Julian," Brady said with the logic of a seven-year-old. All this talk was dredging up memories he'd rather forget. "He looked dead, anyway. So we ran away."

"How did you kill him?" Cody asked.

"He caught me and Brady listening outside the door when he and Mr. Conrad were talking about killing us," Amy explained, picking up the tale. "It wasn't our fault he chased us and fell down the stairs. His legs were all twisted and he was bleeding. We thought he was dead and the law would blame us. We didn't want to go to jail, or be placed in an orphanage, so we ran away."

"And adopted me, fool that I am," Cody muttered beneath his breath. Aloud he said, "So your uncle is alive and trying to kill you, is that what you'd have me believe?"

"It's the truth," Brady vowed.

"Perhaps I should take you back to St. Louis and alert the law to your uncle's machinations."

Amy's eyes grew round as saucers. "No! Please, Cody, don't take us back. They'd never believe us. They'd give us to Uncle Julian. Or make us go to an orphanage. Don't send us away, please! We promise to be good and do everything you say. Just let us stay here with you."

"Aw, she-it. You kids must think I'm a soft touch or something. Don't you know there are men who fear me? When they see me coming they run the other way. I've got a reputation, kids, and I didn't get it from being kind to orphans and widows. I'm half savage. I'm tough, and mean, and ornery enough to send men running in fear."

"You are?" Brady asked, recognizing none of those traits in Cody.

"Aw, she-it! What in the hell am I going to do with you two?"

"You're not like that at all," Amy defended stubbornly. "You're good and kind and—and—

the sort of man we'd like for a papa. We'd prefer our own parents, but since that's not possible, we'll settle for you and Cassie. We like her a lot, too. You like her, don't you, Papa?"

"Don't sidetrack me with your questions," Cody grumbled sourly.

"If you don't like Cassie, why were you in bed with her?"

Cody groaned. This conversation was getting more complicated by the minute. These two kids were as wily as foxes. "Sure I like Cassie, does that answer your question?" *I like her too damn well,* he thought.

"Partly," Amy conceded.

"That's all you're going to get. Let's get back to the subject of your uncle. What are we going to do about him and his henchmen?"

If what the kids said was true, Cody knew he couldn't allow them to be taken away by a man who wanted to kill them. Just because he believed the kids' story didn't mean the law would. Julian Masters sounded like a sly bastard who would be likely to prevail with the law. There was no way he'd let the kids go, no sir. He'd defend them with his life, if need be. He saw the kids looking at him expectantly, hopefully, waiting for his answer.

"Hell and damnation, you're staying right here on the Rocking C. No one's going to hurt you as long as I'm around. If your Uncle Julian turns up, I'll deal with him."

"Oh, Papa—er—I mean Cody!" Amy squealed, jumping down from the bale of hay and throwing herself at him. Unprepared for her exuberant response, Cody stumbled backward, landing hard on his posterior. A moment later Brady joined Amy in Cody's lap, his arms clamped tightly around Cody's neck.

Of their own volition, Cody's arms surrounded the children, holding them close. With his arms filled with squirming, appreciative children, he experienced an enlightening revelation. He actually *liked* being called Papa. It gave him a warm feeling of belonging, something he'd never known before. He'd experienced the same reaction with Cassie, only in a different way. With Cassie there was that sexual, tingling awareness, but the kids imbued him with a feeling of family. They didn't seem to care that he was a rough cowboy more at ease with a gun than with people. Hell, they didn't even care that he was a half-breed.

"It's okay, Amy, you and Brady can call me Papa if you like. I didn't realize it at the time, but I accepted responsibility for you when I paid for your train tickets to Dodge. I won't let anyone hurt you."

Cassie stood in the partially opened doorway of the barn, watching Cody and the children with a wistful expression on her face. Though she couldn't hear what they were saying, the tender moment she was witnessing brought a lump to her throat. It made her yearn for the same kind of affection. Her grandmother, poor overworked woman that she was, had done her best, but Cassie had missed something growing up without benefit of mother or father. At least the kids had Cody, whom they loved unconditionally. The only discordant note in the scenario was Cody's reason for disclaiming his own children. She didn't think she could ever forgive him for that. Didn't Cody know that children were treasures? If she had such treasures, or was ever lucky enough to be a mother, she would hold them in her heart forever.

Deciding not to interfere in so private a moment, Cassie left the barn as quietly as she had appeared.

Chapter Twelve

Hoping he wouldn't regret his decision, Cody asked Reb to take a turn at guard duty Saturday night. That was the night the ranch hands went into town to drink and carouse, and Cody didn't want to leave the house and yard unguarded.

"Do you think you can handle it, Reb?" Cody asked, sensing the man's reluctance. "It only takes one arm to shoot a gun. I know you're fond of the children and wouldn't want to see them harmed."

"I can handle it," Reb muttered, annoyed that Cody had found it necessary to mention his disability. He needed no reminders, living with it every day.

Nor would he tell Cody that he had intended to borrow a horse and go to town Saturday night himself. He knew that Irene would prefer he didn't go to town because she feared he'd lapse back into his old ways, but he was confident he could handle the temptation. He'd give his good left arm for just one drink. Just one, that was all he needed. But Cody's request that he take a turn at sentry duty foiled his plans. And since he'd rather die than give Cody a reason to accuse him of shirking responsibility, he gave a reluctant agreement.

Cody gave Reb a hard look, then went on his way. He intended to patrol himself tonight, but further away from the house, leaving Reb to guard the yard and immediate vicinity. He doubted that anyone could get that close to the house, but just in case they did, Reb would be on hand to prevent an unwelcome invasion by unexpected guests.

Cassie had never felt so helpless. The attempt on the children's lives had left her frustrated and worried. To make matters worse, she felt that she was being left completely in the dark about what was going on. She had no idea that Cody had warned the children to tell no one what they had confided to him, including Cassie. Consequently, some of their natural exuberance fled when they were around Cassie. But Cassie was astute enough to realize she was deliberately being kept in the dark about certain things. And she didn't like it.

When days passed and Cody made no attempt to take her into his confidence, she decided to confront him and get some answers for herself. On Saturday night she saw Cody ride out at dusk.

She thought he was deliberately avoiding her and decided to follow and have that long-overdue conversation. After instructing Irene to put the children to bed at their usual time, she took the rifle from its resting place above the mantel and hurried to the barn to saddle Lady. After placing the rifle in the saddle holster, she rode off in the same direction as Cody.

Cassie knew that Cody had been patrolling nearly every night, so she wasn't surprised when she saw him rein his mount toward the creek. The tall cottonwood trees offered a tempting hiding place for anyone bent on mischief. When Cassie entered the thick cover of trees, a small shiver of apprehension shook her slim frame. Some of the cottonwoods looked like man-eating dragons reaching out gnarled fingers toward her. Her hand fluttered to the butt of the rifle, grateful for the comfort it offered. Thank God she wasn't so stupid as to go out at night without protection.

Unfortunately, she had lost sight of Cody shortly after he had entered the thick stand of trees lining the creek bank. A sudden movement to the right caught her attention and she saw a figure on foot dart behind a tree. Gathering her courage, she slid from the saddle and removed the rifle from the holster.

"Cody, is that you?"

Silence.

"Cody, don't play games with me. I want to talk with you."

More silence.

Growing apprehensive, Cassie cocked the rifle and walked slowly toward the tree where she had seen movement. She had nearly reached it when a figure broke away from the shadows. She knew immediately it wasn't Cody, for the man was too short, not muscular enough, and his furtive movements held none of Cody's measured confidence. That was all Cassie needed to know as she raised the rifle, took careful aim, and fired. She cocked and fired a second time, dimly aware of a third shot fired simultaneously with her second round.

Since the man she had shot at kept running, she realized that the third shot had been fired by another man. She had felt the heat of the bullet whiz past her. On the heels of that shot came another, but this one sounded farther away. She came to the startling conclusion that there was a second man in the woods. That was when she decided it was time to beat a hasty retreat and find Cody.

Cody found Cassie first. Before she reached her horse, he came leaping at her, bringing her down with a flying tackle. Thinking she was being attacked by an unknown assailant, Cassie struggled wildly.

"Damn you! That's the second time you tried to kill me!"

Cassie went rigid. "Cody?"

"Who in the hell did you think it was?"

"Get off me, you big oaf."

He lifted himself off her, dragging her upright. "When are you going to stop trying to kill me?"

"What are you talking about? I didn't try to kill you."

"No?" He picked her gun off the ground where it had fallen. "The barrel is still hot; it's been fired recently."

"Of course it has. I fired twice at someone lurking in the woods. There were two men. I shot at one. Both my bullets missed, but someone shot back at me."

"You're right, there was more than one shot, all of them aimed at me. One of them missed me by scant inches. You're getting to be a damn good shot, Cassie, but not good enough."

"I tell you I didn't shoot at you. I didn't even see you. I did shoot at someone, but I missed him both times."

Cody's disbelief was obvious. "What in the hell am I going to do with you? I've got enough to worry about without you running around taking potshots at me. If you didn't intend to kill me, what are you doing following me?"

"I wanted to talk to you," Cassie insisted, holding her temper in check. "You're deliberately keeping something from me and I want to know what it is. When I saw you ride out I decided to follow and force you to confide in me. Even the children have been secretive, and I feel left out."

"I'll tell you what it's all about if you admit you shot at me."

"That would be lying. I don't want you dead, Cody."

The provocative huskiness of Cassie's voice had always intrigued Cody, and tonight was no exception. As he stared into the sultry depths of her green eyes, he was suddenly, achingly aware that he wanted her, despite the fact that she wished him dead.

"Don't you, baby? How *do* you want me?"

"I . . ."

"Cat got your tongue?"

Her chin lifted fractionally. "I don't want you at all."

He gave her a devastating grin. "I want you. Now. On the ground, with moonlight etching delicate patterns on your sweet flesh. I want to put myself inside you and feel—"

"Stop!" Driven to the brink of madness by Cody's erotic talk, Cassie clapped her hands over her ears. "I don't want to listen to you. While you're talking nonsense, the men who shot at us are getting away."

"There are no men, Cassie, admit it. I've been all through these woods tonight. There's only you and me, and that aching feeling deep in the gut when two people want each other. Is that why you followed me tonight, Cassie, because I've been neglecting you? You didn't have to shoot at me to get my attention."

Her eyes snapped to his. If looks could kill, he'd be shaking hands with the devil. "Let me go!"

"Not yet, not until you admit you want me."

"I don't—"

The words died on her lips as he dragged her against the hard wall of his chest and pressed his mouth to hers with savage intensity. Her senses reeled as pleasure radiated outward from the warm secret places of her body. With that one kiss he had fanned the flames of her passion to match his own. Cassie was dismayed at the magnitude of her own desire, crushed by her wanton response to a man who had the unmitigated gall to accuse her of shooting at him. Nevertheless, she clung to him, needing more of his kisses, wanting everything he had to offer . . . everything.

Recognizing her need, Cody eased her down on a bed of fragrant leaves, his lips still joined to hers. His hand moved under her skirt to skim her thigh, resting atop her hip a tantalizing moment before reaching around to massage the aching warmth between her legs. Cassie was panting raggedly when he released her lips and asked, "Do you want me, Cassie?" His eyes took on a lazy, hooded look. "Tell me, baby."

"No, I don't . . ." She drew in a deep breath to alleviate some of the crushing ache in her chest that came with her blatant lie. Humiliated by her inability to resist Cody's seduction, she tried to turn her face away. But Cody would have none of it. He grasped her chin and forced her to face him squarely. His lips curled into a look of such scathing mockery that she closed her eyes to escape it.

"Look at me, Cassie." His voice was ruthless, hard, unrelenting. Against her will, her eyes flew open. "Can't you tell the truth for once in your life? First you try to convince me you didn't shoot at me and now you say you don't want me." He touched the hard nub of her nipple where it rose prominently against her blouse. "Your body wants me."

"My body lies!"

"I think not." He lowered his head, taking her nipple into his mouth through the material of her blouse, laving it with his tongue. The friction of the material, made wet by his mouth, against the ultrasensitive nubbin of flesh was excruciatingly exciting.

"Oh, dear Lord." The words gushed out on a shaky sigh when Cassie realized that her blouse was unbuttoned and Cody had pushed it aside and released the ties on her shift, exposing her breasts.

"You have beautiful breasts, baby." His expression reflected a heavy, dazed sensuality. When he took a nipple into his mouth and suckled vigorously, a flutter of warmth surged through her and she realized that no matter how much she tried to deny it, she wanted Cody to make love to her.

When he lifted his head and looked at her, his eyes had acquired the stormy blue of a turbulent sea. His sensual gaze fell to her breasts, rising and falling with each labored breath, her nipples glistening wet from his mouth and swollen into erectness.

Cassie groaned and arched her back, fearing he intended to leave her. With her breasts only inches from his mouth, he gave her a cocky grin and started to rise. She uttered a small cry of dismay, wound her hands into the dark thickness of his long hair, and brought his mouth back down to her breasts.

"No, damn you, don't you dare leave me now."

"You're the most aggravating woman I've ever known, sweetheart." It had taken all the willpower he possessed to bring his raging lust under control. He was learning the hard way that he had no control where Cassie was concerned. He was either so damn angry with her he wanted to beat her or so enthralled he couldn't keep his hands off her. "Am I going to make love to you or are we going to sit here jawing all night?"

Cassie drew in a deep, trembling breath. "Shut up and make love to me, Cody."

He grinned cheekily. "I thought you'd never ask. Let's get these clothes off first." He tugged on her skirt. Cassie lifted her hips to ease its passage down her legs.

He was removing her drawers when a frightening thought occurred to her. "Wait! What if those men are still in the woods?"

"Dammit, Cassie, you know good and well there are no men in the woods tonight. It was a good excuse, but I don't buy it. And I give you fair warning, you'll never get another chance to take a shot at me."

"Cody, I didn't—" Her words ended in a gurgle as his mouth covered hers in a demanding kiss.

When it ended he was gasping for breath and Cassie could tell he was approaching the end of his endurance. He rose shakily to his knees and began tearing at his clothes. "For God's sake help me, baby. If I'm not buried inside you soon I'm going to burst."

Rising to her knees beside him, Cassie shoved aside his shaking hands, quickly divesting him of his shirt. When her fingers failed to grasp the intricacies of his gunbelt, Cody groaned and took over the task himself. Within seconds he was beside her again, gloriously nude, brazenly male, beautiful—arousing. Compulsively her eyes moved over all that bare, golden skin, blazing a path along his wide shoulders, broad, muscle-defined chest that narrowed down to hard, flat stomach, and hips that flared out only minimally from his waist.

Black hair swirled around his hard male nipples, was nearly nonexistent on his smooth middle, but below the navel—oh, God—below the navel it grew again in abundance at his groin. Her eyes remained fixed on that private part of his anatomy, mesmerized by the size and thickness of him.

Cody's breath caught painfully in his throat as he watched her through slitted lids, feeling his erection grow larger and harder beneath her stimulating regard. He was suddenly proud of his body and of his ability to please her. A primitive impulse deep inside him stirred to life as he reached for her. "Enough," he groaned raggedly.

Cassie was surprised when he flipped her over on her stomach and ran his hands lightly over the tempting curves of her back, waist, and buttocks. She gasped aloud when his lips followed the course of his hands, kissing, nipping, his tongue leaving a trail of fire on her highly sensitized flesh. When he turned her on her back, Cassie felt as if her world had tilted and spun out of control.

"Cody, please."

"Relax, baby, we've got all night. I want you all hot and wet for me." The torrid heat and throbbing readiness of his big body made a mockery of his statement about them having all night. He was so close to climax he probably wouldn't last another five minutes. But he was so eager to please Cassie that he gritted his teeth and persevered.

Then he was kissing her again, his tongue thrusting deep into the hot sweetness of her mouth, his hands squeezing her breasts, teasing her nipples, until she was whimpering and writhing in sweet agony. And then—then his lips left hers, sliding down the long column of her neck, pausing briefly to worship her breasts with his lips, continuing down her belly—lower.

"Cody, no!" When Cody's mouth settled on the nest of golden curls between her legs, she had a sneaking suspicion of what he intended and she jerked convulsively, trying to escape the hot ravishment of his lips and tongue. People didn't do such things. When his tongue slid into the moist crevice between her legs, she screamed and arched violently upward, consumed by raw liquid fire.

Placing a restraining hand against her stomach, Cody held her firmly in place for the hot ravishment of his tongue while with his other hand he shoved her legs farther apart to give him better access. When his tongue slid against the tiny nub of her femininity, Cassie forgot everything except the searing flame of ecstasy turning her body to ashes. Just when she thought she had experienced the ultimate sensation, Cody carefully inserted a finger inside her, massaging her both inside and out. The resulting explosion shattered her into a million pieces.

When Cody rose above her and thrust into her, her climax intensified with each stroke of his magnificent sex. Convinced that nothing could ever equal the sensations coursing through her, Cassie was shocked when Cody groaned and said, "You're not taking all of me." Rolling over, he carried her with him until she rested atop him and pushed himself deep, deeper still, but it still wasn't enough. Grasping her hips, he pushed her down hard, then up, then down again, finally obtaining the penetration he desired.

Nearly senseless with pleasure, Cassie felt herself contract around him, felt her muscles grasp him tightly as his hot seed spurted against the walls of her womb. She cried out his name.

Cody's body tensed, his control all but shattered as Cassie's hot sheath contracted around him, squeezing him—killing him. Bucking upward again and again, he gave a hoarse shout.

When Cassie gained her wits, Cody was still inside her, staring at her with confusion. "I don't know what just happened but I can truthfully say nothing like that has ever happened to me before. You scare the living hell out of me, Cassie. I wish I knew what to make of it."

Cassie remained mute, utterly beyond speech. Cody wasn't the only one unable to define what had just happened between them. She had never experienced anything so intense, so beautiful, so—so—fulfilling. The fact that Cody felt the same way she did gave her fierce satisfaction. She started to move from atop him but he held her fast, his hands clasping her hips so she couldn't rise. She felt him flex within her and her eyes sought his, surprised that he was still hard. He read the shock on her face and grinned.

"Does it surprise you that I want you again so soon? It sure as hell shocks me. I've always taken pride in my recuperative powers but I've never been this randy before, or ready to perform so quickly." The heat of his blue eyes held her suspended. "What am I going to do with you, Cassie? I've never had a woman as sweet and responsive as you. What am I going to do with you?" he repeated.

Cassie gulped, then uttered something so outrageous it brought a rosy flush rushing over her body. "You could love me again."

He sent her a lopsided grin. "I'll probably dance with the devil in hell for giving you so damn much power over me, but loving you again is what I want too."

With an efficiency of movement he reversed their positions, placing her beneath him. Then he began to move his hips, thrusting within her. Slowly, oh so slowly, he moved until his need was a tormented ache inside him. With a gasping sigh, Cassie surrendered to the burning fury of their mutual hunger.

Favoring his bad leg, Reb circled the house on yet another senseless round of patrolling. The night was too damn long to suit him. His throat was dry as a desert and no relief was in sight. He'd been on sentry duty since sundown and hadn't seen so much as a leaf stir. The house was dark but for one light left burning in the parlor and another in the upstairs hallway, and Reb wondered for the hundredth time why he had agreed to sentry duty when he'd rather be in town carousing with the ranch hands. If he could have one little drink, he thought, licking his parched lips, he'd be satisfied.

Oh, he knew right well that Irene didn't want him to go into Dodge but he could handle it. He hadn't had a drink in so long, his whole body trembled with the need for just one tiny sip of beer or a good slug of whiskey. He had a few coins in his pocket now, a small portion of his earnings as a ranch hand. Hell, he thought derisively, he was no fool. He knew damn well he was barely earning his keep, that Cody was paying him out of pity. Before he had lost his arm he was a real man who could shoot and ride with the best of them. Now he was a cripple, a man to be pitied, of little use to anyone.

If not for Irene . . . Just thinking about the attractive woman brought a smile to his lips. She didn't seem to care that he had only one arm. He had never met a woman quite like Irene. If he weren't a cripple he'd . . . Hell, what good did it do to think serious thoughts about Irene? A drink was what he wanted, all he really needed.

After one more trip around the house Reb had reached a decision. Convinced that all this patrolling was needless, and that if someone was stirring out there Cody would come across the intruder on one of his rounds, Reb decided to borrow a horse and ride into town. If he hurried he'd be back before anyone ever knew he was gone. For one brief moment his conscience protested, but it wasn't as if he were abandoning his post, he told himself; he was merely taking a short leave of absence. His mind made up, he headed for the corral, his mouth watering for the taste of a drink. He had no idea he was being observed when he rode away from the ranch.

"What do you make of it, Dooley?" Conrad asked as he moved from the concealing shadows of the barn.

"Looks like he's hellbent on gettin' to Dodge."

"Hot damn, what a stroke of luck! We know the breed and the woman are down by the creek. I can still feel the heat of the bitch's bullet. She damn near plugged me. If we're gonna snatch the kids we'd better do it now."

"What about the housekeeper? I ain't seen her leave the house yet."

"Shit, Dooley, can't you take care of one helpless woman? A crippled one at that."

"What are we gonna do with the brats after we get them?" Dooley asked. "It's a damn shame Mr. Masters wired us today and told us not to kill them, that the lawyers were gettin' suspicious and wanted to see them. Sure does complicate matters. Wouldn't it be simpler if Masters came after the brats himself? He's their guardian."

"Dammit, Dooley, didn't you hear me when I told you about the man I met at the Longbranch yesterday? Claims he's the half-breed's brother. Half-brother," he amended. "If he was sober he wouldn't have confided in me, but since he did, I listened and learned a helluva lot about the Rocking C Ranch.

"Wayne Carter said that his brother was damn fond of those kids and wouldn't let them go without a fight. You heard them call him Papa. Have you had a good look at the half-breed, Dooley? I sure as hell wouldn't want to tangle with him. As for Masters, he's still too sick to travel, and he doesn't want anyone to know that the kids ran away, or why they ran away. Could raise a big stink."

"So what do we do with them once we get them? We can't just march up to the depot and buy four tickets out of town. I sure don't relish takin' them all the way to St. Louis on horseback."

"We'll ride as far as Wichita on horseback," Conrad said. "Then we'll board a train for St. Louis."

"What makes you think the kids will go meekly?" Dooley asked, still unconvinced.

"We're gonna scare the living hell out of them," Conrad said, grinning maliciously. "Enough talk. Let's get this over with so we can collect our money."

Amy awoke with a start, her senses drugged by sleep, her eyes dull and unfocused. She had been having a nightmare, and when she awakened relief surged through her. She dreamed someone had taken her and Brady away from Cody and had given them back to their uncle. The room was dark except for a gilded shaft of moonlight shining through the open window. She glanced over at Brady's bed, saw that he was sleeping soundly, and tried to concentrate on going back to sleep. Nothing was stirring outside, not even a breeze, and Amy shifted restlessly. Forcing herself into a calmness she didn't feel, she closed her eyes and tried to think pleasant thoughts.

Conrad found the back door open and quietly entered the kitchen, followed closely by Dooley. A light still burned in the parlor and another in the upstairs hallway, lighting their way as they moved stealthily up the staircase. Conrad peered inside two unoccupied rooms before he located the children. Pushing open the door, he stepped inside, cursing beneath his breath when the hinge creaked.

Amy heard the telltale noise and shot upright in bed. "Who is it? Cassie? Irene? Who's there?"

"Shit!" Grabbing a blanket from the bed, Conrad stuffed a corner of it into Amy's mouth, trussing her up in its folds like a Christmas turkey.

The struggle awoke Brady. Too dazed to throw off the mantle of sleep, he was quickly subdued. But before the children could be removed from their beds, Irene came bursting through the door. "Amy, Brady, is something wrong? Did you cry out?"

The poor woman never knew what hit her. She had barely gotten through the door when Dooley grabbed her from behind and Conrad clubbed her with the butt of his gun.

"Let's get out of here," Conrad hissed, "before the half-breed and his woman come back."

Each man hefted a child over his shoulder and they left the house as quietly as they had entered, disappearing into the darkness of the night.

Chapter Thirteen

Cassie stretched languorously. The fragrant breeze felt cool against the torrid heat of her naked body. Her eyes were slumbrous, heavy, her mouth wet and swollen from Cody's kisses. Every inch of her flesh tingled and burned. Only moments ago Cody had been embedded so deeply inside her he had reached every part of her, including her heart. Most especially her heart.

"Are you cold?" Cody loomed over her, resting on an elbow. He stared with rapt enjoyment at her flushed body. He touched a puckered nipple, entranced by the way it rose up to meet his finger.

Cassie's breath caught in her throat as she savored the exquisite sweetness of Cody's caress. What was the matter with her? The way she had responded to him placed her in the same class as Sal's girls. She had wanted him with a wild hunger that frightened her. She wanted to touch him, caress him, give him pleasure—wanted him inside her. She shivered. How could she want him so desperately when she knew he was motivated by lust, not love?

"You *are* cold," Cody murmured. Moonlight bathed her body in shimmering silver, turning the hair on her head and between her legs to pure spun gold. The shiver that ran the length of her body made him aware that they were both lying naked on the damp ground. "We'd better get dressed. I'll take you back to the house."

Cassie stared at him. Hurt curled inside her belly. Where were his sweet words? Now he seemed brusque and anxious to be rid of her. It was obvious to her that once he had used her he had no further need for her—until the next time lust reared its ugly head. If she wasn't naked, still basking in the afterglow of lovemaking and tingling from sweet fulfillment, she'd have sworn they had never been intimate. Her lips were pressed tightly together as she pushed him aside, rose to her feet, and reached for her clothing, hastily discarded just a short time ago.

Cody frowned, aware of Cassie's sudden anger but finding no reason for it. "Are you mad at me?"

She whirled on him. "Should I be?"

He smiled, his eyes glowing so intensely that Cassie felt herself redden beneath his penetrating gaze. Embarrassed, she dropped her eyes, aware of all those arousing, wonderful things he had done to her; of how she had urged him on with small cries of encouragement; of the way she had begged for his touch. She recalled his sensual mouth and how his lips and tongue had pleasured her, and her knees buckled beneath her. He reached out to steady her, but his touch only intensified the feeling of thick heaviness between her legs.

"You have no reason to be angry with me, Cassie. We wanted each other, it's as simple as that. Why shouldn't we indulge ourselves? It's not as if you're still a virgin."

Her eyes glowed with sudden fire. "I would be if not for you."

Cody shrugged as he reached for his shirt and shoved his arms into the sleeves. "If you recall, I did offer to marry you." He made it sound as if marriage was something one did out of obligation, not for love or because being together was the most important thing in the world.

Abruptly she asked, "Did you love the children's mother?"

Rather than go into the somewhat lengthy and complicated explanation of how he had been adopted by the kids, he said, "I've never loved a woman in my life." He would hardly describe what he had felt for Lisa as love, for he knew now that it had been merely infatuation.

"Oh, dear God." It was even worse than Cassie thought. Cody was an animal, driven by lust and utterly heartless. Marriage to Cody would be total hell. She'd never be satisfied with the small part of himself he could spare her.

Cody's brow furrowed as he took note of Cassie's softly spoken oath and realized how callous his words had sounded. He sought to make amends before they returned to the house. He was uncomfortable with the thought that she considered him a heartless bastard without a shred of feeling.

"I don't want to make you angry, Cassie. Lord knows you give me more pleasure than I've known in more years than I care to count. There's no reason why we should argue. I can understand your reluctance to accept my proposal, but that doesn't mean we can't still enjoy one another. And if the need arises, if I do get you with child, you could do worse than marrying me. We already share the ranch, so it would be advantageous as well as desirable to join forces and combine our holdings."

Cassie's temper exploded. "Advantageous! Desirable! You have ice where your heart should be. I told you the only reason I'll marry is for love." She sent him an assessing look. "Do you love me, Cody?"

Cody tensed. Hadn't he just said he'd never loved any woman? Couldn't Cassie leave well enough alone? Why did she insist on badgering him? Since he'd met her his emotions had been in a perpetual state of confusion. He almost wished she had been a whore as he'd originally thought. He could deal with that. He'd always felt more at ease with whores than with decent women. The only reason he'd felt compelled to propose to Cassie after he'd taken her virginity was because she was one of those "decent" women he'd always steered clear of. He wasn't completely without scruples. And he was honest enough to admit he couldn't keep his hands off her.

But was that the only reason he'd proposed? a little voice inside his head asked. Of course it was, he answered, chasing away the little demon with a vigorous shake of his head. Marriage was the last thing in the world he wanted. Suddenly he was aware that Cassie was staring at him, her question dangling between them like an unfinished melody.

"Love is a complicated emotion," he said slowly, carefully. "I want you. When I'm with you I feel . . . exhilarated, strong, invincible. You're beautiful, spirited, and so damn contrary I'd like to strangle you at times. I . . . care for you."

"It's not the same."

"No, I don't reckon it is, but it's the best I can do." His voice turned gruff. "C'mon, let's get out of here."

"Cody, wait."

He turned impatiently. The conversation was making him uncomfortable.

"I can't deny the attraction between us, or the way I feel when we make love, but I won't marry you," she said. "I'm going to try to resist you to the best of my ability, but if I fail, not even becoming pregnant with your child will persuade me to become your wife. I stand by my words. I will only marry for love, and the man I marry must love me in return."

A roguish grin brightened Cody's face. "Are you saying you love me?" In all his life no woman had ever told him she loved him.

"I'm saying I *could* love you. I already love your children."

The breath he hadn't realized he'd been holding hissed out in a swift exhalation of air. Her words rendered him incapable of coherent speech. But no answer was necessary, for Cassie had already turned to mount her horse.

All was quiet when they entered the yard. A single light still burned in the parlor. Nothing seemed amiss, but Cody felt a prickly sensation at the back of his neck and his big body grew tense with unexplained apprehension. Dismounting, he searched the yard with restless eyes. "Where's Reb?"

"Reb?" Cassie was puzzled. "Sleeping, I suppose."

"He's supposed to be on guard tonight. Did you see him when you left the house earlier?"

"No." A jolt of fear slithered through her. She was beginning to experience the same apprehension Cody felt. "Do you think something is wrong?"

"We'll soon find out." His face was grim, his eyes alert. "Reb!" he called out loudly, demanding a reply. If Reb was anywhere in the vicinity he couldn't help but hear and answer. There was no reply. "Where in the hell could he have gotten himself off to? I trusted the bastard."

"I'm going in the house," Cassie said. "Maybe Irene can tell us what happened to Reb."

Cody nodded. "I'll go out to the bunkhouse and see if he got tired of patrolling and went to bed."

Cassie rushed into the house. The parlor was empty, so was the kitchen. Grabbing the lamp from the small table in the parlor, she vaulted up the stairs, her heart pounding furiously. Something was desperately wrong. She felt it with every ragged breath she drew. The door to the children's room was ajar and she stepped inside, holding the lamp high. The beds were empty. A scream rose in her throat. It burst forth in a bloodcurdling screech when she saw Irene lying unconscious on the floor.

Moments later she heard footsteps pounding up the stairs. Cody burst into the room, wild-eyed, prepared to do battle with whatever enemy threatened Cassie.

"What happened to her?"

"The children . . ." Further explanation was unnecessary as Cody's gaze flew to the children's beds, noting that they were empty.

"Sonuvabitch! I'll nail Reb's hide to the wall when I catch him!" When he heard Irene moan, he crouched down beside her. "Irene, what happened? Where are the kids?"

Irene opened her eyes. They were glazed with pain. "My head. Someone hit me."

"Did you see who hit you?" Cody asked more harshly than he intended. "How many men were there?"

With Cassie's assistance, Irene struggled into an upright position. "No, I saw no one. I heard a noise and came to the children's room to investigate. Someone grabbed me from behind when I entered the room and then—I don't know."

"Dammit!" Cody cursed, rising to his feet. "I promised I'd protect the kids, but while they were being kidnapped I was fooling around in the woods like some damn randy animal after a female in heat."

A slow flush crept up Cassie's neck. Cody wasn't the only one ashamed of the way he had acted. She had been just as bad, lolling on the ground, panting and begging him to make love to her. "Why would they need protecting? What aren't you telling me, Cody? The reason I followed you tonight was to make you tell me what was going on. I don't appreciate being kept in the dark. I love the children, too."

"You're right, Cassie," he replied. "You should know what's going on. Take Irene to her room and see that she's comfortable. Come to my room afterward and I'll tell you everything while I pack my gear. I'm going after the kids."

"Alone?"

"It's the only way. I can track a man when there is no trail to follow. I'm an experienced Army scout."

"I'm going with you."

"No, you're not." His eyes glittered hard and flat like hammered steel. "Take Irene to her room. We'll talk later." Abruptly he turned and left the room.

"Mule-headed dolt," Cassie muttered as she helped Irene to her feet. Cody was neither her father nor her husband. He couldn't tell her what to do.

Cody had changed his clothes and was busy packing his saddlebag when Cassie entered his room a short time later. He was dressed in buckskins that hugged the bulging muscles of his torso and thighs like a second skin. When he bent to strap on his spurs, Cassie felt a suffocating heat suffuse her body and quickly looked away.

"I don't have much time, Cassie," Cody said, ignorant of the effect he was having on her.

With considerable effort she willed her eyes upward over the taut firmness of his body to his face. "Tell me about the children. Who is trying to harm them, and why?"

"First, it's important that you believe me when I tell you that those kids don't belong to me. I wasn't lying when I said I never sired any kids. They sort of latched on to me in St. Louis when I came to their aid. I was as surprised as you when they showed up on the train claiming to belong to me."

"That was obvious to everyone," Cassie retorted.

"I couldn't just abandon them in the middle of nowhere, could I? So I went along with their little game rather than raise a ruckus. When we arrived in Dodge there was no place to dump them so I brought them to the ranch. That's the God's truth. They adopted me."

"They call you Papa," Cassie persisted. Cody's story seemed too farfetched to be believed. "Who are they if they aren't your children?"

"That's another long story. I think they miss their own father so much that calling me Papa satisfies a need in them." Then he repeated what the children had told him about Julian Masters, leaving out nothing. "I didn't learn the truth about them until a few days ago."

Cassie was stunned. "How could anyone want to do away with two innocent children? What kind of man is Julian Masters?"

"According to the kids, he's no blood relative. He's greedy and wants their inheritance for himself."

"We should inform the law. The man should be punished for his misdeeds."

"I thought about it, but I'm inclined to agree with the kids. There's no hard evidence that Masters tried to kill them. The law will believe what Masters tells them. He'll say that the kids ran away because they resisted discipline. And once they're back with him, he'll find another way to do away with them."

"Do you think Masters's henchmen took the children?" Cassie asked fearfully.

"At first I thought Wayne was behind it, but the kids set me straight. I don't doubt Wayne wants us all dead, but the kids identified the men who tried to drown them as Masters's hirelings who trailed them from St. Louis. I can only assume that the same two men kidnapped them."

"We've got to find them," Cassie cried with growing panic.

"I intend to do just that. Alone."

"Please, Cody, take me with you!"

He sent her a blistering look. "I couldn't concentrate with you around and I need my wits about me. Stay home and take care of the ranch for both of us. Don't worry, I'll find the kids and bring them back where they belong."

Cassie couldn't help but wonder if Cody realized what he had just said. It sounded as if he had accepted responsibility for the children and meant to keep them. Though he might not think of himself as a father, he sure was acting like one. But if he thought she was going to remain behind while he went after the children, he was mistaken.

"When are you leaving?"

"At first light. I should be able to track them without too much difficulty. Both men are probably greenhorns who have never been west of St. Louis. They aren't smart enough to cover their tracks."

They stood facing one another, the air between them fraught with tension. With sudden insight Cody realized that if he ever had children, he'd like Cassie to be their mother. He started to turn away from the penetrating intensity of her green eyes when he was seized with an incredible need to kiss her. Hooking an arm around her waist, he pulled her hard against him. Then he spanned her jaw with his long fingers, holding her in place as he lowered his head to capture her mouth. Surprised, Cassie parted her mouth, and he sent his tongue deep.

The kiss would have gone on forever if Cody hadn't realized where this would lead and released her with an abruptness that sent her stumbling against the door. "Get out of here, Cassie. I don't need the distraction right now." Then he shoved her out the door before she had time to catch her breath. She stared hard at the closed door for a long time before turning and stomping away, muttering to herself about stubborn men who thought they could handle any situation without help. She had no intention of remaining behind while Cody tracked the children's kidnappers.

The first blush of dawn was a band of pale mauve across the eastern sky when Cody left the house. The wide brim of his hat hid the determination in his eyes. A saddlebag stuffed with gear and trail food hung over his shoulder and a bedroll was tucked under one arm. Cassie watched from the kitchen window as he walked toward the barn. Her own saddlebag was packed and ready to be flung over Lady's back at a moment's notice. The rifle she had carried with her last night was loaded with bullets, and extra ammunition was stowed away in her saddlebag. She had already spoken to Irene and waited now for Cody to leave so she could follow at a safe distance.

The first thing Cody saw when he entered the barn was Reb, passed out on a mound of hay and snoring loudly. An empty whiskey bottle was clutched to his chest and he reeked of the sour stench of overindulgence. Throwing down his gear, Cody reached him in two long strides. His lips were clamped together tightly, his eyes ruthless and cold as ice. Never had he been so angry at another human being. His hands were brutal as he grasped Reb by the collar and yanked him upright.

"Wake up, you worthless sonuvabitch! Where were you last night?"

"Huh?" Still groggy from a night of steady drinking after a long dry spell, Reb blinked at Cody in utter confusion. His eyes were red-rimmed and blurry, his mouth slack. He had only intended to have one little drink, but one led to another and before he knew it someone had handed him a bottle and he had finished it off. If the horse hadn't known the way home, he'd never have made it.

"I want answers and I want them now. Where were you last night when you were supposed to be guarding the house?"

"I—I need a drink, Cody."

"You had a drink. Lots of them, from the looks of you. Because of you the kids are gone. Thanks to your insatiable need for liquor, someone broke into the house last night and took the kids."

"The kids are gone?"

Cody snorted in disgust. He was wasting valuable time arguing when he could be tracking the man or men who had taken the kids. After giving Reb one last vicious shake, he flung him away in utter contempt. Reb rolled head over heels across the floor, coming to a stop against one of the stalls. He watched with racing heart as Cody saddled the large black called Satan's Folly.

"I'll help you find them, Cody, honest," Reb said, finally finding his tongue. "I'm right fond of those kids. Give me another chance."

"You've had all the chances you're going to get. I expect to find you gone when I return. I've done my best for you, but you're too far gone to be saved. It's enough being saddled with two orphans and a mongrel dog without adding a one-armed drunk to my list of responsibilities."

Cody's brutal words didn't convey the way he really felt about the children, but they matched his mood. If anything happened to those kids, he'd find Reb and thrash him to within an inch of his life.

Reb dragged himself up off the floor. He felt responsible for what had happened and couldn't fault Cody for blaming him. He wished he could be the kind of man Cody wanted, but he reckoned he just didn't have it in him. "I'll find them, Cody, I swear I will."

Mounted on Satan's broad back, Cody spared Reb a scathing glance. "I don't need your kind of help, Reb. Just stay the hell away from me."

"What about Irene?" Reb knew that Irene had been in the house with the children last night and he was seized with the sudden fear that something had happened to her. "Is she all right?"

"She has a lump on her head the size of Pike's Peak. She could have been killed."

"I'm sorry," Reb said with head hung low.

Reb's apology seemed to have little effect on Cody as he quickly mounted and rode away. The moment he rode from the yard Cassie hurried to the barn. She was surprised to see Reb staggering out the door. He appeared not to have seen her as he limped slowly toward the bunkhouse. She dismissed him from her mind as she saddled Lady and rode after Cody, keeping far enough behind so as not to be seen.

Fifteen minutes later Reb reentered the barn. He had changed clothes, packed his gear, and saddled the horse he had ridden to Dodge the night before. Within minutes he was trailing both Cody and Cassie, determined to redeem himself in Cody's eyes. Since he'd returned from the war maimed and useless, Cody had been the only person who cared enough about him to try to help him regain his self-respect. And then he had to go and earn Cody's contempt by getting stinking drunk.

Demon whiskey. The devil's brew. Before Reb had cleared the yard he made a solemn vow he intended to keep. He promised never to touch another drop of alcohol.

Chapter Fourteen

Amy was frightened. More frightened than she had ever been in her life. For Brady's sake she tried to remain calm, tried to keep the terror from her eyes, but the farther away from the ranch they traveled, the more difficult it became to pretend. Amy knew a despair so profound it was a struggle to hold back the tears gathering in her eyes. She feared Cody wouldn't be able to save them this time. She wasn't even certain Cody cared enough about them to find them and bring them back. He'd made no bones about wanting to be rid of them when they had followed him to Dodge. The only reason he hadn't was because he had a good heart. He wasn't even aware of the really good person he was, Amy thought.

They traveled all night without respite. Conrad held Amy before him on his horse, his thick arms so tight that Amy could hardly breathe. Brady fared no better, held captive in Dooley's cruel embrace. They slept intermittently, confused, exhausted, and frightened. As they traveled east, subtle changes took place in the landscape. Flat plains and sandy prairie gave way to rolling hills. The typical browns and tans of western Kansas were interspersed with the green of tall cottonwood trees growing in abundance along the Arkansas River and its tributaries. The sun was high overhead when Conrad reined his horse into a thick stand of cottonwoods growing along the bank of a narrow stream.

Amy, who had been dozing in the saddle, was jolted awake when Conrad hauled her roughly from the saddle and dropped her to the ground. Her eyes sought Brady, who had suffered the same heedless handling by Dooley. He sat on the ground, dazed, staring at Amy in mute appeal. He reached out to her, and throwing caution to the wind, Amy crawled to him on hands and knees. Neither Conrad nor Dooley stopped her. The children sat huddled together, holding hands, their frightened little faces turned toward their captors with looks that would have melted the hardest heart. But where money was concerned, Dooley and Conrad had no hearts.

After stretching his legs, Conrad turned his attention to the children, his expression dark and threatening, his eyes narrowed. He knew that getting the brats to Masters wasn't going to be easy, not with Cody Carter breathing down their necks. But once the children were in the custody of their uncle, Conrad was positive that Cody could do nothing to remove them from their legal guardian. Despite Masters's ultimate intention to do away with the children, Conrad knew that the law wouldn't prosecute him and Dooley for snatching the kids from their beds, for it had been done with the approval of their guardian.

Brady could feel Amy's hand shaking, and for his sister's sake he assumed a facade of false bravado. He gave her hand a reassuring squeeze, looked at Conrad squarely, and asked, "What are you going to do with us? If you hurt my sister, you'll be sorry."

Conrad laughed nastily. "We ain't gonna hurt you or your sister, kid. Your Uncle Julian misses you. We're taking you back to him."

Encouraged by her brother's gumption, Amy said, "We don't want to go back. Uncle Julian doesn't like us. We'd rather stay with our papa."

Dooley snickered behind his hand. "Don't that beat all. I think these brats really believe the half-breed is their father."

"Don't call him that!" Brady shouted, his little face red with anger. "You'll be sorry when Papa finds us. Do you know what Indians do to their captives?" Brady wasn't certain what Indians did to their captives, but Conrad must have known, for his face drained of all color.

Adding fuel to the fire, Amy said, "Papa's mean, real mean, when someone does something he doesn't like."

"Shut up!" Conrad thundered, taking a menacing step toward the children. "Let's get something straight right now. Your lives are in my hands, so you'd better not get me mad. If either of you tries to escape or makes trouble, I'll shoot one or both of you. Makes no never mind to me. Do you understand?" He leaned over the children, hands on hips, his teeth pulled back over his lips in a vicious snarl.

Cowering beneath his menacing glare, the children took his threats to heart. Conrad and Dooley had tried to kill them once, and they knew that neither man would hesitate to do so again. For some reason Uncle Julian wanted them alive, for the time being anyway, and they intended to stay that way. But that didn't mean they couldn't devise ways to hinder the two desperados until Cody arrived to save them. If Cody arrived . . . Their little heads wagged up and down in answer to Conrad's question.

"Good, I'm glad we understand one another. You're free to go behind those bushes and do whatever you have to do. When we ride again we won't stop till dark."

Suddenly Brady's stomach growled loudly. "I'm hungry."

"Don't worry, I don't aim to starve you. There's food in our saddlebags. When you return we'll all have a bite to eat."

"A short nap wouldn't hurt," Dooley grumbled as he slumped against a tree. "We've been ridin' all night."

Amy and Brady sidled off behind the bushes Conrad indicated. "Ouch!" Amy exclaimed as she sat down on the ground to nurse her injured foot. They were still barefoot and dressed in night-clothes, having been provided with nothing more appropriate by their captors.

"What's the matter, Amy?" Brady asked solicitously.

"Sandburs. Be careful, the ground is covered with them."

Cautiously Brady peered around the bush. "They ain't watching us. Should we try to escape?"

Amy shook her head. "We couldn't run far without shoes. And when they catch us they might hurt us." Brady's face fell. "We should wait until Papa comes for us," Amy whispered.

"Do you think he will, now that he knows the truth about us?"

"He'll come," Amy said with such firm conviction that Brady felt a surge of hope for the first time since they had been abducted from their beds.

"Hey, are you kids coming out or do we have to come in there after you?" They could tell by Conrad's voice that he was short on patience.

"We're coming, Mr. Conrad," Amy answered. As they were walking from the concealment of the bushes, Amy's gaze fell to the sandburs littering the ground and she was seized with sudden inspiration. Tearing off a section of cloth from the bottom of her nightgown, she told Brady, "Help me gather some burs. Put them in this piece of cloth so they don't hurt our hands."

"What for?"

"Don't argue, Brady, just do as I say. I'll tell you later." When they had gathered a handful of burs, Amy slipped the hastily devised cloth bag into the pocket of her nightgown.

"'Bout time," Conrad grumbled when the kids finally emerged from behind the bushes. He handed them each a piece of jerky and hardtack. "If you want something to drink, there's plenty of water in the stream."

Parched after their long ride, they drank copiously, but the jerky barely satisfied their hunger. After washing their faces and hands in the stream they returned to where Conrad and Dooley were sprawled on the ground.

"Dooley and me need some shut-eye," Conrad growled as he took off his boots and wiggled his toes. "But don't get any bright ideas about running away. Dooley's gonna tie your ankles and wrists so you won't go roaming while we sleep."

Realizing it would do little good to protest, the children submitted meekly to being tied hand and foot. Though they weren't bound tightly, their hands were drawn behind their backs, which proved awkward and uncomfortable. Within minutes both Conrad and Dooley were snoring loudly, their backs propped against a tree and their boots resting beside them.

"Brady," Amy hissed, "scoot over here and try to reach those burs in the pocket of my nightdress." Brady made two tries before he succeeded in withdrawing the small cloth pouch containing the burs from her pocket.

Fumbling clumsily, Amy managed to pick up several burs in her fingers. Then she scooted on her rear over to the men's boots. Struggling to her knees, she turned her back and carefully dropped several burs into both Dooley and Conrad's right boot. Then she shuffled back to Brady so he could replace the burs in her pocket. Once that was done, they lay down on the hard-packed earth and waited.

"There's going to be hell to pay," Brady whispered.

"Don't cuss, Brady."

"Papa cusses so it can't be too bad."

Amy thought about that for a moment, then said, "When you get to be a papa you can cuss all you want. Now go to sleep."

Two hours later Conrad nudged the children awake with the toe of his stocking-clad foot. They were untied and allowed to stretch while Conrad pulled on his boots. They watched in trepidation as Conrad pushed his foot into his right boot. His foot seemed to be stuck halfway down, so he grasped the top with both hands, raised his foot several inches, and stomped down hard.

"Ye-e-e-e-ow!"

Dooley, in the process of pulling on his own

boot, leaped up when he heard Conrad yell, putting his weight on his right foot. His eyes widened and he spit out an oath that rivaled Conrad's.

"Sonuvabitch!"

Both men sat down on their rumps, pulling off their boots with unaccustomed haste. From where the children stood they saw the drops of blood staining the men's stockings and shared a private moment of satisfaction. Cradling his injured foot in his hand, Conrad carefully plucked two wicked-looking burs from his sole and flung them to the ground. Dooley did the same.

"Where in the hell did those come from?" Conrad demanded, glaring at the children in his most threatening manner.

Dooley squinted upward into the branches of the cottonwood tree directly overhead. "I never knew cottonwood trees had burs."

"They don't, stupid." Conrad's gaze was still on the children, who stared back at him in wide-eyed innocence. "I don't suppose you two know anything about this?"

"We were sleeping," Amy offered. "Maybe the wind blew them there."

Conrad looked dubious but didn't press the issue. The brats *had* been sleeping, and tied up besides.

Amy and Brady exchanged relieved looks. The way Dooley and Conrad were limping was enough to keep their spirits buoyed the rest of the day. They stopped that night beside a stream, ate a cold supper of tinned beans and hardtack, then bedded down for the night. Once again the children were bound hand and foot. And once again they tempted fate by hiding the last of the burs beneath the blankets upon which the saddles would be placed.

The following morning Conrad was the first to mount. But before he could reach down to lift Amy into the saddle, the horse bucked wildly, reared up on his hind legs, and pawed the air. Caught off guard, Conrad flew from the saddle, landing on the ground with a thud. Laughing hysterically, Dooley grabbed the reins of Conrad's horse, bringing him under control while Conrad struggled to his feet.

"Shut up, Dooley, before I forget we're friends," Conrad growled, dusting off his pants. "What in the hell got into that ornery animal? He never acted like that before." He turned to glare at the children, his eyes narrowed suspiciously. "You don't suppose the wind blew one of them burs under my saddle, do you?"

Dooley took the hint. Lifting off the saddle, he inspected the saddle blanket and found the burs. "Well, I'll be damned."

"My sentiments exactly. Which one of you brats did this?" Conrad asked, rounding on the children. When neither of them answered, he lifted Brady by the collar of his nightshirt and gave him a vicious shake. "You sneaky little bastard, it was you, wasn't it?" His right hand flew back, intending to deliver a blow that might very well prove lethal.

"Don't hurt him. I did it!" Amy rushed to Brady, shielding him as best she could as she watched Conrad's arm descend in frozen horror. His fist struck her face with such tremendous force that her head snapped backward and she flew across the hard ground, landing in a heap at Dooley's feet, where she lay white and motionless.

Uttering a cry of dismay, Brady dropped to his knees beside his sister. "You've killed her!" he wailed. "You killed Amy!"

"She ain't dead," Conrad spat disgustedly. "But she will be if you brats pull another trick like that." He spun away from Brady and remounted his horse. "Hand the brat up to me, Dooley," he said, nodding toward Amy. "She'll come around, and when she does she'll realize that messing around with us is dangerous."

Dooley obeyed with alacrity, then mounted his own horse. But before he could lift Brady in front of him, he suffered the same fate as Conrad. His rump had scarcely touched the saddle when his horse reared and sent him sailing into the air. Brady cowered against a tree while Dooley, cursing violently, picked himself off the ground and removed the burs from beneath his saddle. Then he cuffed Brady's ears so soundly the lad burst into tears. He could be brave only so long. For Amy's sake he had tried not to break down, but this latest abuse had been too much for him to bear. Looking at Amy now, her face swollen an angry purple, her eye already turning black, he was pitched into the darkest pit of despair.

* * *

Cody had no difficulty trailing the kidnappers. He was close now, so close he could almost smell the foul bastards. Though he had fought it, pure exhaustion forced him to rest the second night. But early the following morning he was back on the trail, realizing by now that his prey were headed toward Wichita, probably to board a train there for St. Louis. It wasn't until the afternoon of the second day that he became aware that someone was trailing him. The first day he had concentrated so hard on tracking the kidnappers that he had become careless. He was too experienced to make mistakes, he chided himself, yet he had allowed someone to tail him a whole day without knowing it.

Aware now of the imminent danger to himself, Cody speculated on the identity of the man or men following him. Could it be Wayne or his henchmen? Catching him in the open country far from home offered the perfect opportunity for Wayne to attack him. Cody was alone and vulnerable, but not unaware of the situation and far from helpless. Pulling his hat down over his eyes and hunching over Satan's back, Cody kept his eyes to the ground and his hand close to his gun. He'd worry about an attack if and when it came and not before. If no one materialized by tonight, he'd prepare a little surprise of his own.

Cassie knew she was close to Cody. Once or twice she had caught sight of him in the distance and deliberately slowed her pace to keep from being seen. It was a miracle he hadn't already discovered her trailing him, for she knew he was keenly aware of everything that went on around him. She attributed his laxity to his worry over the children and was glad for it.

The long summer day didn't give way to darkness until nearly nine o'clock, and Cassie was exhausted when she finally stopped beside a stream to bed down. She knew Cody wouldn't stop until he had taken advantage of every available minute of daylight, and she had forced herself to continue despite her exhaustion. Kneeling at the edge of the stream, she bent to drink deeply of the cool, clear water. The day had been hot and dry; her throat was parched.

The attack came without warning. Her assailant leaped at her from out of the darkness, driving her into the water with the weight of his big body. The breath was forced from her lungs as she was shoved beneath the water and held there. Never had Cassie struggled so desperately for her life. She raged against the unfairness of being deprived of life just when she had found a man she could love. She was dying . . . dying without knowing if Cody could ever love her.

Cody smiled grimly, feeling the fragile bones of the shoulders he was grasping and aware that in another minute or two a life would be snuffed out. Close on the heels of that thought came the sudden realization that the shoulders beneath his hands were too small and soft to belong to a man.

That startling thought brought a return to sanity, and immediately Cody's grip eased as he hauled Cassie out of the water, sputtering and gasping for breath. He paled visibly when he looked into Cassie's terrified face and realized how close she had come to death.

"She-it!" His hands shook, his chest hurt from the effort to breathe. "You stupid little fool! With very little effort I could have killed you! What in God's name are you doing here? Have you been following me?"

Cassie's lungs heaved convulsively. She couldn't speak, could only stare at Cody through eyes narrowed in fury. Her lips moved convulsively but words refused to form. When she began shivering uncontrollably, Cody uttered another curse and lifted her into his arms.

"Where—where are you taking me?" Cassie gasped, searching for her voice and finding it.

"To my camp. I'll come back for your horse later. It's not far."

His arms felt so comforting that Cassie wanted to melt into him, to give herself into his keeping forever. But she also felt anger: incredible, fierce, unrelenting anger.

"You—you bastard! You nearly drowned me."

"How in the hell did I know you were following me? I gave you specific orders to remain at the ranch. And quit using raw language; you know how the children hate it."

Was he smiling? It was too dark to tell, but Cassie had a sneaking suspicion that Cody was deliberately trying to make light of how close she had come to meeting death at his hands. "Damn it, Cody, don't change the subject." Her teeth were chattering so loudly that Cody pressed her closer, offering his own body heat to dispel the chill from her flesh.

Soon they came to Cody's camp, nestled behind some bushes growing close to the stream. He set her on her feet, took his blanket from his bedroll, and handed it to her. "Take off those wet clothes while I go get your horse. There's another blanket in my bedroll if you need it." When Cassie made no move to obey, Cody sighed, lifted unsteady hands, and unbuttoned her blouse. "Let me help you."

With a curious air of detachment, Cassie watched Cody unbutton her blouse and pull it down her arms. Then he released the hooks on her split skirt and slid it down her hips. She stepped out of it, standing before him in her thin shift, shivering not just from cold but from a melting, liquid flame igniting deep inside the core of her. At the moment she couldn't have described what she felt. It was a mixture of icy chill and sizzling heat.

Cody inhaled sharply, his eyes riveted on the coral tips of her nipples clearly visible beneath the wet shift. They seemed to have a life of their own as they rose taut and erect beneath his bemused gaze. Staring into the green depths of her eyes, he reached out and caressed one puckered bud with the pad of his finger. "Take off the wet shift, Cassie, before you catch your death." Then turning abruptly, he strode off through the cottonwood trees.

With shaking hands Cassie removed her shift and wrapped the blanket around her. It felt warm against her sensitive skin, almost like a lover's caress, she reflected dreamily as she hugged the blanket tightly about her. She thought of Cody then—of being alone with him tonight, of the way he had looked at her before he went after her horse, and of the delicious sensation when he had touched her nipple.

She sat down on a fallen log, running her fingers through her sodden hair and speculating on whether Cody was still angry with her for following him. No matter how much he ranted and raved, she was determined to remain until the children were found and returned unharmed to the ranch. She tried not to think about failure, or what would happen if they were taken back into the keeping of their cruel uncle. Distressing thoughts continued to gnaw at her until Cody returned with her horse. To Cassie's chagrin he ignored her all the while he tethered Lady next to Satan and removed her saddle. When he finally turned the intensity of his blue gaze on her, her trembling intensified.

"Are you still cold?" Cody asked. In two strides he was beside her on the fallen log.

"A l-l-little," Cassie stammered.

"Maybe I can help," he drawled lazily as he picked her up and placed her on his lap. Then his arms went around her and the heat of his body overwhelmed her. She sighed and settled her bottom more snugly into his loins. "Damn it, Cassie, how do you expect me to stay angry with you if you keep squirming around on my lap like that?"

"You have no reason to be angry," Cassie replied absently. Her flesh was tingling pleasantly now, the chill she had experienced earlier but a dim memory. "I followed because I want to help find the children."

"You followed because you're too damn stubborn for your own good and too independent to follow orders."

"You're not going to send me back, are you? Because if you do I'll not go. If I can't stay with you, I'll follow behind like I've been doing."

"I should send you back but I won't. It's more dangerous for you alone on the prairie than staying with me." He leaned toward her, his compelling blue eyes glowing with strange inner lights. "I can protect you against wild animals and human predators but I can't protect you against myself," he added in a lower, huskier tone. "That's what I was trying to avoid, Cassie. I told you before, I can't concentrate with you around."

Cassie let out a long, audible breath. "You won't be sorry, Cody, you'll see. I won't distract you in the least little bit."

Cody sent her a startled glance, then tossed back his head and laughed. Not loud enough to carry, but a low rumble that came from deep inside his chest. Not distract him? What in the hell did she think she was doing now with her delicious little bottom planted in his lap with nothing between them but his trousers and a thin blanket? And if that wasn't enough, her squirming around was making him hard as hell. Adding insult to injury, she was looking at him as if she could devour him. Her huge eyes and parted lips were too much for Cody to resist.

Less than a heartbeat later he groaned in surrender and covered her lips hungrily with his. His kiss was urgent yet surprisingly gentle as his tongue pushed past the barrier of her teeth to explore at leisure the sweet recesses of her mouth. Cassie sighed and gave herself freely to the passion of his kiss. What good would it do to protest when he'd have his way in the end? Denying that she wanted Cody was like denying the inescapable fact that she had fallen in love with him. The truth of her startling discovery struck her like a bolt of lightning. Lord, what a predicament—loving a man who didn't love her in return.

But now, with Cody's kisses turning her brains to mush and his hands caressing her bare flesh, it was difficult to explore fully Cody's lack of feelings for her. Now was the time to enjoy. Recriminations would come later.

Slowly Cody peeled the blanket from Cassie's body, his senses reeling out of control as he bared her to his greedy eyes. She was everything a man could want—and more. His lips fell to her neck, pressing warm kisses to the hollow of her throat, her shoulders, the rounded tops of her breasts. Moonlight gilded her skin, giving it an iridescent glow. Cody had the irresistible urge to taste every inch of it. He began at her breasts, sucking and licking the succulent tips until Cassie was moaning with pleasure. But Cody had just begun.

Resting his hand on her stomach, he stretched his fingers, spreading them through the golden fleece between her legs. His index finger flexed, grazing the small bud of feminine desire nestled at the apex of her legs. Cassie tensed, waiting, wanting . . .

"Do you like that, baby?" Cody asked. He touched her again, this time turning it into a brief caress.

Cassie inhaled sharply. "Oh, yes." She tried to move his hand down lower but it refused to budge. "Cody, please."

He took pity on her then, watching her face as he caressed the sensitive nub of flesh with the rough pad of his finger. She shuddered as he nudged her legs apart to give him better access. His finger slid lower, into the warm moist crevice between her legs. "You're wet for me, baby." His strangled voice gave hint to his great need for this particular woman. He thrust a finger inside her, hard, pulled it out and thrust again, harder, deeper. Cassie jerked convulsively, nearly senseless from pleasure as she began climaxing almost immediately.

"Cody!" How could this be happening so fast?

Cody felt tiny rippling tremors pulse against his finger, stunned that he had brought her so quickly to climax. Beads of sweat popped out on his forehead as he fought to control his body's reaction to Cassie's undisguised passion. Having Cassie call out his name at that critical moment brought him a great deal of satisfaction. But he wanted to do more for her, much more. Lifting her in his arms, he laid her on the ground atop the discarded blanket. In a haze of languid contentment she watched as he shed his clothing, her eyes roaming his nude body with slow relish. Then he was bending over her, spreading her legs and kneeling between them. Since she had already had her pleasure, she expected him to take his. But she didn't know Cody very well if she thought that.

Grinning wolfishly, he lifted her legs and placed them over his shoulders. Then slowly, deliberately, he lowered his head to the vee between her legs.

"Cody, what are you doing? I can't, not again."

Cody spared her a wicked grin. "You can and you will. Trust me, baby." Then his mouth was on her and his tongue pierced her.

She trusted him. Completely. He didn't disappoint her. Employing his tongue, his teeth, his lips, and his fingers with incredible dexterity, he sent her on the most incredible journey of her life. Her world was still spinning when he thrust into her, seeking his own pleasure, at the same time reviving those incredible bursts of rapture inside her. Cassie cried out in sweet agony as waves of pleasure thudded through her. Her cry seemed to release something in Cody as his hips pounded against her in frenzied purpose and his breath hissed harshly through his teeth. He cried out her name as the world spun and careened on its axis.

Chapter Fifteen

Dawn was just a breath away when Cassie stirred and opened her eyes. She was lying on her side with Cody's body curved around her and his arm thrown over her. She felt warm and protected, as if sleeping next to Cody was the most natural thing in the world. Turning her head, she saw that Cody was still sleeping. They were both naked. Somehow they had never found it necessary or desirable to don their clothes. They had made love again during the wee hours of the morning and afterward had fallen asleep in each other's arms.

Cassie smiled dreamily. If Cody didn't truly care for her he was an expert actor. She stretched her legs and wrinkled her nose when she felt the stickiness of his seed between her thighs. She thought of the stream just steps away and of how wonderful it would be to bathe in the cool water. If she moved quietly she might not disturb Cody. She could be finished before he awoke. Her movements were slow and careful as she eased from beneath his arm, and she was gratified when he hardly stirred. He looked exhausted, she thought as her eyes roamed lovingly over his dark features. He resembled a nude god she had seen in a book once, his limbs straight and strong, his flesh dark and flawless. Even in repose his manhood lay large and thick against his leg. She trembled with renewed desire when she recalled how magnificent that masculine part of him had felt inside her, how splendidly he had filled her and how sublimely he brought her to climax. Love for this man overwhelmed her. But unless Cody felt the same about her, there was no future for them. The thought of being used merely for gratification the way men used Sal's girls repelled her. She would leave the ranch before becoming Cody's mistress.

A cool breeze kissing her bare flesh reminded Cassie that she was still naked and still in need of a bath. Bending forward, she covered Cody with a corner of the blanket, careful not to awaken him. Sighing, she turned away, retrieved a bar of soap from her saddlebag, picked up the spare blanket from her unused bedroll, and walked through the misty dawn to the stream. She washed and rinsed quickly in the waist-deep water, and by the time she finished, the sun was a big red ball in the eastern sky, heralding the beginning of a new day.

Wrapping herself in the blanket, Cassie walked back to where Cody had made his camp. He was still sleeping, which was unusual for Cody, but she knew he had set a hectic pace for himself these past few days and didn't awaken him. She dressed quickly, then rummaged in their saddlebags looking for something to fix for breakfast. A noise drew her attention back to Cody, thinking he had awakened. He was still lying on his side, his back to the bushes and his chest rising and falling in regular cadence, obviously still asleep. Cassie started to turn away when she saw something that brought the breath hissing through her teeth.

While Cody slept peacefully and unsuspecting, a rattler had crawled from the bushes and lay coiled against his back, seeking his warmth. But Cody must have shifted in his sleep and disturbed the serpent, for its head was raised, its rattles waving in the air. With a sinking feeling in the pit of her stomach, Cassie realized that the snake might have been curled against Cody while she slept at his side. The thought sent a shudder slithering down her spine. Until she recalled that the rattler hadn't been there when she covered Cody with the blanket.

Don't move, Cody, she silently implored. Her steps were slow and measured as she backed toward Cody's discarded gunbelt, which was lying above his head. Her eyes were fixed on the snake as she cautiously bent toward the gunbelt. *Please don't let me miss,* she prayed as she freed Cody's Colt .44 from its holster and aimed it at her target with both hands. *And please don't let me shoot Cody,* she added in silent supplication. The snake was so close to Cody; she didn't know if she was a good enough shot to hit so small a target. She was trembling all over and her palms were slick with sweat.

Slowly, deliberately, she pulled back the hammer. The resulting click sounded like thunder in her ears, though in truth it was barely audible. Using both hands to steady the weapon, she took careful aim.

Cody woke with a start. The sound of a gun being cocked was all too familiar to mistake it for anything else. Trained by years of living on the edge of danger, he awoke instantly from his sound sleep. Seeing Cassie pointing his own gun at him was something out of his worst nightmare.

Cassie nearly lost her nerve when she saw Cody watching her. His fierce expression, filled with astonishment and shock, nearly unraveled her, until she saw the snake poised to strike. *Let him believe what he wants,* she thought distractedly. *I'd rather see him angry at me than dying of snakebite.* She saw his lips thin and his muscles bunch and realized he was preparing to leap at her.

"Don't move, Cody," she said quietly.

The desperate tone of her voice gave Cody pause. He glared at her in mute hostility, his only movement a tensing of his jaw. What kind of woman was she? Cold-blooded and heartless.

Cassie took slow, careful aim at the snake, its head drawn back in a menacing manner. Her lips moved in silent prayer as she tried to recall everything Reb had taught her about shooting a weapon. Her finger squeezed the trigger.

"Cassie, no!" Cody cried as the gun in Cassie's hand spit fire. At such close range he figured he was dead.

His expression turned to one of surprise and disbelief when he saw Cassie lower the gun and realized he was still alive. He had felt the heat of the bullet yet could see no blood on his body, nor did he feel any pain. His gaze flew to Cassie. Her arms were lowered, the gun dangling from one hand. She was staring at him blankly, her mouth slack, her eyes glazed. "What the hell!" Before she had a chance to gain her wits and try to shoot him again, Cody's long muscles uncoiled and he leaped at her, knocking her flat.

Pinned to the ground by the weight of Cody's massive bulk, Cassie struggled for breath, certain she would suffocate before he would let her explain. If she didn't suffocate straight away, he was certainly angry enough to kill her. His face was mottled an ugly red; blazing fury burned in his eyes.

"Damn you, Cassie! I should have known better than to trust you. How did you miss me? At that range you could have blown my head off. Did you have second thoughts at the last minute?"

Shaking her head in vigorous denial, Cassie struggled for breath. The strangling sounds coming from her throat must have alerted Cody to her distress, for he finally eased his weight from her, but not much. Cassie drew in long draughts of air, easing the pain in her chest.

"Get off me, Cody. I can't breathe."

He rolled off her, bringing her with him until she rested atop him. His strong arms held her in place. "What did you think to gain by killing me?"

"Stupid idiot," she hissed, glaring down at him. "I was saving your life, not trying to kill you."

"Excuse me if I misunderstood your intent," he snapped sarcastically. "Usually when someone points a gun at another person it has nothing to do with saving his life."

"It does if that person is in danger of being snakebit."

"What!"

"Look and see for yourself," Cassie taunted. "I swear, Cody, you're the most exasperating man I know. Did you truly think I'd shoot you after making love with you most of the night?"

Cassie hit the ground with a thump as Cody jumped to his feet. He barely heard her howl of outrage as he walked over to the bedroll where he had lain only moments before. His lips spread over his teeth in a grim smile as he grasped a corner of the blanket and gave it a vicious shake. He hadn't expected to find anything, so when the dead rattler came flying out he was too stunned to speak. He swung around and stared at Cassie.

He really *did* think she had tried to kill him, Cassie thought, disgruntled. His face was slack with amazement. He was truly shaken as he stared at Cassie in mute apology. Lifting her chin, she glared back at him, refusing to accept his unspoken apology or to forgive him for thinking her capable of murder. "I should have let the damn thing take a bite out of your thick hide," she grumbled. "He'd probably find it as tough as I do."

"Aw, she-it! I'm sorry, Cassie."

"What? Did you say something?"

Cody gave her a wry grin. Obviously she was going to make him pay for acting like a damn fool. What had just happened with the snake made him realize how stupid he had been for wrongfully accusing Cassie of trying to kill him those times he had been shot at. Obviously someone wanted him dead, but not Cassie.

"I said I'm sorry. How many times must I say it?"

"Until I believe it. I never wanted your death, Cody. I'm more than satisfied with one-quarter of the ranch. It was far more than I ever expected. If you weren't so bullheaded you wouldn't have doubted me."

"I believe you now." He looked so contrite Cassie wanted to throw herself into his arms and tell him he was forgiven, but she decided to make him suffer a little more.

"What did you say?"

He took a step toward her, his arms outstretched. "Dammit, Cassie, what do you want from me? Do you enjoy seeing me grovel?"

There was an unmistakable twinkle in her eye. "That would be a start, but first I'll settle for some breakfast. I'm famished. You can grovel later." She looked up at him, then deliberately let her gaze drift over his nude body, lingering with naughty regard on his loins. His manhood seemed to thicken and lengthen before her eyes. Her face turned a dull red and her gaze flew back to his face. "Perhaps you should get dressed first."

Cody sent her a diabolical grin and lifted one shoulder in a careless shrug. "What did you expect when you stare at me with that dreamy look in your eyes?" Then he reached for her, curling an arm around her waist and bringing her hard against him. "I'd stay naked all the time if it meant having you look at me like that. Dammit, Cassie, I've never known a woman who could affect me like you do. What in the hell am I going to do about it?"

"If you don't know I'm not going to tell you," Cassie said, lifting her lips to his. The invitation was unmistakable as Cody's mouth came down hard on hers. He kissed her so long and hard, with such unbridled hunger, that Cassie grew dizzy and would have fallen but for Cody's strong arms holding her. Suddenly she was free of his embrace and Cody was backing away from her.

"Damn, what am I doing dallying with you when I'm so close to rescuing the kids? That's one of the reasons I didn't want you with me, Cassie. This is exactly the kind of distraction I don't need."

Cassie flushed guiltily. "You're right. Get dressed while I find us something to eat." She turned away, needing more space between them if she was to concentrate on anything besides Cody's nude body and the way he made her feel when he touched her. She should be angry with him, for at no time during their long night of vigorous lovemaking did he mention the word love.

The town of Wichita lay only a few miles to the north. Conrad motioned Dooley off the road behind a small rise lush with trees and a wild tangle of bushes. He wore only one boot—his left one. His right foot was grotesquely swollen, his face contorted with pain.

"Why are we stoppin', Conrad?" Dooley asked as he slid from the saddle. Fortunately for Dooley, the burs had done little damage to the tough sole of his foot. But Conrad wasn't so lucky. His wound had festered and his foot had swollen nearly double. The pain was excruciating and not getting any better.

"We're only a few miles from Wichita," Conrad said, gritting his teeth against the throbbing pain.

Dooley scratched his balding head in consternation. "Ain't that where we're goin'?"

"Of course that's where we're going, idiot. But we sure as hell can't take the brats on the train dressed like they are. And I need to see a doc to get this foot taken care of." He sent Amy a malevolent glare before continuing. "I'll ride into town, buy some clothes for the brats, check the train schedule to find out when the next train leaves for St. Louis, and see the doc."

"What about me?"

"You sit tight and wait until I get back. Tie the brats up so they can't get into mischief and keep your eyes peeled for trouble. You know the kind of trouble I'm referring to," he hinted.

"Yeah, I know." With each passing day Dooley had grown more and more apprehensive, expecting the half-breed to burst upon them at any time. Just the thought of tangling with a man as dangerous as Cody Carter made him break out in cold sweat.

"I should be back in a few hours," Conrad said as he shoved Amy from the saddle and watched dispassionately as she dropped heavily to the ground.

The child hadn't been the same since Conrad had struck her. The entire right side of her face was discolored and swollen to twice its size. Her eye was black and purple, her lips tinged with blood, and she could barely hold her head up. Brady was terribly worried about her, but his pleas on his sister's behalf were ignored by both Conrad and Dooley.

The children watched through dull eyes as Conrad rode away. All hope of rescue had been driven from them by their captors' abuse. When Dooley brought out the ropes and bound them hand and foot, they offered little complaint. Soon they would be on the train to St. Louis and Uncle Julian. Nothing could be worse than that—unless it was the knowledge that Cody didn't care enough about them to come after them. They could accept anything but the thought that Cody had abandoned them.

"They're somewhere in those trees," Cody said as he checked his guns. His face was taut with purpose, his eyes cold. He had tracked the kidnappers to the place where they had left the road and disappeared into the wooded area of the nearby hill. He knew that Wichita lay several miles to the north and that it was probably their destination.

"What are we going to do?" Cassie whispered. Her voice was low and tense, her anxiety almost palpable.

"*You're* not going to do anything," Cody returned. His voice carried a note of finality that brooked no argument. "You're going to wait out of sight while I find the kids." He dismounted, leading his horse into the trees. Cassie followed. He walked a short distance into the woods, then tied Satan's lead reins to a branch. "Wait here. No matter what you hear, don't move from this place."

"But—you may need me!" Cassie cried as she grasped his arm.

Shrugging off her restraining hand, Cody turned on her fiercely. "For once in your life do as I say. I can handle it alone as long as I don't have to worry about you in addition to the kids. I'll be back as soon as I can. Keep your gun handy just in case."

"Cody, wait!" But it was too late; Cody had moved off so stealthily she had no idea in which direction he had gone. "Damn!" Disgruntled, she dropped to the ground beneath a tree, wishing all bullheaded men straight to hell.

It took Cody less than thirty minutes to find the kidnappers' hiding place. Concealing himself behind some thick bushes, he scanned the area, unerringly finding the children. A terrible rage seized him when he saw them lying on the ground a short distance away, trussed up and helpless.

Relief swept through him when he saw the children move. His eyes resembled shards of ice as he turned his attention to the man guarding them. He lounged beneath a tree, his eyes drooping, not really asleep but looking as if he would drop off at any moment. Cody made a thorough search of the area, looking for the second man. He knew there had to be two men, for he had tracked two horses into the woods. But try as he might, he saw no sign of another man. Cautious by nature, Cody waited five minutes, then five more, certain that if the second man had gone into the woods to relieve himself he would have returned by now.

Hovering at the edge of sleep, Dooley let his gun hang loosely from his relaxed fingers. Convinced that the man was alone, Cody angled his way behind the dozing kidnapper, stepped out into the open, and pressed the barrel of his cocked gun to Dooley's temple. Dooley's response was immediate. He tried to reestablish his grip on his gun, but it was kicked from his hand and sent scudding across the grass. Startled, his eyes found Cody, who stood over him holding a gun to his head. What Dooley saw reflected in those cold blue eyes sent his heart plummeting down to his boots. Never had he felt so close to death.

Dooley licked his lips, his mind searching for words to placate this hard man, but nothing came to mind.

"Where is your partner?" Cody's voice, though quiet, had an ominous ring.

"G-gone," Dooley stammered.

"Where?"

"To town to buy the kids some clothes."

Without taking his eyes off Dooley, Cody asked, "Are you kids all right?"

"We're fine, Papa."

The sound of Brady's voice brought a measure of calm to Cody. "Where is the other man?" he asked the boy.

"Conrad went to Wichita," Brady replied.

"Then we'd best hurry." Without a shred of remorse, Cody raised the pistol and bashed it solidly against Dooley's skull. Dooley uttered a single cry and collapsed. Cody hardly spared him a glance as he hurried to the children's side. He took one look at Amy's face and broke down. "Aw, God, no."

Cassie grew restless. It seemed as if Cody had been gone forever. Since he had melted into the woods, she'd neither seen nor heard anything except bird sounds. Now, she suddenly realized, even the birds had stopped singing. Perhaps she should follow Cody, she thought. What if he needed her? She had almost decided to ignore Cody's instructions and follow him when she heard a twig snap behind her. Pivoting on her heel, Cassie was stunned to find a man standing only inches away, his gun pointed at her heart.

"Who are you?"

"You don't know me but I know you." Conrad's leering grin told Cassie he knew far too much about her. "You're the breed's woman. I saw you two down at the creek behind your ranch one night."

Conrad had been returning from Wichita when he saw two horses tethered in the woods. He had taken care of all his errands and seen a doctor about his foot in a surprisingly short time. His foot still hurt like hell; the quack had lanced it, squeezed out the pus, and swathed it in gauze. After pressing some pills in his hand, the doctor had sent him on his way with a word of caution about the danger of blood poisoning.

Cassie realized without being told that this was one of the men who had abducted the children. What was he doing here? she wondered worriedly. What had happened to Cody? Where were the children?

"Have you hurt the children?" Since that question was uppermost in her mind, she blurted it out without thinking.

Conrad smiled nastily. "Now why would I go and do that?" He shoved the gun into her side. "Something tells me the breed's nearby. But as long as I've got you he won't do anything stupid." Cassie flinched as the gun was pressed harder into her flesh. "Move, sister, you're coming with me."

Cassie looked longingly at the rifle in her saddle holster, but she moved forward without protest, anxious to see the children and find out what had happened to Cody. Prodded by Conrad's gun, she walked for several long agonizing minutes. When she heard voices drifting through the stillness of the woods, she stopped abruptly. Conrad heard them too, for he whispered in her ear, "Shh. One word out of you and you'll never see the light of day again." Then he hooked an arm around her waist and shoved her forward.

They burst upon Cody and the children suddenly. Cody was leaning over Amy, his face contorted with grief as he rocked Amy in his arms, repeating something over and over, something Cassie couldn't hear. Seized by a terrible fear, Cassie thought Amy must be dead. Had they been too late?

"Drop your guns, breed, and turn around real slow. I got your woman. If you want her to live, you'll do as I say."

Cody went rigid. The moment he had seen Amy and the appalling abuse she had suffered, his usual caution had deserted him and he ignored years of training to comfort the child. Over and over he repeated his promise to take care of her, never to let anything like this happen again.

Rising to his feet, Cody unbuckled his gunbelt and let it drop to the ground. Then he turned slowly, until he was facing Conrad. His gaze went immediately to Cassie, assuring himself that she was unhurt. He took careful note of her position and of the gun aimed at her back before raising his eyes to Conrad's face. Cody's expression was filled with so much loathing and promised such terrible retribution that Conrad couldn't stop the shudder that traveled down his spine.

"I'm going to kill you for what you did to Amy," Cody said with quiet menace. A snarl pulled back the corners of his mouth.

Cassie could hold back no longer. "Oh, Cody, she's not, she's not—"

"She's alive," Cody gritted out from between clenched teeth.

Dooley began to moan and stir.

"Wake up, Dooley, and get the half-breed's guns," Conrad ordered harshly.

"Huh?" Dooley groaned, shaking his head to clear it of cobwebs. " 'Bout time you showed up."

"Quit yapping and move your butt," Conrad growled. "Kick the breed's guns into the bushes."

Dooley rose unsteadily and did as Conrad directed. "What ya gonna do with them?"

"Tie them up and leave them where they won't be found for a good long time," Conrad said. "No sense killing them and risking a hanging.

Once the brats are with their uncle, these two can't touch them. But first we'll have a little fun with the woman. The train to St. Louis isn't due to leave till noon tomorrow, so we'll have plenty of time to indulge ourselves."

Dooley grinned and wet his lips. "Hot damn!"

Cody's blue eyes clawed Conrad like talons. "If you so much as touch Cassie, I'll hunt you down no matter where you go, no matter how long it takes me. I already owe you for what you did to the kids." His voice was flat, devoid of all emotion, more frightening to Conrad than if Cody had shouted at the top of his lungs.

Suddenly Conrad wasn't as confident as he had been when he had gotten the drop on Cody. "Get the rope from my saddle, Dooley, and tie up the breed. If he makes too much noise, gag him."

Dooley retrieved the rope and approached Cody with caution. He didn't trust the breed, not one damn bit, and it showed.

"Go on, Dooley, he ain't gonna hurt you. If he does, I'll plug the woman."

"Do what you have to do, Cody," Cassie cried. "Don't worry about me."

"Don't you dare hurt Papa or Cassie," Brady shouted.

"Shut up, all of you! Do as I say, Dooley, so I can take the woman behind the bushes and get down to business."

Cody's muscles were coiled into knots, ready to strike. Somehow he had to get them out of this mess or die in the attempt. But Dooley, for once in his life alert, recognized Cody's intention and responded viciously. Using the butt of his pistol, he clubbed Cody across the head, sending him crashing to the ground.

Brady and Amy cried out in unison, fearing Cody had been killed. Though she knew that Cody hadn't been slain, Cassie was filled with despair so profound she was trembling uncontrollably. Without Cody to stop them, Conrad and Dooley could do whatever they wanted with her and the children.

"You used your head for once in your life," Conrad told Dooley. "Tie up the breed while I take the woman behind the bushes. I got something to give her that won't wait."

Dooley holstered his gun while he bent to his task, rolling Cody on his stomach and quickly securing his arms behind him. When he moved to bind Cody's feet, Conrad shoved Cassie roughly toward the bushes. His mouth was slack with excitement, his body already swelling in anticipation.

Suddenly Conrad stiffened, and Cassie felt the slow withdrawal of the gun that had been poking into her ribs. Conrad halted abruptly, and Cassie had the presence of mind to drop to the ground. She was stunned to see Reb standing behind Conrad, his gun poked in Conrad's back.

"Take his gun, Cassie," Reb ordered brusquely. This was a Reb that Cassie had never seen before. Relentless, calm, in complete control of the situation, his hand steady, his eyes clear.

Dooley started to reach for his weapon, but Reb's sharp eyes noted the movement and he said, "If you even move your hand in the direction of your gun, your partner is a dead man."

Conrad turned his head and eyed Reb narrowly, convinced he was faster than the one-armed man. But something in Reb's eyes must have changed Conrad's mind, for he made no protest when Cassie carefully removed the gun from his hand.

"Now go get the other man's guns, take the clips out, and throw them in the bushes." Cassie did as she was told, stepping gingerly around both Dooley and Conrad as she slipped the clips into her pocket and tossed the guns as far as she could throw them. "Untie Cody and see if he's okay."

When Cassie knelt beside Cody, she saw that his eyes were open and he was staring at Reb as if he had never seen him before.

Chapter Sixteen

"Untie me." Though still groggy from the blow he had taken on the back of his head, Cody was aware that Reb's unexpected appearance had come at a critical time.

Cassie fumbled clumsily with the knots on the ropes binding Cody's wrists behind his back and nearly screamed with frustration when they refused to give. "There's a knife in my boot," Cody instructed. "Use it."

Cassie found the knife in a sheath on the inside of Cody's boot, carefully removed it, and began to slit his bonds. It was razor sharp and freed him in a matter of seconds.

Free of the ropes, Cody struggled to his feet, still dizzy from the blow to his head. "I'll never underestimate you again, Reb. Thanks."

"Glad to oblige," Reb returned, grinning from ear to ear. It had been many years since he'd been of use to anyone.

The moment Cody was free, Cassie scrambled over to the children and quickly sawed through their bindings. Their relief was enormous as they threw themselves into Cassie's arms, nearly bowling her over. As Cassie hugged the children fiercely, she got her first good look at Amy's face—and gasped in dismay.

"Amy! Your face! What did they do to you?"

"Conrad hit me after we put burs in their boots," Amy explained, managing a weak smile despite her painful injuries.

Cassie glanced at Cody, wondering if he had heard. She could tell by the tightening of his jaw that he had.

"Where are my guns?" Cody asked.

"Behind the bushes," Reb replied.

Within seconds Cody had his guns strapped on and was advancing on Dooley, his blue eyes dark with menace.

"Wha—what are ya gonna do?" Dooley asked fearfully.

"Take care of you so you can't hurt anyone again."

"You can't kill us. We ain't done nothing illegal," Conrad said. "We were hired by the kids' guardian to bring them back home. They're runaways. The law will see it Masters's way."

Ignoring Dooley, Cody glared at Conrad. "You're

going to get special treatment, Conrad," he promised, "for what you did to Amy."

Grasping Dooley by the scruff of the neck, Cody threw him to the ground, placing a booted foot in the middle of his back. "You got a rope handy, Reb?"

"Yeah, on my saddle. You'll find my horse in the woods." He motioned with his head in the direction where he had left his horse.

"I'll get it," Cassie offered, scrambling to her feet. She found Reb's mount tethered nearby, calmly munching grass. He made no protest when Cassie unhooked the rope from the saddle and handed it to Cody.

Cody made short work of Dooley, trussing him up like a Christmas goose. Then he turned his stormy gaze on Conrad, held motionless at the end of Reb's gun. "Give Conrad your gun, Reb. I'm gonna give the bastard a fighting chance. That's more than he gave Amy."

Reb looked startled. "Cody, I don't think . . ."

"Do it, Reb! Then you and Cassie take the kids into the woods. Cassie, show Reb where we left our horses. I'll join you as soon as I can."

"Cody, don't!" Cassie didn't trust Conrad. A man who would abuse a child would employ every dirty trick in the book against Cody. "He's not worth it. Tie him up and leave him with his friend."

"You heard me, Reb. Give Conrad your gun. Then take Cassie and the kids the hell out of here." Cody's voice was hard and relentless, his lips stretched over his teeth in a humorless smile.

"I can take care of myself. Been doing it for fifteen years. Besides, the bastard needs a lesson."

Reluctant to place his weapon in Conrad's hand, Reb tossed it on the ground several feet away. Conrad stared at it with glittering eyes while Reb and Cassie picked up the children and carried them into the woods.

"Pick up the gun, Conrad," Cody said quietly. His jaw was clenched, his eyes narrowed.

"I ain't no match for you, Carter. How do I know you won't plug me while my back is turned?"

Deliberately Cody holstered his gun. "You'll have the same chance I do. I won't draw until you're ready."

Conrad suppressed a smile. If the breed expected a fair draw he was crazy. Conrad knew the only chance he had of winning was by acting quickly and taking the breed by surprise. He sidled toward the gun lying in the grass scant feet away. His fingers flexed, relaxed, and flexed again, his eyes never leaving Cody's as he bent to retrieve the gun. But instead of rising, he crouched, pivoted, cocked the gun with his left hand, and fired with his right. The moment Cody noticed the subtle change in Conrad's expression, he tensed, dropped to one knee, drew, took aim, and fired. Two shots rang out simultaneously, scattering the birds resting in the trees.

Cassie, Reb, and the children had reached the spot where Cody had left their horses when the reports of gunfire cracked through the air. Cassie let out a strangled cry, ready to rush to Cody's defense, but Reb stopped her. "He'll be back," Reb said confidently.

"But Conrad could have tricked him! Cody could be lying dead right now."

It was the wrong thing to say. Both Brady and Amy began to wail. "Did Conrad kill Papa?" Brady asked, his voice rising on a note of panic. "What's going to happen to us?"

For the children's sake Cassie held her emotions tightly in check. "I'm sure Cody is fine. He knows what he's doing."

To take the children's mind off Cody, Reb picked up a bundle he found lying on the ground, turning it over in his hands. "What's this?"

Cassie shrugged. "I don't know. Conrad was carrying it when he sneaked up on me."

Reb tossed it to her. "Open it."

Tearing the paper away, Cassie was surprised to find an assortment of children's clothing. "He must have bought these in Wichita."

"Conrad said he couldn't take us on the train in our nightclothes," Amy explained.

"You might as well put them on," Cassie said. "It's a long way back home." The children scrambled behind the bushes and pulled on the clothes while Cassie watched anxiously for Cody to appear through the trees.

Reb patted her arm awkwardly. "Don't worry, Cassie, he'll be back. You're mighty fond of Cody, aren't you?"

"Is it that obvious?"

"To me it is. Maybe it's because I feel the same way about Irene. She's a fine woman. Too good for the likes of me."

"That's not true, Reb. If not for you, no telling what would have happened to me and Cody. Not to mention the children, whose lives wouldn't have been worth a plug nickel once they were back in their uncle's custody."

"I've been following you and Cody ever since you both left the ranch," Reb admitted sheepishly. "I swore I'd redeem myself, and now I have. But as soon as Cody returns I'll move on. Would you give Irene a message for me?"

"Of course I will, but you don't need to go anywhere. I'm sure Cody will want you to stay."

"And do what? I'm no good as a ranch hand. I can't tend cattle properly. I'm a helpless cripple, for God's sake! Just tell Irene I—I, aw, hell, don't tell her anything. What good would it do?"

"Why don't you tell Irene yourself, Reb?" Cody stepped into view, his lips curved into a lopsided grin.

"Papa!" Amy reached him first, hurling herself against him. He dropped to his knees, pulling both Amy and Brady into his arms.

A flood of relief swept through Cassie, nearly overwhelming her. Until that moment she hadn't realized how deep her love for Cody ran. Then she saw the blood on Cody's shirt and a strangled cry slipped past her lips. "Cody, you're hurt!"

"Just a scratch," Cody said, shrugging away his

wound as if it were nothing. "I've injured myself worse shaving."

"What happened?" Reb asked, his eyes shining with admiration.

"I was expecting a trick, and Conrad didn't disappoint me. What did surprise me was how accurate a shot Conrad was."

"Is he—did you . . . ?"

"If you're asking if Conrad is dead, the answer is no. But I doubt he'll be using his shooting arm again any time soon. Are you ready to leave?"

"Let me bind your wound," Cassie said in a voice that brooked no argument. Without waiting for Cody's reply, she rummaged in his saddlebag and found a spare shirt, which she ripped into strips.

"Hey, that's my best shirt!"

"Sit down, Cody, while I get some water from the stream."

Cody had been right, the wound wasn't serious. In fact, it had already stopped bleeding. The bullet had entered and exited the fleshy part of his left arm without disturbing bone or muscle. It would be sore and stiff for several days, but barring infection it should heal with no lasting effects.

Reb hovered nearby while Cassie tended Cody's wound, waiting for the right moment to speak. "Well, I reckon I'll be moving on."

Cody frowned. "Where in the hell do you think you're going?"

Reb shuffled his feet. "I don't rightly know. Back to Dodge, maybe."

"To do what?" Cody demanded to know.

Reb shrugged. "Same as I did before, I reckon. An odd job here and there."

"Don't you like ranch work? Irene will miss you."

Reb flushed. "She's better off without me. I ain't no good to anyone the way I am."

"You sure as hell saved my skin. And kept Cassie and the kids from suffering Lord knows what. I'm willing to give you another chance, Reb."

Reb hung his head. "I don't deserve it, Cody. It's my fault the kids were taken away in the first place. How do you know I won't crave a drink again and sneak into town like I did before? I can't even promise it won't happen again."

"Do you care for Irene, Reb?"

"Damn right I do, but I ain't good enough for her."

"I agree," Cody said, "but for some reason the woman cares for you. I'm counting on your love for her to keep you sober and straight. Besides, I can't ignore the fact that you saved my skin back there. You could have gone and gotten drunk when I kicked you off the ranch, but you didn't."

Reb's chin rose with a hint of the old pride that was once his. "I couldn't do that, Cody. I owed you."

"Now I owe you."

"Please don't go away, Reb," begged Brady, who had grown quite fond of the one-armed veteran. "Papa said you'd teach me how to ride a horse."

"Well, I'll be danged," Reb said, clearly at a loss for words. "You won't be sorry, Cody. I've still got a good right arm and two legs."

"C'mon," Cody said, tousling the kids' heads, "let's go home."

Amy's face remained swollen and discolored many days after they returned to the Rocking C. Her nightmares began almost immediately. Either Cody or Cassie spent part of each night by her bed, reassuring her that she was safe and no one was going to take her from them. During the day Cassie did her best to keep the children's minds occupied so they couldn't dwell on their recent ordeal.

Cody immediately fell into the routine of arising early and working late. There were cattle to brand, bulls to castrate, and fodder to be purchased and stored for the winter when grazing land was covered with snow and ice.

To Cassie it seemed as if Cody had deliberately been avoiding her since their return. And on those rare times they were together he appeared troubled. She wondered if he regretted making love to her. On those occasions when they had made love she could have sworn he cared for her. But since their return he had deliberately avoided talking about their times together.

If not for the children, Cassie would have left the Rocking C. She could have lived quite nicely off her quarter profit from the ranch. After her grandmother had died she had managed just fine on her own. Or so she tried to tell herself.

Cody had no illusions about himself. He wanted Cassie with a fierce need that made a mockery of his desire for any other woman, including Lisa. But, aware of his bastardy and the way most women felt about his Indian blood, he feared to express the fledgling love he felt for Cassie. Once it burst into full bloom it would set him up for more heartache than he could bear. Ridicule from Cassie was the last thing he needed. Yet he knew that things couldn't go on the way they were. One day soon he'd be forced to face his own demons and come to grips with the fact that he and Cassie couldn't live in the same house like brother and sister. What he felt for Cassie was far from brotherly love.

A few days after their return to the ranch Cody expressed his intention to go to town to pick up mail and supplies. Since Cassie had made plans to help Irene bake the children's favorite cookies, she declined Cody's offer to accompany him, though she gave him a list of staples to be purchased at the general store.

When Cody reached Dodge he left Cassie's list with the store clerk and made his own purchases at the hardware and feed stores. Then he picked up the mail. He was surprised to find a letter from St. Louis waiting for him. It was from a lawyer he had never heard of. With shaking hands he tore it open and read it quickly. When he finished he was as pale as death. Ignoring the postmaster's concern, he turned on his heel and left abruptly.

Five minutes later he was shaking the letter in Lawyer Willoughby's face.

"For God's sake, Willoughby, can they do this? Is it legal? What can I do about it?"

"Sit down, Cody, and let me read the letter," Willoughby said, plucking the letter from Cody's fingers. Then he settled back to read the missive while Cody, disdaining the chair Willoughby had offered, paced the office like a caged animal.

"The kids have more stability here than they've had since their parents died," Cody said when Willoughby finally set the letter down.

"Did you know the children had an uncle in St. Louis? According to his lawyer, Mr. Baxter, Julian Masters spent considerable time and money searching for them."

"I didn't know about Masters until just recently. The man hired two thugs to kidnap the kids from the ranch and bring them back to St. Louis. The kids told me the whole story. They were to be returned to St. Louis and paraded before the estate lawyers. Afterward Masters planned to do away with them and make it look like an accident. He'd already tried it once but hadn't counted on me coming to their rescue."

Resting his elbows on his desk, Willoughby tented his fingers and sat back in his chair. "Sit down, you're making me dizzy. What you've just told me is incredible. Why don't you begin at the beginning? If there's any way to help you, I'll find it."

Reluctantly Cody sat in the chair opposite Willoughby. Clearing his throat, he began the story by relating how and when he had first seen the children and all the events that had taken place up to date.

"Are you sure this Conrad and Dooley had no idea Masters was dead when they kidnapped the children from their beds?" Willoughby asked when Cody had finished his tale.

"I'm sure they didn't know," Cody said thoughtfully. "They had no reason to take the kids to St. Louis without Masters there to pay them. According to the letter, Masters died of blood poisoning the day after the kids were kidnapped. The estate lawyers didn't know where the children were until they found a telegram from Conrad in Masters's effects stating that the kids were living with me at the Rocking C. Dammit, Willoughby, I'm not going to let them put the kids in an orphanage."

"There's not much you can do about it," Willoughby said with a shrug. "You're no kin to those kids."

"They don't want to leave. Isn't that enough reason to keep them with me?"

"Not according to the law, I'm afraid. They're considered runaways. They're also orphans, albeit rich orphans. When they come of age they'll inherit a lot of money."

"I don't want their damn money! I'll sign a paper relinquishing any claim to their fortune. I can take care of them without using their money. Those kids would hate being confined in an orphanage. Is there nothing I can do? Mr. Baxter is coming to Dodge within the month to take the kids back to St. Louis. How in the hell do you expect me to tell them that they're going to an orphanage? I gave them my solemn promise, Willoughby, that they could stay at the Rocking C, that no one would ever hurt them again."

Deep in thought, Willoughby rubbed his jaw as he contemplated Cody and his dilemma. "You seem mighty fond of those kids, Cody."

"Well—uh," Cody hedged, "they're damn good kids and they don't deserve to be shut away in an orphanage. They've had a rough life after their parents died. I gave them my *word,* Willoughby. My solemn oath."

"There is something you can do," Willoughby said with marked reluctance. "Though there's no guarantee it will work, it might very well help your cause. How serious are you about keeping those kids?"

"Serious enough to take them away where they can't be found," Cody said evenly.

"That's against the law and you know it, Cody. What I'm going to suggest is legal and might work if you get a sympathetic judge."

"Are you going to tell me or do I have to drag it out of you?"

"You don't have a snowman's chance in hell of getting custody of those children without a wife. It's as simple as that. Children need stability, and no judge this side of the Mississippi is going to award the custody of impressionable children to a single man whose life thus far has hardly been exemplary."

Renewed hope bolstered Cody's flagging confidence. "Are you saying that if I get hitched a judge will give me custody of the kids?"

"I can't promise, you understand, but it sure as hell can't hurt to take a wife. You got someone in mind?"

Some of the grimness left Cody's features. "Maybe, if she'll have me."

"You take care of the details. Meanwhile, I'll prepare custody papers to present to Mr. Baxter when he arrives," Willoughby said. "Good luck, son. Keep in touch. Let me know as soon as Baxter hits town. Better yet, send him a telegram instructing him to get in touch with me the moment he arrives in Dodge."

Twenty minutes later Cody had picked up his order at the store and was on his way back to the ranch. When he arrived he left the supplies for the hands to unload and went in search of Cassie. He found her in the study, going over the account books. When he burst into the room, she looked up from her work, startled by his intense look. He was staring at her strangely and looked upset. Her brow creased in a worried frown.

"What is it, Cody, is something wrong? Was there trouble in town?"

Not one for mincing words, Cody blurted out, "We've got to get married."

Cassie's mouth dropped open. It was hardly the kind of proposal she had dreamed of, and there was certainly nothing romantic about it. "Married?" Her heart did flip-flops. "What in the world brought that on?" Had Cody finally discovered that he loved her as much as she loved him?

"Here, read this," he said succinctly. He tossed Baxter's letter on the desk.

Cassie picked it up and read it quickly. "Oh no, they can't do that! The children belong here."

"Willoughby said I might be awarded custody of the kids if I had a wife." His terse explanation sent her heart tumbling down to her shoes. It hurt dreadfully to know that Cody wanted to marry her because he needed a wife for the kids' sake, not because he loved her. "I can't explain how I feel about those kids, Cassie. In a short time they've become important to me."

At least he was being truthful about *something,* Cassie thought, disgruntled. What really pained her was that his words confirmed her belief that he didn't love her, that all he cared about was the children. He enjoyed making love to her because he was a lusty animal with healthy appetites. Her eyes flashed in sudden anger, and she wanted to hurt him in the same way he had hurt her, even though she knew that ultimately she would marry him. He wasn't the only one who loved the children. Her sacrifice would be worth it, if one could call their marriage a sacrifice. But before she accepted his rather callous offer, she wanted him to know exactly what she thought of his hasty proposal.

"I wouldn't marry you if you were the last man on earth, Cody Carter!"

Cody froze, his face contorted by an emotion Cassie couldn't identify. Had she been able to look into his mind she would have realized just how deeply she had wounded him. Her words were close enough to Lisa's to send him back in time, to that terrible day when the woman he cared about, the woman he hoped to make his wife, had laughed in his face. She had been repulsed when he confided that he had Indian blood flowing through his veins. Or had it been his bastardy that had turned her away? And Cassie was no different.

"Does my being a half-breed bother you so much?" Cody asked tightly. His eyes looked like chips of ice. "It didn't seem to make any difference to you when we were making love. Or is it because I'm a bastard?"

Cassie was dumbfounded. She couldn't recall ever giving Cody the impression that his mixed blood bothered her. Not after she had come to know him, she amended silently. If he had told her he loved her, she wouldn't have hesitated a moment. "You know those things mean nothing to me."

Cody gave her a scornful laugh. "You could have fooled me. I wouldn't have asked you to marry me if I wasn't desperate. I've known for a long time that marriage wasn't for me, even though I would have married you if I got you with child." He glared at her, too angry to realize that he was adding insult to injury.

Stifling a sob, Cassie leaped to her feet, sending papers scattering. "Leave me alone, Cody! *Just leave me the hell alone!*"

"You're damn right I will!" Cody yelled back. "There must be someone in this damn town willing to marry me." Turning on his heel, he stormed from the room.

Dashing the tears from her eyes, Cassie was tempted to run after him, then decided that she would let him sulk for a while before she accepted his proposal. Even though Cody didn't love her, Cassie felt she had enough love in her heart for both of them. And maybe, in time, he could learn to love her. For the children's sake she was prepared to make the ultimate sacrifice of marrying a man who didn't love her.

Cassie was on the verge of leaving the study to go in search of Cody when she glanced out the window and saw him riding hell for leather toward Dodge.

Chapter Seventeen

Cody looked at the drink in his hand in brooding silence. Two hours had passed since he'd slammed through the swinging doors of the Longbranch, ordered a bottle, and proceeded to get rip-roaring drunk. At this time of day the saloon was nearly deserted, which suited his mood perfectly. The more he drank and the longer he sat there, the harsher and more damning Cassie's words seemed.

"I wouldn't marry you if you were the last man on earth!"

Of course she wouldn't marry him. Though she hadn't come right out and said it, what she really meant was she didn't want a half-breed for a husband. Or a man who had no legal right to his last name. He was born a bastard and would remain one for as long as he lived. He saw things more clearly now. Cassie was like Lisa and every other "decent" woman. He was good enough to give them pleasure but not respectable enough to marry. The hell with decent women, he thought bitterly. The kids seemed to like him, and that was all that mattered, wasn't it?

With shaking hand he upended the bottle and splashed the last of the liquor into his glass. He took a healthy pull, then set the glass down, staring morosely into the amber depths.

Holly and Wayne paused at the top of the stairs. They had just emerged from Holly's room where they had dallied the afternoon away. It was the only time of day Holly could spare for Wayne, for her nights were reserved for the men who came to the Longbranch seeking good whiskey and lusty women and were willing to pay for both.

"Well, well," Wayne said, eyeing Cody with bitter resentment. "Looks like my little brother is drowning his sorrows. Now what do you suppose could be bothering him? He has everything he could ever want in the Rocking C."

"He sure doesn't look happy, does he?" Holly observed. "I don't think I've ever seen him drunk before. What do you think is wrong?"

No matter how drunk Cody was, Holly still thought him the best-looking man she'd ever seen. Or likely to see in a town like Dodge. All he had to do was crook his little finger at her and she'd give Wayne the boot. She'd been Wayne's girl for over two years and he hadn't mentioned marriage once in all that time. She rather enjoyed working at the Longbranch and being fawned over by men, but she wasn't getting any younger. She realized she wasn't always going to be desirable—looks faded fast in her business—and if Wayne kept putting her off, she was going to start looking for a permanent replacement.

"I don't know what's wrong with Cody, but I intend to find out," Wayne said as he descended the stairs.

"Do you think he'll tell you?" Holly asked. Wayne stopped abruptly, giving her an assessing look.

"You're right, Holly, I'm the last person little brother would trust. But you, my sweet little whore, are an expert at drawing things out of men." He chuckled, laughing at his play on words. "I'll wait here while you go down and do what you're so good at. Get Cody to tell you what's eating at him. Who knows, maybe it's something I can put to good use."

Frowning, Holly continued down the stairs. She was as curious as Wayne, but for a different reason. Cody wasn't the type to lose control, and she wanted to know what had sent him over the edge. It had to be something serious, she surmised, to make him drown his troubles in a bottle. Hips swinging in jaunty invitation, she tugged the neckline of her bodice down another inch to reveal the rosy tips of her nipples and sashayed her way over to Cody. Her endeavors to gain his attention were wasted, for Cody didn't spare her a second glance.

"Howdy, Cody," Holly rasped huskily. "What brings you to town?"

Cody glared at her through blurry eyes, grunted, and took another swig of whiskey. If he was going to get drunk he might as well do it up right.

Ignoring his rejection, Holly pulled out the chair next to him and sat down. "Would you like some company, handsome?"

Cody cocked an eyebrow and said, "Suit yourself. I reckon I'm not very good company right now."

"Something bothering you, honey?"

"You could say that."

"Wanna tell me about it?"

"No."

Holly glanced toward the top of the stairs where Wayne was lingering in the shadows and shrugged in a manner suggesting she was having little luck. Wayne urged her to try harder with an impatient motion of his hand. She returned her attention to Cody. He appeared so forlorn she wanted to run her hands through the inky crispness of his hair, to pull him to her soft breasts and soothe him.

"I'd really like to help you, Cody."

A strange expression came over Cody's face as he looked her straight in the eye and said, "I need a wife. You interested?" Then he laughed uproariously at such an outrageous notion.

"Marry you?" she asked in astonishment. "Do you really mean it?"

"Aw, hell, don't pay any attention to me."

"No, Cody, tell me more. Why do you need a wife?"

"It's a long story."

"I—I really do want to help you." Hell, yes, she wanted to help if it meant getting a man like Cody.

Cody sat back in his chair and regarded Holly through narrowed lids. Perhaps Holly *could* help him. His head was spinning dizzily and he wondered why his mind seemed unable to function coherently. He couldn't remember: Had he just asked a whore to become his wife? Why not? Whores were his kind of women; he had no business messing around with the decent ones who objected to his mixed blood and bastardy.

"Cody? Did you hear me? I really want to help you."

"Huh?" His brains felt like mush. He stared at Holly through bleary, bloodshot eyes, trying to recall what it was he wanted to ask. His eyes narrowed in concentration. Oh, yeah, he remembered now. "Ya wanna get hitched, Holly?" His words were so slurred that Holly had difficulty understanding.

"You want to marry me?"

He shrugged. "Why not? Ya know a preacher?"

"What's this about a preacher?" Having grown impatient, Wayne had descended the stairs and approached the table in time to hear Cody's last sentence.

Cody stretched his neck up to look at Wayne. It took several seconds before his brother came into focus. "Hello, Wayne."

"Did I hear right, Cody? Did you just ask for the preacher? Is someone at the Rocking C sick or dying?"

"Cody just asked me to marry him," Holly said breathlessly. If she ever got her clutches into Cody she'd never let him go. He might be drunk now and unaware of what he was saying, but she intended to latch on to him before he sobered up.

Flabbergasted, Wayne stared at Holly as if she had lost her mind. "Cody did what? Either you're crazy or I am. Why would Cody marry *you?*"

Holly winced. "I don't know, ask Cody."

Wayne turned his astounded gaze on Cody. "Are you joshing, little brother, or did you really mean it when you asked Holly to marry you?"

Cody shrugged. "Reckon I must have. I need a wife and better a whore than—than . . . " He left the sentence dangling, but the implication was there.

"Did you and Cassie have a fight? I thought you were sweet on her."

"Forget Cassie. I asked Holly to marry me."

"Why?"

Cody gazed moodily into his empty glass. "I sure could use another drink."

Wayne nodded at Holly, who quickly rose and got another bottle from the bartender. She filled Cody's glass, then sat back down. Cody upended the glass and drained it. In order to go through with this farce he needed to be too drunk to know what he was doing.

"I asked a question, Cody. Why do you want Holly to marry you?"

"Huh? Oh, yeah, I remember now. If I don't have a wife, they'll take the kids away from me."

"Who?"

"Those fancy St. Louis lawyers The kids couldn't stand living in an orphanage. Besides," he mumbled disjointedly, "I promised . . . I promised . . ." His voice fell off and his chin dropped down to rest against his chest.

"Well, I'll be damned. Who would have thought a tough bastard like Cody had a soft spot for kids."

A soft snore blew through Cody's lips, and Wayne gave Holly a speculative look. "Why are you looking at me like that?" Holly asked.

"Do you want to marry Cody?"

Holly sent Wayne a startled look. "Are you kidding? What woman wouldn't? It sure as hell beats working at the Longbranch. Besides," she said pointedly, "by the time you get around to marrying me I'll be an old woman."

Wayne's mind worked furiously, exploring the possibilities of a marriage between Holly and Cody and how he might use it.

"I think it's a wonderful idea," Wayne said, beaming.

"You do?"

Suddenly Cody snorted and awakened. With considerable effort he pulled himself upright in the chair and peered at Holly in confusion. Where in the hell was he? Oh, yeah, he remembered now. The Longbranch. He had wanted to get rip-roaring drunk and here he was, sober as a judge. His head started to sag and he jerked upright, and was immediately sorry. The room began spinning and suddenly he saw three of Holly.

"Cody, you've made me so happy," Holly gushed when she saw that Cody had come out of his stupor.

Cody stared at her. What in the hell was she talking about?

"I'll get the preacher," Wayne offered. "We can hold the wedding right here. Give Cody another drink, Holly. I'll be back before long."

"Yeah, the preacher," Cody mumbled, having no idea what was going on. Nor could he rouse himself enough to care.

Wayne gave Holly a speaking look and left the saloon with great haste. His mind was a seething cauldron of ideas and possibilities. With Cody safely married, he could court Cassie himself. Marrying Cassie was one way of regaining part of the ranch, a small part, but nevertheless it was a start. And maybe, just maybe, Cody might be willing to sell his share of the ranch once he, Wayne, married Cassie. That way he wouldn't have to do anything illegal. By the time Wayne reached the preacher's house, he was chuckling and rubbing his hands together in gleeful anticipation.

"I'm sorry, Mr. Carter, but my husband isn't home. He was called to Garden City and I don't expect him back for at least three days. He'll be here for Sunday services, though." Mrs. Lester, the preacher's rotund wife, smiled pleasantly at Wayne, wondering what he wanted with her husband. To her knowledge, Wayne Carter had never been inside the church or sought a private word with the preacher before.

"Damn," Wayne muttered beneath his breath. Three days would be too late. By then Cody would have slept off his drunkenness and he'd have second thoughts about marrying Holly. Cody would realize that marrying a whore wouldn't influence the St. Louis lawyer one damn bit.

"What did you say, Mr. Carter?" Mrs. Lester looked down her nose at Wayne, through glasses set askew on her chubby face.

"Er, nothing, Mrs. Lester. I'll see your husband when he returns." Tipping his hat, he hurried away.

Wayne was halfway back to the Longbranch when he remembered the justice of the peace. But once again he was thwarted when he read a sign on the door stating that the office was closed due to illness. Then he recalled that the justice of the peace had nearly died of a burst appendix and was gravely ill. Turning away, he racked his brain for an answer to his dilemma.

Wayne took his time walking back to the Longbranch. When he saw a crowd of people gathered around a man standing on a crate, waving his arms and sermonizing, he stopped to listen. He started to turn away—it was just another itinerant preacher spouting hellfire and brimstone. But then a burst of insight told him that this man could very well be his salvation. The preacher's long, gaunt frame was slightly bent, his shoulders hunched beneath his baggy clothing, and he waved a dog-eared Bible in the air to emphasize his words. His hair was long and shaggy and streaked with gray; his untrimmed beard reached nearly to his waist. But it was his eyes that captured Wayne's attention. Obviously the man was a zealot, and completely mad.

The preacher's eyes were black and shiny as glazed glass, with tiny fires burning deep within their centers. His feverish intensity was relentless; he displayed the religious fervor of a man totally committed to saving sinners. When the crowd started to drift away, Wayne approached the man.

"Can you perform marriages, Reverend?" Wayne asked hopefully.

The preacher grunted. "Could if I had a license. Still can, but it won't be legal. I'm more interested in savin' poor lost souls and showin' them the way to heaven."

Wayne's mind worked furiously. If the preacher wasn't around tomorrow to answer questions, who would know he wasn't an honest-to-God preacher? "I'd be happy to donate to your cause, Preacher, if you'd perform a marriage for my brother and his girl."

The preacher stared at him with burning eyes. "I told you before, it wouldn't—"

"It doesn't matter," Wayne interrupted. "It's merely a practical joke I'm playing on my brother. The woman is a whore, and I'll tell him it wasn't legal when he sobers up. It's to teach him a lesson so he'll stay away from alcohol."

The preacher looked indignant. "I want no truck with whores. They're an abomination in the sight of God. So is demon alcohol. I spit on them." He spat a brown wad at Wayne's feet.

"You'll find my donation quite generous."

The preacher's eyes seemed to burn holes in Wayne. "How generous?"

Wayne smiled thinly. Money worked every time. Fortunately, he had enough money stashed away to keep him comfortable for a long time. He dipped into his pocket and removed two shiny ten-dollar gold pieces. "Is this enough?"

The preacher's eyes burned even brighter as his tongue darted out to moisten his lips. Briefly he debated asking for more, but wisely decided that twenty dollars was fine—more money than he'd seen in a good long time. He nodded, holding out his hand. No sooner had Wayne deposited the coins in the preacher's outstretched palm than they disappeared somewhere in his rusty black jacket that hung in loose folds on his gaunt frame. Leading the way to the Longbranch, Wayne fought the urge to laugh. Wait until the preacher learned the wedding was going to take place in a saloon. It might cost him another gold piece, but it would be worth it.

This was going to be rich, he laughed to himself. Soon his brother would find himself married—or thinking he was married—to a whore. He debated whether or not to tell Holly about the hoax, and at the last minute decided to let her in on the joke. He didn't want her to get the idea that she was really married to Cody.

Cody moved his head, and the resulting burst of pain brought a groan to his lips. His mouth tasted like the inside of a spittoon, and his eyes felt as if they had been glued shut. He must have really hung one on last night, he thought miserably. Where in the hell was he? He recalled being in the Longbranch and getting drunk, but the latter part of the evening remained a blank. He tried to move, but a heaviness on his chest pinned him to the bed. He knew he should open his eyes but feared what he'd find when he did.

Suddenly he felt the sensual brush of warm flesh against his own, and the aroma of stale perfume wafted up to him. The scent was heavy and cloying and unpleasant to his senses. He shifted positions to escape it, throwing his arm out across the bed, and was rewarded with a startled yelp.

"Ouch, that hurt."

Cody's eyes flew open, and he turned his head despite the crushing pain. He tried to rise and realized that a naked woman—Holly?—was draped inelegantly across his chest. To his horror, he saw that he was likewise naked.

"What the hell! What are you doing here, Holly?"

Holly's red lips came together in a teasing pout. "Is that any way to talk to your wife?"

Cody shook his head, certain he was hallucinating. "I didn't hear you right. Did you say my wife?"

"You heard right, honey. Don't you remember? We were married yesterday. Wayne was your best man and Betsy from the Longbranch was my attendant."

Cody plopped back against the pillow and closed his eyes, hoping he was having a bad dream, but when he opened them again, nothing had changed. "How did it happen?"

"You came into the Longbranch and said you needed a wife. When you asked me to marry you, I accepted. I'm thrilled to be your wife, honey, really thrilled. The preacher thought we made a good-looking couple." What she didn't say was that the self-proclaimed preacher had to be bribed to enter the saloon at all.

"We were married by a preacher? Did he give you a marriage license?"

"Well, no, not exactly," Holly hedged. "He said he was plumb out of proper marriage licenses, but he wrote out a paper that says we're married."

Cody couldn't think straight. He recalled coming to town and getting drunk, even remembered why he had felt the need to get drunk. Cassie had refused to marry him and he was about to lose the kids. Hell! He must have been desperate to have asked Holly to marry him. And where did Wayne fit into all this? "Anything else I should know, Holly?"

"Oh, Cody, you were wonderful last night." She sighed dreamily. "I've never had a man like you."

A groan of dismay slipped past Cody's lips. How could he have made love and not been aware of it?

"Was this Wayne's doing?"

Holly returned Cody's query with an innocent stare. "Wayne found the preacher, but getting married was your idea. Don't you remember? You said you needed a wife so you could adopt the kids. There were several witnesses to the wedding."

"She-it! I don't ever recall being that drunk before. I've got to get out of here. What time is it? Where in the hell am I anyway?"

Holly giggled. "It's morning, honey, and you're in my room." What Holly didn't tell him was what a struggle it had been getting Cody up the stairs to her room after the brief ceremony. Nor did she explain that he had passed out as soon as he hit the bed. Wayne had suggested that she pretend the marriage had been consummated, but that was no more the truth than the legality of the marriage itself. She had gone along with the pretense, since Cody had no way of learning what had really happened. "It will only take me a few minutes to pack," she added as Cody struggled to sit up.

Cody sent her an oblique look. "Pack?"

"I'm your wife, honey. You're not going to leave me behind, are you?"

"Hell and damnation! I can't even think straight. What's Cassie going to say when I show up with a wife?"

"Cassie? Isn't she your whey-faced stepsister who inherited part of the ranch? Buck Carter must have been crazy to make the girl his heir. I didn't know she was still out at the Rocking C."

Whey-faced? Cassie? She might be a lot of things but she certainly wasn't whey-faced, Cody thought as he pushed himself out of bed and got shakily to his feet. What in the hell was the matter with him? He needed a wife, didn't he? And Cassie had turned him down flat. He had known for a long time that whores were more honest in their feelings than so-called "decent" women. What did he care what Cassie thought about Holly? It wasn't her place to wonder about anything he did. She had had her chance and had told him in no uncertain terms that she wanted nothing to do with a half-breed bastard. So be it. He only hoped Willoughby wouldn't be too upset by his choice of wife.

"Pack up. I'll meet you downstairs in an hour," Cody said brusquely. "You can ride, can't you?" Holly nodded eagerly. "I'll rent a horse for you."

"I'll make you happy, Cody, just you wait and see."

Cody pulled on his pants, then turned to face Holly, his expression devoid of all emotion. "I don't know what in the hell went on between us in that bed last night, Holly, but I want you to know where you stand with me. I married you for one reason and one reason only: to gain custody of the kids. I have no intention of getting drunk again, so this will never happen again. As soon as I'm awarded custody of the kids, we can divorce and go our own ways. Bedding you just doesn't appeal to me."

The dark pits of Holly's eyes turned to flame. "Ain't I good enough for you, Cody? You didn't seem to care last night when you made love to me. You've got no call to look down on me when you're nothing but a half-breed who's not even entitled to his last name. At least mine's legal."

Cody went still; his hands were coiled into fists at his sides and he looked ready to explode. "Why did you marry me? I was in no condition to force you." His voice was taut with barely controlled fury.

Holly blanched. The last thing she wanted was to make Cody mad at her. He was her ticket to a good life, and she intended to hang on to him. Legal or not, this "marriage" was her last-ditch effort to escape the Longbranch before her looks and youth were gone.

"I'm sorry, honey," she purred silkily. "You know I didn't mean it. I know why you married me, but I don't see why we can't enjoy one another as long as we're man and wife. I got the hots for you, honey, you ought to know that." She sidled up beside him, rubbing her naked breasts against his chest. "I'm gonna try real hard to change your mind, Cody, real hard." Her eyes held the glittering promise of passion.

"Get dressed," Cody said, deliberately moving away from the cloying heat of her body.

He could smell her arousal and felt nothing but contempt. Holly was nothing like Cassie, nothing. The heavy paint she used on her face was caked and stale, emphasizing the hard lines around her mouth and eyes. Nothing about her was fresh or clean, and she didn't smell sweet and feminine like Cassie. A few months ago it wouldn't have mattered, but after making love to Cassie he couldn't stomach bedding Holly, or any other woman.

Cody rode in silence the entire way out to the Rocking C, his mind in a turmoil. After he left Holly he had gone to Wayne's house and questioned him closely about his "marriage." Wayne had verified everything Holly said. When he tried to find the itinerant preacher who Wayne said had married him, the man seemed to have disappeared into thin air. But several men who had wandered into the Longbranch during the ceremony confirmed that the preacher had been in town yesterday and had performed a marriage between him and Holly.

Cody stole a surreptitious glance at Holly, riding beside him on the horse he had rented at the livery, and his expression grew even darker and more bleak. She was dressed conspicuously in red satin trimmed in black lace, one of her more demure gowns, he assumed, since the neckline and hemline were both modest. But she still looked like a whore. Cody could still hear Willoughby's roar of shocked disbelief when Cody had informed the lawyer that he had married Holly the night before.

"You what!" Willoughby had thundered. "Holly Gilbert from the Longbranch? Are you loco, Cody? Every man in Dodge has had the woman, including me. I told you to get yourself a wife, not a whore."

It had taken Cody several minutes to calm the man down, and when he left Willoughby's office fifteen minutes later, the lawyer was still mumbling to himself. Cody spared Holly another glance, wondering why he hadn't thought to buy her something decent to wear before they had left town.

Cody's thoughts took many directions on that long ride to the ranch as he tried to imagine Cassie's reaction to his wife. She probably wouldn't care one damn bit, he thought bitterly. If she hadn't turned him down, he wouldn't have gotten drunk or suggested this marriage of convenience. Had Cassie accepted his proposal, their marriage could have been a real one. He truly cared about Cassie and thought she cared about him. Hell, he couldn't even recall proposing to Holly, or marrying her, or bedding her. She-it!

Cassie had spent the long night regretting her hasty words to Cody. She loved Cody and wouldn't have hurt him for the world. She had no idea what had possessed him to think that her refusal had anything to do with his mixed blood or the accident of his birth. But he'd never even given her a chance to explain before rushing out of the house as if the devil were after him. And he had been gone all night. It had been difficult to explain to the children why he had taken off so abruptly, and harder yet excusing his failure to return. If he didn't return soon, Cassie intended to send Rob to town to look for him.

It was midafternoon when Cassie looked out the window and saw two riders approaching. "That looks like Cody's horse, doesn't it, Irene?"

Irene walked to the window, squinting at the two riders. "It is Cody. I wonder who that is with him? It isn't like him to remain away all night without telling us."

Cassie flushed guiltily. She hadn't told Irene about the bitter words between her and Cody that had led to his flight. Cody's callous proposal had hurt too much to share it with another person.

Cassie left the window and walked outside to await Cody and his guest. She had a lot of explaining to do. She just hoped Cody would understand. She was no different than most women in yearning for a romantic proposal. What she had received from Cody was a cold-blooded offer totally lacking in love or warmth. A woman wanted to hear tender words, she wanted commitment, neither of which was evident in Cody's terse proposal.

"Is that Papa?" Brady and Amy had seen the riders and joined Cassie. "Who is that with him?"

"I don't know," Cassie admitted in a hushed voice. Though she had no idea why, she felt a sinking feeling in the pit of her stomach. Tiny fingers of apprehension marched down her spine and she was overcome with a sudden inexplicable chill. When she realized that it was a woman accompanying Cody, her anxiety increased.

Cassie saw the woman's garish red dress before she could make out her features. She had seen dresses like that many times in the past. Nearly every girl who worked for Sal owned one.

Cody's heart slammed against his chest when he saw Cassie and the kids standing in the yard waiting for him. He had hoped for a brief respite before making his explanation, but he saw that it wasn't to be. Hell, he might as well get it over with, he thought glumly. Postponing the inevitable would only make things worse. But when he was close enough to see Cassie's face, he panicked and almost turned and rode away.

Cassie's face expressed anxiety and concern. But there was more. She actually appeared glad to see him, even after the angry words they had exchanged yesterday. It was almost as if he could look through her eyes into her soul, where she had laid bare her heart for him to see. The moment their eyes met and locked, he knew. He *knew!* Cassie didn't hate him at all! No matter what she had said yesterday, she cared for him. Seething anger raged through him when he realized that neither of them had been truthful with the other. He was angry at himself, at Cassie, at the world.

He dismounted, helped Holly from her horse, and finally found the courage to look at Cassie and the children, all of whom were regarding Holly with open hostility.

A heavy sigh hissed through Cody's lips as he said, "Cassie, kids, this is Holly—my wife."

The moment Cody revealed the woman's name, Cassie knew who she was. She had seen Holly hanging over the balcony of the Longbranch on more than one occasion. She was a whore.

She was also Cody's wife. He had done exactly what he had threatened to do. He had gone to Dodge and found a wife.

Stifling a sob, Cassie turned and ran into the house.

Chapter Eighteen

For a brief moment Cody's eyes revealed the incredible anguish inside his soul before the cold, remote mask descended once more. What was done was done. He couldn't change things. In a moment of drunken madness he had married a woman he cared nothing about, and now the woman he really cared for despised him. Yet he wasn't entirely to blame. Oh, no, Cassie had started his slide toward insanity with her refusal to marry him. It was unfortunate she had chosen to use the same words that Lisa had flung at him. The hard planes of his face were bleak as he watched Cassie run into the house, her elegant back stiff, her head held high.

"What was that all about?" Holly asked once Cassie had disappeared through the door. She had immediately sensed a rival in Cassie and was secretly pleased at her obvious distress.

Cody was saved from answering when Irene came limping through the door. She had passed Cassie in the hall and come out to see what the commotion was all about.

"What's wrong with Cassie? I just passed her in the hall and she—" Irene's words slid to a halt and her black eyes grew round when she saw Holly standing beside Cody. She had lived in Dodge long enough to know who the woman was and how she earned her living. What was wrong with Cody, she wondered, to bring such a woman to the Rocking C? No wonder Cassie was upset, as well she should be.

Just then Reb arrived to add to the confusion. "Cody, I was just fixin' to come looking for you. Cassie was worried and—" His eyes fell on Holly. "Hell and damnation, what is that woman doing here?"

Only too aware that he deserved their indignation, Cody said, "Holly is my wife. We were married last night."

Reb let loose a hoot of laughter. "C'mon, Cody, quit joshing. We all know you wouldn't marry a woman like Holly." Suddenly realizing how unkind that sounded, Reb sent Holly a contrite look. "No offense, Holly, but we both know you ain't a fit wife for Cody."

Holly glared at Reb and sidled closer to Cody, rubbing herself against him in an indecent display of possessiveness. It was definitely not suitable behavior in front of impressionable children, and Amy and Brady stared bug-eyed at Holly, unable to grasp all that was happening. "It's the truth, Reb," Holly purred, eyeing Cody with an expression that could only be described as lust. "Me and Cody were married yesterday. Or are you too drunk to understand what I'm saying?"

Reb's eyes narrowed indignantly. "I'm as sober as a judge. What did you do to Cody, drug him?"

"Enough!" Cody shouted, embarrassed by the furor he had caused but unable to do a damn thing about it. "Irene, take Holly to the spare room. I'm sure she'll want to . . ." he raked her red-clad figure with distaste, "freshen up for dinner." When Irene continued to stand there, her face a mask of disbelief, Cody rasped, "Now, Irene."

Holly started to protest, but when she saw the black look on Cody's face she felt it in her best interest to comply. Since she was going to be the mistress of the house for a long time, at least until someone discovered the trick she and Wayne had pulled on Cody, there was plenty of time to assert her authority. And the first order of business once her authority was established would be to get rid of Cassie. Cassie was too young and beautiful to remain in the house with Cody.

But before she turned and flounced off, she looked down at the children and said, "So you're the brats who have turned Cody inside out. It's obvious he spoils you outrageously. Now that I'm here, you'll receive proper discipline. Children should be seen and not heard."

Amy's little face screwed up into a frown as she watched Holly sashay into the house, her hips swinging in blatant sexual invitation. "Did you really marry that woman, Papa? I don't think I like her very much."

"What's di-di-ci-pline?" Brady asked, perturbed. "If Holly is going to give it to us, I don't want it. Why didn't you marry Cassie?"

Cody's face softened as he dropped to his knees before the children. "Don't worry about Holly; she's only here for a short time. Nothing is going to change."

"Is Cassie leaving?"

"Leaving?" The thought hadn't occurred to Cody. Even if she wanted to leave, he wouldn't let her. "No, Cassie definitely isn't leaving. You're both too young to understand what happened, and even if you weren't I wouldn't expect you to understand when I don't know myself how this all came about."

"Why didn't you ask Cassie to marry you?" Brady asked, repeating his previous question.

"I did," Cody said quietly. "She wouldn't have me."

"Now wait a dang minute," Reb interjected, taking exception to Cody's words. "I find that hard to believe."

Not wanting to argue with Reb in front of the kids, Cody said, "Why don't you kids go play with Blackie while I talk to Reb. We'll discuss this later. Meanwhile, try to get along with Holly until—" he was going to say "until the lawyer arrives from

St. Louis," but instead he said, "until things are resolved."

Reluctantly the children ran off, leaving Reb and Cody facing one another. "All right, Reb, spit it out. I know you've got more to say."

"Damn right," Reb said. "I know I ain't got no right to criticize, nor stick my nose in your business, but what you did defies all logic. How could you go and marry a whore when you've got a good woman right here in the house? Cassie cares for you, Cody."

"Like hell she does," Cody said sourly. "I asked her to marry me after Willoughby told me my chance of getting custody of the kids would be better if I had a wife, but she refused."

"Then you ran off to town and asked the first woman you saw," Reb charged disgustedly.

"It wasn't exactly like that."

"Did you give Cassie time to explain? Or did you go off half-cocked?"

"What was there to explain? Cassie doesn't want me."

"Hell and damnation, Cody, there's got to be more to it than that. Why don't you talk to Cassie about it?"

"Maybe I will," Cody grunted, signaling the end of the discussion. He didn't like the turn of events any more than Reb did, but it was done. At least he had the wife Willoughby said he needed. After he was granted custody of the kids, he'd decide what had to be done about his unwanted marriage. Not once did he consider the possibility that he wouldn't be named the children's guardian, for that would make his marriage more of a farce than it already was.

Cassie didn't leave her room the rest of the day. Not even the thought of joining the children for supper could coax her from her private refuge into the hell of sitting at the same table with Cody's wife. Bringing home that whore had been a terrible blow to Cassie's self-esteem. *How could Cody have done that to me?* she wondered indignantly. She had no idea her rash rejection of his proposal would send him riding hell for leather into the arms of another woman. Why couldn't he have waited until she had cooled down enough so they could discuss things like two mature adults?

Once Cassie realized that Cody's terse proposal had been the result of his anxiety over the children and his eagerness to keep them from being placed in an orphanage, she regretted her callous words. For some reason the specific words she used had released some pent-up animosity in Cody. Had someone else rejected him with those same words? she wondered astutely. Someone he had cared about? Unfortunately, it was too late for second thoughts. Cody was married, which meant that Cassie could no longer remain at the Rocking C. The problem remained of finding somewhere else to live. An even bigger problem was trying to forget Cody.

Cassie had no idea that her absence at the supper table had placed a strain on Cody and the children. Cody groaned aloud when Holly sailed into the dining room, her tight poison-green dress adorned with pink flounces barely covering her nipples. The children, who usually chattered non-stop during the evening meal, fell silent beneath Holly's intimidating presence, while Cody did his best to keep them from staring at the front of Holly's dress. If not for the children he would have taken supper with the hands in the bunkhouse. But he didn't have the heart to leave the children alone with Holly, who obviously had little experience with youngsters.

Cody kept glancing at Cassie's empty place, missing her more with each passing minute. In a way he couldn't blame her for absenting herself, but in another way it was her fault, for none of this would have happened if she had agreed to marry him. They could be sharing supper tonight as husband and wife, with the children's future secure.

Cody rose from the table the moment the meal was finished, expressing his need to attend to pressing duties. Holly took exception to his abrupt leaving.

"Cody, honey, we're newlyweds. Can't you find someone else to do your chores? What about Reb? I know that drunken cripple ain't worth much, but there must be something he can do to earn his keep."

"Reb is teaching me how to ride a horse," Brady defended stoutly. Reb was his friend, and it hurt to hear him spoken of in so disparaging a manner. "He saved our lives."

"He helps Papa a lot," Amy added, "and he isn't a drunk. Not anymore, anyway."

Holly frowned as the children hastily left the room. "Cody, you're going to have to do something about those brats. They really are too forward. Since I'm the woman of the house, I'll see that their manners improve."

A warning cloud settled on Cody's features. "Leave the kids alone, Holly. Cassie and Irene have been caring for them quite adequately, and I don't expect things to change."

Holly's mouth took on an unpleasant twist. "I doubt your stepsister will want to stay on now that you have a wife. With me here to take care of you, she's no longer needed." Her words implied more than they actually said.

"I don't expect things to change where Cassie is concerned," Cody said evenly. "Nor do I expect you to alter things that are no concern of yours. For the time being we're married; let that suffice."

Holly took a deep breath, adjusted her smile, and said, "Of course, Cody, whatever you say. You and Cassie can handle the kids in any way you please. Kids always did make me nervous; that's why I never had the desire to have any. Until I married you, of course," she quickly amended when she noted Cody's stormy expression.

Sleep eluded Cassie. Vivid pictures of Cody engaged in passionate lovemaking with the sultry, sexy Holly kept her mind working overtime.

In the past few hours she had called Cody every vile name she could think of. She wanted to hear from Cody's own lips why he had married Holly when he knew how it would hurt everyone, but she was still too angry to confront him. In fact, she wasn't certain she wanted to talk to him ever again. She would truly hate leaving the children to fend for themselves, but she could see no alternative. Despite her resolve to bury her hurt deep inside and not let anyone know how badly she was suffering, a series of wrenching sobs burst from her throat.

Cody tiptoed down the hallway, careful not to make any noise when he passed by Holly's room. The soft glow from the lamp left burning on a table in the hallway lit his way as he paused briefly at the children's door and peered inside. Since the hour was late and they both slept soundly, he didn't bother them. He had deliberately stayed away from the house tonight until he was certain everyone was asleep. He had no intention of sleeping with his "bride" tonight or any night, no matter how much she pouted or cajoled. The only woman he wanted was Cassie, and she had rejected him.

Cody had to pass Cassie's room on the way to his own, and he would have walked on by if he hadn't heard heart-wrenching sounds coming from behind her closed door. When the door opened noiselessly beneath his hand, he slipped inside, standing a moment with his back against the door while his eyes adjusted to the darkness.

Since it was a bright, moonlit night, Cody could see the bed and the outline of Cassie's body beneath the sheet. He was startled to see that the sheet was shaking, and even more surprised to discover that the noises he had heard sounded like sobs. Was he the cause of Cassie's distress? The thought brought a stabbing pain to his heart. But at the same time, the notion that Cassie cared enough about him to become distraught over his marriage gave him a warm feeling. With all his heart he wished he could undo the damage done by his marrying Holly.

"Cassie." He hadn't realized he had spoken aloud until Cassie's sobs turned into a startled gasp. He hadn't intended to frighten her.

"Cody?" Cassie thought she was dreaming, that she had conjured him up. When he pushed himself away from the door and walked to the bed, she knew her imagination wasn't playing tricks on her. "What are you doing here? Won't your bride miss you?" Bitterness and resentment made her voice hard.

"You were crying."

Cassie sat up, hugging the sheet to her chest. "I was not."

He was standing so close she could see his eyes darkening as he searched her face. She inhaled sharply, stunned by the nearly tangible heat of his body, by the musky odor of tobacco, horse, and maleness clinging to him, and her pulse leaped in response. No matter how often or emphatically she denied loving Cody, the truth revealed itself in the racing of her blood and the erratic cadence of her breathing. The moon provided sufficient light for her to see a blaze kindle in the blue depths of his eyes, hot and wanting, making her skin tingle and her heart leap.

"Why did you send me away, Cassie? Why did you turn down my proposal? I need to know for my own peace of mind."

"You didn't waste any time finding another woman," Cassie returned bitterly. "I could have understood if you had chosen someone decent, someone the children could have loved and respected, who would have loved them in return. Why, Cody? Why Holly?"

"I still don't understand what happened," Cody said slowly. "I got drunk. I feel like a hypocrite for the way I raged at Reb about his drinking when I'm no better. I don't even recall getting hitched until I woke up with . . . well, never mind, needless to say I was stunned to learn I had married Holly." He sent Cassie a look that spoke clearly of his anguish and disillusionment. "Why should it matter to you? You made your feelings clear."

"You assumed too much," Cassie claimed. "Didn't it occur to you that I might prefer a proposal that spoke of love and commitment instead of cold words that spoke only of your need for a mother for the children? It's not very flattering to think that the only reason you asked me to marry you was because I was handy and Mr. Willoughby suggested it was expedient that you find a wife before the lawyer arrived from St. Louis."

Cody frowned. "I didn't mean for it to sound that way. What do you think it did to me when you turned me down flat? You can say what you want, but the reason for your refusal was clear enough. I'm a half-breed, not good enough for 'decent' women. I'm not even entitled to my last name." He shrugged. "I more or less expected to be turned down. I understand women like Holly. She had no qualms about marrying a half-breed bastard."

Cassie sighed, wondering who had made Cody so cynical. Had some woman in his past hurt him to the point of making him doubt his own worth? Had he always been so touchy about his illegitimacy and mixed blood? She knew that Cody's half-brother treated him with contempt and wondered if her own mother had added to Cody's misery while she had been married to Buck.

"Nothing I can say will change the fact that you're married to Holly," Cassie replied. "You'd better go to her. She's probably waiting for you."

"I don't give a damn about Holly. I never have. Nor do I intend to share a bed with her. I haven't looked at another woman since the day we met." He perched on the edge of the bed, reaching out to smooth the back of a finger down the satin surface of her cheek and across her full lips. "I want you as much now as I ever have."

"You're married."

"I have no memory of the marriage. I have only Wayne's and Holly's word that I was married. The itinerant preacher who married us wasn't even around the next morning to confirm that he had indeed performed the ceremony. All I have is a handwritten paper that supposedly makes it all legal."

"What about Reverend Lester? Why didn't he perform the ceremony?"

"He was out of town, and the justice of the peace was recovering from an illness. Wayne says he ran across the preacher on a street corner."

Cassie chewed on that for a while. But in the end it made little difference who had married Cody and Holly. She told him as much. "Please leave, Cody, this isn't right. You can't just come into my room any time you please. I think I should leave the Rocking C."

"No!" His voice was like thunder. "No," he said again more reasonably. "This is your home. Are you such a coward that you'd let Holly chase you away? What about the children? They need you. Besides, as soon as Lawyer Baxter leaves, I plan on divorcing Holly. I've told her as much."

"I don't think I can remain in the house knowing you and Holly—that you and she are . . ." The words stuck in her throat.

"I already told you I'm not going to bed her. I don't want Holly in that way. If you had accepted my proposal instead of acting as if I'd insulted you, things might have turned out differently. Blame me all you want, Cassie, but remember that some of the blame is yours. I thought—that is—I hoped you cared for me."

"It's too late for recriminations or conjectures," Cassie said with scathing sarcasm. "Admitting that I care for you will only complicate matters. What's done is done. It doesn't matter now what I feel for you." It was difficult to maintain a facade of anger when what she really wanted was to throw herself into Cody's arms and beg him to make love to her, to make her feel all those wonderful, exciting sensations again.

"It's never too late, sweetheart," Cody said, his voice husky with emotion.

There was something so intimate about sitting in a darkened bedroom with Cody that Cassie found it difficult to argue against his peculiar logic. He was sitting close, much too close. Her thin linen nightgown clung damply to her skin, which had grown so sensitive that the mere touch of the thin material felt like burning brands on her flesh.

"You'd better leave." Her words were strangled, her voice strained.

Cody smiled, pulled the sheet from her shaking hands, and drew her into his arms. "You don't really mean that, Cassie."

"Maybe not," she admitted frankly, "but it's the way it has to be."

Cody wasn't going to take no for an answer. He hadn't intended to come into Cassie's room tonight; it had just happened. But now that he was here he couldn't leave without one kiss from her sweet lips. "Perhaps you're right, Cassie, but dammit, it's not what I want. This is what I want."

Grasping her shoulders, he pulled her hard against him, pressing his head against the fragrant curve of her neck and breathing deeply of her soft, warm skin. She smelled delicious, of flowers and springtime, and he recalled that she tasted delicious, too. That thought brought a spurt of hot blood pounding through his loins.

With frantic urgency he dropped soft, teasing kisses on her forehead, her eyes, her nose, the pulsing hollow of her throat; but soon that wasn't enough. Her tempting red lips drew him like a bee to honey as his mouth took hers with savage hunger. His tongue traced the fullness of her lips before plunging inside, hot and probing, all his frustration and thwarted desire evident in one soul-searching kiss that seemed to go on forever.

Dimly Cassie thought about resisting, but she wanted Cody with all her heart and soul. She felt herself being pressed back against the mattress, felt her nightgown being ripped open and Cody's hands drift down the quivering length of her body and back up again to her breasts. When he finally broke off the kiss and slid his mouth over her breast to suckle a rosy nipple, Cassie's startled protest ended on a trembling sigh. But she did manage a half-hearted attempt to push him away.

"Don't stop me, sweetheart, you want me as much as I want you." The harsh rasp of his voice eloquently conveyed his need.

"Cody, this is . . ." His mouth came down hard on hers, silencing her most effectively. Without knowing how or when he had removed his clothing, Cassie felt the searing heat of his bare flesh against hers.

And his hands. Oh God, his hands. They knew just where to touch her, how to caress her and when to stop, leaving her needy and aching for more. With his mouth covering hers and his hands spreading and probing, she was consumed by the fires of hell. And if she allowed a married man to make love to her she'd truly be damned. When Cody slipped a finger inside her, she desperately wanted to succumb to the devil driving her. But that core of honor that had been instilled in her by her grandmother won the hard-fought battle to evict the devil from her soul.

"No, Cody, please don't do this. I'd never be able to face myself again if I allowed a married man to make love to me."

Cody froze, nearly past the point of no return. "What?" He reacted slowly, as if both his body and mind were drugged. How could Cassie ask him to stop when to do so would push him past the limit of human endurance? Did she get perverse enjoyment out of teasing him and then dropping him cold?

"You're married! Don't you understand? I—I can't do this."

"You sure as hell could have fooled me," he snorted disdainfully. "In another minute my fingers would have brought you to climax. And in another minute after that I would have been inside you, bringing you even greater pleasure.

Touch me, Cassie, feel how much I want you." He grasped her hand, dragging it to his groin, forcing her fingers around him.

An agonized gasp hissed through Cassie's lips. He was enormous, the pulsing tip of his manhood filling her palm. With a will of their own her fingers moved down the shaft of velvet-covered steel, then up again. Suddenly Cody flung her hand aside and leaped from the bed, his body trembling, his face contorted into a mask of sweet agony. With slow, jerky movements he gathered up his clothes and pulled on his pants and boots. Before slamming out the door, he paused and flung Cassie a scathing look.

"I won't bother you again, Cassie. I wish you joy in your lonely bed. You can damn well believe mine won't be lonely." Then he flung open the door and disappeared into the dark shadows of the hallway. Cassie had no way of knowing that frustration and pain made him say things he didn't mean. Despite his words to the contrary, no matter how needy he was he'd never turn to Holly for satisfaction.

Making his way down the hall, Cody entered his own room. He was still seething as he flung his clothes onto a nearby chair and stomped to the bed. When he sat on the edge to remove his boots, he felt something warm and soft slide against him. Force of habit sent him reaching for his gun, which of course wasn't where it should be.

"You're late, honey." The voice was rich and husky with promise. "Where have you been?"

"Holly? What are you doing here?"

"You're my husband, remember?"

"Only too well. Why aren't you in your own room?"

She sidled closer until she was pressed snugly against his back. She was naked, her flesh hot, her breath ragged. "I want you, Cody. We're man and wife, there's nothing wrong in that."

When her hands found his erection, she gurgled happily. With a strength of will he didn't know he possessed, he shoved her hands aside. "I don't want you, Holly. This marriage was a mistake. I'm sorry, but that's the way it is." It took every ounce of fortitude he possessed to control his response while his body literally screamed for relief. A relief he wanted only from Cassie. But Holly wasn't easily discouraged. Her hot little hands continued to roam freely over his torso.

After Cody had left her room, Cassie found sleep impossible. She pulled on a fresh nightgown and tried desperately to recall all the reasons why she couldn't allow Cody to make love to her. Her tingling body made the task difficult. If she didn't love him so much it wouldn't hurt so much to deny him. Why couldn't he understand that they couldn't be together while he was still married to Holly?

Cassie's restless tossing ceased abruptly when she became aware that she wasn't alone. Had Cody returned? Oh, no—if he had returned she wasn't certain she had the strength of will to deny him again. When a plaintive voice reached her from the shadows, she heaved a shaky sigh of relief. Amy.

"I'm frightened," Amy said in a small voice. "I heard noises coming from Papa's room. Do you think he's all right?"

Cassie stifled a groan. She knew without being told what kind of "noises" were coming from Cody's room. Obviously he hadn't wasted any time in bedding Holly once he left her. So much for his lie about wanting no other woman.

"I'm sure Cody is fine, Amy," Cassie assured the child. "He's a big boy and can take care of himself. Shall I take you back to your room?"

"Yes, please," Amy said, somewhat mollified but still not convinced Cody wasn't in trouble. "Can we stop at Papa's room first and make sure he's all right?"

Cassie swallowed past the huge lump that had formed in her throat and said, "No, honey, I don't think that would be a good idea. You're going to have to take my word for it that Cody isn't in any kind of trouble."

Cassie took Amy back to her room and sat with her until she fell asleep. Then she quietly tiptoed out the door.

"Get the hell out of here, Holly," Cody thundered, shoving her from the bed. She fell to the floor with a thud. "And don't come back unless you're invited."

"It's Cassie, isn't it? If she wanted you she

would have married you. Obviously you're not good enough for her," Holly taunted spitefully. "When are you going to learn that people like us belong together?" When Cody made a menacing move toward her, she scrambled to her feet and fled.

"Yeah, Cody," he chastised himself bitterly, "when *are* you gonna learn that you're not good enough for decent women?"

Cody would have been stunned to know that Cassie had seen Holly slip from his room. Cassie had just let herself out of the children's room when the light in the hallway illuminated Holly's naked form poised in the doorway of Cody's room. And as luck would have it, Holly knew she had been seen. Taking advantage of the moment, she boldly turned and preened in all her naked glory before a stricken Cassie.

Chapter Nineteen

The dagger-edged slice of sunlight stabbing into her eyes told Cassie it was time to get up. She had slept little the night before and felt drugged and listless. Refusing to surrender to her despair, she dragged herself from bed and prepared to meet the day.

Her head held high, Cassie descended the steps a short time later, as ready as she'd ever be to face Cody's wife in spite of her breaking heart. She knew that Cody was already up and gone because the room to his door was ajar and his bed empty. The children were also out and about, but Holly's door was still closed. Why hadn't Holly spent the entire night with Cody? Cassie wondered dimly. If she was Cody's wife she'd share his bed all night every night, like a loving wife should.

Cassie went directly to the kitchen, attracted by the metallic sounds of pots and pans banging against one another. Irene was alone, taking out her frustration on various cooking implements.

"Good morning," Cassie greeted with forced cheerfulness.

Irene wasn't fooled by Cassie's ebullient facade. She had but to look at Cassie's wan face to know that she had spent a sleepless night. Her skin was pale and drawn, her eyes, surrounded by violet smudges, were dull and lifeless. She looked so fragile and vulnerable Irene's tender heart went out to her.

"Good morning, Cassie." Irene sent Cassie a sympathetic smile. She tried but found it difficult to be cheerful after the shock they had all received yesterday. "Are you hungry? Sit down, I'll fix breakfast for you."

The mere thought of food made Cassie ill. "Not really, Irene. Perhaps a cup of coffee and one of those biscuits sitting on the stove. Have the children already eaten?"

"Eaten and out with Reb," Irene said, placing the biscuits before Cassie and setting out a bowl of freshly churned butter.

The yellow blob nearly turned Cassie's stomach, so she nibbled at the dry biscuit, washing it down with hot black coffee. "What are Reb and the children up to today?" she asked dully.

She was finding it difficult to concentrate; her head was fuzzy and her stomach roiled dangerously. Had Cody done this to her? Had his bringing home a wife upset her enough to turn her physically ill? Obviously it had, for her meager breakfast was lodged in her throat and she had to swallow convulsively to keep from spewing it out in an undigested lump.

"Reb took Amy and Brady to watch the branding," Irene explained. "He thought they needed a diversion after yesterday."

"Don't we all," Cassie mumbled morosely.

"Cody left at daybreak," Irene continued. "He said he'd have breakfast with the hands in the cookhouse." She slid Cassie a sidelong glance to see how she reacted to that bit of information. When Cassie showed little emotion, she added, "And he said not to wait supper for him. He didn't look very happy to me."

Cassie lifted her hands in a gesture of helplessness. "Cody made his bed, he'll have to lie in it."

"What's this about Cody's bed?" Holly walked into the room, looking wantonly disheveled with her dark hair tangled about her face and her inappropriately sheer dressing robe barely hiding her more than ample charms.

Irene deliberately turned her back on the voluptuous woman and resumed banging pots with increased vigor.

"You know more about Cody's bed than I do," Cassie said spitefully. "You're his wife."

Holly grinned, inordinately pleased by Cassie's admission. "I'm glad you recognize the fact that I'm the one entitled to share Cody's bed. I know you were—close to Cody before we married, but from now on I'm the only one who's entitled to share his life—and his bed." Abruptly she turned to Irene. "I'm famished." Her plaintive voice made Cassie even more ill than she already was. "I'll have bacon and eggs and hotcakes. And coffee, with lots of cream. I've worked up a terrible hunger." Neither her sly innuendo nor malicious grin was lost on Cassie.

"If you'll excuse me," Cassie said, rising unsteadily to her feet. She'd had about all of Holly's snide remarks that she could take.

"Wait," Holly said. Her voice was hard, her eyes narrowed. "This house isn't big enough for two women. I strongly suggest you find other accommodations. Cody and I are newlyweds. Your presence in the house is somewhat—inhibiting, if you get my meaning."

"Perfectly," Cassie said tightly. Without another word she turned on her heel and stormed from the kitchen, her head held high, her chin quivering only slightly. She prayed she'd reach her room before she lost her meager breakfast.

Three days passed before Cassie packed her belongings in a battered suitcase and announced her intention to leave. There was a boardinghouse in Dodge where she planned to rent a room until she decided what to do with her life. As soon as she moved she planned to consult Lawyer Willoughby and arrange for her share of the ranch profits to be forwarded to wherever she moved. She even toyed with the idea of going back to Sal's, since she had no other place to go.

When she was packed and ready she bid a tearful and emotional good-bye to Irene and the children and asked Reb to drive her into town. When Reb tried to talk her out of leaving, Cassie set her chin at a stubborn angle and refused to be dissuaded. At the last minute she decided to take Lady and tied the mare to the back of the wagon by her leading reins.

As luck would have it, Mrs. Smith, a plump, dimpled widow, had a large front room available, which Cassie paid for immediately.

Reb waited until Cassie disappeared up the stairs with Mrs. Smith before leaving the boardinghouse. He was so damn angry at Cody that he felt the urgent need to turn into the Longbranch and have a short snort to take his mind off the trouble at the ranch. Without conscious thought his feet carried him through the swinging doors of the saloon. His nose twitched appreciatively as he sniffed deeply of the beery, boozy smell of the saloon, and his mouth began to water in avid anticipation. It had been a long time since a drop of liquor had teased his palate, and the temptation to indulge now was a pounding ache inside him.

"Howdy, Reb." A fixture at the Longbranch for several years, the bartender recognized him immediately. "Ain't seen you in here in a long time. What'll ya have?"

Reb's tongue twitched with the need to tell the bartender to pour him a whiskey, but for some unexplained reason the words stuck in his throat. He pictured Irene, Cody, and the children and how disappointed they would be if he fell off the wagon. He had been dry for several weeks now, finding no need to drink himself into a stupor. Irene's gentle giving and the children's warm regard, not to mention Cody's trust and friendship, had combined to lend him the strength of will needed to resist the demons driving him.

"Nothing," Reb replied, "nothing at all." Pulling his shoulders back and raising his head high, he seemed to gain stature and presence before the bartender's startled eyes. When he walked from the dim interior of the saloon into the bright sunlight, Reb felt that he had just fought the toughest battle of his life and won. His step was jaunty, his eyes bright. He felt like a new man.

Cody couldn't recall when he'd ever been so tired. He'd been married all of three days and already it felt like forever. His nights were a nightmare and his days a living hell. When he returned home after long, exhausting hours in the saddle he had nothing to look forward to. He couldn't face Holly, whose sexually charged invitations sickened him. The children hardly spoke to him. Irene acted as if he had committed a foul deed, and Reb's outspoken criticism was wearying. As for Cassie, he couldn't even let himself think about her. Seeing Holly and Cassie together had made him realize the vast difference that separated the two women and what a terrible mess he had made of his life.

He wanted Cassie. He ached with wanting her. He'd always want her. There was no question of substituting Holly for Cassie in his bed, for he doubted that he could perform with Holly while Cassie filled his thoughts. He recalled the husky quality of her voice that he loved so well, and the way it grew even huskier when they made love. And her eyes. Her eyes had the ability to suck the soul from his body.

She-it! he thought disgustedly as he rode into the yard. How had he gotten himself into such a tangle?

He had returned to the house early today, thinking to have supper with the kids since he'd seen so little of them these past few days. Dimly he wondered if he'd see Cassie, and brightened considerably at the thought. Why in the hell was he destined to love a "decent" woman? he wondered miserably. Life would be much simpler if he could love Holly, or someone like her.

Cody was pleased to see that the children were in the yard playing with Blackie. He hadn't had a private word with them since he'd brought Holly home and decided to remedy that situation now. His brows drew together in a quizzical expression when the children barely acknowledged his presence. He quickly dismounted, but when he walked over to join them, they deliberately turned their backs on him. He paused uncertainly, wondering if something else besides marrying Holly had upset them. When the children scampered away toward the barn, Cody's temper exploded.

"Just a minute. Where do you two think you're going?"

Amy turned and gave Cody a look of lashing contempt. "Did you want us for something?"

"I want to talk to you. Are you too busy to spare me a moment?"

Brady turned, refusing to look Cody in the eye. "Are you going to send us away like you did Cassie now that you have a wife?"

Cody's mind was spinning with bewilderment. "What in the hell are you talking about? I didn't send Cassie away. This is Cassie's house as well as mine, and she's going to stay."

"Then Holly must have sent her away, because Cassie said she had to go away, that she wasn't wanted here," Amy accused. "Ask Irene, she'll tell you how Cassie was crying when she left. Reb took her into town this morning. She moved into the boardinghouse."

"She what! Why wasn't I told about this?"

"Told about what, honey?" While Cody and the children had been talking, Holly had spied them from the window and walked out to see what they were talking about.

Cody rounded on her. "The kids tell me Cassie left today. What happened? Did you say something to her?"

"Me?" Holly said, her eyes wide with feigned innocence. "Why would I do something like that?"

"You did too!" Brady accused hotly. "Don't believe her, Papa, she's mean. I want Cassie to come back."

"You vicious little brat!" Holly lashed out. Giving vent to her explosive temper, she threw caution to the wind and boxed Brady's ears soundly.

Swiftly Blackie launched himself at Holly, tearing at her skirt with his sharp little teeth and growling ferociously.

Holly screeched, fearing she'd be torn to pieces by the small dog. "Get him away! Cody, help me!"

After the way Holly had struck Brady, Cody thought it would serve her right if Blackie tore huge chunks out of her hide. But fortunately for Holly, the small dog wasn't capable of inflicting that kind of damage. "All right, kids, pull your dog off Holly."

"But Papa, she hit Brady," Amy said indignantly.

"Let me take care of it, Amy. Just take Blackie into the barn. I have to go into town."

Amy's eyes lit up. "Are you going after Cassie? Can me and Brady come along?"

"Yes, I am going after Cassie, and no, you can't come along. Now do as I say. I want to have a private word with Holly before I leave."

"Are you going to punish Holly?" Brady asked hopefully.

Cody gave him such a stern look he turned and fled, dragging Blackie with him. Amy followed, remaining long enough to toss a parting shot over her shoulder. "I don't think Cassie will come back as long as Holly is here."

"She'll come back," Cody promised through the tightness of his throat. When he finally turned to face Holly, his face was like a thundercloud. "I'm only going to tell you this once, Holly. Don't ever touch the kids again."

"They're spoiled," Holly sniffed. "And they ain't even yours."

"Be that as it may, consider yourself warned. Now, about Cassie. There must be some truth to the kids' accusation. Did you or did you not tell Cassie to leave?"

"Well," Holly hedged, suddenly frightened by Cody's fierce look, "I didn't say that exactly."

"Exactly what did you say?"

Holly shrugged, looking everywhere but at Cody. "I might have hinted that you and me would like some privacy, seeing as how we're newlyweds and all."

"She-it! Get out of my sight, Holly, before I forget that I never strike women. I was willing to try to get along with you for the children's sake, at least until the lawyer from St. Louis arrived, but your jealousy and cruelty sicken me. I'm going to town to get Cassie, and when I return I expect you to behave."

"I'm your wife, Cody," Holly complained in a fretful voice. "I don't deserve to be treated this way."

"I don't feel married and I'm not even sure we are married. For all I know, you and Wayne dreamed this all up."

"I have the marriage paper," Holly returned shakily. "It's signed and dated and perfectly legal. And there were witnesses." She prayed that Cody would never learn about the deception she and Wayne had perpetrated.

"If I had the time I'd search for the preacher who conveniently disappeared the morning following the ceremony. But until things are settled with the kids, I'm obliged to stay here and make the best of this 'marriage.' I'm going into town now and try to make amends with Cassie."

"Cassie," Holly spat derisively. "You were good enough for her to bed but not to wed. Let her go, Cody. People like you and me belong together."

"You're probably right, Holly, but unfortunately for both of us I don't want you. Now if you'll excuse me, I'd best get going if I want to get back before dark."

Cody had no idea that Reb had overheard his conversation with Holly. Reb was just leaving the barn when he spied Cody and Holly talking and he ducked into the shadows. He knew he shouldn't listen, but in the circumstances he felt no guilt over eavesdropping. After Cody walked away and Holly returned to the house, his expression grew thoughtful. Then abruptly he smiled. He had just had a glimmer of an idea about how to help Cody and couldn't wait to tell Irene about it. He and

Irene had grown close these past few weeks and he wouldn't dream of going off without seeking her advice first.

"Irene, can I speak with you a moment?" She looked up from her work and smiled when she saw Reb standing in the doorway. She thought he was looking exceptionally well these days and hardly showed any signs of his former dissipation.

"Sure, Reb, come on in." When he took his battered hat off, she noticed that his expression was quite intense. "Is something wrong? Besides the obvious, I mean," she added, thinking of the tense situation between Cassie and Cody.

"I just overheard Cody saying that if he had time he'd look for that preacher man who was supposed to have married him. Maybe Cody don't have time, Irene, but I do. I aim to set out tomorrow and find that man, no matter where he's got himself off to. I don't trust Holly. Nor Wayne Carter, for that matter. If Cody has doubts about being married, then I aim to find out if he really did get hitched."

"Oh, Reb, I hope you're right. I hate to see Cassie and Cody so unhappy. How long do you expect to be gone?"

"Until I find the preacher. Does anyone know the man's name?"

"No, but I can find out. Holly has the marriage paper in her room. I'll find it and let you know later."

"Has Cody signed it?"

"He must have or it wouldn't be legal, if it is

legal. Are you going to let Cody know what you're doing?"

"No, I aim to ask for a few days off to visit relatives in another county. I don't want him to get his hopes up in case the man proves to be legitimate or I fail to find him. But if I do find the varmint I'll bring him back to Dodge even if I have to hogtie him."

Irene's warm brown eyes softened. "You're a good man, Reb. I'm glad Cody brought you here."

Embarrassed, Reb flushed. "I've only got one arm, Irene. But if I was a whole man I'd ask you to marry me."

"If I wasn't lame I'd accept," Irene flung back.

Reb looked stunned. "What has your lame leg got to do with how I feel about you?"

"About as much as your having one arm has to do with how I feel about you."

A slow smile spread across Reb's lips. "Then you don't think I'm an old fool?"

"I think you are a man who was lost for a while and found himself."

"I owe it all to you and Cody. When I get back we'll talk more about this—if you're willing," he added hopefully.

"More than willing, Reb."

"You're one helluva woman, Irene." Reb grinned, pulling her against him and planting an exuberant kiss on her lips.

Cassie barely had time to unpack her suitcase before Mrs. Smith arrived at her door to tell her she had a visitor in the parlor. Cassie couldn't imagine who besides Reb, Irene, and the children knew that she had left the ranch and taken a room at the boardinghouse. It couldn't be Cody, she reasoned, for he'd still be working at this time of day. Deciding the only way to find out was to go downstairs and meet her visitor, Cassie ran her fingers through her honey-colored hair, smoothed the wrinkles from her dress, and told Mrs. Smith she'd be down directly.

Wayne Carter was the last person Cassie expected to see looking out the window of Mrs. Smith's elegant parlor. His back was to her, and she paused in the doorway a moment, comparing him to Cody. There was absolutely nothing about Wayne to suggest that he and Cody were related. They might have the same father, but obviously Cody resembled his Indian mother. Wayne's sandy hair and light eyes lent him a youthful appearance despite his forty-odd years. Where Cody was tall, broad, and handsome, Wayne was of medium height, slim, sleekly muscled, and attractive. Aware of the part Wayne had played in Cody's marriage to Holly, Cassie felt nothing but contempt for him.

As if sensing her arrival, Wayne turned slowly and smiled at her. "Cassie! How good to see you."

"Hello, Wayne. How did you know I was here?"

"News travels fast. You're not angry, are you? It would be remiss of me not to stop by and see how my stepsister is settling into her new lodging.

Weren't you happy at the ranch? Has my brother done something to annoy you? By the way, how are Cody and his new wife getting along?"

His obnoxious smile set Cassie's teeth on edge. Wayne knew exactly why she had left the ranch. "As far as I know, they're doing just fine."

"Cody is just full of surprises, isn't he? But enough of Cody, it's you I'm concerned about. I got the impression that you were fond of my brother. I'm sorry if he has disillusioned you. But you have to admit he and Holly are perfect for one another. You're much too good for a half-breed."

"What do you want, Wayne?" Cassie asked.

"Why, I'm merely expressing brotherly concern, Cassie. Your mother and I were quite—close at one time. It would be remiss of me to neglect her daughter. I'd like to take you to supper."

Having supper with Wayne was the last thing Cassie wanted to do. She could barely stand the man. Besides, she didn't appreciate his sly innuendoes about her mother. Why didn't he just come out and say what he meant? "I'm not very hungry, Wayne." It was true; she just couldn't seem to get rid of her upset stomach.

"Are you afraid of me?"

"Should I be?"

"Of course not. I want to help you. Is there anything you need?"

"No, thank you."

"Are you sure you won't reconsider supper? The hotel prepares an excellent meal. There are some important matters I'd like to discuss with you. I think you'll find them most interesting."

Despite her reluctance, Cassie was intrigued. She couldn't help but wonder what Wayne had up his sleeve and if it somehow involved Cody. "Very well, Wayne, I suppose it won't hurt to have supper with you."

Wayne's eyes kindled. "Shall we leave then?" He offered her his arm.

A pearly gray twilight descended over the city as Cody rode into Dodge. His hat was pulled low over eyes dark with anguish. The stark planes of his face were hard and determined as he dismounted before Mrs. Smith's boardinghouse. He nearly frightened the poor lady to death when he asked for Cassie in a grating voice that left no room for refusal.

"Why, why, Cassie isn't here," Mrs. Smith stammered.

"Where is she?"

"I believe she went to supper with her stepbrother."

"With Wayne?" Cody's voice was ripe with contempt. "My brother wasted little time in making himself available to her."

"Your brother?" She stared at Cody over the round wire rims of her spectacles. "You must be Cody Carter." She thought him every bit as frightening as people said. "It's heartening that you and your brother are so concerned over your stepsister's welfare, but she's perfectly safe here.

I'll tell her you were asking for her."

"I'll wait," Cody said tersely.

"Yes, yes, of course." The dimpled woman was truly flustered now. "You may wait in the parlor, Mr. Carter."

Cody glanced toward the staircase. "Which room belongs to Cassie?"

Mrs. Smith stiffened in outrage. "Men aren't allowed to visit the rooms of women guests, not even male relatives. If I recall, Cassie is merely your stepsister, not a blood relative. You may wait in the parlor or not at all, whichever you prefer."

Cody sighed heavily. He could see that Mrs. Smith wasn't going to budge on this issue, so he tried a different approach. "I just wanted to make certain she was comfortable. I wouldn't want to see her given a tiny little room with no ventilation."

"I'll have you know I gave Miss Fenmore my very best room facing the front of the house. It has two very large windows and a tree shading it from the afternoon sun. I'm sure she'll be very happy there."

"I'm sure she will," Cody said, trying hard not to smile. There was more than one way to gain information. "And now I'll bid you good night."

"Good night? I thought you wanted to see Miss Fenmore."

"It can wait until tomorrow. I'd appreciate it if you didn't tell her I was here. I'd like to surprise her."

"Of course," Mrs. Smith agreed, feeling great relief now that the dark, dangerous man was leaving. "Anything you say."

Cassie was surprised at the superior quality of food served at the Dodge House. And despite what she had told Wayne earlier, her stomach felt better with some food in it. She sat over coffee and dessert now, waiting for Wayne to tell her what it was he wanted to talk to her about.

"Do you like the Rocking C, Cassie?"

Cassie frowned. His probing question startled her. "Of course I like the ranch. When I lived with my grandmother I used to dream about it and how happy I had been before Buck sent me away."

"Then why did you let Cody drive you away?"

"He didn't. I merely found living there not as attractive as it once was."

"Because Cody is married?"

What good was it to lie? "Partly."

"How would you like to buy out Cody?"

"What? That would take a lot of money. Surely you must know I have only what I earn from my quarter share of the Rocking C."

"I have a proposition you might find attractive."

Cassie's eyes assumed a wary expression. "What kind of proposition?"

"Marry me. I have enough money to buy Cody out, and together we'll own the Rocking C. That ranch belongs to me, dammit. I should have been named Buck's sole heir. Cody has no right to what's mine." Silence. "Did you hear me, Cassie? If you're thinking about Cody, forget him. He's married to another woman."

"Cody would never sell out to you. It's a wonderful place to raise children."

"If it's the children you're worried about, you and I can adopt them. We'd be more likely to be awarded custody than a half-breed bastard married to a whore. Just say yes and I'll have my lawyers work on the papers now." More silence. "You're a beautiful woman, Cassie. I'd be lying if I said I didn't want you."

"You're wasting your breath, Wayne," Cassie said, trying to hide her revulsion. Just thinking about bedding Wayne was repulsive. "I have no desire to marry you."

"Think about it, Cassie," Wayne urged. "I can wait for your answer. You do want those kids, don't you? Cody will never get them, not as long as he's married to Holly."

"Take me home, Wayne," Cassie said, bringing an end to the conversation. She couldn't deal with Wayne now. She was still too hurt, her emotions too raw. Cody's marriage had devastated her. She felt numb, discarded, destroyed, empty.

Cassie had to admit, though, that Wayne was probably right about Cody's marriage. No judge in his right mind would award custody of the children to an unlikely couple like Cody and Holly. Did she really want the children to be placed in an orphanage? Though Wayne had offered a remedy for the problem, the cure was too bitter a pill to swallow.

Wayne walked Cassie back to the boarding-house, and she waited until he left her at the door before letting herself into the darkened hall. She glanced into the parlor on the way up the stairs, saw that it was empty, and continued on up to her room. Evidently Mrs. Smith and her other boarders retired early. Which was just as well, for Cassie had no desire to stop and chit-chat with anyone right now. She had too much to think about.

Cassie knew that Cody would be devastated if the children were sent away to an orphanage, which she feared would happen if Lawyer Baxter found out about Holly's former profession. Just the fact that Cody was a half-breed would work against him. The only way the children could be saved would be if she married and filed for custody herself. She had to admit that Wayne's suggestion had merit, but she was repulsed by the thought of marriage to a man she didn't love, didn't even like. Her thoughts were in turmoil when she unlocked the door to her room and stepped inside.

A thick blanket of darkness greeted her, and she wondered why she hadn't thought to leave a lamp burning. Feeling her way to the table, she found the lamp and matches sitting beside it. Though darkness had never bothered her in the past, tonight the ominous curtain of black disturbed her. Even the silence seemed ominous. Her keen senses spiraled crazily, and it was impossible to steady her racing pulse. When the lamp flared and filled the room with flickering light, Cassie saw immediately what had caused her flesh to tingle and the skin at the back of her neck to crawl.

Cody.

Sprawled across the bed, his head resting on a stack of pillows, Cody was staring at her, his face dark and remorseless, his eyes cold. "Did you have a good time with Wayne?"

His voice was devoid of all emotion, and she felt a chill despite the warm night.

Chapter Twenty

Cassie didn't know what to make of Cody's question. "The meal was very good."

"I wasn't referring to the meal. What did you and Wayne discuss? He has a way with women, you know. I suspect that's why our father disowned him."

A spark of anger turned her eyes a dark, stormy green. "What are you doing here, Cody? How did you get into my room? I know Mrs. Smith didn't let you in, for she has strict rules about not allowing male visitors in female guests' rooms."

Cody uncoiled his lean length from the bed to tower above her. "I have my ways."

"My door was locked," Cassie maintained.

Cody glanced toward the window. "The tree was quite accommodating."

Cassie gasped, recalling that the room had been stuffy and she had left the window open when she left. "You'd better leave before someone hears you. Besides, I'm sure Holly is anxiously waiting for you at the ranch. She doesn't strike me as a particularly patient or understanding woman in regards to her husband."

Cody's fingers combed through his hair distractedly. "I don't feel married. I'm not even sure I am married."

"You were certain enough when you introduced Holly as your wife a few days ago."

"I've had time to think since then. I'm not sure I could have married Holly even if I was too drunk to know what I was doing."

"It seems like a match made in heaven," Cassie observed, wanting to hurt him as he had hurt her. "Obviously you had no qualms about bedding her."

Cody slanted her a quizzical glance. "I haven't bedded Holly since I brought her to the ranch. But I'm not here to defend myself. I came to Dodge to get you. Pack your clothes. I'm taking you home."

"This is my home."

Cody gritted his teeth in frustration. "You belong at the Rocking C. The children miss you. Hell, they're so mad at me they won't even talk to me. Irene has too much to do to act as buffer between Holly and the kids."

"Buffer?" Cassie asked curiously. "What do you mean?"

"If I hadn't been there when Holly struck Brady, the boy could have been hurt worse than he was."

"Holly hit Brady?" Cody had found the one argument that could sway Cassie. "Is he all right?"

"He's fine," Cody replied, "but who's to stop Holly from doing it again? Lord knows I can't be around every minute to monitor her, and the kids insist upon aggravating her."

Cassie nearly succumbed to Cody's logic, until she recalled the smug look Holly had given her when she was leaving Cody's room. It was difficult to believe that Cody hadn't bedded Holly, for she'd seen proof of it with her own eyes. "I won't go back to the ranch, Cody. You can't make me."

Cody's face hardened. "I'm not going to argue with you, Cassie. You'll leave even if I have to carry you out of here over my shoulder."

He was standing so close that Cassie could feel his determination. But she was equally determined. "Why should you care if I choose to live in town?"

"I cared enough to ask you to marry me, even if you did turn down my proposal. I foolishly believed my Indian blood wouldn't make any difference to you."

"It doesn't," Cassie responded softly. "I was upset by the coldness of your proposal and spoke prematurely. Who hurt you, Cody? What woman turned you down because of your Indian blood? She was a fool."

A stillness came over Cody. "It doesn't matter. I should have known better. I'm the kind of man parents warn their daughters away from. It happened a long time ago when I was naïve enough to think a woman would want me for myself."

Cody's pain was like a physical blow to Cassie. For the first time the full impact of what her callous rejection had done to him struck her. Her face must have reflected her feelings, for Cody said, "Don't feel sorry for me, Cassie. I'd rather have your anger. I deal far better with anger than with pity. And don't change the subject. You're coming home with me, and that's final."

Cassie wanted that too. She just didn't think she could handle it, loving Cody as she did and knowing she had no right to him. They had both spoken foolishly, and it had cost them dearly. "I don't think that's wise, Cody."

"I don't intend to stay married to Holly, if that's what's worrying you. You and the kids need only put up with her until Baxter arrives. I intend to talk to Willoughby tomorrow about starting divorce proceedings. I just hope it doesn't hurt my chances of adopting the kids."

"When Holly is no longer your wife I'll come home," Cassie said in a hollow voice.

"No, sweetheart, you're coming home with me now. I don't trust Wayne. He's up to something."

Cassie could tell him exactly what Wayne was up to but refrained. There was already enough bad blood between the brothers. "I don't trust Wayne either."

"He wants you, Cassie, can't you tell? He wants to pick up with you where he left off with your mother."

Cassie searched his face. When she spoke, her voice was strained. "What do you mean? What about Wayne and my mother?"

Cody groaned, realizing that Cassie couldn't possibly have known why Buck had disinherited Wayne. To make matters worse, he still felt incredible guilt over his own one-time encounter with Linda. "It doesn't matter. It happened a long time ago."

"No, it does matter, Cody. I want to know."

"Come home with me and I'll tell you everything I know."

Cassie stiffened. "I won't be bribed. Don't tell me; I think I already know anyway. Young as I was, I have no illusions about my mother. She and Wayne were—they were lovers, weren't they? That's why Buck disowned his own son. The man is disgusting. He cuckolded his own father."

What would you say if I told you I did the same thing? Cody thought guiltily. It would just give Cassie one more reason to hold him in contempt.

Cassie looked as if she wanted to burst into tears, and only her strength of will kept her from breaking down. Her bottom lip trembled and she looked so damn brave and adorable that Cody acted instinctively. His arms went around her and he pulled her to him. When his lips came down hard on hers, the swiftness and intensity of her response took them both by surprise. Her arms came around his neck and her mouth parted sweetly beneath his.

His short groan of pleasure was muffled in the hot sweetness of her mouth. They stood in the dimly lit room, their lips locked together, their bodies touching from breast to thigh. The blood rushed to his loins and he hardened against her as his lips traced a line from her neck to her shoulder. Burying his face in the fragrant fall of her hair, he breathed deeply of her sweet scent. He had missed her desperately.

Cassie inhaled with sharp pleasure, the feel of his lips against her flesh bringing back memories she had tried to deny. She loved Cody. No man could ever take his place in her heart. The frenzied delight she experienced in Cody's arms transcended all knowledge of right or wrong. To be in Cody's arms now, when she thought she'd never glimpse heaven again, was sweet agony. For nothing had changed; Cody was still married. She made a valiant effort to remove herself from his embrace.

With one arm he bolted her to him, his hand splayed at the base of her spine, holding her firmly against the hard ridge of his erection. "Ah, Cassie," he groaned, "it's been so long. I need you, sweetheart, I need you so damn bad. I've gone through hell these past few days. Let me, Cassie, let me . . ."

She wanted to let him, dear Lord, she wanted to let him. She needed to feel him throbbing inside her, loving her, filling her with piercing pleasure, sating her with perfect bliss. Then the choice was taken from her as Cody began stripping her with a swiftness that took her breath away. No sooner were her bodice and shift shoved down to her waist than Cody wrapped his large hands around her rib cage and lifted her up to him. His hot mouth closed over her breast; his teeth captured a nipple and tugged at it.

Cassie cried out, mashing her aching loins up to his, needing to feel the hardness of him against her, inside her.

"Oh, baby," he groaned against the soft flesh of her breast. "If I'm not inside you soon I'm gonna explode."

He was thrilled by the fury of her response. Lifting her higher, he swept her clothes away, spread her legs, and placed them around his waist. Cassie's arms tightened around his neck as she braced herself against him. Holding her with one hand, he used his other to release his throbbing member.

"I'm sorry, baby, I've got to be inside you right now. It's been too damn long." Long-repressed desire scorched through Cody as he held her in place and thrust inside her. "Oh, God, you feel so good. So damn tight, like a velvet glove clenching me."

Cassie threw back her head and moaned, her nails biting into his shoulders as his largeness stretched and filled her. She was aware of nothing, not the wrongness of making love with a married man or the rightness of being with Cody again. She could only feel. Feel herself grow slick and wet, feel Cody grow huge and hard inside her, feel him pounding against her womb, feel tiny spasms burst deep within her.

Feel love, overwhelming, soul-destroying, terrifying, wonderful.

"Cody, I can't hold back! I—I—oh, God, it's happening." Her sharp cry was delivered on a shuddering sigh.

"C'mon, baby, come to me, come to me now."

Still needy, still unfulfilled, Cody waited until her trembling ceased, then pulled out of her and lay her gently down on the bed. Stripping quickly, he stretched his long body in the cradle of her thighs, waiting for her ragged gasps to subside into normal breathing. Then he began moving his mouth hungrily over her body, stopping in his journey to suckle a puckered nipple before moving down to nuzzle the smooth white skin of her stomach. Lower still, to the silken tuft of her womanhood. His fingers followed his lips in an intimate caress that made her jerk against his hand. He rotated his palm in a motion so arousing that Cassie would have cried out if Cody hadn't placed his other hand against her lips in warning. Suddenly the pressure of his hand below was removed, replaced by the delicious warmth of his mouth.

She felt slick, hot moisture gathering again between her thighs. She was shivering, burning, arching into the sweet warm liquid of his mouth.

His tongue was a flaming torch, lashing her into a frenzy of need. Moments before she succumbed to shattering climax, Cody removed his mouth and thrust into her.

He moved inside her with sweet surging strokes, his hard length driving deeper and deeper with each thrust. He held her hips and raised her higher, burying himself to the hilt, using the powerful thrust of his thighs to piston himself forward. Each downward stroke brought him closer to explosion. He felt like a cocked gun with a hair trigger. Aw, hell, he wasn't going to be able to wait for her . . . he could feel the tension build deep inside him. Moments before unleashing himself, he felt Cassie stiffen and saw her eyes widen. Then he exploded, vaguely aware of Cassie's climax as shattering spasms gripped him in waves of hot pulsing rapture.

As their breathing returned to normal, Cassie felt like crying. She had made love with a married man. She was no better than Sal's girls except that she wasn't being paid to sleep with Cody. She'd done it of her own free will and had to live with her conscience from now on.

"I was afraid I'd left you behind, sweetheart," Cody said as he slipped from atop her to rest at her side. "I can't ever recall losing control of myself like that. I'm helpless when it comes to you. I've just made love to you and I want to do it again."

"You didn't leave me behind."

He gave her one of those rare, devastating smiles. "Good." He grew silent, his hand resting against the taut firmness of her stomach, his breathing even.

Sleep was just seconds away when Cassie said, "Cody."

"Hmmm."

"You can't go to sleep. You have to leave before Mrs. Smith or anyone else sees you."

He rolled over, suddenly wide awake. "I'm not ready to go yet. I want to love you again."

Cassie dragged in a shuddering sigh. "I don't think I can."

He sent her a look that made a mockery of her words. Then his hands were on her breasts and his mouth on hers, touching her, kissing her, over and over, wildly, bringing her quickly and easily to the pinnacle of ecstasy. Lost in a haze of euphoria, Cassie was barely aware that Cody had reversed their positions, placing her on top and spreading her legs. When he lifted her bottom and eased her onto his erection, she cried out, bowing her back and bringing him even more deeply inside her.

"Oh, baby, you're so hot," he gasped as he filled her with himself.

His hands were clasping her buttocks, holding her in place as he pumped furiously, going deeper than he had ever been before. Her eyes glazed, Cassie quickly set the rhythm, bracing her hands against his chest and grinding her loins against his groin as he came into her again and again.

When he raised his head to suckle her breasts, her eyes rolled back and she went wild atop him.

"Come now, baby, I can't wait!" Though barely aware of what he said, she obeyed instantly, without hesitation, her muscles clenching and relaxing in spasm after spasm of raw sensation.

Though desperately eager to unleash himself, Cody grew still when Cassie cried out, "I love you, Cody!" But the moment was lost as he thrust forward, his seed spewing forth in hot, molten spurts.

Afterward they lay sprawled in each other's arms, replete, too drained to move. When their breathing returned to normal, Cassie glanced at Cody through lowered lids. He appeared so pensive, so utterly bemused, she feared something was wrong. But before she could ask, Cody said, "Did you really mean it?"

A puzzled frown worried her brow. "Mean what?" Had she said something to anger Cody while they were making love? Funny, she couldn't recall saying anything.

"You said you loved me. Is it true?"

Oh, Lord, she'd gone and done it now. It must have come out in the heat of passion. She had no business telling Cody she loved him while he was married to another woman.

"Is it true, Cassie?" Cody probed, determined to hear the answer to his question. It was too damn important to him.

Her reply came on a trembling sigh. "Yes, I love you. I've loved you for a very long time."

"I'm a half-breed and a bastard. I'm rough, unrefined, and crude. Most women consider marriage to a half-breed repulsive. Even you, who just confessed to loving me, rejected me when I proposed."

"I told you why, Cody. I thought you wanted me for the children's sake, not because you really cared for me."

"We certainly made a mess of things, didn't we?" he observed bitterly. "We love one another yet can't be together as we'd like, and all because of pride and a few hastily spoken words."

Cassie inhaled sharply. "You love me?"

"I reckon I do. Fear of rejection kept me from saying anything before. I relived a nightmare when you turned me down. When I rode hell for leather to Dodge and got drunk I swear I had no intention of returning with a wife. I hope you'll be patient while I get this mess cleared up."

"I'm so afraid the children's lawyer will reject your petition to adopt them," Cassie said frankly. "Holly isn't exactly the best of mothers for the children. I think the lawyer will recognize that right away."

"I've thought of that," Cody said worriedly. "But divorce takes months. I can't file papers until the lawyer comes and makes that judgment for himself. If only . . ." What good would it do to dwell on what might have been?

"I'm sorry, Cody. I hate to see the children sent to an orphanage." She grew silent, debating whether to tell Cody about Wayne's proposal.

Finally she blurted out, "Wayne asked me to marry him. He's willing to adopt the children. He said he and I would have a better chance of gaining custody of them than you and Holly."

Cody reared up on his elbow, glaring down at her. "I hope you told him to go to hell! He thinks he can take you like he did your mother."

There it was, finally, the truth about her mother. "I already guessed that Wayne and my mother were lovers. Is that why Buck disinherited him?"

Cody flushed. He hadn't meant to tell her so bluntly. "I don't want to hurt you, sweetheart."

"It happened a long time ago," Cassie said gently. "I've already reconciled myself to the fact that my mother was no angel."

"It's my belief that Wayne and your mother were lovers, that Father disinherited him for that reason." And then Cody confessed something that he'd never told anyone before. Something he never intended to reveal. "I left home because Linda came to my bed one night and initiated me to sex. It was my first sexual encounter. I couldn't face my father after what I had done. I was fifteen, for God's sake, a green kid.

"I knew I didn't have the guts to resist if it happened again, so I left home. Father didn't really care; he had Wayne. I was merely a bastard son he tolerated because I carried his blood. And Wayne hated me. After my mother died, I had no one. I'm not excusing what I did, just trying to make you understand how it happened. I shouldn't have told you, but I want no lies between us."

Cassie's heart contracted with pain. In her mind she pictured Cody, a lonely, neglected child, different from other children, despised by his brother and merely tolerated by his father. He couldn't handle the guilt when Linda took him to her bed, and because he loved his father, he had left home. How could she blame Cody when her mother had been the seductress? When Cody left and Wayne returned from school, Linda had wasted no time in taking Wayne to her bed.

Vaguely Cassie recalled her mother's funeral and Buck's bitter words at her graveside. It occurred to her now that the child Linda had died birthing had probably been Wayne's child, not Buck's.

"I understand, Cody, and I don't blame you. I hardly remember my mother except that she was very beautiful. As for Wayne, I could never marry him, not for any reason."

"Then you'll wait for me? Until I can have my marriage to Holly dissolved?"

A sudden thought occurred to Cassie and she grew excited. "Cody, why can't you have the marriage annulled? If you never slept with Holly, it shouldn't be too difficult to undo your mistake."

Cody groaned, wanting desperately to tell Cassie he hadn't slept with Holly, but if Holly was to be believed they had consummated the marriage in her room above the Longbranch even though he had no recollection of it.

"Cody, did you hear me?"

His voice was flat and emotionless. "I heard. The marriage can't be annulled."

A small, hurt cry slipped past Cassie's lips. "You lied! Holly was right. You did bed her."

"Not at the ranch, Cassie, I swear it. It happened, or was supposed to have happened, I don't recall, after the ceremony in Holly's room. I woke up in Holly's bed and she swore we had made love. Truthfully, I doubt I could have performed under those circumstances, but I can't prove it."

A deep clenching ache shattered inside her. Just the thought of Cody doing all those wonderful things to Holly that he did to her made her physically ill. Gorge rose in her throat and she had to swallow repeatedly to keep it from spewing forth. Getting sick to her stomach was becoming a habit of late and she didn't like the feeling.

Cody sensed her distress and asked, "Are you all right?"

Unable to speak, Cassie nodded.

"I wish I didn't have to leave. I want to lie beside you all night and hold you. I want to wake up at dawn and love you again. Trust me, sweetheart, we'll be together one day soon."

She wanted to trust him; it was Holly she didn't trust. "You must go now, Cody, while it's still dark enough for you to leave without being seen."

With marked reluctance Cody heaved himself upright. "You're right, of course. It wouldn't do for me to be seen in your room. I'll come back for you in the morning, after I've spoken with Willoughby.

I saw Lady at the livery when I left my mount. I'll bring her around. Have your belongings packed and ready."

Cassie seemed deep in thought while Cody found his hastily discarded clothes and dressed. When he was completely clothed he sat on the bed and pulled her into his arms. "Why so quiet, sweetheart?"

"I don't know if it's such a good idea for me to return to the ranch."

"Of course it is. The kids need you, I need you. I'll need your help when I tell the kids that their uncle is dead and their lawyer is coming to get them."

Cassie looked stunned. "Haven't you told them yet?"

"I couldn't seem to find the right words. They were upset enough about Holly, and I didn't want to add to their distress. What do you say, will you return home with me?"

Flushing, she confessed, "I—I can't control myself where you're concerned."

Cody grinned. "Nor I you. If things work out like I hope, we'll soon be together in every way. You and me and the kids. Meanwhile, who's to know what we do in the privacy of our rooms?"

"If I come home, Cody, we can't be together like this until your marriage is dissolved. It isn't right. I couldn't live with the guilt. Even though your marriage to Holly was a mistake and you don't love her, it is legal and binding. Do you still want me to return under those circumstances?"

Reluctant agreement came hard on the heels of keen disappointment. "If that's the only way I can get you back home, then I agree. The kids will be ecstatic."

"What about Holly?"

"Leave Holly to me. I'll see that she gives you no trouble. Try to get some sleep now. I'll return later today." He kissed her hungrily, realizing it might be the last time for a long time. He left her then as he walked to the window and perched gingerly on the edge. He turned and waved once before sliding onto an outstretched tree limb. Within seconds he had disappeared into the murky darkness of night.

The children had seen Cassie and Cody approaching the ranch long before they arrived. Cassie had only been gone a day but it had seemed like forever. She had missed the children, and Irene, and Reb, and even missed the little white mutt inappropriately named Blackie. Mrs. Smith had been quite confused when Cassie announced her intention to leave so soon after she had rented a room, but was too intimidated by Cody to inquire further. She had merely nodded and wished Cassie well.

"I told you the kids missed you," Cody said when he saw them waving and calling to them enthusiastically. They bounced up and down until Cassie dismounted, then threw themselves into her arms.

"I knew Papa would bring you home," Brady crowed delightedly.

"Holly said you didn't belong here, but I told her this was your home," Amy said importantly. She glanced around to see if Holly was nearby before adding, "I don't think Holly likes you, Cassie. I know she doesn't like me and Brady 'cause she boxed Brady's ears and made him cry. I don't know why Papa married her."

"That's enough, kids," Cody said. "Let Cassie catch her breath before you worry her with your complaints."

"Well, you're back. I thought I'd seen the last of you." Holly stood on the porch, hands on hips, dark eyes snapping at Cassie. Her voluptuous curves strained at the seams of a garish satin dress the most hideous shade of puce Cassie had ever seen. "I should have known a man of Cody's appetites needed more than one woman to satisfy him. We'll have to make out a schedule, Cassie, if we're to share him."

"Holly!" Cody's roar of outrage nearly blasted the paint off the house. "The kids don't need to hear that kind of talk."

"They don't need to be taken to an orphanage either, Cody, but that's what will happen when the lawyer arrives from St. Louis and learns that you have a mistress living in your house."

"Papa, what's a mistress?" Amy asked, picking up immediately on Holly's words. "Are you sending us to an orphanage? Or back to Uncle Julian?"

"Aw, she-it, now you've gone and done it, Holly. I meant to tell the kids, but not like this."

Brady began to shed real tears. "I don't want to leave. Why are you sending us away?"

"Cody isn't sending you away," Cassie soothed as she sent Holly a withering glance. "But something has happened that you both should know about. It concerns your uncle."

Amy looked frightened. "What about him?"

"C'mon in the house where we can talk," Cody said, herding them toward the house. They all trooped into the parlor except for Holly, who walked purposefully toward the bunkhouse. She wasn't accustomed to being so long without male companionship and knew that one or two of the hands would be glad to oblige her. Since most of them had visited her at the Longbranch at one time or another, she figured she had probably slept with a good many of them. If Cody wouldn't give her what she needed, she'd find someone who would. She'd been so damn long without a man it was making her cranky.

Once the children were seated in the parlor, Cody told them that their uncle had died of complications from his broken leg. And since they had no living relatives, their lawyer was coming to Dodge to take them back to St. Louis.

"Is it our fault?" Amy asked in a frightened voice. "Will we be put in jail for killing Uncle Julian?"

"None of what happened is your fault," Cody said fiercely. "Julian Masters deserved his fate. He hired thugs to kill you so he could inherit your money. Don't ever feel guilt over what happened to him."

"How did the lawyer know where to find us?" Brady asked.

"He found a telegram from Conrad in your uncle's belongings. It was sent from Dodge and said you could be found at the ranch. I received a letter from the lawyer saying he would arrive soon to take you back to St. Louis."

"I won't go!" Brady insisted stubbornly.

"I'm hoping you won't have to," Cody replied. "My lawyer said I had a good chance of gaining custody of you if I was married."

"Is that why you married Holly?" Amy asked, aghast. "Don't you like Cassie?"

Cody sighed heavily. "It's a long story, one I don't even understand myself. But, yes, I reckon Holly is here because of that. As for Cassie, I love her. I love her very much."

"You're right," Amy admitted, shaking her head, "I don't understand. Will Holly be our mother? If Cassie is your mistress, will she be ours too?"

"Aw, she-it."

"Papa, remember your language," Brady cautioned.

"I don't know how to answer, kids, except to say that one day, when this is all settled, Cassie will be your mother. And maybe there will be a brother or sister or two to make our family complete. Would you like that?"

"Oh, yes," Amy said brightly. "I love babies." Her expression grew thoughtful as she searched

Cody's face. "But please, Papa," she implored, "don't give babies to Holly. I think she'd make a terrible mother."

Cassie choked on a gasp.

Cody looked stunned, then roared with laughter.

Chapter Twenty-one

Cassie knew it wasn't going to be easy living in the same house with Cody. The following days were more of a strain than either of them had anticipated. And Holly's cold resentment was so palpable, the children were careful to stay out of her way. One night Cassie heard Holly knocking on Cody's bedroom door and held her breath, fearing Cody would succumb to her pleading. But after a few minutes of fruitless pounding and doorknob rattling, Cassie realized that Cody had meant what he said. He truly didn't want Holly. The thought was immensely gratifying.

One day Wayne appeared at the door asking to speak with Cassie. Cody had ridden out early that morning and wasn't expected home till suppertime or later. Cassie greeted Wayne in the parlor, hoping to get rid of him in short order.

"Did you wish to speak with me, Wayne?"

"I was shocked to learn you had returned to the ranch with Cody. Mrs. Smith told me you left the very next morning. I can't imagine why you let him talk you into returning. I don't suppose Holly is too pleased about you being here."

Cassie had no intention of divulging her reasons to Wayne. "Is that all you wanted to say, Wayne?"

"No, I want an answer to my proposal of marriage. You left without telling me what you had decided."

Cassie frowned. "I gave you my answer right after you asked."

"I thought you might have changed your mind after you had time to think about it. Marriage to me makes sense, you know. You led me to believe you were fond of those kids. Cody hasn't a snowball's chance in hell of gaining custody of them. There are too many strikes against him."

"My answer still stands," Cassie maintained. "I won't marry you under any circumstances, Wayne. Now if you'll excuse me, I promised the children I'd help them bathe Blackie."

Wayne's pale eyes turned icy as he watched Cassie walk from the room. The rigid line of her back brought the bitter taste of defeat to his tongue. Nothing was going as he had planned. Because of Cassie's whoring mother he had been disinherited and lost the only thing that mattered to him. It was as much principle as it was loss of property. And now Linda's daughter had defied him, bringing insult to injury.

Why should Cody, a half-breed and bastard, be rewarded with something as valuable as a prosperous ranch? Wayne wondered spitefully. *He* was Buck's legitimate heir, not Cody. Lord knows he had tried to rid himself of his arrogant half-brother. Twice he had shot at him, and twice his shot had missed. His aim had never been very good. And now Cassie, the whore's daughter, was defying him. He had thought that the bogus "marriage" he had arranged between Cody and Holly would cause a rift between his brother and Cassie. A rift big enough to allow him a free hand with Cassie. A quarter of the ranch was better than none.

Wayne wondered if Cassie was still a virgin, and an idea began forming in his brain. A moment later Holly entered the parlor, closing the door quietly behind her. "I'm glad you're still here, Wayne." She sounded almost desperate.

"What is it, Holly? Are you having second thoughts about being married to Cody? Is he brutal? Savages usually are. They have none of the finesse that white men possess. Still, I wouldn't think a little brutality would bother you."

"How in the hell would I know if Cody is brutal?" Holly hissed angrily. "He won't even allow me into his room. Nor does he come to mine. I never had a problem with men back at the Longbranch. I was one of the most popular girls there."

Wayne stared at her, his face a mask of disbelief. "Isn't Cody bedding you?"

"Would I be complaining if he was? Hell no, he isn't bedding me. I can't even get close to him."

Wayne laughed mirthlessly. "That's rich, Holly. With your experience one would think Cody would be panting after you night and day." Suddenly his eyes narrowed. "Is he bedding Cassie?"

"If he is, I have no knowledge of it," Holly conceded. "He locks his bedroom door, and I've even stayed up late every night listening for him to leave his room and go to Cassie, but he never has."

"Do you think Cassie is still a virgin?" The plan Wayne had hit upon earlier looked more promising with Holly's disclosure.

"I wouldn't doubt it," Holly sniffed. "I think she's turned Cody inside out flaunting her virginity before him like a red flag. The prissy little bitch wouldn't know what to do with a man between her legs if she had one."

"She's about to find out," Wayne said, rubbing his hands together in avid anticipation. "And you can help me. All you have to do is get Cassie out to the barn tonight after dark."

"How in the hell am I gonna do that?"

"I don't know. You're inventive, just do it. It will be worth it, Holly. We'll both get what we want."

"I don't understand."

"Do you want Cody or not?"

The pink tip of Holly's tongue flicked out to moisten her lips. Getting Cody into her bed was a matter of pride as well as a driving need inside her. The longer she remained in Cody's house, the hotter she got to bed with him. "I want Cody."

"Then do as I say. If I marry Cassie, she'll no longer be available to tempt Cody. Don't fail me, Holly. I'll be waiting in the barn."

Cody failed to return in time for supper. He sent a message to the house with one of the hands that he would bunk down with the hands tonight. Holly appeared inordinately pleased by the turn of events, which puzzled Cassie. Was Holly finally reconciled to the fact that Cody wanted nothing to do with her? Cassie wondered. Later, after Holly had gone to her room, the children had been put to bed, and Irene had retired to her little cottage behind the bunkhouse, Cassie settled down with a book in the parlor. She must have fallen asleep, for the next thing she knew Holly was shaking her awake.

"Cassie, wake up. I just saw the children going out to the barn. Aren't they supposed to be in bed?"

Still groggy from sleep, Cassie leaped to her feet. What Holly said didn't make sense, but in her dazed state she didn't stop to analyze the logic of Holly's statement. "Are you certain?"

"Positive. I happened to look out my window and saw them sneaking from the house. You must have been sleeping and didn't hear them. Where do you suppose they're going?"

"I don't know but I intend to find out."

Stifling a smile, Holly turned away as Cassie hurried from the room. She had no idea that Blackie, who had been curled at Cassie's feet, trailed behind Cassie as she left the house.

There was no moon to light Cassie's steps as she carefully made her way to the barn. The bunkhouse was dark, since the hands usually retired early and arose early. When she reached the barn she peered through the gaping door. It was pitch black inside, and Cassie wondered what had possessed the children to come out here at this time of the night.

"Amy. Brady." Silence. She walked inside, trying not to collide with obstacles she couldn't see. She started violently when the door closed behind her and she heard the dull thud of the bar being shoved into place. "All right, children, enough of your games."

Suddenly a light flared in front of her, held aloft by some faceless being she couldn't see because of the clever placement of the lamp. "Who are you? Where are the children?"

Cassie followed the movement of the lamp with her eyes as it was carefully placed on a nearby bale of hay. When she looked up she was startled to see Wayne standing before her, leering at her in a most disconcerting way.

"The brats are in bed where they belong this time of night," Wayne said as he took a menacing step forward. Cassie turned to flee, but Wayne was too fast for her. Grasping her arms, he hauled her up against him.

"What do you want, Wayne? Why are you doing this? What can you hope to gain by terrorizing me?"

"I'm going to take you, Cassie, right here on the barn floor like an animal. I'm going to pretend I'm loving your mother. I miss her, you know. I haven't had a woman as good as her since she died. When I'm done you'll have to marry me. You're a virgin. What if I make you pregnant? Cody is a proud man. Do you think he'll still want you after I've had my fill of you? Or left a babe in your belly?"

What in the world made Wayne so certain she was a virgin? "Wayne, I'm not—"

Her words ended in a yelp when Wayne pulled the kerchief from around his neck and stuffed it into her mouth. "I can't afford to have you screaming." Then he shoved her to the floor and fell heavily atop her, tearing at her clothes like a madman.

Outside the barn, Blackie sniffed at the door and tried to scratch his way inside. When he heard Cassie cry out, he paused in his efforts and stared at the closed door with his head cocked to one side. When he heard a strange voice inside, he started barking ferociously. He kept it up until a light flared in the bunkhouse and Cody appeared on the threshold, barefoot and clad only in his trousers.

"What in the hell are you barking about, Blackie?" His voice betrayed his agitation as he looked toward the barn where the little white dog was raising such a racket. "Go to sleep, you damn inconsiderate mutt." When Blackie made no effort to cease, Cody's anger exploded. "She-it! Have you got a possum cornered in the barn? Is that why you're carrying on?"

The persistent little dog ignored Cody's angry tirade. Finding no help for it, Cody stalked to the barn, turning the air blue with his salty language. When he cut his foot on a sharp twig he promised all kinds of dire punishment for the pesky mutt. What was Blackie doing outside anyway? The dog could usually be found either curled up in the parlor or lying at the foot of one of the children's beds.

Grasping the mutt by the scruff of the neck, Cody was on the verge of taking him back to the house when he noticed a light coming from beneath the door. When he tried to pull the door open and found it bolted, a jolt of raw fear seared through him.

Too far gone with the need to thrust himself into Cassie, Wayne heard Blackie barking but paid him little heed. Dogs often barked at night. It was what they did best. He had succeeded now in stripping Cassie nearly bare and sat back on his haunches to admire the play of lamplight on her pale skin. When Cassie began struggling beneath him, he calmly tore a strip of cloth from her blouse, bound her wrists, and tied them to a nearby post.

"I'm going to enjoy this," he said as he began tearing off his clothes. "Afterward I'll take you into town and we'll be married."

Cassie shook her head in vigorous denial. Nothing Wayne could do to her would make her marry him. Not even rape. She too had been aware of Blackie barking outside the barn door, but unlike Wayne, she prayed the noise would awaken someone in the bunkhouse, which wasn't all that far away from the barn.

Poised outside the barn door, Cody heard the sounds of struggle, and when he found the door bolted from the inside, quickly looked around for another means of entry. Running around to the back, he saw a hay wagon pulled up beneath an open window and quickly vaulted onto the high seat. From there he levered himself through the window and dropped noiselessly to the floor. Blackie followed in his footsteps, leaping from the wagon through the window. What Cody saw in the flickering light froze his blood.

Cassie lay on the floor, struggling beneath Wayne's partially clothed body. Her arms were stretched above her head and tied to a post; her shredded clothing was strewn around her nearly nude body. Shouting in outrage, Cody flung himself at Wayne, pulling him from Cassie and pounding him mercilessly. Wayne fought back desperately, realizing Cody was angry enough to kill him. He struggled to his knees, trying to escape from Cody's wrath, but Cody was at him again.

"Damn you, Cody," he spat in his half-brother's face. "Twice I tried to kill you, but each time you escaped. You lead a charmed life."

Realizing now that Wayne had been the one who had shot at him both times, Cody wrestled him to the floor. Trying to rise, Wayne lurched against a bale of hay, the one upon which he had placed the lamp, and it toppled to the floor. Flames licked at the dry straw littering the floor, which ignited the bales of hay used as fodder for the animals. Within minutes the whole interior of the barn was ablaze.

The terrified animals began screeching in fright, and Blackie was barking furiously. Cody looked into Cassie's wild eyes and knelt to try to untie her. He didn't see Wayne coming at him with a pitchfork. But Blackie saw and reacted instinctively. He leaped at Wayne, sinking his sharp little teeth into Wayne's hand. Wayne let out a howl and dropped the pitchfork mere inches from Cody's back. Cody whirled, and delivered a punch that rendered Wayne senseless.

Turning to Cassie, Cody pulled the gag from her mouth and worked frantically at the ropes binding her to the post. He was shaking so badly it took him precious minutes to release her from her bonds. He started to take her up into his arms when Cassie said, "I can walk. Set the animals free."

Her urgent request galvanized him into action. Racing from stall to stall, Cody released the animals while Cassie, wrapping herself in a horse blanket she found draped over one of the stalls, lifted the bar and shoved the barn door open.

The blast of air pouring into the barn fed the fire, sending crackling flames into the loft where additional hay was stored. Cassie barely had time to step aside as the crazed animals stampeded past her into the open. When she looked back into the barn she saw a blazing inferno and no sign of Cody.

By now men were pouring out of the bunkhouse, and the ramrod, Sandy Blaloch, had already organized a bucket brigade, though in truth it was too late to douse the blaze. The best they could hope for was to contain it to the barn and prevent it from spreading to the house, bunkhouse, and Irene's cottage. But none of that mattered to Cassie as she watched anxiously for Cody to appear. When she didn't see him emerging through the nearly impenetrable murkiness of smoke and flame, she started to rush back inside. One of the hands saw her and held her back.

"Cody's inside!" Cassie screamed. "I've got to go to him!" She was so distraught by Cody's failure to appear that she never gave a thought to Wayne, or to her own injuries.

"Cody is inside?" the ramrod asked. Thrusting Cassie into another man's keeping, he wet his kerchief in a bucket of water, tied it around his nose and mouth, and rushed inside the burning barn.

Irene appeared at Cassie's side, the children clinging to her skirt. "Are you all right, Cassie? What happened? Where is Cody?"

Cassie took one look at the terrified children and said, "I'll tell you about it later, Irene. Cody is still inside the barn. I don't know what happened to him. He was letting the animals out of the stalls and then he just disappeared."

"Papa is inside the barn? Oh, no! Where is Blackie? I don't see him anywhere." Amy tried to pull away from Irene but the woman clung to her, preventing her from running into the burning barn.

Just when Cassie had given up all hope of ever seeing Cody again, she saw Sandy dragging him from the inferno. Blackie came dashing out behind them. Brady opened his arms and the mutt jumped into them.

Once in the fresh air, Cody revived quickly, though both men were coughing and gasping for breath. Cody saw Cassie, and his face lit up. Then they were in one another's arms.

"Are you all right, sweetheart?" His voice sounded raw from the acrid sting of smoke.

"I was just about to ask you that same question."

"Did Wayne hurt you?"

"No." Suddenly the roof fell in on the blazing barn. Cassie looked at Cody, her eyes wide with the knowledge that only two men and a dog had escaped the inferno, and that Wayne was still inside.

"I tried to save him," Cody said, aware of Cassie's unspoken question. His voice was troubled, his eyes bleak. No matter how vile Wayne had acted, they still carried the same blood in their veins. "I was dragging him out when a beam fell, pinning him to the floor. I tried to free him but was overcome with smoke. I must have passed out, for I knew nothing more until the air hit me and I revived. By then it was too late to tell Sandy that Wayne was inside."

"Couldn't Sandy see Wayne?" Cassie wondered.

"I'm lucky he stumbled across me," Cody said slowly. "The smoke was so dense that in another minute Sandy would have had to leave or lose his own life. If not for Blackie's whining, I wouldn't be here talking to you now. That's how Sandy was able to locate me. I owe that mutt a big steak."

"Where's Wayne? What happened to Wayne?" Holly ran up to them, nearly frantic. She had waited in the background for Wayne to come out of the barn, and when he didn't appear she guessed what had happened. "You've killed Wayne!" Tearing Cassie away from Cody, she began pounding on his chest, calling him all kinds of names.

Grasping her arms, Cody shoved her away. She fell to the ground, where she sat weeping.

"You knew what Wayne intended tonight, didn't you, Holly? If you didn't you wouldn't know that Wayne was in the barn."

Holly looked up at Cody through bleary eyes. "He wouldn't have hurt Cassie. He wanted to marry her. Wayne was my friend. I only agreed to help him because of you."

"Me?" Cody roared. "How did I fit into Wayne's vile plans?"

"Wayne wanted to marry Cassie. He said that once he and Cassie were wed you'd turn to me."

"You're dreaming, Holly. I'd never turn to you. Count yourself fortunate that Cassie wasn't harmed, for I have a suspicion that you're responsible for sending her out to the barn tonight where Wayne could attack her. Get out of my sight, Holly, before I forget you're a woman and take out my anger on you."

Lifting herself from the ground, Holly turned on her heel and ran into the house. By now nothing was left of the barn but blazing embers, and the men began drifting back to the bunkhouse, having at least succeeded in saving the house and outbuildings. Tomorrow they'd face the arduous task of rounding up the horses that had fled the fire. Dawn hovered on the edge of the horizon, leaving precious few hours for sleep. Once the children were assured of Cody's safety, Irene herded them into the house and tucked them in their beds. Cody put his arm around Cassie's shoulders and led her back to the house.

"Cody, what about—about . . ."

"The ashes will have to cool before Wayne's body can be removed. I'll see that he has a proper burial next to our father."

Cassie gave an exhausted sigh and sagged against Cody. He reacted by sweeping her into his arms and carrying her in the house and up the stairs to her room. He laid her gently on the bed. It wasn't until he lit a lamp that he noticed the deplorable condition of the horse blanket that covered her. The edges were tattered and smoldering, obviously the victim of licking flames, and in places fire had scorched clear through the rough material, reddening her tender flesh.

Cody gasped and whipped the blanket away from her, fearing she had been burnt and that shock had prevented her from feeling pain. Relief shuddered through him when he saw several raw places on her body but nothing serious enough to require a doctor. Though he didn't realize it, his own burns were far worse. There was one blistered welt across his back that begged for attention, and his hands and bare feet were seared an angry red.

After carefully inspecting her body, Cody said, "Thank God you weren't seriously burned." He turned away and poured some water in the basin to wash away some of the soot and grime covering her body.

"Oh, Cody, your back!" She put her hand to her mouth, frightened by the blistered, oozing burn on his back. And his feet! They looked as if he had walked across a bed of hot coals. "I know where Irene keeps her medicines. Wait here, I'll be right back." Stopping long enough to pull on a robe, she raced from the room. Within minutes she was back, carrying a small chest.

"There must be something in here to soothe your burns."

"Don't fuss, Cassie, I'll be fine."

Cody watched in rapt bemusement as Cassie opened a jar of ointment and began slathering it over the burn on his back. He couldn't recall when someone had expressed concern for him. He was somewhat embarrassed when Cassie washed his feet, then lovingly spread ointment on them, and he gave her a foolish grin.

"I was so frightened," Cassie said when she finally looked up from her chore. "I feared you had perished in the fire."

"I nearly did," Cody said grimly. "But I couldn't leave Wayne there to burn to death. I had to try to save him."

"He tried to kill you. More than once," Cassie reminded him. She had heard what Wayne had told Cody in the barn.

"I'm sorry," Cody said, sending her a repentant look. "I knew you weren't capable of shooting a man in cold blood. It's just that—well, at first I didn't know what to think. Can you forgive me for accusing you of shooting at me, sweetheart?"

"Oh, Cody, hold me, just hold me," Cassie begged. "I was so afraid I'd never see you again."

His arms went around her. "You can't begin to know how I felt when I saw Wayne abusing you in the barn. It must have been terrifying. Do you want to tell me what you were doing in the barn at that time of night? I have a notion Holly is somehow involved."

"I fell asleep in the parlor and Holly awakened me. She said the children had gone into the barn and thought I should know. I guess I was too fuzzy from sleep to doubt her, or ask questions. I trudged out to the barn like a lamb to slaughter." She shuddered. "Wayne said once he'd had me you'd no longer want me, that he was going to plant a baby inside me so I'd be forced to marry him. He figured a quarter interest in the ranch was better than none at all."

"Wayne was wrong," Cody said tightly. "I'd want you no matter what Wayne did to you."

Cassie's face glowed with happiness, until she remembered Holly. "What about Holly? You're still married to her."

"I'm sending Holly away tomorrow and starting divorce proceedings. After what she did to you, I can't bear to have her in the house. I don't want her anywhere near the kids."

"But—what about Lawyer Baxter? He'll probably arrive soon and you'll need Holly."

"Holly is no asset. I must have been mad to think she would be. I can do just as well without her. When the lawyer arrives, I'll make my own case for adoption. You can help by promising to marry me as soon as my divorce is final."

"Oh, Cody, yes, yes, I'll marry you. I'd be proud to marry you. If I hadn't been so damn stubborn, none of this would have happened. You wouldn't be married to Holly and in danger of losing the children."

"You know," he mused thoughtfully, "I can't explain my feelings where those kids are concerned. From the moment I met them they struck a chord deep inside me. I rarely thought about kids at all, and was certain I'd never have any. Maybe I saw them as an extension of myself and couldn't bear the thought of someone trying to harm them."

"Maybe it's because you just love children. You'll make a wonderful father, Cody."

Cody beamed. "I can't wait to make some of our own. Meantime, we can practice. If you're willing." The magnetic blue of his eyes pierced her where she was most vulnerable. She felt her heart melting with love. Denying him now was out of the question.

"You're hurt, you should rest."

Cody grinned cheekily. "Nothing hurts bad enough to keep me from making love to you."

"What about Holly?"

"Holly be damned. In my heart I'm not married to her. I want only you."

Cassie caught her breath, then let it out in a slow hiss. The look in her eyes gave Cody all the permission he needed. He was still sitting on the edge of the bed, with Cassie kneeling at his feet, having just spread ointment over his burns. He pulled her up by the shoulders, dragging her between his spread legs. With shaking hands he peeled the robe from her body. Cassie stood perfectly still while he looked his fill. Her breasts were just the right size to overflow his hands, her waist narrow, her flaring hips giving way to slender, shapely thighs. And between those enticing thighs, thick curling hair lay like golden fleece atop her woman's mound.

"I want to touch you," Cassie said, tugging at his belt. "I want to give you pleasure too."

Her erotic words aroused him instantly. He started to rise, but Cassie pushed him back down, realizing that his feet must be paining him dreadfully. She knelt at his feet and unfastened his pants. He raised his hips so she could slide them down his legs. She tossed them aside to join her robe on the floor. Sending him a smoldering glance, she bent her head and nuzzled his stomach, touching her tongue to his belly button. Beneath the clinging odor of smoke his skin smelled fresh and clean, as if he had bathed in the stream before he had gone to bed.

"I don't know if I can stand what you're doing to me," Cody groaned between clenched teeth. Cassie merely smiled and traced her finger down the line of hair below his navel to the rich dark forest covering his groin. Cody sucked in a ragged breath; his stomach clenched and his manhood jerked convulsively. Then her hand found him and her palm closed around him. When her head lowered, Cody felt his world tilt. He knew he'd die if she touched him.

But she did touch him, lovingly, with her hands and mouth. "No!" he cried out, but it was too late. Cody could no more stop her than he could stop breathing. Which he nearly did from the pleasure Cassie was giving him.

When Cody had all he could take of her tender torment, he lifted her from her knees and brought her beneath him on the bed. "Now it's your turn, little temptress. Turnabout is fair play."

Shoving her legs apart, he buried his face between her thighs. Cassie cried out, his mouth sending waves of delicious rapture singing through her veins. When he sent his tongue inside her, she nearly jumped off the bed. Abruptly he withdrew and slid full length atop her. Still aching, still needy, she squirmed while he took her nipples, first one then the other, into his mouth and bit down just hard enough to send a spasm of pure pleasure surging through her. Then he laved them with his tongue, soothing the hurt.

"Cody, please." How could he make her want him so desperately? she wondered distractedly. He knew exactly how and where to touch her to bring her the most pleasure. Her hands slid over his hot, hair-roughened flesh, over rippling muscles slick with sweat, and she wanted him inside her—now.

"Roll over on your side, baby," he instructed in a hoarse growl that spoke eloquently of his own urgent need. She obeyed instantly, wondering what he was going to do next. She felt the heat of his body pressed against her back, the swollen length of his manhood prodding her, and then he was parting her legs and thrusting deep inside her. A delicious languor spread through her as he began moving slowly, oh so slowly, making love to her as gently and tenderly as his big body was capable of.

Then she felt his hand between her thighs, parting her golden curls and rubbing the tiny nub of flesh, sending raw fire through her veins. The erotic friction sent her over the edge. When she convulsed, her body gripping him in a series of hot pulses, Cody exploded in his own shattering release.

Chapter Twenty-two

Cassie kept the children away from the smoldering remains of the barn the next day while Cody and some of the hands sifted through the ashes. When he returned to the house later, his face was bleak and he looked more grim than she had ever seen him. She followed him upstairs to his bedroom so they could talk in private.

"I sent Sandy to town to notify the sheriff and bring the preacher back," Cody said in a flat voice. "We'll hold the funeral immediately. Damn, I wish Reb hadn't gone off to visit relatives. I could have used him these past few days."

"You found Wayne?" Cassie asked, ignoring the reference to Reb. She was beginning to think he'd never return.

"We found his body, or what was left of it.

Sandy is bringing back a pine box for the burial." He sounded tired. Lord knew that neither of them had much rest the night before.

"I'm sorry, Cody."

"I know Wayne brought it on himself, but he was my brother. When I was very young I looked up to him. Until I learned how much he despised me for being a half-breed. I think he always feared that our father would name us both heirs to the ranch. That's why he treated me so abominably. He must have been relieved when I ran off and remained out of touch all those years."

"Have you seen Holly? Is she still upset over Wayne's death?"

"I spoke with her this morning. I told her to pack her belongings, that she was returning to town with Reverend Lester. I gave her some money and told her I'd notify her when the divorce was final. Tomorrow I'll go into town and talk to Willoughby about filing for divorce."

He plopped down on the edge of his bed. "God, I'm tired. And the worst is yet to come. There's still Baxter to contend with." He took her hand, pulling her down beside him. "What if Baxter rejects my petition to adopt the kids?" His voice sounded hollow.

"How can he? This is a perfect place to raise children. And don't forget, they chose you, you didn't choose them."

"You're overlooking all my faults, Cassie. I've never had much in the way of possessions, never felt the need for them. But you were right when you said children were treasures. Those two kids have made me a wealthy man, not in money but in ways that count. The feeling is so foreign to me it boggles the mind. And you, Cassie, you bring everything together. I can't wait to rid myself of Holly. I swear I'll never take another drink again."

He held her close, kissing her so tenderly it brought tears to her eyes. When he started to ease her down onto the bed, Cassie resisted. "No, Cody, we don't have time. Reverend Lester will be here soon and you need to clean up. Your clothes smell of smoke and—death."

It started to rain shortly before the funeral. The small group of mourners assembled behind the house in the tiny fenced-in plot where Wayne's father and mother were buried. Linda, Cassie's mother, was buried there too, and the dead babe that had never been given a name. Cassie had visited the place several times since her arrival at the ranch.

The rites were blessedly brief, due entirely to the rain, for Reverend Lester could be annoyingly verbose at times. Holly, the mourner most affected by Wayne's death, sobbed openly throughout the ceremony. At the last minute Cody had decided that the children shouldn't attend; they were confused enough as it was. Most of the hands were present, though, since Wayne had been their boss not too long ago. Irene had remained at the house to look after the children.

The sheriff was present too, having arrived

with the reverend. After private conversations with both Cody and Cassie, the sheriff appeared satisfied that Wayne's death was accidental. He stayed for the funeral and left immediately afterward while the others trudged back to the house, their clothes sodden from the steady drizzle. After a light meal provided by Irene, Reverend Lester prepared to leave in his buggy. Holly waited for him in the hall, her suitcase sitting at her feet.

"Would you be good enough to take Holly back to town with you, Reverend?" Cody asked as he paid the man of God for his services.

The preacher cast a jaundiced eye at Holly and grimaced. She looked every bit the fallen woman, dressed inappropriately in a tight red dress with a neckline cut nearly to her nipples. "Well, er, this is rather irregular, Mr. Carter."

"You'd be doing me a great service, Reverend," Cody said in a voice that gave little room for argument.

"Isn't Miss, er, Mrs. Carter your wife? It's my understanding that you married her."

Cody gave him a tight-lipped smile. "That's debatable."

"Oh, I see, I think. Well, then, I suppose it's my Christian duty to be of service. Come along, Miss, er, Mrs.—er—Holly, you're welcome to share my buggy."

Flinging Cody a hostile glare, Holly flounced after the preacher. Cody stood on the doorstep until the buggy was a small speck in the distance.

With Holly gone he felt as if a great weight had been lifted from him.

The following day Cody called on Willoughby. The lawyer agreed to start divorce proceedings but warned Cody that it could cost him custody of the children.

"I'm not certain Holly would have helped your cause any, but without her there's virtually no hope of adopting those children," Willoughby said regretfully.

"I'm going to marry Cassie as soon as the divorce is final," Cody revealed. "That's how it should have been in the beginning. So many things conspired to keep us apart. For one, my damn pride got in the way."

Willoughby beamed. "From what I know of Miss Fenmore, she is a good woman. Good luck. Did you write and tell Mr. Baxter to call on me when he arrives in Dodge?"

"I wrote."

"Good. I'll present your petition of adoption to him upon his arrival. The rest is up to you."

Two days later Denton Baxter arrived aboard the 10 a.m. train from St. Louis. According to Cody's instruction, he called upon Mr. Willoughby first. An uncompromising, pompous man without a sentimental bone in his body, Baxter perused the petition of adoption and listened to Willoughby's most eloquent plea in Cody's behalf without expression.

"Is Mr. Carter married?" he asked bluntly.

"Well, sort of," Willoughby hedged.

Baxter gave an impatient snort. "Either the man is married or he isn't."

"At the moment he is," Willoughby conceded, giving nothing away.

"I suppose I'd better get myself out to the ranch and talk with Carter myself," Baxter said. "I can promise nothing, you understand, for it will be up to a court to decide. There's a lot of money involved here. The children are quite wealthy."

"I'm sure money isn't the reason that Cody wishes to adopt the children. He truly cares for them. The decision might not be yours to make, but I'm certain you have influence with the judge and that your recommendation will be taken into consideration."

"Well, yes," Baxter acknowledged, puffing himself up importantly. "I'll rent a buggy and leave as soon as I have a decent meal. Can you recommend a tolerable place to eat?"

"Try the Dodge House. You won't be disappointed."

Replete after a satisfying meal, Denton Baxter strode past the Longbranch saloon on his way to the livery and happened to glance up and see a fetching brunette leaning over the balcony, her breasts nearly spilling from her bodice. When she smiled and winked at him in a most provocative manner, he looked at his watch, decided he had plenty of time to dally, and sauntered inside, his step jaunty. As formidable and portentous as he was, he wasn't above a tumble or two when the occasion presented itself. At least he didn't have to worry about his wife finding out in a god-forsaken place like Dodge City.

Holly stood at the top of the staircase, beckoning to the man who looked like a prosperous dandy in his expensive suit. Baxter grinned foolishly and bounded up the stairs. Within minutes he was unclothed and grunting over Holly's naked body. It was over fast—it always was—but was nonetheless satisfying. While he dressed, Holly asked idly, "I've not seen you in Dodge before, honey. Are you new in town?"

"Oh, I don't live in Dodge, my dear, I'm here on business. Do you happen to know Mr. Carter? Cody Carter? My business is with him and I'm on my way to the Rocking C now."

Holly blinked, sitting up straighter and paying closer attention. "You have business with Cody? Are you by chance from St. Louis?"

"Why, yes, how did you know?" Intrigued, Baxter gave her his undivided attention. "Are you acquainted with Mr. Carter?"

Holly grinned slyly. She owed Cody for discarding her like so much garbage after she'd done her damnedest to make him happy. And for being responsible for Wayne's death. "Very well acquainted. I'm Cody's wife. I know you've come to Dodge to get those kids he's so fond of."

Astounded, Baxter stared down at Holly, his eyes bugged out in disbelief. She was naked, her body sprawled without a shred of embarrassment across the bed in a most revealing pose. "You're married to Cody Carter? I don't understand. What are you doing here?"

"The ranch ain't doing so well, Mr. Baxter. I'm merely earning a little extra money to help out," Holly lied blandly. "Besides, Cody has a mistress living out at the ranch and I didn't like sharing him. I get more attention here, if you get my meaning." She winked at him.

Baxter let out a choking gasp. "His mistress? He has a mistress?"

"Oh, am I telling you something I shouldn't?" Her eyes widened with feigned innocence. "Everyone knows Cassie Fenmore lives at the ranch and is Cody's mistress. She's also his stepsister. Quite a mess, isn't it?"

"My dear girl, I never heard such a scandalous story," Baxter exclaimed, outraged. "Imagine, his stepsister." Though Baxter looked scandalized, he was clearly titillated.

"It is rather hard to understand," Holly sighed with exaggerated dismay. "But Cody is so handsome, I doubt there's a woman alive who can resist him. It must be his Indian blood that attracts women."

That really got Baxter's attention. "Indian blood!" He was all agog to hear more, and Holly happily obliged.

"Didn't you know? Cody is a half-breed; his mother was Cheyenne."

By now Baxter was so flustered he put his vest on backward and shoved his hat down past his ears. He had heard enough. Reaching into his pocket, he tossed some greenbacks on the nightstand and bid Holly a hasty good-bye. When he reached the sidewalk he withdrew from his pocket the petition of adoption that Willoughby gave him, tore it into pieces, and scattered them to the wind.

Cassie was in the henhouse when she saw the buggy approaching. She knew without being told who it was and sent one of the hands to find Cody. Then she went into the house to prepare the children for Lawyer Baxter's visit. Cody arrived at the house almost at the same time Baxter was levering his somewhat portly frame from the buggy. Cody's friendly greeting was met with a chilling glare that sent his heart tumbling down to his shoes.

"Mr. Carter," Baxter nodded curtly. "I've come for the children. If you would be so kind as to present them, I'll be off."

"Now wait a damn minute, Baxter," Cody growled. "You can't come here and take the kids just like that. Didn't you speak with Mr. Willoughby first? Didn't he tell you I wanted to adopt the kids? They don't belong in an orphanage. They've been happy here."

Cassie saw Cody's face go rigid and she rushed out of the house to see what was being said and try to help in any way she could. "Mr. Baxter, Cody has been a good father to the children. Ask them, they'll tell you themselves how much they care for Cody."

"I suppose you're the mistress," Baxter said condescendingly. "Isn't it rather awkward, what with Mr. Carter having a wife and all?"

Cody groaned, wondering where Baxter had obtained his information. Certainly not from Willoughby.

A dull red crept up Cassie's face. Being referred to as Cody's mistress stung, even though in a sense it was true. Drawing herself up proudly, she said, "I'm part owner of this ranch, Mr. Baxter. I have a perfect right to be here."

"How fortunate for you," Baxter said, unimpressed. "About the children, are they prepared to leave?"

"Won't you even consider my petition?" Cody asked tightly. It was all he could do to hang on to the shredded remains of his temper. "Has someone been giving you false information about me?"

"I won't discuss it," Baxter refused tersely. "I've already destroyed the petition of adoption." He wouldn't care for it to be known that he had spent his first hours in Dodge City with a whore.

Cody's face was as dark as clouds before a violent storm. Hoping to defuse the situation, Cassie said, "Won't you come inside, Mr. Baxter? It's a long drive out here. I'm sure you could use something cool to drink."

"Well, yes," Baxter acquiesced. "That would be nice. The children need to become comfortable with me before I take them away. I'm not an inconsiderate man, you know. I have children of my own."

"Please come inside," Cassie invited, "and you can meet the children."

Several minutes later Baxter was sipping lemonade while Cassie went for the children. Cody, too upset to sit still, paced the room like a restless animal. How dare that pompous ass insult Cassie? he thought resentfully.

"Please sit down, Mr. Carter, you're making me nervous. Since we're alone, there are a few questions I'd like to ask. Mr. Willoughby led me to believe you were married. Is your wife out of town?"

Disregarding Baxter's request, Cody towered over him, glaring at him in such a ferocious manner the poor man choked on his lemonade. "Whether or not I'm married is no concern of yours."

"I would say it's of great concern." Baxter smirked smugly.

"Look here, Mr. Baxter. My concern is for the kids. I want to adopt them. They'd have a good home with me. Living in an orphanage would destroy their spirit."

"There's a lot of money involved here," Baxter hinted.

"I don't want their damn money!" Cody roared. "Put it in trust for when they turn twenty-one, do whatever you want with it, I don't care. I'm perfectly capable of providing them with everything they need, including love."

"What about a mother?"

"I won't be raising them alone. There's Cassie."

"Ah yes." He sent Cody an oblique look. "I must admit you lead a most—interesting life, though hardly the kind of environment I would approve of for children." Baxter gave Cody a speculative glance. "I understand you're a half-breed." He made it sound like a dirty word.

Cody went rigid. One more disparaging remark from the bastard and he'd toss him out on his ear. "What if I am?"

Cody's expression was so fierce, so utterly savage, that Baxter felt an immediate retreat was called for. "Why, nothing about it, I just mentioned the fact, that's all."

"Where in blazes did you get the notion that Cassie was my mistress?" Cody queried, unwilling to let the matter drop.

"I—I heard it in town," Baxter hedged. His high collar was suddenly too tight and he ran a nervous finger beneath it.

"You didn't by any chance visit the Longbranch, did you?"

A dull red crept up Baxter's neck. "Well, er, I might have, now that you mention it."

Cody didn't have time to remark on that statement as the children bounded into the room. "You wanted to see us, Papa?" Amy asked, casting a furtive glance in Baxter's direction.

"Is that the lawyer from St. Louis?" Brady wanted to know. More direct than his sister, he wasted no time slicing to the heart of the matter.

"This is Mr. Baxter," Cody said, barely able to control the fury in his voice. How dare this compassionless, utterly heartless man make decisions that could affect the lives of two innocent children without considering what was best for them?

"Hello, children," Baxter greeted. "I'm very glad to see you. Are you ready to return with me to St. Louis?"

Amy sent Cody a pleading look. "Do we have to go, Papa?"

Brady was much more adamant in his refusal. "I'm not going! I don't want to leave Papa and Cassie. And what about Blackie?"

"Blackie?" Baxter looked confused.

"Our dog," Amy said with a hint of exasperation.

"Well, a dog, well, we can't very well take a dog with us on the train. No, that won't do at all. The dog will have to stay here with your, er, with Mr. Carter."

"We're not going anywhere without Blackie," Amy insisted stubbornly. "Why can't we stay with Papa?"

"Mr. Carter isn't your father," Baxter explained, growing impatient. "Wherever did you get that idea?"

"We adopted him," Brady said proudly. "We chose him because we knew he was a good man and would save us from Uncle Julian. Uncle Julian wanted to kill us, you know."

"Be that as it may," Baxter said, "Mr. Carter doesn't have the qualities one would hope for in a father."

"He does so!" Brady disagreed vehemently.

Baxter shrugged his elegantly clad shoulders, as if Brady's opinion made little difference in his decision. "Arguing with children is pointless. If your things are packed, we'll leave directly. I have tickets on the evening train; we'll just have time to make it."

Amy's chin trembled as she regarded Cody with soulful eyes. It nearly broke Cody's heart. "Won't you reconsider, Mr. Baxter?" he asked as reasonably as he knew how. "The children will have a mother. Cassie is a wonderful mother."

Baxter grimaced distastefully. "I don't consider this a wholesome atmosphere for raising children. In any case, the decision isn't up to me. I'm here merely to return the children to St. Louis. In due time a judge will decide what's to become of them."

"I won't go to an orphanage!" Amy cried out in panic. "Don't let him take us away, Papa!"

Cody sent Baxter such a black look the man felt obliged to say, "The law is on my side, Mr. Carter. I can bring the sheriff out here if you insist. But for the children's sakes, I suggest you allow them to leave without hindrance."

Gazing from Cody to the children, Baxter began to wonder if he was wrong, if that whore at the Longbranch hadn't been feeding him lies. Even Willoughby, a respected man in the community, seemed impressed with Carter and hinted that he'd make a good father for the children. The children themselves appeared happy and healthy and extremely fond of the half-breed.

"I don't like it, Mr. Baxter, but I won't disobey the law. I had hoped to find you a reasonable man, but I can see that nothing is going to dissuade you from taking the kids from me."

"Yes, well, harrumph, I always thought of myself as a reasonable man. But the law is the law. I can only repeat, a judge will decide the children's fates. My firm merely represents their interests. But I can see how fond you are of the children and they of you. May I make a suggestion?"

"Please do," Cody said hopefully. By now he was truly desperate.

"The children are to be taken to St. Vincent's Orphanage in St. Louis. It's a respectable institution run by the good nuns. Within the month the court will review the case, and if no guardian is appointed they will remain at St. Vincent's until they reach their majority. If you feel you have a good case for adoption, then I suggest you appear in court on the appointed day and state your case. But I feel obliged to add that if you have no wife you have virtually no chance of gaining custody. And by wife I mean someone who will make a good impression on the presiding judge. Do I make myself clear?"

Since Baxter had already seen the woman who claimed to be Cody's wife, if that whore was really his wife, he suspected there wasn't much chance of Cody gaining custody. That hot little number at the Longbranch could never pass for anything but a whore. Carter couldn't possibly rid himself of one wife and marry another in so short a time.

Cody's spirits plummeted. Baxter's advice made him realize how hopeless his cause was. No matter how badly he wanted the kids to remain with him, fate was against their doing so. "I reckon you've made yourself clear enough," Cody granted. "Since I have little choice in the matter, I reckon I'll have to let the kids go with you."

"Papa, no!" The children's protests tore at Cody's soft heart, a heart he hadn't even known he had until he met Amy, Brady, and Cassie. Not too long ago he had considered himself a rough cowboy who lived from day to day and made sure his back was always protected. He had killed men in self-defense and thought nothing of it. He had lived with the stigma of being a half-breed, and after Lisa had turned him down he'd figured that marriage and a family were for other men, not him.

Dropping to his knees, he hugged the kids fiercely. "Listen, kids, it's only temporary." Though he meant what he said, he wasn't foolish enough to believe he could change the judge's mind. But for the kids' sakes he couldn't let them suspect the hopelessness of his cause.

"Do we have to go?" Amy asked. For Brady's sake she fought bravely to stem the flow of tears hovering so close to the surface.

"Will you come to St. Louis and get us?" Brady asked hopefully. Despite his fear of separation, for Amy's sake he tried to show a brave face.

"I'll come to St. Louis," Cody promised. "You can count on it."

If Baxter wasn't such a cold, unemotional man he would have been touched by the scene. As it was, he could hardly wait to be off. He didn't relish missing the train and having to remain the night in Dodge with two whining children. His own children, though already in their teen years, were obedient and well-behaved.

The parting was heart-wrenching and tearful, but mercifully brief due to Baxter's impatience. By the time the buggy disappeared down the road, even Cody's eyes looked suspiciously moist. Neither Cassie nor Irene attempted to hide their tears.

"Reb is going to feel terrible that he wasn't here to bid the children good-bye," Irene said, wringing her hands in her apron. "I hoped he'd be back by now."

"He's taking his own sweet time visiting those relatives of his," Cody complained. "He's probably holed up in some saloon getting stinking drunk." Venting his spleen on an absent Reb was better than dwelling on his loss. Irene recognized Cody's need to lash out at someone and did not defend Reb as she was wont to do.

"Cody, come inside," Cassie urged, hoping to distract him from his brooding anger.

"I don't need your pity," Cody lashed out as he whirled on his heel and headed toward the corral.

"Cody, wait!" She started after him.

"No, Cassie," Irene said, restraining her with a gentle touch. "Let him go. He's hurting right now. He's just encountered a situation he can't control and needs to come to grips with it."

"That's why he needs me," Cassie tried to explain.

Irene regarded her with sympathetic eyes. "He'll come to you, Cassie, but let it be on his own terms. Anything that smacks of pity right now will only send him deeper into despair."

Realizing that Irene was right, Cassie watched Cody ride from the yard, her eyes bleak. When he disappeared over a distant rise, she sighed unhappily and went inside the house. It was going to be terribly lonely around the house without the children, she silently lamented. Even Blackie sensed the loss, for he sat down by the fence, staring into the distance and howling.

Cassie awoke to the certain knowledge that she wasn't alone. The room was dark. She had undressed and gone to bed hours earlier, having grown tired waiting for Cody to return. Then she saw him, his big frame limned in the light shining through the window.

"Cody?"

"I need you, sweetheart."

She held out her arms and he came to her instantly. "I've been waiting for you." She tugged at his shirt. "Let me help you." Together they removed his clothes and he slid into bed beside her.

"I couldn't bear it if I'd lost you too," Cody said in a raw voice. "I don't deserve you, sweetheart. Baxter made me feel like dirt. Somehow he found out I was married to Holly, though I admitted nothing. He made me doubt my own worth. I always considered myself a rather arrogant bastard with a thick skin, until you and the kids found a soft spot inside me I didn't even know existed."

Cassie smiled in the dark. "Being vulnerable isn't the worst thing in the world."

"It is when you're a half-breed without a last name. I made my reputation being tough and ruthless. I always knew I had few redeeming qualities."

"I love that vulnerable place you've tried so hard to hide. I even love the uncompromising inflexibility and pride that make you the kind of man you are. I guess I just love you."

Cody groaned and pulled her into his arms. "I want to make love to you, baby. To hold you and know you're with me in this."

"That's what I want too, Cody. I want to be here for you."

He stared down at her. Her thick-lashed eyes were seductively dark against the cream and rose of her complexion, and he realized how lucky he was. When he kissed her, his mouth was sweet and thoughtful, sending shivers of delight racing through her. When his slow, drugging kisses grew more urgent, she abandoned herself to his growing ardor. His touch was light and exquisitely tender as he sought to bring her the greatest pleasure. But soon their playful teasing gave way to a raging hunger that swept them away on a surging tide of magical splendor.

Afterward, Cassie lay quietly beside Cody, her lips tingling in remembrance of his kisses, her body languorous and sated. She had something to tell Cody but feared that her news would upset him. She had finally recognized the symptoms and realized that she was carrying Cody's child. Yet she resisted telling him, fearing he would slide deeper into despair when he realized he couldn't marry her. And he had so many things on his mind right now, so many problems to grapple with, that he didn't need her adding to his woes.

She knew how much he had always despised being called a bastard and realized that was exactly what their child would be if they weren't married before she delivered. Cassie knew little about divorce, but she imagined it was a rather lengthy process. No, she decided resolutely. She would keep the news of her pregnancy from Cody as long as she could and pray that everything would work out in the end.

Chapter Twenty-three

Heartache followed Cody the following days, despite his best effort to conceal it. He placed Sandy Blaloch in charge of raising a new barn and set the hands to their normal ranch chores in an attempt to keep everything running smoothly while he was away. He had promised the children he would do all in his power to convince the court to award him custody, and he wouldn't let them down. He fully intended to be in the courtroom to present his petition for adoption. And he wanted Cassie with him.

Not for the first time Cody wished Reb was back from his mysterious trip to take over some of the burdensome duties of running the ranch. Despite his limitations, the one-armed man had proven his worth.

Cassie's heart went out to Cody. When he asked her to go to St. Louis with him she had agreed instantly, ignoring the fact that their relationship might be exploited by people unaware of the love they bore one another. She knew she would be considered Cody's mistress, but it didn't matter. He needed her and she wanted to be with him.

About a week after the children's departure, Cody prepared to ride into Dodge to buy tickets to St. Louis and call on Lawyer Willoughby. Since Mr. Baxter had destroyed his petition for adoption, Cody needed to have another drawn up before his trip. He was already mounted when he saw two riders approaching. He dismounted and waited with growing impatience for his visitors to arrive. It wasn't until they entered the yard that Cody recognized Reb. Though the tall, gaunt man with Reb looked vaguely familiar, Cody couldn't recall where he had met him before. Cody stirred uneasily, trying to dredge up a name from his memory.

"About time you showed up," he greeted Reb sourly. "Where in the hell have you been?"

Reb gave him a red-faced grin. "I'm sorry, Cody, but it took me longer than I thought to find Reverend Wescott. I finally caught up with him in Garden City, and he wasn't too happy about coming back to Dodge with me. He got downright nasty when I insisted."

Preacher Wescott sent Reb a fulminating look. "I am a man of God, sir, not some rowdy to be ordered about or threatened with a gun." He straightened his sparse frame, peering down his long nose at Cody.

Cody's dark brow quirked upward. "What's this all about, Reb? It better be good 'cause it's keeping me from business in town."

"Oh, it's good, Cody, damn good," Reb assured him. "Reverend Wescott is the man who married you and Holly."

Cody went rigid. So it was true. He and Holly really had been married. He had hoped—well, never mind, it was too late now. "What are you trying to prove, Reb? The man who performed that abominable ceremony is the last man in the world I'd care to meet."

"You're gonna change your mind when I tell you that Reverend Wescott is no reverend at all. He's a self-proclaimed preacher without authority to perform marriages. He's never been properly ordained."

A great shudder traveled the length of Cody's body. His riveting blue eyes settled on Wescott, and the man shifted uncomfortably beneath Cody's penetrating stare. "Is that true, Wescott?" Cody asked tightly. "If you knew the ceremony wasn't legal, why did you agree to perform it?"

Wescott glared back sullenly. "Your brother told me it was a joke, that it would teach you to avoid liquor and whores in the future. He said he'd tell you it was all a joke as soon as you sobered up. You were roaring drunk, Mr. Carter. It was all we could do to get you to sign the marriage document."

"And I assume my brother paid you dearly to get you to perform the bogus ceremony," Cody challenged.

"The money was used for God's work," Wescott declared. The preacher's face was taut, his eyes bright with religious fervor, and Cody realized that the man was a half-mad zealot with little sense of reality. It would serve no purpose to exact any kind of retribution from the crazed man. The only thing Cody would insist upon was that Wescott sign a deposition stating that he had no license to perform wedding ceremonies. Willoughby could take care of the details.

"You'll never know the harm you've done with your practical joke, Wescott, and I expect you to publicly acknowledge the wrong you've done me."

Wescott looked dubious. "How?"

"We're going to visit my lawyer in Dodge. He'll know what to do." Then he turned to Reb. "Why didn't you tell me what you intended before you left? Why the story about going off to visit relatives?"

"I didn't want to get your hopes up in case I couldn't find Wescott." He looked at Cody squarely. "But I wanted to do this for you, Cody. You've given me back my self-respect and I owed you. If not for you I could have died in that alley behind the Longbranch. You and Irene have made life worth living again."

Shrugging off Reb's praise, Cody said, "What made you decide to try to find Wescott in the first place?"

"Something you said about not believing you were really hitched. I got to thinking that Holly and Wayne could be lying, that they made up a wedding. The only way to find out for sure was to find the man named on the marriage document Holly had in her possession."

"I—I don't know how to thank you, Reb."

"Don't thank me. I'm the one who should thank you." Suddenly Reb looked around, his face puzzled. "Where's the kids? I missed those little scamps. I saw Blackie down by the gate, but he didn't even wag his tail at me."

Cody's expression grew bleak. "The kids are gone, Reb. That fancy St. Louis lawyer came and got them a few days ago."

Reb blanched. "You mean if I had gotten here sooner they'd still be here?"

"I'm afraid even that wouldn't have helped. Baxter would have taken them to St. Louis no matter what. They've been made wards of the court until a judge decides what's to be done with them. My petition for adoption was rejected out of hand, and the kids are going to an orphanage until their fate can be decided."

"Aw, hell, Cody, life just ain't fair. Those kids really love you. What kind of man would take kids away from a good home and people who care for them?"

"A black-hearted lawyer who interprets the law with cold precision. He couldn't see beyond the kids' fortune or the legal aspects of the case. And I strongly suspect that Holly got to him first. I don't know what kind of lies she fed him, but he came out here with his mind already made up about me and Cassie. I won't go into details, but suffice it to say he treated Cassie abominably."

Reb shook his head regretfully. "What are you gonna do?"

"I promised the kids I'd be in St. Louis for their court hearing. And you, my friend, have just provided me with the best piece of news I've had in a good long time. When I leave Dodge it will be with Cassie as my wife, the way it should have been if not for a stupid misunderstanding."

"At least something good has come of all this." Reb grinned. "When's the wedding?"

"Immediately. As soon as I can break the news to Cassie and ride to town."

"Reb, you're back!" Cassie came bounding from the house, Irene hard on her heels. After giving him a quick hug, Cassie asked, "And who might this be?"

"This is the preacher who married Cody and Holly," Reb said. "Only he ain't no honest-to-God preacher. The marriage isn't legal, Cassie. The ceremony was a sham." All the while he spoke he had eyes only for Irene, who stared at him in open adoration.

"I am a man of God," Wescott said indignantly. Being maligned by these people didn't sit well with him. "Being ordained means nothing."

"Maybe not, Wescott, but by your own admission you had no right to perform marriages. Why don't you and Reb go to the kitchen for something to eat while I talk to Cassie. We'll leave for Dodge in an hour."

Reb agreed with alacrity. He couldn't wait to get Irene alone so he could tell her how much he had missed her, how desperately he loved her. When Cody and Cassie returned from St. Louis there would be another wedding at the ranch, if Irene would have him.

"Come inside, sweetheart," Cody said when the others disappeared into the house. "There's much we have to do before we leave for town." Instead of stopping in the parlor where they could be overheard, Cody led her upstairs to his bedroom. When the door was closed firmly behind them, he took her into his arms. "I have an important question to ask."

Cassie waited expectantly, her eyes shining with happiness.

"Will you marry me?"

"Oh, Cody, yes. I've already said I would."

"I don't mean in the future. I mean now. Today. I want you to be my legal wife when we go to St. Louis. It nearly killed me when Baxter referred to you as my mistress."

When Cassie hesitated longer than Cody would have liked, he quickly added, "I'm asking because

I love you, Cassie, not because of the children. If having a wife helps my cause, then good, but I learned my lesson. You're the woman I want to spend the rest of my life with. If we can't get custody of Amy and Brady we'll start our own family. I'd never thought much about it before, but I'd like to have children of my own. Not that I'll love Amy and Brady any less."

"I know that, Cody, and it makes me love you all the more."

Cassie almost burst with the news that she was already increasing, that his wish for having children of his own was closer to fulfillment than he thought. But still she refrained from blurting out the truth, unwilling to burden Cody at a time when he needed all his wits about him. And he might insist she not endanger their child by traveling in her condition. Cody needed her, and she fully intended to be at his side when the court hearing was held in St. Louis.

Cassie thought Cody had never looked more handsome when they stood before Reverend Lester at four o'clock that afternoon as he pronounced them man and wife. Reb and Irene were witnesses, and it was obvious from their dreamy expressions that it wouldn't be long before they stood before the preacher themselves.

Cassie could hardly take her eyes off her tall, dark husband, finely garbed in suit, white shirt, cravat, and shiny black boots. The fancy clothing had been purchased at the mercantile just minutes before the ceremony. She felt certain the judge would be impressed when Cody appeared before him dressed in his finery.

Cody's blue eyes glowed with admiration and pride as he watched his bride. She was a vision in a fine lawn dress sporting tiny capped sleeves and a sweetheart neckline in a becoming shade of blue, embroidered with tiny white rosebuds. She looked so damn sweet and innocent that Cody wondered how a rough cowboy like him had been lucky enough to capture her love.

Immediately following the ceremony they boarded the evening train for St. Louis. They had already visited Lawyer Willoughby before the wedding, dragging a reluctant Reverend Wescott with them. Once Wescott had signed an affidavit attesting to the fact that he had no license to perform marriages, he was free to go. He made a hasty departure, voicing his intention never to return to Dodge City any time in the near future. Willoughby had notarized the document and wished Cody and Cassie well. Now, with a legal marriage license in his possession, as well as Wescott's affidavit, Cody entertained the hope that his petition for adoption would be looked upon favorably.

Cassie couldn't help grinning when Cody engaged a room at one of the best hotels in St. Louis, registering them as man and wife. After their rocky beginning it didn't seem possible that they were married, especially after all the heartache and misunderstandings they had endured. But it was true. She wore his ring on her finger and Cody had their marriage certificate in his pocket.

Their room was spacious and comfortable, but Cassie barely had time to admire it before Cody hurried her out the door. He wanted to call on Lawyer Baxter before the office closed for the day. Baxter was just preparing to leave when they entered the offices of Baxter, Bartholomew and Merriweather. The clerk had already departed, and Cody pushed open the inner door to Baxter's private office.

"Mr. Baxter, I'm glad I caught you before you left."

Startled, Baxter looked up, his eyes widening when he saw Cody and Cassie standing in the doorway. "Why, Mr. Carter, I believe. Have you come for the hearing?" He kept glancing toward the door, as if eager to escape now that the workday was nearly over.

"Yes. I promised the kids I'd be here for the hearing," Cody explained. "It hasn't been held yet, has it?"

"As a matter of fact it hasn't. It's scheduled for—" he opened an appointment book on his desk and checked the dates "—a week from today. At ten o'clock in the morning. But if you're thinking of attending, it will be a waste of time. Bringing your, er, companion with you—" he slanted Cassie an oblique look "—will do more harm than good. It could have a harmful impact on the judge's decision."

Cody wanted to punch the officious man in the nose, but restrained himself. "I insist that you apologize to my wife. Your disparaging remarks are uncalled for."

"Your wife? But—but I was led to believe this woman was your mistress."

"May I ask who told you such a lie?" Cody asked with deceptive calm. "I told you Cassie wasn't my mistress when you made that outrageous accusation."

"I—I—you didn't say she was your wife."

"Would you care to see our marriage license?" Cody's voice was cool and clear as ice water, and Baxter felt a chill slip down his back. He was convinced that if Cody lost his temper it wouldn't be pretty.

"No, no, I believe you. I offer my humblest apologies, Mrs. Carter." What had ever possessed him to believe that that tempting little baggage at the Longbranch could be Carter's wife? he wondered. Normally he acted with more discretion. His only excuse was that it had been a long, tiring train ride from St. Louis and he had wanted to pick up the children and return without delay. "Is there something I can do for you?"

"As a matter of fact, there is. I had another petition of adoption drawn up and I want to present it to the court. And of course Cassie and I want to see the children. Can you arrange it for us?"

"Well, now, harrumph, that isn't possible. As one of the children's lawyers I can't legally represent you. You'll have to find another lawyer. Your petition must be in the judge's hands immediately for it to be even considered. As for visiting the children at St. Vincent's, I wouldn't recommend it. They are settling in nicely, and a visit from you would just upset them."

Cody grew rigid. He didn't believe Baxter, not for one damn minute. "Regardless of what you say, Mr. Baxter, Cassie and I fully intend to visit Amy and Brady. We didn't come all this way just to hear you tell us we'd upset them. We've never upset them before."

"Things are different now. They're starting a new life at St. Vincent's."

"Not if I can help it," Cody muttered beneath his breath. "Besides, I doubt you can stop us from visiting. They're not in jail, after all. Good day, Mr. Baxter. We'll see you in court."

Cassie could feel the tension building in Cody as they left Baxter's office. Would nothing ever go right for them?

"Damn pompous ass," Cody mumbled darkly. "If he wasn't such a pitiful specimen I'd knock him on his ear."

"That wouldn't help matters," Cassie consoled. "I doubt the nuns at the orphanage will deny us a visit with the children. And any judge worth his salt will see immediately that they're better off with us. What are you going to do about a lawyer?"

"Find one. Fast."

"Any ideas?"

"Yes. When I lived in St. Louis there was a young, enthusiastic lawyer just out of law school. I met him when he rode the Butterfield Stage to town. I rode shotgun on that run and we struck up a friendship of sorts. His name is Parker Granger. His office is just down the street in one of the less expensive rent districts, if he's still here. His office might not be as fancy as Baxter's, but I'm willing to bet he'd take our case."

They found Parker Granger still in his office, his full head of dark, unruly hair bent over a thick law tome. He regarded them through intelligent brown eyes and invited them to sit down.

"We feared you'd be gone," Cody said. "I'm Cody Carter. We met some time ago when you arrived in St. Louis aboard the Butterfield Stage. I rode shotgun. This is my wife, Cassie."

Granger's rather gaunt features lit up, his friendly smile telling Cody he did indeed remember him. "I recall the occasion, Mr. Carter, very well indeed. It's a pleasure to see you again and meet your beautiful wife. What can I do for you?"

Cody cleared his throat, gave Cassie's hand a squeeze, and said, "We need your help." Though he could tell by the shabbiness of the office that Granger received a pauper's share of the legal business in town, he felt comfortable with the intense young man. For one thing, they were close to the same age and Cody felt that Granger would be supportive of his petition.

"Why don't you tell me about the nature of your problem?" Granger invited. He sat back in his chair, tented his hands in a contemplative manner, and nodded for Cody to begin.

Cody began at the beginning, leaving out nothing. Granger's eyes widened when Cody revealed how he had arrived in Dodge with two strange children in tow and quickly added a one-armed drunk and a half-starved dog to his entourage. But Granger merely nodded his shaggy head and waited for the next fascinating detail. Cody talked for nearly thirty minutes. When he finished he was hoarse, but he had gained Granger's support as well as his admiration.

"I'd be honored to represent you in court, Mr. Carter. What you've done for those poor children goes far beyond simple duty. I can tell you care for them very much."

Cody gave an embarrassed grin. "They sure caught me unprepared. I never even thought about kids until those two came into my life. Now here I am, ready to adopt two half-grown sprouts and maybe have some of my own." He shook his head, as if trying to come to grips with the strange turn his life had taken.

"Cody is a wonderful father," Cassie felt obliged to add.

"Yes, well, let's not jump the gun," Cody said, growing serious. "What are my chances, Mr. Granger?"

"Your chances are very good, Mr. Carter, but we have to act fast. I must take your petition to the court immediately if we want it considered. I only hope we get a sympathetic judge. The hearing will probably be a private affair held in the judge's chambers. Where are you staying? I'll be in touch as soon as the details are worked out. Meanwhile, I see no reason why you can't see the children. If you have a problem, let me know and I'll get a court order."

Cody gave Granger the name of their hotel, handed him the petition of adoption drawn up by Willoughby, and shook hands. "We'll be waiting to hear from you, Mr. Granger."

"If I may make a suggestion, Mr. Carter?"

"Please call me Cody."

"Very well, Cody. I think it best that you wait until tomorrow to see the children. It's rather late now and the good sisters might not let you visit so late in the day. Have dinner and get a good night's rest. You both look exhausted."

Granger's advice was sound. Cody and Cassie had dinner at the hotel and retired immediately afterward. In the privacy of their own room, Cassie came into Cody's arms easily and naturally. It would be their first night together as man and wife, and Cassie savored the special feeling that being Cody's wife gave her. Yet despite all that, their coming together was an explosive burst of mutual hunger and driving need. Cody's mood demanded a quick, urgent release, barely giving her time to take off her clothes before pressing her down onto the bed and thrusting inside her. But Cassie had needed little preparation. She was already wet and hot as she opened herself to his hard, frantic thrusts.

He rode her fast, furious, repeating her name over and over, driving her, tearing off the rest of her clothes as he brought them both to shuddering climax.

He collapsed on his side, panting, pulling her with him. "I'm sorry, baby, I didn't mean for it to be so fast. Give me a minute to catch my breath and I promise it will be better next time."

"Don't worry, Cody. I was ready for you."

"It's just that I'm so damn frustrated. Despite what Granger said, I don't feel confident about all this. In times of stress I seem to need you more than ever." He sent her an apologetic smile.

Raising up on her elbow, Cassie leaned down and kissed him full on the mouth. "Are you rested yet?" Her eyes twinkled with devilment.

"Oh, baby, I don't need much rest with you in my arms."

After a leisurely breakfast the next morning Cody hired a hack to take them to St. Vincent's Orphanage. The carriage stopped in front of a large, austere, three-story building whose gray stone exterior promised little in the way of comfort. The tall, narrow windows were devoid of curtains, and a kind of desolate emptiness was reflected in the dingy panes. Cassie's heart beat in trepidation as she and Cody trudged up the stone stairs and paused before the door. Cody gave her a tentative smile as he lifted his hand to the brass knocker.

Several minutes passed before the door was opened by a solemn-faced woman swathed in a gray habit that blended with the home's exterior. She peered at them though myopic eyes. "May I help you?"

"We've come to visit Amy and Brady Trenton. We're Mr. and Mrs. Cody Carter."

"You'll be needing permission from the Reverend Mother," the nun said. Though she wasn't exactly unfriendly, her welcome was far from warm.

"We've come a long way to see the children," Cody replied, refusing to be intimidated.

"I will take you to the Reverend Mother. Please follow me to her office." She turned abruptly and scurried along, her beads jangling against her skirts as she walked.

It was so quiet in the halls that one could hear a pin drop, and there were no children in sight. Cassie wondered how young, active children could exist in such a gloomy atmosphere, and her heart went out to the homeless waifs forced to live within these dreary walls. Oh, they were probably well fed and properly clothed, and their spiritual needs met, but what about love? At the end of the long hall they were ushered into the Reverend Mother's outer office and bidden to wait while their guide disappeared into the inner office. Within minutes she was back, her face expressionless.

Did no one smile around here?

"The Reverend Mother will see you now."

The Reverend Mother was short and plump and wore rimless glasses perched at the end of a long nose. She looked over those glasses now to study her visitors. Her pleasant face was mildly curious. "You wish to see Amy and Brady? Sister Michael said you were the Carters. I assume you're the same Carters the children mention."

"We're Cody and Cassie, sister, er, Reverend Mother," Cody said. "We've come a long way to see the children. How are they?"

The Reverend Mother frowned. "Healthy," she said, revealing nothing of what Cody wanted to hear. "Have they always been so quiet and uncommunicative?"

"Quiet!" Cassie gasped. "Uncommunicative! That surely doesn't sound like Amy and Brady. What have you done to them?"

"I assure you, Mrs. Carter, we have done nothing to the children," she said indignantly. "Our aim is to raise children into well-adjusted adults, with the help of God, of course. We require obedience and respect and promote a healthy fear of evil and the devil's works."

Cody grew impatient. "That's all well and good, Reverend Mother, but may we see the kids now?"

The Reverend Mother stared at them a moment, then said, "I suppose it will do no harm. Please remain here while I prepare them for your visit."

Cassie and Cody exchanged worried glances as the stout nun bustled from the room. "Do you think the children have changed?" Cassie asked fearfully. "They've only been here a short time, surely not long enough to affect them."

"Even a day in here is too long," Cody muttered. It pained him to think of spirited kids like Amy and Brady being subdued in this gloomy atmosphere.

Suddenly the door opened and Amy and Brady appeared in the doorway. They stared at Cody blankly, their eyes dull, their faces devoid of all emotion. The Reverend Mother stood behind them. She pushed them inside, then backed away, softly closing the door behind her.

Cody stood up awkwardly, waiting for the children to say something—anything. When they remained mute, he cleared his throat and said, "I said I'd come and here I am."

"Hello, Cody," Amy said dully.

Cassie cried out in dismay while Cody swallowed past the lump in his throat and tried again. "Aren't you glad to see me?"

Brady stepped forward, his face belligerent. "You let them take us away. Reverend Mother said we have to stay here until we're eighteen. Why did you come, Cody?"

Oh, God, Cody thought, it was worse than he had imagined. The kids had never called him Cody. He had always been Papa to them and he had grown accustomed to it. "I didn't let them take you away, Brady, I had no choice. But I'm here now to try to fix things so we don't ever have to be parted again."

A glimmer of hope lifted Amy's pinched features. Cassie thought she looked as if she hadn't been eating properly. "Really?"

"Your papa would never allow you to remain here," Cassie said.

"Cody isn't our papa," Brady observed sullenly. "The Reverend Mother said our father is dead. What are you doing here with Cody? Why isn't Holly with him?"

"I'm Cody's wife now," Cassie explained. "We both want you back at the ranch." How could the children have become so embittered in such a short time? Cassie wondered miserably. It nearly broke her heart to see them like this. They'd already been through so much. "Holly is gone. You'll never be bothered by her again."

Cassie's words coaxed a small smile from Amy. "I didn't think Cody wanted us to call him Papa."

"It grew on me," Cody shrugged, grinning foolishly.

"And you want us back?"

"More than anything. Both Cassie and I want to take you home with us."

Brady began to warm to the conversation. "How is Blackie? We're not allowed pets at St. Vincent's. There aren't even any cows or horses."

"Blackie is just fine," Cassie replied, "except that he misses you."

"We miss him too," Brady sighed wistfully. He sent Cody a guarded look. "Do you really want us, Cody?"

Cody groaned, wondering if it was possible to earn back their trust. They seemed to have grown so cynical. "More than you'll ever know."

Just then the door opened and the Reverend Mother bustled inside. "Time is up, children, you should be at your lessons."

Amy's bottom lip quivered. "Will we see you again?"

"Cassie and I will be at the hearing, Amy, you can count on it. I've already hired a lawyer to work in our behalf." Then he dropped to his knees and hugged them fiercely. Cassie did the same. It nearly broke her heart to see their drooping faces when the Reverend Mother ushered them out the door.

Chapter Twenty-four

Nearly every seat was taken in the judge's private chamber the morning of the hearing. Cassie sat beside Cody, holding his hand and smiling encouragement. Parker Granger, their lawyer, was present, as was Denton Baxter, representing the children's interests. Judge Fedders was to hear the case, which seemed to please Granger. He was regarded as a harsh disciplinarian but a fair man whose decisions were made with compassion and wisdom.

The judge sat behind his desk, perusing the papers before him. From time to time he raised his head and looked at Cody from beneath shaggy gray brows. After several moments of tense silence, the judge cleared his throat and said, "I believe I have all the facts firmly in my mind now.

I've been studying this case for a week and find it almost beyond belief that the Trenton children's guardian had planned their deaths. The man was a most foul villain, and were he before me today I'd not hesitate to punish the man according to the law. But God in his wisdom has seen fit to remove the demon from this earth, and now we must consider his wards and what's best for them.

"I have before me a petition of adoption, presented by Lawyer Granger in behalf of his clients, Cody and Cassie Carter." He paused, regarding Cody and Cassie with unfeigned interest. "I find the circumstances of the case fascinating, and before I make my final decision I have a few questions for Mr. Carter."

Cody's attention sharpened, and he squeezed Cassie's hand so hard she had to bite back a cry of pain.

"Are you aware that the Trenton children are quite wealthy, Mr. Carter?"

"Yes, Your Honor," Cody replied, "I am now, but of course at first I had no idea who they were, for they refused to divulge any information about themselves."

"I find it rather strange that an unmarried cowboy, who by his own admission is somewhat of a drifter and ne'er-do-well, would befriend two homeless waifs without thought of reward or compensation."

"When I pulled them from beneath the wheels of a runaway carriage I thought I'd seen the last of them. After I came to their aid a second time I assumed it was a coincidence and promptly forgot them, since I was leaving town immediately. Finding them aboard the same train, claiming to be my children, overwhelmed me. I must admit I didn't appreciate their intrusion into my life at first, but that ended when I brought them out to the ranch and got to know them."

Judge Fedders glanced back down at the papers spread across his desk and said, "According to Mr. Granger, the children called you Papa."

Cody's taut features relaxed into a reluctant smile. "They've called me Papa from the very first. It seemed to make them happy, so I didn't insist on any other form of address."

"Hmmm, yes, well, I understand that until you met the children you had little contact with youngsters."

"That's true, Your Honor, but I learned fast. Cassie helped me understand."

"Ah, yes, your wife." He cast an oblique glance at Cassie. "Mr. Baxter told me a rather mixed-up tale about your marriage. Do you consider your marriage one of convenience? Perhaps undertaken for the purpose of gaining custody of the children?"

"Certainly not!" Cody protested indignantly. "I married Cassie because I love her." When he turned and smiled tenderly at Cassie, not one person in the room had reason to doubt his love for his wife.

"I believe I have concluded my questions, Mr. Carter, except perhaps for one that would ease my mind considerably." Cody waited with bated breath, wondering if the judge would ask about his mixed blood. He didn't. His question was much simpler, yet a thousand times more difficult to answer. "What makes you think you're the right father for the children?"

Beads of sweat appeared on Cody's forehead. Many answers came to mind but nothing seemed appropriate. Not only did Cody want to impress the judge, he wanted to speak from the heart. He had little experience with children, nor had he led an exemplary life. He was a half-breed, the bastard son of a prosperous rancher; he'd led a fast and dangerous life and along the way had acquired an unsavory reputation. Besides that he cussed too much. On the credit side he genuinely loved the kids and had married a wonderful woman who loved them as much as he did. And if that wasn't enough, he could provide a home where they would have the freedom to grow strong and healthy.

After considering all the pros and cons, Cody unwittingly gave the only answer that could have swayed the judge's decision in his favor. "I know I'm the right father for those kids because no one else, besides Cassie, of course, loves them like I do. They'd have everything they could possibly wish for at the ranch. And one day I hope to give them brothers and sisters."

"Nicely said, Mr. Carter." Judge Fedders nodded. "Now I will speak with the children. Mr. Baxter, please bring in your clients."

Baxter rose and disappeared into the outer office, returning directly with the children. They bounded into the room, saw Cody, and rushed to embrace him.

"Papa! Cassie!" Amy cried happily. "You did come. I told Brady you'd be here. Can we go home now?"

The judge bit back a smile. "Children, children, please sit down, the hearing isn't over yet."

Amy took a seat beside Cassie, but Brady, wanting to show Cody that he was sorry for the way he had acted at their last meeting, crawled into Cody's lap. Cody's arms closed around him, and Judge Fedders made no effort to have the boy set down.

"Could you tell me in your own words, Amy, why you want to live with the Carters? You're old enough to know that Mr. Carter isn't your real father, aren't you?"

Amy regarded the judge as if he had lost possession of his mind. "Of course we know Cody isn't our real father, but me and Brady adopted him because we knew he was a good man and would take care of us."

"How did you come to that conclusion?" the judge asked curiously. "You hardly knew the man."

"He saved us from Uncle Julian and let us keep Blackie. He helped Reb and chased away the two men who tried to kill us. Besides—" she slanted Cody a shy glance "—we knew in our hearts."

"And just who are Blackie and Reb?"

"Blackie is our little white dog that Papa rescued, and Reb is a one-armed man Papa found drunk and beaten up in the alley behind the saloon. But Reb doesn't get drunk anymore. Papa brought both Reb and Blackie home and nursed them back to health."

The judge's eyes widened, trying to make sense out of Amy's words. "A white dog called Blackie and a one-armed drunk named Reb. After everything else I've heard or read thus far concerning this case, your words make a curious kind of sense."

"We can't have a dog at St. Vincent's," Brady piped up, shifting the limelight from Amy.

"Don't you like St. Vincent's, Brady?" the judge asked kindly.

"It's all right, I reckon, but it's not home. Blackie isn't there. Did you know Reb is teaching me how to ride a horse? The Reverend Mother said we haven't got a real father. I told her that we know our real father is dead, but if we couldn't have him or our real mother, then Cody and Cassie were the papa and mama we wanted."

"May I say something in behalf of my clients, Your Honor?" Baxter boldly interrupted, anxious to say his piece.

"Go ahead, Mr. Baxter."

"You must remember that these are young, impressionable children who have lived with Mr. Carter for many weeks. I'm certain he has influenced their thinking. But we must consider the fact that Mr. Carter is an unlikely candidate for fatherhood. You are aware, of course, that he is a half-breed, born out of wedlock to a full-blooded Cheyenne woman who lived with Mr. Carter's father."

Until that moment Cassie had remained quiet, letting Cody answer the judge's questions. But after hearing Baxter's words she could no longer withhold comment. "Your Honor, may I respond to Mr. Baxter's charges?"

"Certainly, Mrs. Carter, please forgive me for ignoring you. I'm most interested in what you have to say."

"My husband is the most honorable man I know. The accident of his birth is not worthy of consideration. He's a proud man with a strong sense of family and justice. He takes his obligation to the children most seriously, which he has had occasion to prove many times. And I am prepared to be as good a mother to them as I will to my own child when it arrives."

"What!" This from Cody, who stared at her dumbfounded. "What in the hell are you talking about?"

Cassie smiled placidly. "I was going to tell you at a private moment but decided this was as good a time as any."

"Congratulations on the impending birth of your child, Mrs. Carter," the judge said, trying to keep a sober face. "Your loyalty to your husband is to be commended."

"Thank you, Judge, I'm thrilled at the prospect of becoming a mother and giving Amy and Brady a brother or sister. I love Cody and am proud of the kind of man he is. We'll be a real family. The children will prosper and grow strong in the loving atmosphere that Cody and I can provide."

"Very well, I think I've heard enough. If you would all step into the outer office I will make my decision. The bailiff will summon you when I'm ready to deliver it."

The moment they all trooped into the outer office, Cody said, "All right, Cassie, I want the truth. Are you expecting a child or aren't you?" Parker Granger had taken the children aside to allow Cody and Cassie a private word.

"We're going to have a baby in seven months," Cassie announced happily. "I wanted to tell you before but hated to add to your responsibilities. You already had so much to worry about."

"I ought to wring your sweet little neck," Cody said, sending her a tender look that belied his words. "If I had known you were expecting I'd never have brought you on this trip."

"That's another reason I didn't tell you," Cassie acknowledged softly. "I wanted to be with you. Come on, let's join the children. They're looking quite neglected."

Hand in hand they approached Granger and the children. "What do you think of our chances?" Cody asked the lawyer.

"Excellent," Granger observed, patting the children's heads fondly. "These two made wonderful witnesses in your behalf. Even Baxter seemed impressed, for he objected little beyond those few sentences he uttered at the end of the hearing."

Brady kept staring at Cassie, a puzzled expression in his brown eyes. "Do we have to wait a long time for a baby brother or sister?"

"Of course we do, silly," Amy chided with a hint of exasperation. "Don't you know anything? Babies take time to grow."

Brady eyed Cassie with misgiving. "If it grows too big, how will it get out?"

Cody groaned with dismay.

"Oh, my," Cassie gasped, her eyes growing wide. Being a mother to these two inquisitive children was going to be a challenge. Albeit a wonderful one.

They were saved from answering Brady's probing question by the bailiff, who opened the door to the judge's inner chamber and ushered them inside.

"I have reached a decision," Judge Fedders said once they were all seated. "After listening to testimony from everyone involved in the adoption petition presented in behalf of the Carters, I find that the Trenton children made the choice long before I did, and the court has no authority to deny them. By their own admission they adopted Mr. Carter of their own free will, and despite all odds Mr. Carter grew to love them as much as they obviously love him and his wife. It would be remiss of me to take them from a loving home and place them in a cold atmosphere lacking in all but the essential elements necessary for their survival.

"Therefore, I see no reason to deny Mr. Carter's petition for adoption. The children's fortune, though, is another matter. I will do as Mr. Carter suggested and place the money in trust for the children until they reach their majority. If at any time Mr. Carter finds that he has need of any part of that money for the children's upbringing, he may appeal to the children's estate, which will continue to be administered by Mr. Baxter's law firm."

Absolute quiet reigned while Cody and Cassie took time to wade through the judge's words.

"Does that mean we can go home, Papa?" Brady asked plaintively. "I'm hungry." His seven-year-old mind had quickly gotten to the heart of the judge's decision and was now ready to get on to more important issues.

"That's exactly what the judge means, son," Cody said, savoring the word that suddenly gave his life new meaning. The responsibility was awesome, but he felt ready and willing to tackle it. In a few short weeks he had gone from rough cowboy to husband and father of two, soon to be three. Most men would be overwhelmed by the commitment, but Cody felt a sense of belonging he had never experienced before. With Cassie beside him he could accomplish miracles.

"The children were exhausted," Cassie said when she returned to the room she and Cody shared. Cody had rented a suite at the hotel, and the children had already retired to the adjoining room. Since a celebration was definitely called for, they had gone to a fancy restaurant and treated the children and Parker Granger to the best meal in town. When they returned to their suite they tucked the excited children in bed immediately. It would be a long trip back to Dodge, but they looked forward with relish to their return trip home the next day.

"Now maybe I can have a private conversation with the children's mother," Cody said with mock severity. He pulled her into his arms, his body already hard for her. But he was determined to have some answers about their baby before succumbing to the need to make her his again in the most basic way.

"I'd rather not talk right now," Cassie purred huskily as she wound her arms around his neck.

"Oh, no, you don't," Cody said, picking her up and carrying her to the bed where he sat down with her in his lap. "I'm still angry at you for not telling me about our child. How long have you known?"

Cassie's head fell to his shoulder as she stared up at him. "I suspected it weeks ago while you thought you were still married to Holly. It wasn't until just recently that I became convinced that I was carrying your child."

"Dear Lord, it frightens me to think what would have happened to you and our child if I was really married to Holly. I might not have been able to obtain a divorce before the child was born. That would make him . . ." He shuddered, unable to repeat the word that had caused him so much grief throughout his life.

Cassie placed a finger across his lips. "Don't say it, Cody. Our baby was conceived in love no matter what had happened with Holly. I don't want to talk about it anymore. This has been a memorable day in more ways than one. We're a family now, and nothing is going to change that. I want to celebrate by showing you how much I love you."

"No, sweetheart, let me show you how much I love *you.* Loving you has changed my entire life. What I thought I felt for Lisa is nothing compared to what I feel for you. I want to love you, Cassie. Being inside you brings me the kind of happiness I never expected to experience in this life. It won't hurt the baby, will it?"

Cassie lifted her face, inviting his kiss, telling him without words how very much she wanted him. "How could your loving possibly hurt either me or the baby?" Cassie said moments before his lips descended on hers.

He kissed her deeply, moving his mouth over hers, devouring its softness, tasting her sweetness as his tongue delved inside. Gently he eased her down on the bed, removing her clothing with shaking hands. "Every time we make love I discover something new about you," Cody whispered against her lips. "For instance, did you know you have this utterly fascinating little mole beneath your right breast? He kissed the tiny spot beneath her breast, then licked it with his tongue, sending shivers of desire racing through her.

"And did you know you have an intriguing dimple in your right cheek?" Cassie gasped in response. "It's only visible when you smile."

He sent her a devastating smile, making his dimple even more pronounced. "I love your body; you fit me so well."

"You won't be able to say that much longer. Soon I'll be big and clumsy and waddle when I walk."

"Ducks waddle. To me you'll always be graceful. When you're big with my child you'll be even more beautiful in my eyes."

His hand rested on her stomach, his riveting blue eyes hazy with images of the child he and Cassie had produced. Then he was kissing her again, more urgently this time, his hands finding all those places on her body that gave her the most pleasure. He kissed her and fondled her until she grew dizzy with need, until her lips were swollen and trembling and her breath came in soft little pants, until she was flushed with heat and he could feel the hammering of her heart against his chest. He removed himself long enough to strip away his clothing, then lowered himself full length atop her.

"Open your legs, baby, I'm coming home."

He thrust once and entered her fully. She felt the throbbing heat of him stretch and fill her, felt his pulses pound and his heart thud against her breast. Wrapping her legs around his hips, she drew him deeper inside her, taking all he had to give and urging him to greater heights. Her excitement escalated when he lowered his head to her breasts to give suckle, his teeth and lips nipping and pulling at the tender buds.

"Cody!"

"Soon, baby, soon," Cody gasped, nearly senseless with the need to release himself inside her.

"I can't wait!"

A great roaring filled her ears as her body shook and vibrated with the beginning of her climax. Cody realized what was happening and grasped her hips, lifting and pulling her hard against him as he surged deeply, oh so deeply, inside her. Her release was instant and rewarding, drawing him along with her as he exploded almost violently inside her.

"I love you, sweetheart," Cody said when his breathing steadied to a dull pounding. "If I died a pauper I would die knowing that in my lifetime I've possessed the only treasures worth owning. You and the children are in my heart to stay."

Epilogue

"This is taking an awful long time," Brady complained as he glanced nervously toward the stairs.

"Papa says it usually does," Amy replied with the superior wisdom of a ten-year-old. They were sitting in the parlor before the fire on a cold wintry day, awaiting the long-anticipated arrival of Cassie's baby.

"Do you want a boy or girl?"

"I'd like a girl, but both Mama and Papa said they don't care as long as the baby is healthy."

"Well, I want a boy," Brady declared firmly, "so I can teach him all I know about ranching."

Amy snickered behind her hands. "What makes you think you know so much?"

"Reb told me I know almost as much as he does, and Papa said I was getting big enough to help with the branding."

"Ugh," Amy said, grimacing with revulsion. "You can brand all the cows you want, but I bet I know something you don't."

"That's not fair, Amy. We promised a long time ago not to keep secrets from one another."

Amy considered a moment, then said in a conspiratorial tone, "You promise not to tell?"

"Cross my heart."

She leaned toward him. "Well, Irene is going to have a baby. I heard her telling Mama."

"Aw, she—"

"Brady!"

"Heck," he amended, "I knew that. Reb already told me. What's so secret about married people having babies?"

Disgruntled by being upstaged by her younger brother, Amy sniffed indignantly. "I'll bet you don't know how babies are made."

Amy had finally captured Brady's undivided attention, as well as earned his respect. "No, do you?"

"Of course, it's simple, really. A baby grows from a tiny seed that is planted when two people love each other."

"Like Mama and Papa?"

"Yes. And Reb and Irene."

Brady looked skeptical. Amy's explanation stretched his imagination beyond his meager capabilities. "How is the seed planted? Who told you?"

"Mama did, silly. I don't know exactly how it is

planted, but she said I'd understand one day."

"Understand what?" Cody had entered the room in time to hear Amy's last sentence."

"How babies are planted," Brady replied with casual unconcern. It hardly seemed like anything he'd need to know about any time soon.

Cody choked on a gasp. "What!"

Amy sent him a smug smile. "Ask Mama if you want to know more about it. She knows exactly how it's done." She sounded so knowledgeable Cody had difficulty remaining calm. He definitely had to have a talk with Cassie about their precocious daughter.

"I surely will talk to Mama about it, honey, but not now. I came to tell you you have a new baby sister."

Amy clapped excitedly. "A sister! It's just what I wanted." She sent a condescending smile at Brady, who looked definitely piqued.

"Can we see her? What's her name? Does she look like you or Mama?" Amy's questions came fast and furious.

"Whoa, sprout, one question at a time. I reckon you can take a peek at her. And she's beautiful, just like your mother. As for a name, we haven't decided yet."

The children tiptoed up the stairs behind Cody, definitely awed at the prospect of seeing the tiny being that Cassie and Cody had created. Cassie was sitting up in bed, looking exhausted but happy, holding a small bundle against her breast. The doctor was gathering up his paraphernalia, preparing to leave. Cassie motioned them toward the bed and held out the babe for them to see.

"Papa is right," Amy said reverently, "she is beautiful like you."

"Yeah," Brady agreed. Enchantment with his tiny sister was quickly replacing his disappointment over not having a brother. "Look, she has blond hair, just like Mama."

Cassie sent them a weary smile. Her labor had been long and painful, but having Cody beside her all the time had helped. And once she had seen her daughter she could no longer remember the pain. She supposed it was thus with all mothers.

"Your mother needs to rest, kids," Cody said as he ushered them out the door. "Tomorrow you can have a longer visit."

The doctor exited behind the children, leaving Cassie and Cody alone with their baby.

"You're not disappointed that our first child is a girl, are you?" Cassie asked when Cody returned to her bedside. His expression was one of such bemusement she didn't know what to think.

"She's exactly what I had hoped for," Cody said, sending her that devastating grin that had intrigued her from the beginning. "Have you a name in mind?"

"Truth to tell, I had been expecting a boy and hadn't picked out any girl's names."

"I have. My mother's name was Bright Star. I'd like to call our daughter Starr."

Cassie looked down on her bright eyed, blond

daughter and felt the rightness of the name immediately. "It's perfect."

"So are you, sweetheart. Thank you for another treasure to add to my collection."

MADELINE BAKER

"Madeline Baker's Indian romances should not be missed!"
—Romantic Times

Handy with six-guns and fists, Creed Maddigan likes his women hot and ready. But the rugged half-breed isn't used to innocent girls like Jassy McCloud who curtsy and make ginger snaps. Then Creed is falsely jailed for a crime he didn't commit, and he can think of nothing besides escaping to savor Jassy's sweet love.

Alone on the Colorado frontier, Jassy can either work as a fancy lady or hope to find a husband. But what is she to do when the only man she hopes to marry is a wanted renegade? For Jassy, the decision is simple: She'll take Creed for better or worse, even if she has to spend the rest of her days dodging bounty hunters and bullets.

_3832-3 $5.99 US/$7.99 CAN

Dorchester Publishing Co., Inc.
65 Commerce Road
Stamford, CT 06902

Please add $1.75 for shipping and handling for the first book and $.50 for each book thereafter. NY, NYC, PA and CT residents, please add appropriate sales tax. No cash, stamps, or C.O.D.s. All orders shipped within 6 weeks via postal service book rate. Canadian orders require $2.00 extra postage and must be paid in U.S. dollars through a U.S. banking facility.

Name____
Address______________________________________
City ____________________ State______ Zip______
I have enclosed $______in payment for the checked book(s).
Payment must accompany all orders.☐ Please send a free catalog.